Kobo Presents

Year's Best Crime & Mystery Stories 2016

Selected by
Kristine Kathryn Rusch & John Helfers

Kobo Presents

TORONTO

Published By:
Kobo Writing Life
Rakuten Kobo Inc.
135 Liberty St S. Suite 101, Toronto, ON M6K 1A7
www.kobowritinglife.com

Publisher's Note: This is a work of fiction. Names, characters, places, and incidents are a product of the author's imagination. Locales and public names are sometimes used for atmospheric purposes. Any resemblance to actual people, living or dead, or to businesses, companies, events, institutions, or locales is completely coincidental.

Book Layout © 2014 BookDesignTemplates.com

Year's Best Crime & Mystery Stories 2016
Kristine Kathryn Rusch, John Helfers. -- 1st ed.
Trade Paperback ISBN: 978-1-987879-43-8
eBook ISBN: 978-1-987879-42-1

For my brother, Fred Rusch, and my sister, Sandra Hofsommer, who just might love mysteries even more than I do.
- Kristine Kathryn Rusch

To Martin H. Greenberg and Ed Gorman, who taught me everything I know about creating anthologies.
- John Helfers

Contents

Foreword: John Helfers

Welcome to the first in a series of the best crime and mystery stories of the year, edited by the incomparable Kristine Kathryn Rusch and myself.

When it comes to putting together "Year's Best" anthologies, I learned everything I know from two unparalleled masters of the craft: Martin H. Greenberg and Ed Gorman. Working at *Tekno Books*, Marty's book packaging company, for more than fifteen years, I assisted in assembling incredible anthologies of mystery stories covering a vast range of authors, theme, genre, and styles. Through many volumes, and more than a few publishers along the way, each Year's Best collection was a true microcosm of the field for that year. I learned a lot about what it took to put such a collection together, but didn't think I'd ever have the chance to actually put one together myself.

Enter Mark Leslie Lefebvre from Kobo Books. At a workshop on the Pacific Coast last year, we were discussing ways his company could enter the original publishing business, and one of us (I'm still not sure who) suggested doing a *Year's Best Mystery* volume as a kind of test run. It seemed a fairly safe bet; culling the best of previously-published works in a popular genre with (ideally) a range of authors from bestselling to midlist to independents would ensure that our potential audience would be wide enough to, if not guarantee success, at least garner enough interest for the series to launch successfully.

That was how I returned from the workshop with a pending deal for a *Year's Best Crime and Mystery* anthology—something I had worked on dozens of times, but never as the editor. While I didn't feel completely lost, I knew I'd probably need some help in this.

At *Tekno*, one of the things I'd learned was to utilize the vast network of contacts made during decades of book packaging to find a co-editor to help me out. Fortunately, I didn't have to look very far. The same workshop where Mark and I hatched our cunning plan is run by Kristine Kathryn Rusch and Dean Wesley Smith, both of whom I've known for many years, and with whom I've been working with on the *Fiction River* series of anthologies (a bit more on that later).

It didn't take long for me to set my sights on Kris, a multiple award-winning writer of mystery short fiction, as well as an omnivorous reader of the same. After a short discussion about a potential issue that could make her co-editing a bit sticky (patience, that part is still to come), she agreed to join me on this venture. We worked out terms for the volume with Kobo, and started reading toward the end of last year.

That was when I got my first true realization of just how much work putting together one of these volumes could be. Back at *Tekno*, Marty and Ed (mostly Ed, to be honest) put together the table of contents, and my job was to go forth and clear the stories for use, assemble the manuscript and all its particulars, and send it off to the publisher.

Now, however, I found myself responsible for all of the above, *plus* actually having a voice in choosing which authors made the final cut. This was complicated by several things. First, there is the incredible volume of short stories that are published in a calendar year. It turns out that the digests are only a small portion of that. Between independent magazines, anthologies, and authors publishing their own short fiction, we were soon swamped with submissions, and I *know* we didn't receive or find everything that came out in 2015. But we tried to get ahold of everything we could for consideration. The only restriction we placed on our submissions was that the story first had to appear in print during the 2015 calendar year. How it got published, whether on paper or electronically, didn't really matter, as long as it had appeared somewhere else before it came to us.

With the stream of stories growing every day, Kris and I gamely waded in. She tackled the digests (probably a million words of fiction, if not more, right there) and selected anthologies of interest, with me picking up the rest.

About halfway through, I was seeing short stories in my sleep. Every time I turned around, there was always the next traditional or self-published anthology to review, the next downloaded story to read, dozens, hundreds of them. We both read a lot of excellent fiction, ranging from the quietest cozy to stories that pushed right up to the edge of horror. And when all was said and done, we'd managed to carve out a far-too-large selection of stories we both wanted to reprint.

That's when the horse dealing began. Those who have attended the coast workshops know that Kris and I have fairly different tastes in the mystery genre. That was the other reason I chose her for this series, to ensure that we covered the widest range of stories possible. And indeed, when it came time for us to do our final cuts, I was mentally bracing myself for some potential knockdown, drag-out fights over why *this* story should go in over *that* story, and vice versa.

However, I am delighted to report that that was not the case. It turned out that from our first culling, there were enough stories that we both agreed on to make a superlative volume. Of course, we each had to let go of stories that were personal favorites and, as Kris mentions in her introduction, we would have included if the anthology has been a little (okay, a lot) bigger, but the line had to be drawn somewhere, and so we did, and the book you're reading right now is the result.

And what a result! I don't think we could have been more pleased with how it turned out. There's truly something for everyone here, from stories firmly in the classic mystery genres to tales that edge into fantasy, science, fiction, and horror; all written by authors ranging from worldwide bestsellers to people you may never have heard of, but who wrote and published some of the very best short mystery fiction of the year—at least, according to us.

That does lead me back to the *Fiction River* series of anthologies that, full disclosure, I both edit and write for, and which are published under the discerning eye of Kris and Dean, the series editors. Initially, that was the reason Kris was hesitant about joining me for this project, given her involvement in the series. We discussed the issue, and came up with what I think is an eminently workable solution.

There are several stories in this volume from various FR anthologies published in 2015. I took the lead in selecting them from those qualifying anthologies (none of which I edited myself) with no advice whatsoever from Kris or Dean. Once that particular shortlist was complete, we discussed them as part of the larger shortlist we'd created, and the final selections were agreed upon by both of us.

Ultimately, however, it is now up to you to peruse our selections and make up your mind for yourself. Both Kris and I are very comfortable in saying that we think this anthology contains some of the very best crime and mystery short stories published in 2015—not all of them, of course, because that anthology would probably be three times as large—but certainly a representative selection of the year as a whole. And we hope that, whether you agree or disagree with our choices, that you enjoy what we've put together, and perhaps it will lead you to finding a wonderful new author that you might not have known existed.

I cannot express enough thanks to Kris for agreeing to undertake producing this volume and for Mark Leslie

Lefebvre and the wonderful folks at Rakuten Kobo for publishing a Year's Best volume.

And here's hoping there will be many more in the future, because I know there will be a multitude of excellent crime and mystery stories published in 2016—and we don't intend to miss a single one.

—John Helfers
Green Bay, WI
March 13, 2016

Introduction: Kristine Kathryn Rusch

I started editing and publishing in grade school. I was one of those kids who mimeographed a newspaper for the neighborhood, and sold it for five cents. Very entrepreneurial and probably too revealing of my family's foibles.

But I don't know when the idea of editing fiction first crossed my mind. I'm guessing it was in my first year of college. I ended up as one of four editors of my college's literary magazine, an eye-opening experience in awfulness. Not with the other editors. They were good people and easy to work with. The stories.

I wrote it off, thinking college students couldn't write good fiction. I continued to consume good fiction, particularly short fiction, which I loved then and I love now.

One thing I do recall about the days before I became a professional editor was the way I thought about the job. *Imagine*, I thought, *reading for a living*.

Editing is usually much more than just reading. I learned that working for publishing houses, editing the revolutionary *Pulphouse: The Hardback Magazine*, and then *The Magazine of Fantasy & Science Fiction*. Ignore, for a moment, the other editorial duties that involve sales forces and contracts and math (there's a lot of math in editing, believe it or not). Just contemplate the reading.

Editing original material involves a lot of scanning. Not real reading, and not reading what you like. Scanning for something catchy, something half-way interesting, something that will—

And then, suddenly, you find yourself in the middle of this grand adventure, filling with amazing people and startling ideas and great vistas—and then you hit a bump. Kind of a *what? What did that just say? Really?*

Those stories are seriously flawed, but they have a lot of good pieces. If they have a more good than bad or if they simply went awry for a page or two, they can be fixed, if you feel asking the writer to fix the story is worth your time. Otherwise, it's all encouragement and onto the next promising manuscript.

Day in and day out, except for the brilliant stories that leap off the page. Again, the grand adventure, the marvelous characters, the breath-taking vistas, the ideas you'd never ever contemplate on your own—and suddenly, you're at the end, wondering where's the next story? And, if you're a good editor, how do I make sure I get the next story? And if you're a savvy editor, how do I make sure I get *this* story?

That kind of editing is akin to mining for gold. You stick your hands in ice-cold water and sift through a lot of rocks before you find anything even promising.

The only job in editing even akin to the way I had imagined editing to be way back when is this one. For *The Best Crime and Mystery Stories 2015,* John Helfers and I divided up the mystery and crime stories *published* last year and read, and read, and read.

Very little of what I read was bad. Oh, yeah, editor me might have asked for a revision here or a tweak there on some of the stories, but my job as editor of *this* volume involves no tweaking or revisions. I get to paste a gold star on one of my favorite stories, share it with John, and then discuss.

We started this project late, in the second half of 2015 by the time the project went from a glimmer in the eyes of Mark Lefebvre of Kobo Books to commissioning John who then asked me to coedit. We had to gather materials in the fall, and read like college students cramming for an exam. I usually spend the month of December reading Christmas short stories. This year, I read about murder and mayhem, stabbings and decapitations.

I enjoyed myself immensely.

The variety of stories that get published under the mystery and crime heading surprise me. The stories aren't all dark and depressing. Sometimes they're funny or at least witty. And they all explore human nature in all its variations.

Perhaps that's what I love the most about mystery and crime stories—the way that they explore how our humanity works or doesn't work.

Because John and I write and read in multiple genres, we both know that the strict genre lines have broken down in the past ten years. One of my favorite detectives, Jim Butcher's Harry Dresden, solves magical crimes with all the wit and verve and sadness of Raymond Chandler's Philip Marlowe. One of the best novels I read in 2015, *All-American Boys*, by Jason Reynolds and Brendan Kiely, was marketed for teens ages 12 and up, and as far as I could tell, never got mentioned in the mystery press at all.

Romance writers from Nora Roberts to Fern Michaels have continuing series that are, for all intents and purposes, suspense novels with a touch of romance. For more than a decade now, Roberts, under her J.D. Robb pen name, has combined mystery, romance, and science fiction for her Eve Dallas *In Death* books.

Mystery writers themselves have brought in other genre elements as well. Half of Robert Crais's novel from a few years ago, *Suspect,* is from the point of view of Maggie, a German Shepherd. Some of the science in Jeffrey Deaver's Lincoln Rhyme series is so cutting edge that it almost feels like science fiction.

John and I are both aware of this trend, so when we had our first discussions about the volume, we decided to publish stories from other genres if we felt they were primarily mystery or crime stories.

We have a few of those stories here. I'm not going to point out which ones, because that would ruin the surprise. As I read one of the stories in this volume, I believed the author couldn't wrap the piece up without finding the ghost. There was no ghost—no fantastical ghost, anyway. Not in that story. There's a ghost in another story. Or is there...?

John and I initially thought the hardest task facing us was agreeing on what stories to include. We were wrong. We agreed on almost everything. We had the most trouble *eliminating* stories. If only Kobo had given us an anthology double this size—

Well, no. That would have led to fewer eliminations, but we still would have had to eliminate stories. In my opinion, 2015 was a banner year for mystery short fiction. We have a list of honorable mentions that we hope you look up after you finish reading this volume.

I've never quite had an editing experience like this one. For the first time ever, the experience matched my teenage imagination of editing. Reading, and then recommending.

Thanks to John and Mark for being such great partners. And huge thanks to the writers who published stories in 2015 for making our task extremely difficult.

—Kristine Kathryn Rusch
Lincoln City, Oregon
February 25, 2016

The Best Man: Tendai Huchu

First published in *Ellery Queen's Mystery Magazine*, August 2015

VaMhashu sat in his office, staring blankly at the piles of papers, invoices, letters, contracts, receipts that lay on his desk. In his left hand was a rocker glass with a finger of whiskey, straight. Mavis, his secretary, stood at the door. She'd been there for a minute or two, watching him anxiously, waiting for instructions. VaMhashu looked up and nodded.

"You can tell the superintendent to come in now," he said in a quiet voice.

Mavis turned and gestured with a simple sweep of the hand to allow the man waiting outside to enter. The superintendent walked in. He waited next to the chair across the desk. Mavis closed the door as she left.

"I would stand up, old friend, but I haven't the strength," said VaMhashu, motioning to the empty chair in which Superintendent Chiweshe sat down.

Chiweshe took off his hat, revealing a head speckled with grey hairs. He sat in silence for a while, not even bothering with the lengthy greeting rituals that were expected of him.

"You have found my son?" VaMhashu said. He raised the glass to his lips, but fell short before it reached them and let it drop back to the table again. "Well?"

Chiweshe looked at the hat in his lap.

"We found him at dawn," the policeman said in a grisly voice, "on the shores of Lake Chivero, near a picnic site on the northern bank."

VaMhashu looked up at the ceiling; a film of moisture in his eyes made them shine under the lights. He was a short, robust man, with a bald spot at the back of his head, and wore a moustache. He took several long breaths as he waited for the inevitable blow.

"We've been through war together, my friend, seen men who were like brothers to us die, but I don't know how to break this to you. . . ." Chiweshe's voice trailed a little and he cleared his throat. "Your son, they did things to him. I don't know if it was before or after . . . I am sorry. I am so, so sorry."

VaMhashu gritted his teeth and buried his face in his hands. He trembled like a man on the verge of a fit.

"I am sorry," said Chiweshe.

"I don't want your sorrys. I don't want stories. I want you to find the person who did this!" VaMhashu shouted.

"That's why I came here personally, to give you my word as a man who once served under you that I will not rest until I find the person who did this."

"You are not going to do that sitting in this office, are you?"

The superintendent took this as his cue to leave. He stood up stiffly, straightened his uniform, turned, and marched to the door. Just as he reached it, VaMhashu called to him:

"And when you find him—" VaMhashu reached into his desk and brought out a Mamba pistol from the drawer on his right-hand side, which he pointed at Chiweshe's head as he clicked the safety off.

VaMhashu's home was a large colonial bungalow in Highlands, which stood on a few acres of land, surrounded by tall bougainvillea hedges. It had a sheet-metal roof, box-profile style, which made noise as the rain fell on it.

On the veranda was a group of men drinking Chibuku. VaMhashu and some of the older men sat on old-fashioned wrought-iron chairs, while the younger men sat on the floor. From inside the house, where the women were, a popular funeral dirge poured into the night:

Mambo Jesu, hande, vakataura,
Hande, ndavekuenda,
Asi basa ndasiya ndapedza . . .

He could hear a voice weeping louder than the rest. It was his ex-wife, Runako, the boy's mother. They didn't have the body yet. It was still with the ZRP. The superintendent would escort it himself, in a sealed casket, when the time came. VaMhashu would rather have had solitude, but when there was news of death, there was no way to prevent relations and friends from swarming in like ants.

The garden boy, stationed near the gate, opened it. A Series IIA Land Rover cast its lights on the garden. Even from that far, the metal grinding of its buggered gearbox reached the veranda, as the driver put it in gear, and it crunched along the pebbled driveway. It parked behind the other cars on the lawn. The driver, a tall silhouette in the night, got out and slowly walked to the veranda, not bothered by the rain.

VaMhashu followed the figure as it drew closer until it reached the light cast from the veranda. It was a woman. A woman taller than any he had seen in his life. She walked with a stoop, as though trying to mask her height. She had short hair, wore a brown suit, a white blouse, and had a small handbag awkwardly drooped near her waist. When she reached the veranda, she stopped, curtsied the old-fashioned way, and clapped her hands, right over left. The men responded by clapping as well.

VaMhashu got up and went to her. He barely reached her chest.

"Nematambudziko," she said to him, as custom dictated.

"Akaonekwa," he replied.

He didn't recognise her. In the chaos of these things, she could have been a distant relation, or a friend of a friend, or someone just coming along for the free food.

"I know this is not a good time, but can we talk?" she said.

"And who are you?" he asked.

"Detective Munatsi from the CID—Superintendent Chiweshe sent me."

VaMhashu laughed. "I thought he said he was getting me his *best* man."

"I am she," Detective Munatsi replied in a flat voice, the kind that said she was used to this reaction.

VaMhashu wearily led her into the house, past the praying women, to his study. He sat on his desk and did not offer her a seat. The study had a bookshelf with some old volumes, a world map on one wall, and another wall lined with wooden face masks.

"I need to ask you some questions about the day Tinashe went missing," she said.

"Is this some kind of a joke? I already answered that when I filed the missing-persons report. You should have it in your files!"

"I know this is a difficult time for you, but if you want us to catch this guy, we have to do this now," she said. "Look, I've been pulled off another case just for you." She sighed. "Okay, I want to know what happened on the day Tinashe disappeared."

"It was Saturday, two weeks ago. He goes to play cricket at St. John's, where he's—he was doing his form one. I went to pick him up and he wasn't there."

"What time do you normally pick him up?"

"I don't. The driver usually does that," said VaMhashu. He explained that he had told the driver not to go on that particular day because he wanted to spend time with the boy. Tinashe was having trouble in school since the divorce and he thought it would be a good way to spend time with him.

"When did you get divorced?"

"Last year."

"And you're already remarried."

"That's none of your business."

"I noticed your ring. I'm just thinking the new setup might have disturbed him. Maybe he could have run away and then fallen in with the wrong people. We live in a violent age."

The detective walked over to the wall and inspected one of the masks. It was a light teak piece, an imitation by a local artist of a West African design. She stared into its hollow eyes, the white wall behind.

"After he went missing, did you receive a ransom note?" she asked.

"No."

"A phone call, text, e-mail, anything?"

"Nothing of the kind," VaMhashu replied, exasperated.

The detective moved to the side of the desk, took a copy of the day's *Herald* and tore a neat piece off. She reached into her handbag, brought out a pouch of tobacco, and sprinkled a pinch on the paper. She rolled it and sealed it with a lick. Then she lit up with matches and took a drag.

"You see, that's unusual. *Gororos* grab a rich kid and don't look to make a quick buck. That doesn't make any sense to me. If it was me, I'd have ransomed him." She blew out a plume of smoke. "Do you have any enemies?"

"Everyone has enemies, *Detective*," he said.

"Someone you strong-armed in the past, *munhu wamakavhara padhiri*, a contract gone wrong, someone you cut off in traffic. I want you to write me a list of their names. That will be a good starting point." VaMhashu scribbled some names on a pad. The detective continued, "You were told what they did to him? They took a pound of flesh: his hands, the heart, the gallbladder, his genitals, and the eyes. The eyes are the most important of all."

The midday sun was blazing overhead when Detective Munatsi arrived in Domboshawa. She parked near the five huts that made up the kraal. The heat made her sweat. Keeping her foot on the brakes, she opened the door, picked up a large rock, and tossed it behind the front tire. The hand brake was loose. She got out of the car, found another rock, and wedged it in front of the tire. It was going to take awhile to get an appointment with the lazy bastards at the

VID to sort out the problem.

The sound of drums came from beyond a grove of muzhanje trees. She picked up her handbag and slammed the door. A little girl in a tattered dress came out of one of the huts and ran to her. The girl smiled, revealing brilliant white teeth. *"Mauya kunhamo?"* she said, and the detective nodded.

The little girl took her by the hand and led her towards the sound of the drums. The huts had thick thatch with wavy designs. The walls were perfectly circular and the windows had glass panes. This was the homestead of a family that was doing well. A couple of chickens scurried past. In the distance, a boy herded a flock of goats. The detective remembered her own more modest upbringing in Manhenga.

A group of a hundred or so sat on a *dwala*. The men were at the right and the women to the left. Only the old men had stools to sit on. The detective joined the women, and sat at the back, from where her tall frame allowed her to see over the doeks, weaves, and perms of her fellow women. The *dwala* was hard, rough, and hot.

"Have you come from Harare?" an old woman turned to ask her.

"I am a friend of the family," Detective Munatsi replied.

"Such a tragedy, for one so young. A great hammer has struck the earth. These days it is us, the old, who bury the young."

The gathering was mostly made up of old people and little children. The men and women had gone to Jonhi or Harare North to seek their fortunes. A prophet with a Bible stood at the front. He was a crisp man in an Italian suit. There was a row of graves below the *dwala*, on brown earth. A freshly dug one was close to the prophet. The casket stood on a small table.

"For this tragedy to happen to the Mhashu family is nothing short of a sin. These are the end times, my brothers and sisters. VaMhashu is a devout Christian, a member of my church, God's own church. Let me tell you this, no one is a better Christian than this man. Last year when he bought a Benz, he remembered God, and bought me the exact same type, same colour, same everything, because he knows God is great and he remembered the servant of God. Now I am here to tell you that God will punish the wicked. God will wipe the tears from your eyes. God will raise Tinashe up to the heavens, because didn't He say, 'Let the little children come unto me'? The God we worship is a living . . ."

Affirmation and sobs from the congregation punctuated the sermon. Detective Munatsi's heart was wrenched by the wailing of the boy's mother. This is what she did on every case she worked. She went to the funeral to see the family. It made her more determined to see justice. It made the case personal.

After the burial, as the congregation walked down to huts, VaMhashu came up to her. He looked up, beads of perspiration on his brow, eyes red from tears shed.

"What are you doing here?" he said. "You should be out there chasing down my enemies, finding out who did this."

"I came to see if you had any enemies here," she replied.

"Among these old people? What kind of policeman are you?"

"I'm sorry. I didn't mean to cause you any more distress. I have men canvassing the city as we speak. We are doing everything we can. I came to offer my condolences."

"Let her stay, let her see a mother's sorrow," said Runako, who had crept up behind them. A small group had formed around. Her voice was hoarse, broken from moaning. "My child, my only child is gone, Detective. Can you bring him back to me? Will you dig up the earth and return him to my bosom?"

Runako turned and left before the detective could find anything to say. VaMhashu was led away by a group of men to the *dare* where they drank *mupeta*. The detective lingered by the fresh grave. She scooped up some earth and sprinkled it on the mound. Then she smoked a rollie. The plains in the distance were a mix of rocky outcrops and scrub. She went to the huts and joined the women. Taking off her jacket, she helped the *varooras* cook *sadza* in huge pots on open hearths outside.

In the early evening, as the crowd thinned down, the detective announced she was leaving. Funerals made her miserable. A couple asked for a lift to Harare and she obliged. Her Land Rover kicked up dust under the starlit sky.

VaMhashu lay in bed under soft satin sheets. He watched his wife, Tasara, remove her earrings and necklace. She had her back to him, sitting at the dressing table. It was full of cosmetics: strange foreign bottles containing elixirs he knew nothing about. The silver jewelery box he bought her for their wedding took its place of pride in the center, near the mirror.

He was ashamed of his desire, seeing the beads of her spine on her back as she undid her dressing gown. It slipped onto the stool. She studied her face in the mirror, using it to look back at him, triumphant in winning his attentions. When she was done removing her makeup, she came to bed.

"You have so much on your mind," she said, and kissed his cheek. "I wanted to come with you to Domboshawa but you wouldn't let me."

"Runako has rights," he replied.

"I don't care about her or your family. It's you I worry about. Tinashe was my stepson too. We were just beginning to get along when—"

"Please, don't say it," he said, bowed his head and sighed.

"Come here." She took his head and laid it on her chest. He could hear her heart beating. She massaged his head with her fingers and kissed him.

Tasara was only twenty-three. Her youth restored him. After Runako failed to give him more children, he had come to the decision that he would take another wife. It was not a decision he came to lightly. A man of his status could not be expected to have only one child. Runako should have understood. She was *vahosi* and Tasara would be *nyachide*. It would have worked, he thought, if only she had given it a chance.

He still loved Runako. How could he not after twenty years of marriage? But children mattered as well. It was a cultural obligation, a biological yearning.

Even Abraham had taken Hagar. Now he had lost his only child. Still, lying on her soft, youthful breasts, he knew Tasara would give him others. He was ashamed of these thoughts.

"ZRP are useless. I'm thinking of hiring a private detective," he said bitterly. "I don't even know why I turned to the police. Unprofessional. Corrupt. Underpaid. Useless. Useless."

There was no answer. He turned to Tasara and found she was already sleeping, breathing lightly. Sleep is the blessing of youth, he thought. He watched her for a while. And when he was sure he would not wake her, he got up, crept out of bed, and left the room.

He walked down the corridor, past the maid's bedroom, to the last door. The sweet pong of adolescence hit him as he opened it. He switched the light on and looked around the room. The bed was unmade. A pair of dirty trainers lay on the carpet. Dirty clothes thrown to one corner. Posters of American singers and movies on the walls. A desk with exercise books, textbooks, and school things. Tinashe's room was exactly as he had left it, frozen in time.

VaMhashu shut the door and turned the light off. He walked to the single bed and lay down in it. The mattress sagged under his weight and the springs squeaked. Alone at last, in the dark, he began to cry. Large tears ran down his face, soaking the bed, as he embraced a pillow tight against his chest.

Southerton was a postapocalyptic mausoleum of its former glory. Decaying factories that once churned out goods for export fell to pieces. Gone were the men in boiler suits and steel toecaps who walked these streets en masse. Their place was taken by the forlorn unemployed going to and fro aimlessly. The factories and warehouses were empty shells. Broken windows. It was silent, the machines within sold, smashed, or stolen. This was Harare's industrial heart.

The security guard who opened the gate wore blue overalls and had a baton stick dangling against his thigh. He stood to attention and saluted Superintendent Chiweshe. Chiweshe gave him a nod. The idea of returning a salute to someone outside the forces was abhorrent to him. Detective Munatsi followed a step or two behind. Her height made her look like a faithful Doberman trailing its master. Unlike the superintendent, she did not wear a uniform.

They walked past rows of construction equipment. Mostly it was heavy earth-moving hardware, front-end loaders, Caterpillar graders, tractors, tippers, and dumper trucks. Big vehicles with faded yellow paint. The metal was rusty and dented from years of use. Three road rollers were parked side by side. A driver in one of the machines lounged while reading *Kwayedza*. Detective Munatsi patted a drum and her hand came away black with dirt.

"I should have gone into business after the war," said Superintendent Chiweshe. "Look at all this equipment. It's fantastic."

"Boys and their toys. It's old, junk," she replied.

"Reliable, that's what it is. They don't make them like they used to. Look at your Land Rover. How old is it?"

"Nineteen sixty-three."

"Older than you are, and it's still going. My Hyundai will be buggered long before that car."

"Talking about cars, here's his Benz, so we know he's in," she said.

"Great work, Detective, but I simply called ahead." He laughed. "We have these things called cell phones now. Heard of them?"

She laughed. If the superintendent was making jokes, it was because he was nervous. She knew VaMhashu had called him last night, bawling down the phone, demanding answers. They'd pulled men off other cases for this one. Nothing had turned up yet. If it was a kid from the townships, they might not have bothered. A rich kid from the northern suburbs was another matter altogether.

They went into the brick double-story office building. Emblazoned at the front was the name:

MHASHU CONSTRUCTION & ENGINEERING LTD
Tel: 665546/7/8 Fax: 665308 www.mhashu.co.zw

The receptionist told them they could go straight up.

"Perhaps you'd like me to wait here, Sup. I'm not sure he'll be very happy to see me just now," said Detective Munatsi.

"*Pfutsek*, you're coming up to face the wrath with me. Every slap I'm taking is coming down on you, Munatsi," he replied. Then he smiled. "It's called victim support. Didn't you do the course?"

"ZRP, serving the nation in the twenty-first century, Sup."

Any mirth Superintendent Chiweshe had in him was all gone by the time they got to the lobby and waited for Mavis. She opened the door for them and let them into VaMhashu's office. VaMhashu stood up, came round his desk, and shook Superintendent Chiweshe's hand. The superintendent almost winced under the firm grip.

"You have news for me?" VaMhashu said straightaway. "I want results."

"We came to update you on the progress of the investigation, yes," Superintendent Chiweshe answered diplomatically. He felt like it was the war again. Then, he was a guerrilla fighter and VaMhashu was his commander.

"Results are not an update," said VaMhashu.

"We are very, very close. New leads are coming up every day. That's why I brought the chief investigating officer, whom you have met, to debrief you." He deflected the heat to his subordinate.

"Hang on. What size shoes do you wear?" VaMhashu asked the detective in

a puzzled voice.

"Pardon?" she said.

"Your shoes. They're big," he said.

"So are my feet," she replied. "That's why I wear these Grasshoppers, men's shoes; because it's hard to find women's shoes that fit me."

"Go on."

VaMhashu turned away and looked out the window. The back of the complex had a large yard filled with more equipment. Bare earth with clumps of lawn. The sun reflected off the windows and metal there. He held his hands behind him and waited for the report.

"This is a complex case. We have had no real leads to go with, so we've had to do old-fashioned policework. That means heavy canvassing. I'm sure you've seen the reports on the news. We had appeals in the newspapers, both state and independent . . ."

"All at the department's expense, if I may add," Superintendent Chiweshe said. VaMhashu snorted.

"As I was saying," Detective Munatsi continued, "we've had public appeals.

We've also held interviews with children, parents, and teachers at St. John's. No one saw anything unusual there. Then we covered potential witnesses near Lake Chivero at the time."

"Over a thousand man-hours in the last fortnight alone," Superintendent Chiweshe added.

"We're getting closer—" Detective Munatsi said, only to be interrupted again.

VaMhashu turned his head slightly to the side: "So what have all these interviews yielded?"

Superintendent Chiweshe coughed several times, brought out a handkerchief, and spat in it.

"Have you checked with the list I gave you?" said VaMhashu. His voice held the tremor of a man fighting to hold back his fury.

"There are seven names on the list," said Detective Munatsi. "I have interviewed four of them, but can't seem to find who Cai Pingjie, Wu Kai, or Jack Ma are."

"Gross incompetence. That's the reason this country has gone down the drain. Laziness. I wake up at five every morning. At quarter past six, I'm the first one here. I built everything you see around you through sheer hard work. And what do you people do—hang about in your offices all day long, waiting for bribes? They are business-men, Detective. Chinese businessmen. How hard is it to find a Chinaman in this country!" VaMhashu banged his hand on the window sill and turned around.

"Thank you," Munatsi said.

"No, thank you, for nothing," he replied.

"I will have a name for you within the week," she said.

"I'm engaging a private detective. Someone who knows what they are doing."

"Sir—"

"Get out of my office, both of you. Get out! Out!" He pointed to the door.

Superintendent Chiweshe gave a slight bow and turned round stiffly. Detective Munatsi followed behind, stooping to avoid hitting the lintel above the doorway. As they left, Mavis stood up and rushed to close the door behind them. The superintendent shook his head all the way to the car park outside. He hit the roof of his Hyundai with the palm of his hand. After waiting a few moments to calm down, he turned to the detective and said:

"Go. Find those damn Chinamen."

The hit drama *Timi naBhonzo* was playing on TV when Runako arrived at the Highlands home. She walked in without knocking, just as she had done when it was her house. VaMhashu and Tasara were in the lounge, watching the show. He was startled to see her and abruptly stood up from beside his new wife.

"What are you doing here?" Tasara asked.

"Will you tell your little pet that I don't speak to dogs; bitches, that is," Runako said, the venom dripping from her voice.

"Who are you calling a bitch?" Tasara turned her hand and showed the large rock on her fourth finger. "You should learn to knock. Pity you're not house-trained."

Runako clenched her jaw. "I swear to God, if I hear one more word, I'll burn this house down."

"Ladies, please," VaMhashu said awkwardly. He'd always arranged matters so that they didn't meet, like at the wake and funeral when he made sure Tasara was away at her parents' so there'd be no friction. "Tasara, can you please go to the bedroom."

She took her time, spending more of it eyeballing her rival than she did getting out. The house was big, but not big enough for two mistresses. When she was gone, VaMhashu turned to his ex-wife. Runako's eyes were narrowed into little slits, her lips were pursed.

"So what brings you here?" he said.

"It's still my house—half of it, anyway. I can come here anytime I want." Her voice was cold. Subzero cold.

"I thought we settled that when you took the Malborough house. Is this about money?"

"Ha." She laughed. "You haven't got any. I came here to get my son's things. I told you to give my child to me, but you wouldn't. I'm going to hate you for the rest of my life. Nothing your little whore can give you will ever replace Tinashe. Nothing!"

VaMhashu covered his eyes with his hand. His head was throbbing. She pushed past him and went to the bedroom. He followed her and watched from the doorway as she rummaged through Tinashe's things. Almost by instinct she stepped up to the bed to make it, but stopped herself. She collected his favourite Nikes, a poster from the wall, his rugby jersey, a book, and a jar filled with his baby teeth. She turned, gave the room one final look, and walked out. Only then did VaMhashu know she'd never come back to the house again. The house they'd bought together when he was still just starting out in business.

Detective Munatsi didn't bother with the other *tsotsis* and *gororos* in Southerton as she waited on Motherwell Road. It was cold. She drank Tanganda tea from a thermos—black, no sugar. A lorry passed by carrying a load of bricks. Then she saw the Benz going along Douglas Road. She sipped her tea patiently and waited.

Twenty minutes later, she pulled up at the yard a hundred meters or so away. The night guard, who didn't recognise her, challenged her. She pulled out her badge and said two words: "ZRP. CID." They didn't invoke the same terror as "CIO," but the way the guard rushed to open the gate was fine by her.

She took her time, walking in her usual languid gait. Her little handbag made a jingling noise as though it was full of coins. Not that there were any still in circulation those days. She was dying for a rollie. She checked her watch—06:40—as she walked through the reception.

Then she went up to the second floor and knocked.

"What?" VaMhashu shouted.

"Can I come in?" she said, opening the door.

"It's you." He couldn't mask his irritation. "I thought it was the guard. What do you want?"

She took a seat opposite his desk. "I told you I would come back within the week."

"I hope you're not wasting my time, Detective. Don't you have bribes to chase?" he said. She took the newspaper on his table and tore off a bit of the front page. She got the tobacco from her handbag and rolled one. Then she dropped the cigarette back in her handbag. VaMhashu cracked his knuckles.

"This is how it went down." She spoke in a low tone, but it carried clearly in the quiet of morning. "Tinashe went to school and played cricket that Saturday. He scored twenty-one runs, and his under-fourteens won by thirty-nine against St. Georges. He was watching the first team with his friends when he said goodbye and went to the car park.

"You showed up later, and he was gone. You called home, and he wasn't there. Then you checked with his friends. No one at the school noticed anything unusual."

He interrupted her. "We know all this already!"

"Yes, we do. We also know he was picked up by a black Benz, just like the one outside," she said.

VaMhashu turned grey. "I didn't pick him up!"

"No. You didn't. This is what we also know. Your business is failing. You're not making any money. You have all this equipment outside lying idle, rusting. The Chinese have come in hard. They have modern equipment. They bring in their own labour, cheap labour. They work faster. They are more efficient. They undercut and take shortcuts. Crucially, they can pay more in bribes.

"You see, the list you gave me of your enemies—it was all your rivals in construction and civil engineering. The three Zimbabwean firms and the South African on the list are looking much healthier than you are. You relied on government contracts; now the state is 'Looking East' and you don't have what it takes to beat the Chinese. They are the future; you're yesterday."

"I don't see what this has to do with anything!" VaMhashu got up. His eyes narrowed, a vein in the middle of his forehead pulsed. "I am going to call your boss and have you fired!"

"I'm not finished yet," Detective Munatsi said calmly. She stared him in the eye. "You did what any man of faith would do; you turned to your spiritual advisor. The prophet told you that just as Abraham sacrificed Isaac, you must give up Tinashe. The ritual medicine to save your business would be more potent if it was someone closest to your heart. Your back was against the wall. With a new wife, a man can make more children. But not just any man. A man used to sacrificing pawns on the battlefield. A man who knows what it is to send other men to their deaths, wake up in the morning, and start over again."

VaMhashu bared his teeth. His nostrils flared; he was shaking like a reed in a heavy storm.

"It was the prophet who picked up the boy in his Benz. No one noticed anything unusual. And so Tinashe was the sacrificial lamb. And this is what you got: his hands—for work; his heart—to entice clients; his gallbladder—so your enemies could taste bitterness; the genitals—so your wealth could multiply. And the eyes. The eyes are the most important of all. His eyes—so no one would see what you have done. His eyes—so his *ngozi* would wander in the wilderness, blind, and never return to avenge you. His eyes—so the law could not find you. That is what the prophet gave you."

VaMhashu reached into his drawer and pulled out his Mamba. The steel glistened under the light. Detective Munatsi froze. He pointed the gun at her, in the space right between the eyes.

"I built this company from the ground up, with my own hands. You have no idea how hard I worked for this. How would you feel if everything you'd built your whole life crumbled to dust? Wouldn't you do anything?" he said.

"Including murdering your own son?"

"So my legacy can live!" Spittle flew out of his mouth. He checked his watch. "But no one else will know because you won't be there to tell them."

"So, that's the plan. Murder me and get rid of me. The guard might hear the shot. No doubt you will bribe him, make him an accomplice, and get him to help you dispose of the body before the staff get here." She nodded. "That confirms my theory. But at least let me have one last smoke before you kill me."

He ground his teeth. "Okay. Move your hands slowly. No sudden movements."

She opened her handbag. In a flash her hand reached in and quickly withdrew. But she was too slow, too slow for a man like VaMhashu with military experience. He might have been old, but the reflex was still there. He pulled the trigger.

There was a click. He pulled it again. Another click. Detective Munatsi raised her hand, and in it was a rollie. She put it to her mouth, lit up, and began to laugh.

Superintendent Chiweshe walked in.

"The Rhodesian-made Mamba is known for being unreliable. Lousy design, poor workmanship—the alignment is off, which causes feeding problems. That's why only two hundred were ever made," said Chiweshe. "But yours might well have gone off if I hadn't removed the bullets."

Detective Munatsi patted her handbag and it made a jingling sound.

VaMhashu swayed and sat down in his chair. His face turned grey. The superintendent went to the cabinet, took out a glass, poured a double of whiskey, and gave it to him.

"You murdered your son. You tried to kill an officer of the ZRP. The war is over, but it seems we're still fighting it, my friend," said Superintendent Chiweshe in a melancholic voice. "I told you she was my best man. Now it's Chikurubi Maximum for you, and after that, the gallows. Out of the love I still bear for you, I will give you a choice."

Detective Munatsi took out one 9x19mm from her handbag and put it on the desk. She took a drag and exhaled the smoke up to the ceiling. The superintendent touched her shoulder. She got up and they walked to the door. She took the key, closed the door, and locked it from outside. The two walked past the plant equipment, towards the gate. The superintendent was quiet, his face drawn to a tight mask. Detective Munatsi trailed a step or two behind.

"You must have known he'd done it when he first came to you," she said.

"I don't know what I know anymore," he replied. "At least I have you."

"Let's go get the prophet for real now and end this," she said.

"No. We can't touch him, you know that. The prophet has political friends way above our pay grade. In this country, you learn only to pick the fights you can win. There's always a bigger predator in the jungle. This was the best possible outcome. The honour of my friend is preserved. The papers tomorrow will say he killed himself out of grief for his son. You never solved this case, Detective. It will go down as a blemish on your record. Go home, have a beer, tomorrow you start on a new case."

There was a loud bang as they reached the gate. The guard looked startled, but said nothing. The detective and superintendent did not look back; they were homicide, not suicide. A few cars drove along Douglas Road. Day was breaking in Harare—the Sunshine City.

Tendai Huchu was born in 1982 in Bindura, Zimbabwe, and is a podiatrist living in Edinburgh, Scotland. The *Hairdresser of Harare* was his first novel, and was first published to acclaim in Zimbabwe and South Africa in 2010, followed by translations into Italian, German, Spanish, and French. His most recent novel is *The Maestro, the Magistrate, and the Mathematician*. His short fiction in multiple genres and nonfiction have appeared in *The Manchester Review*, *Ellery Queen's Mystery Magazine*, *Gutter*, *Interzone*, *AfroSF*, *Wasafiri*, *Warscapes*, *The Africa Report*, and elsewhere. In 2013 he received a Hawthornden Fellowship and a Sacatar Fellowship, and was shortlisted for the 2014 Caine Prize for African Writing.

(disc.): Genevieve Valentine

First published in *Hanzai Japan*

I went alone to Greenland, because I'd already gone exploring Nara Dreamland with Lars and Cormac and Eddie Leaper, and they'll make you done with anything.

I'd started the drive in the dark, and the light was still barely enough to take photos by, and it was so foggy — the mountain fog that hangs so heavy it seems impossible you can't push it aside with one hand and let it swing shut behind you – that when I saw the man on the carousel it took me ten seconds to realize he was dead. I hoped it was Leaper.

He was propped with his back against the pillar, head lolling slightly, like he'd died admiring one of the horses still clinging to its post. I didn't see any blood, not then, but his eyes had clouded over so he'd been dead at least overnight. (At the time I didn't know how I knew, and I was already in the car headed back when I realized it was condensation on his corneas, like back in New York on the windows that faced the garden, and I braked so hard I spun out.)

There was no bag near him. I imagined his friends panicking and making a run for it, which seemed sadder than him actually dying until I realized he might not have been an explorer at all, just dragged here because no one would find it.

I took a few pictures without thinking, an establishing shot and a few angles and details to sort out later, like I did with any corner of a *haikyo* that struck me. I had forty-three photos of the room where the maple had gone to seed.

For all the urban explorers who go into mental hospitals and come out with storied of chalk that writes by itself and faucets that turn on and off an the certainty that someone's there with you, I'd never heard of someone finding a dead thing larger than a fox. Were you supposed to call the police? You were probably supposed to call the police.

There were no tire tracks. There were no footprints but mine. The plants were undisturbed for fifty paces in every direction. I started breathing through my mouth, because it made less noise.

He had a postcard in his vest pocket with Nara deer on the front. On the back, someone had written "Let them ear from your hand." The receipt in his pants pocket was from a highway stop two years ago, he had directions written on it in English that mapped to the middle of the pacific. When I set them on his legs to take a photo, they looked like leaves.

At Nara Dreamland, the first time I ever went anywhere with them, Lars and Cormac had dared each other up the Aska coaster – Lars had seen someone else's photos and was trying to top them by scaling the whole drop, and

Cormac had taken some pills and was mostly just climbing because he couldn't stand still. Eddie spent three hours trying to convince me to stay there overnight with him.

"It's really beautiful at night, I've seen pictures," he's said, as I was taking photos of peeling paint on the Main Street shops. "Do you remember it from when you came here?"

I had been five years old back then, on a trip home with my parents, and I mostly remembered the plane rides and my grandparents' faces. I should never have told Lars I'd been here. Lars couldn't keep secrets, even from people who should clearly never be told anything.

"I have work tomorrow, Eddie."

He's twitched and gone quiet for a while, like he always did when I used his real name. ("It's mostly just Leaper," Eddie had said when Lars introduced me, like it was an honorific someone else had given him that he was bashful about.)

"But we could –" he said, and then something cracked and Cormac was shrieking and we had to run to help.

All the way across the park, my bag banging against my shoulders and my camera smashed to my chest with both hands, I was thrilled that Cormac was shouting and cursing. That meant he was probably fine, and I didn't have to worry about how relieved I'd been to hear him falling just for something else to do.

Haikyo hunting only works well if you're with the same type of people. Maybe you need one thrill seeker to be the first one over the gate, but otherwise, you stick to your own kind.

But I don't get the thrill of crossing a threshold that some people get, and I don't have any skill at photography. The Japanese kids who do haikyo respect the condition of the buildings, but it's still a detective story to them, and white guys who came to Japan just to see haikyo were all pretty terrible, and they were all interested in the next place or the hardest place, so I still hadn't found anyone of my kind.

I might just be a bad explorer. We'd moved back to Yokohama before I got started, so I'd never done any of the haunted hospitals in the States, but I've never seen the point of going someplace just to terrify yourself. Some people like to go rooftopping or memorize forty miles of tunnels just to see if they can make it out alive without a map. Cormac told me UK explorers scan maps looking for the (dis.) notation – disused, the final mark that a place has been abandoned – and the first to get into the place gets the bragging rights. Plenty of abandoned places still had security, and for some people that was more important than the place: Witanhurst, military bunkers, anything they had to sneak into. Some people got off on the thrill of arrest.

I just like being in places that human decision has emptied out. They're quiet in a way nothing else is quiet, like even the animals left them alone for a while – some mourning period that still lingers after the foxes gnaw through the walls. It was a place that was chosen for a while and then it was unchosen; you can count its ribs, you can wonder at the little stack of plated left behind by people who must have known they were never coming back and what made those four plates the thing they could live without.

There was a local haikyo team I met up with once, but while we were in the factory they were talking about the last place and the next place and how hard it had been to find this place, and five voices murmuring is still five voices. I didn't last long with them. Shouldn't have lasted with Lars and Cormac and Eddie either, but it's dangerous to go places by yourself, and it's definitely more comforting to go places with people you kind of hate.

It's fine. I don't mind coming back to the same place over and over. Sometimes the quiet goes – kids find it and start hanging out there, or it gets refurbished, or it gets demolished until it's just a pile of timber and glass – and then I look for new places, but there are some small houses in the mountains that I've been to a dozen times, so quiet I can sit and watch the foxes burrowing. I don't need things to be showy.

Yokohama makes me feel carbonated. Maybe New York would have made me feel the same way if we'd stayed there, but who knows. Yokohama has a few places that feel like New York – Akarenga sometimes, maybe – but just seeking them out makes me feel guilty for wanting Yokohama to be something it's not, something I wasn't really old enough to know. When kids at school asked me about the States, there was nothing to tell; it just felt like I had moved from one city into another

city that sometimes mapped over its ghost, two dimen-
sions into three, and I hadn't ever stretched to inhabit it
like I was meant to.

It's good for me just to be in one of these gone places
for a while, to wander through something so deliberately
still, with all its hopes gone. I take pictures of the branches
that have broken through the roof: saplings in the middle
of a hotel lobby, a carpet of maple leaves in a dining
room. I never show them to anyone – no point, maybe,
but no need. I like having places just for myself; that's why
I ever go out to haikyo at all.

(Lars runs a forum for exploration photos. When he hit
a hundred thousand shots six months ago, he drew the
number in the ground on some dirt outside an unknown
site and challenged anyone to find it. He set up a subfo-
rum for the people who are trying. It's the most popular
thing on the site.)

Maybe I understand the archivist kinds a little. The
ones who go to libraries and historical societies and buy
atlases looking for forgotten places, or who spend six
weeks tracking down a family out of a photograph, just to
see if they can. Not that I'm any good at it (you have to
have a network to be good at it), but I understand. It took
me weeks to get up the courage to go to Takakanonuma
Greenland, but by then I could have told you the layout of
that park with my eyes closed.

The difference between the Greenland and the
Dreamland amusement parks is that Dreamland exists in
a way you can track. There are pictures of soldiers and

families visiting when it was still open. There's video foot-age of people riding the rollercoasters and the swings and wandering down Main Street, holding children who have that slightly bewildered look at children tend to get at amusement parks, surrounded by so much fun that will soon be over and that's out of your control – the birth of some lifelong dissatisfaction.

But not Greenland. When you go looking for Green-land, the park might as well have been haunted since it opened for all the pictures you can find of it in its heyday. That place had been born empty in the mist and stayed that way, like it had been made for the ivy to devour.

I made notes and looked at maps and made some ar-chives requests of the train stations near Hobara pretending I was studying civil engineering and decided where I had to go. And after the Nata Dreamland visit I took all the extra precautions you made when going someplace solo; I didn't want any of them coming with me, but I knew things could get out of hand if you went exploring alone.

I don't remember driving back from Greenland, that first time. I had the police number programmed into my phone, a call never sent that whole five-hour drive. I de-leted it when I got home, and then I sat on my bed and scanned through fifty pictures of the corpse. His hair looked like a businessman's, gone a little to seed; too long between cuts. My notes from the car, almost too shaky to read, were that he was chubby, but when I was at home and flipping through the photos I realized he might just be swollen. I set down my camera for a while.

He had no tattoos on his forearms. Someone had rolled up his sleeves to the elbows to prove it. My first thought was that he had rolled them up himself, before, but it was cold enough that his eyes had frosted over- night, so he wouldn't have. Most likely someone dressed him after.

I thought about that for a long time, sitting cross-leg- ged on my bed. I wondered if he really had just died of natural causes, like a cat that runs away from home when it knows the end is coming. He was young, maybe he re- membered the park from childhood and had wanted to come back here, and hadn't bothered to bring much with him because there wasn't much he'd need. Maybe he'd been humming carousel music until his heart stopped.

I doubted it. His shoes were worn nearly through – in one of the pictures the sole was peeling near the arch, and it looked like a sheet of vellum, there was so little left of it. But they were untouched: not a spot of mud, not a blade of grass.

Someone had killed him, and washed the body clean, and dressed it carefully – sleeves rolled up for testimony. Someone had carried him through the castle gates like a new bride and chosen the carousel for him, and set him gently against the post so he could look at the horses until he was found.

And he must have been meant to be found. There were so many of us looking for places, looking for this place, looking for things to take photos of, that whoever killed him had staged him to be seen. My establishing shot was at an awkward angle; I couldn't tell if he was really looking at the horse, or if he was meant to be looking at whoever approached.

Lars sent me a message at two in the morning. *Hey, you haven't been around much. Cormac's out of his cast. Feel like going out?*

We went up to some abandoned factory housing that took us nearly five hours to get to. Lars kept the coordinates secret as long as he could, shaking his head and giggling when Cormac asked him, hinting at things it wasn't.

When Lars got to "No one will get smallpox," I said, "Lars, just tell us or don't."

He blinked for a second before he admitted what it was. After that I put headphones on and ignored everybody from the front seat, which I always got to sit in, because Lars's GPS was broken and I had to translate signs.

("Good thing you've turned local," Lars had said when he pulled up, like he always did, "or we'd die of old age in Yokohama."

We all waited the tree seconds it usually took for Eddie to remind everyone it was also nice to have a girl around in case security stopped you, but he must have still been upset I wouldn't fuck him in Dreamland, and he kept quiet.)

"Where have you been anyway?" Cormac asked me eventually. "You haven't been in the forums. You going anywhere?"

"I'm never in the forums. I don't care who finds Lars's number."

"Jealous, you are. There have been eighty guesses so far. Somebody did a counterfeit just to see if Lars would return to the real one to check on it. Idiots." He leaned forward. "Lars told me where it was."

"He'd tell anyone," I said, and Lars laughed like I was trying to be funny and said, "I could tell you, too," and I shook my head and turned up the volume.

"Let's just find someone else who likes this shit," Cormac said at some point, between songs. "Anybody Japanese could read the fucking signs, she's not worth it," and it was a solid two seconds before Lars answered, "It's fine, she's fine."

The homes looked about eighty years old, which made sense when I thought about it but still surprised me. The roof had fallen in on the kitchen of the first house, and we couldn't get into the biggest bedroom because the door had swollen and molded shut to the frame, so Lars, Cormac and Eddie all took turns getting artistic shots of the panes without paper and whatever they could manage of the room beyond.

I went into the smaller room, which had to have been a child's, it was so small. It had been wallpapered in Moga postcards that had crumbled or bubbled or warped, so it looked like the wall was swelling with huge grubs that had black bobs and lipstick for camouflage, rolling down the wall in herds.

There hadn't been nay grubs in Greenland. No flies, no beetles, none of the things you'd think would be interested once someone had died. I didn't remember him smelling like anything; nothing rotten had coated my mouth, like the smells of dead things do even when you try to keep them out. Had he been there long enough that the smell was gone? I imagined a scar down the center of his chest, right along the placket of his shirt, where someone had taken the innards out, so the rest would last longer.

But his eyes had been pristine, milky and round and still glistening, not an eyelash disturbed. The insects couldn't have taken over. Not by then.

"You thinking of stealing one?"

I jumped. "What?"

Eddie gestured to my camera, where it hung forgotten over my sternum. "Taking nothing but photographs, remember. Leave the postcards for posterity."

"I wasn't going to steal anything," I said, but Eddie was already taking a photo of the wall like it was evidence he could use later if the Missing Eighty-Year-Old Postcard Council called him into court.

The woods around the houses were deep and quiet, the trees nearly interlocking, which gave everything a grim darkness shot through with bands of light, and I took pictured of that every ten minutes, watching the puddles of sun across the ground and wondering how late in the morning it was before the condensation on his eyes warmed and disappeared, until Lars came out shouting for me because they thought I had fallen through the floor to the cellar and fainted.

The Ferris wheel at Greenland is at the farthest edge from the sad castle entrance, so you have to work to reach it – my civil engineering class would have frowned on having something so distinctive so far away – but it's worth it. A ring of circular cars, like a model of an atom or a cartoon firework before it bursts. And decay has only made it quainter, pastels and patina and the entrance nearly blocked off with feathery plants like nature can't wait to crowd inside. It's already made it into the lower cars – the saplings have gotten big enough to push in-side, their branches trailing leaves against the seats. When I went back to Greenland, alone, I made myself take photos of it again before I went to the carousel. I was an explorer, the Ferris wheel was as good as anything.

I couldn't look directly to see if he (it, he) was still there, o I watched the ground for prints (there were only mine, softened by the damp but still marked where I had stepped across the green), and then looked through the viewfinder as I rounded the curve, until I saw the slumped silhouette. Then the shutter sounded like doors slamming shut right on my heels, there was so much blood in my ears. My hands were shaking. I pressed my elbows to my sides, to keep the shots steady.

He had no tattoos on his ankles or his neck. I hadn't been willing to do more than lift his collar to see if he had anything lower on his back; the glimpse was enough to tell if he had affiliation tattoos, and it would have been rude to drag him onto the ground to check for any on his thighs.

I set his head to rights afterward, so he could look at the horses. The mist had shaken loose from his eyes, and it made him look more interested in everything. (I knocked some air loose from his nose when I pushed him up. He smelled like the floor of the forest, sour and wormed. When I pulled back from it I saw the calluses where his glasses should have been.)

His shirt was from Uniqlo, which meant nothing, and when I undid his buttons there was no easy scar on his stomach where he'd been emptied out. *Be brave*, I thought, *he's like any other unchosen place,* and so I slid my hand lightly around his ribs – I winced when I pressed in; I was ticklish and always sympathized – and felt a scar that was still raised. Either very old, or very new.

His fingernails were as clean as my father's, and he had a callus on his right index finger from writing too much. His mouth had been sewn shut with careful, invisible stitches behind the lips, so tight you couldn't get a look at the teeth. I ran my way over his lips to count the stitches (fifty-two), and then along his jaw to count his teeth (three missing).

The postcard was gone.

I froze with my hand still in the pocket of his vest, my first thought was, *Maybe he moved it to another pocket*, and when I realized I laughed too loudly and covered my mouth with my free hand. Then I checked his other pockets anyway, in case I had put it away wrong, and then underneath him, even through the cracks in the boards, just in case. But it was missing.

The receipt was still there, and I took it out with the sides of my fingers – too late to worry about fingerprints, but still – and got half a dozen photos, just in case.

I was glad I had taken so many shots on my way in; my hands were shaking and I would never have been able to put his vest and collar the way I had found them without some reference to go by.

I waited until I reached Utsunomiya to pull over, and found a café where I could sit with my computer. (I couldn't look up any of this from back home.)

Looking for someone who's gone missing is like looking for a building that has. The news only reports it if he's famous enough, and in that case you have to think his corpse would get a bigger example than being left in some mostly-forgotten amusement park. You can't call district police and start asking questions about dental records, but you never call looking for maps directly, either. You go to the library and make up some excuses and start hunting, if you don't have anything to go on, you take the first map you can find and look for anything (dis,).

I started at Nara. The postcard could mean anything, but if he'd been at one of the deer parks, someone could have caught him. He must have died long enough ago for the first round of flies to have been in him and gone, not quite enough time for the second. Hair already shaggy, wearing glasses. I started pulling photos.

It took me under a thousand to find him, in the background of someone's shot of the red Temukeyama gate.

He still had a watch, then, and she carried a small draw-string backpack, and his button-down shirt was checked in threads of navy. (It probably hadn't made any differ-ence to whoever had left him, but I was glad he'd been dressed in a style he liked even after someone killed him.)

My computer could go closer than my phone, and the coordinates from the receipt put me on Manuae, which was so small I had to be zoomed in completely before I could see anything but water. it was an atoll shaped like a ring. This close, Manuae had a little (dis.) at the end of its name.

There was an extra four-digit number tacked on to the end of the coordinates – the hour on a clock. A lock code. Number of people. Kilos of cocaine.

I felt with every guess like I'd felt in the plane on the way to Yokohama at thirteen, watching movies in Japa-nese because I couldn't sleep, refusing to put on subtitles and getting a bigger knot in my stomach with every word I didn't understand. All of this was just missing vocabulary – I didn't want my share of anything, I didn't want justice for whoever he was. He was an abandoned hotel, he was a peeling shrine, he was a stack of plates; I was closing a window that had no panes in it.

As I was checking into the hotel for the night, my father called. He wanted to make sure I was still alive, he said on the message, his voice fading bt the end of it like he was already hanging up.

Lars messaged me: LEAPER THINKS YOU DON'T LIKE HIM.

A little later: WANT TO DO ANOTHER AMUSEMENT PARK?

WHICH ONE?

GULLIVER MAYBE? OR GREENLAND. OR RUSSIAN VILLIAGE BUT CORMAC ALREADT WENT.

I WENT WITH SOME PEOPLE TO GREENLAND LAST YEAR, I wrote, because nothing takes the shine off for most explorers like knowing someone's already been there. IT WAS BORING. WE SHOULD DO GULLIVER. OR THE SEX MUSEUM IN HOKKAIDO?

SEX MUSEUM COULD BE FUN, said Lars, after a pause where I could almost hear him looking up other pictures to see if it was worth it. BUT TOO FAR AWAY. CORMAC'S TEACHING ENGLISH TWICE A WEEK NOW. WE COULD DO THE GRAND MOULIN?

HEARD IT WAS DEMOLISHED.

It had been beautiful; a hotel built three stories high and decorated like New Orleans, balconies like lacework and the floors hardwood under the peeling brocade carpet. Moss has grown on it in patches, and the gold-stamped wallpaper was peeling in wide coils like doll's hair. There were still some desk chairs in rooms on the third floor, and you could sit and look out at the treetops and understand exactly what had happened with a hotel set so far back in the woods it felt like you were the only living soul for a hundred miles. The birds had come back, and after a few hours I saw a rabbit race from the front door into the cover of trees. They said the owner killed himself and that's why it was empty, but no ghosts moved, there are anywhere.

I'd driven back over when I heard it was demolished, to see if it was true. Sometimes people see one fallen wing and assume the whole building is unstable, or someone will say a place is gone just to discourage others from going, you never know. But it had been eaten, a crater among the trees with a few piles of brick and lacework still waiting to be carted away. There were no birds nearby; there wouldn't be.

☹ TOO BAD. WHAT ABOUT A LOVE HOTEL?

WITH EDDIE?

LOLOL. HE'S FINE. WE SHOULD TRY YUI.

Yui was where the murder happened. Supposedly. That room was scorched out down to the beams. Some explorers had her ghost burned it down, and the story struck. You can't keep explorers out of there, now, and Lars's forum has a whole section dedicated to it with photos of the red handprints that half of them swear that paint and the other half swear are blood.

MAYBE. SEE WHAT CORMAC SAYS.

Cormac said the Fuurin motel was closer, and so that's where we went. I pulled my mask up and pretended the rubber seal made it hard to talk, and half-heartedly took pictures as Cormac and Lars dared one another to get aerial shots from the roof.

I stood for a while in the Japan room, which looked like a set from a Bond movie right down to the TV in one corner, like what I remembered Japan looking like even after I had been home to meet my grandparents as a kid, before that half-memory space filled up enough for me to reconcile it.

From the medieval Europe room, Eddie and Cormac were taking turns getting their pictures with the suit of armor. There was a spider on the wall beside them. They hadn't seen it; it was as big across as my hand and utterly still except when Eddie laughed and then it raised one leg, as if deciding whether or not to strike.

Watch out, I almost said, or *Behind you*, but even if they listened they'd probably just kill it. Take nothing but photographs, kill nothing but insects.

Some of the roof had fallen in, but it wasn't yet decay, just neglect. The garden courtyard outside the Japanese room hadn't yet been overtaken by the plants. It was one good cleanup away from being usable again, and seemed to be clinging to its chances; the sort of place that hasn't yet gone quiet the way it needs to for me to be happy in it.

I looked over my shoulder. On every wall that was still whole, spiders, holding perfectly still.

It was almost a week before I could get the time to rent a car and go back to Greenland. By now the spine of the coaster didn't even give me the thrill of having found it. I was just relieved it was still there, and I was the only living thing in it.

The body was breathing. I took two steps back before I did the math and remembered it was about time for the second round of insects inside him. (Or the first round, if he had been preserved before he got here. Nearly anything could disrupt decay. The more research I did the more I thought something had been wrong with this body.) They must have been inside the stomach cavity, making homes for themselves; his lower chest shifted in and out an inch at a time.

The postcard was back in his pocket. Nothing else was written on the back. I had expected another line, some dialogue or a strikethrough when the message was received, but the only sign it had been touched was that one corner had snagged in the pocket and folded when they slid it back in. I took pictures, just to compare later. There was a dot of black marker on the front, and I couldn't remember if it had been there before. It would probably be enough for whoever came back.

And they would come back. The only one of them who had respected the quiet was the dead man, whose wrists sometimes stretched as if there was still a pulse beneath them, thanks to the worms and the ants. He was an abandoned hotel, an empty place; he understood. It was the others who didn't. The people who made the place had decided this place un-existed, and they had deliberately left it behind. It was cruel of them to interrupt it.

I wrote, "This place isn't safe" on the back of the postcard, my kanji unsteady (just as well, if you're trying to look terrified). I walked out backwards, used a branch behind me to cover the worst of my footsteps. There weren't many. I was learning.

Inside the Ferris wheel car, hidden by brush and with a missing door in case I had to run for it, I wrapped myself in the emergency blanket I kept in my rucksack. It was cold, and it was only going to get colder, but I wanted to wait, and condensation on your eyes looked pretty enough, if you died.

They would come overnight – tonight, maybe, or the night after. They'd see the note and take him away, with the insects burrowed warmly inside him. When I came back out into the park, tomorrow morning or the morning after, there would be only the Ferris wheel behind me and the carousel horses ahead, and the kind of quiet that would slowly become birds.

When I reached to turn off my phone, Lars had sent a message: BACK TO DREAMLAND? AN OVERNIGHT. EDDIE'S ASKING.

SURE. TONIGHT. MEET YOU THERE.

I should call the police, I thought. All three of them should be arrested. Leave that place alone.

Greenland was beautiful in the dark. The rollercoaster snaked against the stars, and the curtain mist settled over everything along the ground. If they came to get the body, I wouldn't even see it. If they came looking for me, I wouldn't know until it was too late. If it was other explorers who had taken the card and put it back in a fit of conscience, then it would serve them right to piss themselves and get on a plane back home.

If there was no one, and it was just the corpse and me and some card that had gone missing and come back all by itself, I'd be waiting a long time. That was all right. It was neither one place nor another, until somebody came.

A spider crawled across my shoe; then it stopped, perfectly still.

Genevieve Valentine's first novel, *Mechanique: A Tale of the Circus Tresaulti*, won the 2012 Crawford Award and was nominated for the Nebula. Her second novel is the speakeasy fairy tale *The Girls at the Kingfisher Club*. Her third novel, the political thriller *Persona*, is out now from Saga Press. She has currently the writer for *Catwoman* for DC Comics. Her short fiction has appeared in *Clarkesworld*, *Strange Horizons*, *Journal of Mythic Arts*, *Lightspeed*, and others, and the anthologies *Federations*, *The Living Dead 2*, *After*, *Teeth*, *Hanzai Japan*, and more; her short stories have been nominated for the World Fantasy Award and the Shirley Jackson Award, and have appeared in several Best of the Year anthologies. Her nonfiction and reviews have appeared at NPR.org, *The AV Club*, *Strange Horizons*, io9.com, *LA Review of Books*, *Interfictions*, and *The New York Times*, and she is a co-author of pop-culture book *Geek Wisdom* (Quirk Books).

Autobiographical House: Amity Gaige

First published in *Providence Noir*

I moved into the Armory District in the springtime of my fourth year of college. A handwritten sign on the door of a beat-up china-blue historic home on Dexter Street: *Attic/One Bedroom.* At the time, the area was full of dropouts like me – storied young people, generously tattooed. I like to think it had a tang of Berlin to it, circa 1990 – I mean the contradictions, especially between Broadway and Westminster: RISD types mixed with Dominican muscle men mixed with gay professionals, with a couple defiant elderly people lording over each block. It reminded me a little of old Woonsocket, a place I no longer felt I could return to. For several months before Dad and Ma discovered I'd left Brown, I walked the district, content to be alone. What I loved best was the building itself – the Armory – a castle-like structure running an entire block of Cranston Street, bookended by two crenellated turrets. In the daylight its brick were tacky yellow, but in the nighttime the Armory building filled up the West End with the medieval shadow, and remained, since it had been in disrepair for decades, unlit; you could almost hear the dripping of pipes in the great hall. Nobody came in or out.

I had been happy once or twice, and these moments were also associated with large buildings.

1999: The Metropolitan Opera House. Mémé in a stole. I was ten. "Champagne for me," Mémé had whispered to the barman in her Woonsocket French accent, "and champagne for the child." I did not watch the ballet; I watched the hall itself, five fan-shaped levels studded with gold lights, red velvet everywhere, a thousand rapt faces and no one looking back at me. The air was smoky with rapture. As the starburst chandeliers rose up on their pulleys I knew they would rise up in my dreams for years afterward. Was it the champagne? I don't think so. Later, when I was inside other big buildings, not nearly as pretty as that, I felt a similar weightlessness, a deep, wheezy, excited freedom, tinged with the illicit. I am a watcher. I don't like to *be* watched. Mémé would put her two fingers to her eyes, then move those fingers to my own. *I know you.* Later, as identification made me quite uncomfortable.

How I got from Woonsocket High to College Hill is a short story. I worked like a devil is how I did it. I studied until bedtime and set the alarm for four a.m. and got up and studied again. Every once in a while the gatekeepers at Brown would admit a Rhode Island native for good measure, and one year in the early aughts, that native was me. Mom and Dad shelled out for a party at Amvets, and all of Woonsocket came. Brown hadn't taken a single kid from Woonsocket since Frannie Archambeault in 1994. A great party except for when Ma raised a shaky glass to Mémé, and Dad had to shoo her into the powder room, both of them drunk on muscatel. Of course, come September, I was glad to be gone.

They didn't know what to make of me at Brown. Ma had taken me shopping for clothes but our approximation of what a Brown student would wear turned out pretty badly off the mark. I showed up with half a dozen cardigans from Apex, but they didn't suit my low-class haircut nor cover my jaw-dropping chest, which was, to be honest, an attribute my family discussed openly, because it presented many problems, some of them just logistical, like how to get a seat belt over it or how to buy a jacket for it, and some problems historical, because Mémé had exactly the same legendary bust size, and consensus was that it had ruined her life. I worked so hard to be a good girl. In high school, I'd worn the Woonsocket version of a burka – shapeless tunics over cotton leggings, everything a couple sizes too big. It was within me, always in my mind, that I should work extra hard against whatever it was Mémé recognized in me.

Professor K- was my freshman advisor. Dad and Ma were happy about Professor K- because he was a famous architectural scholar (they read this on the website), and ever since I was a kid I'd said I wanted to be an architect. In photographs, he looked like a cross between Albert Camus and a *Dukes of Hazzard*-era Tom Wopat. He was forty-two at the time I came under his influence, walking straight up to his desk with my hand out, like Dad had instructed me, my notebook pressed against my chest. I might as well have said, *Here I am, the dope you have been waiting for, an absolute fool.* His smile, after a pause, was warm and youthful. He was a very warm man when you first meet him, and naturally, he had a brilliant mind. He had written a seminal text on Walter Gropius; I'd read it closely, at age sixteen, and upon hearing this he signed me up for his popular lecture course, The Autobiographical House.

He was Viennese. When he first referred to himself with the term, I didn't know what it meant. I thought maybe it meant he was from Venice, but he sounded like a German. Why not just call yourself Austrian? But this was the first of many such moments at Brown. Words in English that were not in my vocabulary. Everyday allusions more difficult to parse than anything out of *The Wasteland*. Every time I pretended to understand was a minor betrayal of myself, and all the people of Woonsocket, but it never once occurred to me to ask anyone to clarify. Looking back now there was a lot of buried anger, layer under layer, but I did not feel any anger at all until I left school and moved to the Armory. And then I felt a lot, quite a lot.

Anyone but me would have seen it coming. Any girl who'd read Thomas Hardy novels or attended private school or owned a passport would have read the signs. Not me. Once, he even grabbed my wrist as I tried to leave Sayles Hall after The Autobiographical House, whispering, "Stay." Another time, during one of our meetings, he'd languorously opened a coffee-table book of Franz von Bayros's erotic paintings and asked me what I thought of them. ("Technically proficient.") Yet I persisted in seeing ours as a collegial relationship. I struggled quite a bit, however, once he finally for me down on the floor.

There was strenuous physical resistance and clear use of triggering words. So it was a violent coupling – the only pause originating in his awestruck expression upon penetration – and after that, well, I never struggled again. We had both experiences revelations: hi, that I was a virgin, and mine, that my personal sovereignty was completely irrelevant. The situation dragged on, and on, and on – three years – a month off here and there, one semester of liberation (Austrian Sabbatical), all of it a marathon of denial. As a junior, I suffered through one excruciating semester as his TA in Vienna: City of Dreams, during which I developed a case of eczema so profound I felt I was cursed. Who'd cursed me – his wife? God? I never had any sexual pleasure. He was always rough and loveless. I told no one, and did not pursue other boys. Back in Woonsocket for holidays, I took my place around the noisy table, drawing a blank when anyone asked me how school was going.

"She's too modest," Ma said, dragging her cigarette. "So smart they made her an assistant to the *teacher*."

Faces flipped toward me like dominoes: eyes, nostrils, mouth – five holes.

I tipped back my glass of muscatel.

"Jake, Jake," my aunt said to my cousin, waving, "tell the story of how you got arrested at Brown."

"Not arrested-"

"He was on a *job*," my aunt said. "A couple weeks ago. A racoon or something got into the crawl space so they called us. Some chick called campus police and said a white male was trying to dig his way into the building. Un-identified white male."

"That's me," said Jake. "Unidentified."

"Fucking eggheads"

I believe that I know what a *relationship* is. I know that it implies two people with individual wills meeting one an-other in some kind of mutually-agreed-upon psychic territory, and in the material world, at certain places and times, i.e., "Let's meet at two o'clock at the Coffee Ex-change." I even understand that a relationship can encompass moments of sacrifice and duty and even un-happiness and still be mutual. But then there are relationships that mimic relationships, and even if you are one of the parties involved, you have no clue that you are not, in fact, in a relationship. You are a kind of excruciat-ingly convincing performance.

It was not until my junior year, when, pausing outside a plate-glass window on Thames Street in Newport, I ex-perienced a moment of clarity at this point. I stood in an oversized raincoat, my hair in the kind of childish kinks it develops in humidity, and a man came up behind me and stood there breathing over my shoulder. I thought we were both looking at our reflection, the two of us. A calli-ope hooted eerily from somewhere in the fog-bound bay. By then, I was skinny and pale and miserable and so self-hating as to be radioactive, and I thought, *I am so terribly unhappy. I am going to have to kill myself, I am going to have to kill myself if I don't get out of this.*

Professor K- put one aged hand on my shoulder. "I will buy it for you," he said. I blinked. *What*? He gestured at the charm bracelet that now appeared to me on the other side of my reflection. "I will buy it for you on one condition," he said. "I will tell you when we get back to the hotel room." I nodded, though I had not been listening, and he disappeared inside the store.

In the chronology of things, I do not believe that what he did to me in the hotel room in Newport had any sort of bearing on subsequent events. It hurt me, and I bled. But I was from Woonsocket. I'd blinded myself throughout my life there, but suddenly I realized that all the violence was inside me anyway, a branching may of transgressions, crimes, betrayals. The community was full of the passions of any semi-isolated cultural subgroup on the economic downslope. We are full of rage. We were trying to kill one another as a form of relief. I remember what my own father said of Mémé the morning after we returned from the ballet those years ago. "She for you drunk? She got you *drunk*?" He ripped open the front curtains, as if she'd still be standing on the front porch hours later. "Where is she? I'm going to kill her. I'm going to do to her what she did to Claude. That crazy fucking Nipmuc."

A shame, really. Uncle Sam was wasting forty-two grand on my senior year. Pallid, unwashed, I stalked the edges of that aristocratic campus, moving around largely at night. I was a ghoul. I clung to the low wall that ran along Charlesfield, I watched normal boys hee-hawing through the windows of the social dorms (*that's* how you wear a cardigan), I watched attractive semiotics majors smoking Gauloises. And then I just left. Left my things in my room and rented my place on Dexter Street which remained for years, almost completely unfurnished.

I met Edgar in the park new the Armory. He owned an ugly dog back then, something he'd rescued, and the mutt dragged him around Dexter Field with the other dogs at the end of the workday. I was sitting on the swing set – no real kids ever used it – and watched the beauty with which Edgar threw the mutt a stick. He was a tall, broad man with a very neat trim of dark hair, the tattoo of a tentacle or a vine reaching out from under his collar and up the side of his neck. He flapped his Carhartt coat open and closed when he talked with the others. He was very expressive, and the cluster of people laughed whenever he joined them. He looked like any other twenty-something day laborer, but later, from the shadows across the street, I saw him step out of his house in tight black pants and a fierce trench with a fur collar, swinging an actual cane around his arm and singing – loud – some kind of bachata; he was probably the most attractive man I'd ever seen.

He was the sort of man who had deep, destroying affairs, and I loved hearing about them, my head against his chest, and after a while we both started to suspect that the best part of the affairs was talking about them afterward, together, under the oblique streetlight, on the mattress, in the dark – with the *stories*, the violence, the kisses, the breaking glass, the running, the crying, the begging. I was not at all surprised when he told me what his uncle did to him as a boy. I think I knew this the first moment I saw him in his Carhartt and work boots making people laugh in the park. Ours was a deep fidelity and a complete exception to our otherwise brutalizing relationships – his, in their number, mine, in their absence. Because I loved him, I hated his pederast of an uncle. One day I told him that I wanted to find his uncle and do to him what my Mémé had done to her long-ago lover Claude. I told him what I would do with the knife.

"Ah," he sighed, "my darling. You can't. Somebody already had the pleasure, when he was in prison for something else."

I felt relieved that the man was gone from the world, but was also disappointed.

"Too bad," I said. "Don't you wish you could have watched?"

It did not take us long to get around to Professor K-, and for me to pour out the sad story I had never uttered to anyone. After that, all we had to do was formulate the terms of restitution. Edgar really had nothing – less than nothing – to lose. As for me, I'd been paralyzed for nearly four years, estranged from my family, my architectural dreams reduced to breaking into the Armory to sit in its great, leaking hall. I was an expert on this building – I could have told you where the structure needed maintenance and where the steel tresses would first collapse – but I knew nobody would ever ask me what I thought about this and anything else.

We caught up to him in the late afternoon of an astonishing autumn. He was leaving his office, and I was right to assume his attachment to a regular schedule would be unchanged four years later. He was, naturally, on his wat home to dinner with his wife. Edgar came up and slipped his arm companionably through the professor's, and I did the same. Professor K- was tall, but Edgar was taller, and had about fifty pounds on him. Edgar smiles winningly as I'd seen him do so many times, so many people in awe of him physically, and him just having the time of his life, knowing it all leads to death – even pleasure. The professor's expression, of course, was one of confusion. We walked together, arm in arm, like chums. The professor looked from Edgar to me, and back to Edgar, then me.

"How are you?" I asked him.

"He's great," said Edgar.

"He'd have to be, on a day like this," I said, whistling. "What a stunner."

"What are you doing?" the professor whispered.

"Yes siree, he's feeling great," Edgar continued. "He's blessed with so much. A high-class job. Summers off. A loving wife."

Professor K-'s expression clouded. He pulled back on our arms, but of course we did not give him any slack.

"Our car is just over there," I said. "Don't worry. It's not far."

"He doesn't think it's far," said Edgar. "He's happy to walk. On a day like this. He knows how lucky he is. And look at his shoes. Comfortable. European."

"Viennese," I said.

"He doesn't look Vietnamese," said Edgar.

"Oh poo," I said.

"You *cannot*," said the professor. "You can*not*-"

Edgar opened the door to his Charger, arm still hooked through Professor K-'s, whose mouth was opening and closing in disbelief.

"We can't?" Edgar smiled at me tenderly. "What was Obama's slogan, honey?"

I smiles at Edgar. We were going to heal ourselves. "*Yes we can.*"

Plans had been laid and abandoned for the Armory building numerous times. Given up by the National Guard due to upkeep, it functioned, for a time, as a soundstage for a couple Hollywood movies. In 2004, a proposed bond issue to finance renovation was placed on the ballot; it did not pass. Standing inside of it, feeling the dank, perpetually wet air, one realizes that it will never be renovated because there is something *wrong* about it, something dark and un-American. It brings to mind torture. It reminds me in design of the Stasi building in Struttgart, a building on which I'd written a paper for – who else? – Professor K-.

Had he ever been inside before? I asked him, when we were settled.

He did not answer me. He was sitting on a folding chair with his hands clasped together, looking at his shoes. He hadn't said anything in a while, and looked a little pathetic, so small in that grand space, storage containers stacked to the windows on either side, with only a camp light to see by in the falling light. Edgar approached and stood behind him. I winced, but all he did was cup the professor's neck lightly with one hand. He bent down and whispered, "Are you all right?"

Professor K- laughed shortly. "No," he said. "No, I am not."

"Okay, okay." Edgar began to rub his shoulders. "It's okay,"

Edgar looked at me and smiled sympathetically. I alone knew what this smile meant. It meant it was time to go forward, to live. Before I knew it, he'd the professor over to an old industrial desk – some remnant of the National Guard – and softly instructed him to grab onto it.

Did I want to watch? No.

I just wanted to listen.

There were no words at all, of course, only the shuffling of feet, the friction of clothing, the occasional sound of Edgar's murmur, and a cry or two – the professor – something like the cry of a person stumbling upon an unspeakable vision. Watching the last of the sun face through the western windows, I thought about what the professor had really taught me: he'd taught me that the body was a *design*. A brilliant design, a very tidy machine, a collaboration of limbs and joints, all working together to get itself down the street, or to raise a glass to its lips, or to crouch in a corner and hide. No need to get too emotional about it or march around campuses and in general take things too much to heart. A belt buckle clattered to the floor. The desk juddered as it was pushed a little farther. The professor cried out again, a warble of pain. I wondered how Edgar and I would speak of this later, on the mattress, under the streetlight.

We drove the professor back to College Hill. Up onto Benefit Street, left at the Athaneaum, arriving at the back gated of the main quad, where graduates egress with diplomas each May. He say in the back, not saying a word.

When we pulled in front of the professor's building on George Street, Edgar turned and put his hand over the seat bench.

"Which one's your car, honey? He asked Professor K-
.

Professor K- stayed silent.

"Hey," Edgar said, swatting his leg.

The professor jumped. He looked at me. "I don't understand this," he said, and started to cry.

"I know you don't," I said. "I know you don't."

"Which one is your car?" growled Edgar.

The professor looked around. He started shivering. "That one," he said.

"Good," said Edgar, leaning over the backseat and opening the professor's door for him. "See you next week."

"What?" said the professor.

"We'd like to see you again," said Edgar. "Does next week work for you?"

"Again?"

I turned around. George Street was behind us, leading gently uphill to the heart of the campus, a bower of aged trees, a vision of New England worthiness.

I said, "If you don't show up here again this same time next week, I will tell you wife about what you did to me, and I will tell the chair of your department what you did to me."

Professor K- looked at me without recognition.

"He understands," said Edgar. "He understands the terms. After all, he's a very smart man. He's an expert. He's a professor."

Not infrequently, in these relationships-that-are-not-relationships, there can be very graceful victims. That is, people who can smile and appear happy and even grateful, even when there's a metaphorical gun to their ribs. I used to think these people were all women. But recently I have come to think, no, men can do it too, men can be graceful victims, and it made me feel more warmly toward them actually. Every time Edgar and I pick up Professor K-, I feel a rush of sympathy for him, the way he stands with one hand cinching his coat together against the cold, or when he troubles to bring an umbrella, and as we pull up in front of his office on George Street, he looks off into the treetops, almost politely, as if he is writing poetry in his head, as if things are going precisely as he planned.

Amity Gaige is the author of three novels, *O My Darling*, *The Folded World*, and *Schroder*, which was shortlisted for The Folio Prize in 2014. To date, *Schroder* has been published in eighteen countries. It was also named one of Best Books of

2013 by *The New York Times Book Review*, *Washington Post*, *The Wall Street Journal*, *Kirkus*, *The Women's National Book Association*, *Cosmopolitan*, *Denver Post*, *The Buffalo News*, *Amazon.com*, *Bookmarks*, and *Publisher's Weekly*, among others. She has won many awards for her previous novels, such as Foreword Book of the Year Award for 2007, and in 2006, she was recognized as one of the "5 Under 35" outstanding emerging writers by the National Book Foundation. She's the winner of a Fulbright Fellowship, fellowships at the MacDowell and Yaddo colonies, and a Baltic Writing Residency. Her short stories, essays, and reviews have appeared in publications such as *The Guardian*, *The New York Times*, *The Literary Review*, *The Yale Review*, *One Story*, and elsewhere. Listen to Amity at the 2013 National Book Festival, All Things Considered or on The Diane Rehm Show. She lives in Connecticut with her family, and is the currently the Visiting Writer at Amherst College.

Rusch & Helfers

The American Flag of Sergeant Hale Schofield: Kelly Washington

First published in *Fiction River: Hidden in Crime*

This is my father's story and it starts long before I was born, but I become the narrator as we stand at the foot of a grave.

Not my father's. Not even someone I'm related to, but one of his war buddies.

The year was 1985 and I was ten years old.

"I'm sorry, Billy," said my father, his voice shaking. He spoke not to me, but to the headstone that was placed in the ground seven years before I was born.

Ever since I was a small child, I've always wondered what he was sorry for. My father and I have come to this particular site so many times that the name etched into the headstone is as familiar as my own name.

William Bryan Halverston, US Army, Private First Class, Vietnam, Nov 21 1949 to Mar 25 1968.

He died in the Vietnam War.

Whether through guilt, or love, or some combination therein, my father named me after this soldier.

Willamina Brianna Schofield. I preferred to be called Willa.

Row upon row of white granite headstones lined the perfectly trimmed lawns of Arlington National Cemetery. Small American flags furled and unfurled with the wind, creating a fabric-snapping cadence like that of an erratic heartbeat.

I knew the names of the fallen on either side of Private Halverston. With my Polaroid camera, I took pictures of the nearby headstones, and whispered the names of the men and women who served their country, some of whom died while doing so.

In a way they were my family.

My father, Hale Schofield, fought for his country. He fought and *survived*. Yet, in a surreal way, the soldier in the ground was more alive to me than my father.

When the sun fell behind him, I lifted the camera. I captured his anemic profile, the downturn of his lips, his closed eyes.

My father may have returned from the war, but the war never left *him*.

One day would I bury him here, too?

With heavily scarred arms—burned during the war— my father reached down to remove the flag from Private Halverston's grave and handed it to me. He cannot bear to look at it.

Twirling it in my hands, I rolled the Stars and Stripes around its thin, plastic pole, and placed it gently in my tie-dyed satchel. The top of the flag poked out.

My father wasn't unpatriotic. He was angry, sad and, at times, hopeless.

"I'm a goddamn son of a bitch," my father said through clenched teeth. His voice reminded me of demonic undertow that pulled him further and further into hell.

I studied him. Once he might have been a handsome man, but he no longer cared about his appearance. His hair was long, thin, and stringy, and, even though he wasn't old, it was white.

His dark beard was rough and patchy, like black straw.

An old olive army jacket billowed around his thin frame and he smelled like the paper mill factory where he worked: glue and wood pulp.

It wasn't an unpleasant smell. I've known it all my life.

He was a hard worker. It was how he showed affection, by putting food on the table and clothes on our backs.

In return, I loved my father enough to stand silently beside him at Private Halverston's grave. I wasn't here because I wanted to be here. I was here because he needed me to be.

I slipped my hands around one of his. It was scarred, leathery, and cold.

"Are you ready to go, Daddy?" I asked. The sun was setting and in his reflective, brown eyes, I saw what he could never say aloud: *I'm afraid to love you.*

I know, Daddy.

He blinked away unshed tears.

"One day I'll escape this concrete river, Willa, but I don't know how." He leaned on me as we walked out. His frame was a slight one, but I felt the heavy burden in his soul. "I don't know how."

His albatross was *my* albatross as I thought about the small American flag tucked inside the satchel.

In three days, when we returned to Texarkana, he would burn the flag.

My earliest memory is that of my father lighting a fire in the metal barrel behind our house. I was two. From the back porch I watched, transfixed, as my father dropped the flag into the flames. His mouth moved but I couldn't hear. Was he reciting something?

Names? Prayers?

I asked, but he told me to go back inside. Before I slipped back inside, he said, "This is a protest I must do on my own, Willa, even if the folks I'm protesting never know about it."

Every year I was merely a spectator. However, this year, when we got home, I would document it with my camera.

I didn't know that burning the American flag was illegal, but I knew it wasn't right. Thinking about it made my insides feel funny, as if I knew a secret that I should never, ever tell.

This ritual—this burning ceremony—made him feel better, as if he absolved himself of some wrongdoing. Though the effects were temporary.

It wasn't until years later that I understood why.

***

Every March we drive from Texarkana, Texas, to Washington, D.C., to visit Private Halverston's grave and to rub his name on the Vietnam Veterans Memorial.

This year's trip coincided with the Cherry Blossom parade. My stepmother, Evelyn, said we should do something fun. It was her second trip with us and she was trying to be optimistic.

Evelyn, who was twelve years my senior, was a nurse. Being optimistic is in her blood. Otherwise I didn't know how she put up with my father's constant moodiness.

My birth mother couldn't and one day, three years ago, she stood at the doorway, suitcase in hand, and said, "I can't do it no more, Hale. Willa, at eleven, you're old enough to take care of the house, but don't neglect school too much." And without so much another syllable, the screen door smacked the frame, signaling her departure.

Last I heard, she was living in Nevada, waiting tables.

After she left, I got pretty good at taking care of my father. I woke him up in time for work. I made sure he ate breakfast, even if only a slice of toast, and I ensured he took all of his medicine. He could be stubborn.

In the evenings, I tucked him into bed, praying for an uneventful night.

My prayers rarely came true.

He suffered from nightmares. As he woke up screaming, I would lay on top of the covers, dry his face, all the while assuring him in a practiced, calm voice, that he was safe.

Safe from what, though, I could only guess at by the way he called out Billy's name, over and over.

Did he yell to *save* Private Halverston, or to rebuke him for some offense?

I never asked and ten months later, when Evelyn came into our lives, she took on the responsibility of my father. I was only too glad to let her assume the role.

He needed a nurse and she needed a patient.

And I got a brother out of the deal.

I cradled Michael's tiny form as we piled into our baby blue peace-sign-stickered station wagon and made the three-day trip through Arkansas, Tennessee, and Virginia.

Evelyn was a quiet driver, my father slept, so other than keeping Michael entertained, I read V.C. Andrews' Flowers in the Attic and hoped that Evelyn couldn't see my expression in the rearview mirror.

No doubt she'd object to a thirteen-year-old reading about the horrible things being done to the Dollanganger children, but my father abhorred censorship of any kind. If she raised a stink, he'd go right out and buy ten copies to hand out to my friends.

So, if she noticed anything, she didn't say a word. We had a partnership, of sorts. I attended all the events with my father and she turned a blind eye when I occasionally did something I wasn't supposed to.

When I looked up from the last chapter, my father was turned around in the passenger seat, and his eyes were arrested on my face.

I shut the book fast. On the cover, Cathy Dollanganger's blonde head peeked through the attic window. I wondered if I mimicked her startled expression.

"Did you bring the tracing paper, Willa?" he asked urgently. His voice was croaky from sleeping so long.

Tomorrow we would rub Private Halverston's name onto the tracing paper, a custom we started when the wall was built in 1982. Well, I would rub it. My father's hands shook too much.

This was my thirteenth trip to his gravesite, sixth to the wall, but it was only Evelyn's second and Michael's first. It was strange to think how we each had our own unique journey with the deceased soldier.

"Yes, Daddy." I kept my voice even. "It's time for your medicine."

I handed him an assortment of pills and an army canteen filled with water.

Beside me in the backseat, Michael stirred awake but barely made a sound as I changed his cloth diaper. My father watched wordlessly as I wrapped the used diaper in a newspaper.

He was afraid to hold Michael. In fact, other than when he was born, I don't think my father ever held his son in his arms.

"And the black chalk, Willa? Did you remember to pack that as well?"

"Yes, Daddy."

From my pocket, I removed three black chalk sticks, still wrapped in plastic.

His face flooded with relief. Evelyn let out a long sigh, as if maybe she had been holding her breath, waiting for me to answer. Once, when I was seven or eight, I forgot the chalk, and my father turned the car around even though we were already in southern Virginia.

I was old enough to understand that there were different types of love and wondered at Private Halverston's hold on my father. Did they have a brother-like relationship? Or was it something more? Were they in love?

In my mind, I created my own romantic, fictional tale where the young private died a hero, saving my father's life.

I was also old enough to understand that the front-lines of war were not drawn with pastel watercolors, but with blood.

Michael cooed, his words gibberish and delightful. I put him on my lap and he reached out to touch our father's red, puckered arm.

My father flinched and his whole body jerked away. Thinking it a game, Michael clapped his hands as I gently bounced him on my knees.

"Sometimes, when I look in Michael's dark brown eyes..." My father said haltingly, as if he wasn't sure he should continue on. His face softened, then hardened. I noticed that Evelyn snapped her head his way before returning her eyes to the road. "I see their eyes. Scared, huge, defeated. Those children saw deep into my soul, Willa, and I glimpsed my own future staring back at me."

I swallowed hard. Was this why he never wanted to hold Michael?

"What did their eyes say?" I whispered, instantly on edge and worried.

Did the children's eyes tell him he'd never sleep through the night again, that he would develop unexplained illnesses, and that he would shun affection?

"Willa," Evelyn said, her voice a gentle warning. "Please don't."

In his own way, I knew my father loved us. But at a distance. A *safe* distance where we couldn't hurt him.

Or maybe it was so he couldn't hurt us.

I didn't like thinking about what he might have done in the war. The people he might have killed, and the friends he lost. All I knew was that the man formerly known as Sergeant

Hale Schofield would gladly trade places with Private William Halverston.

And that made me very sad.

I touched my father's arm to bring him back to the present. For a moment, his mind disappeared. His glazed eyes refocused on me and then on Michael.

"I was supposed to die over there," he said, finally, but without emotion, though there was a tone of truthfulness in his voice.

When my father talked of his time in the army, he would dance around the edges of war. He might tell me about the bugs, or the heat, or how he could survive on C&C—coffee and cigarettes—for weeks at a time.

And except for the time he placed his Purple Heart medal on Private Halverston's headstone, this was the most he'd ever come close to talking about the war itself.

I placed my hand over his, and he didn't pull away.

"Then you wouldn't have had me or Michael. Whatever you saw in the children's eyes was wrong, Daddy."

"You weren't there, Willa." He closed his eyes and I thought, for a moment, that he had fallen asleep. But I was wrong. "None of us should have been there."

He fell silent and eventually his soft snores filled the car.

"He's lucky to have you as a daughter, Willa," Evelyn said, looking at me through the rearview mirror. It was already dark outside. We'd be in Washington, D.C. soon.

With my free hand, I brushed away an errant tear. With my other hand, I held his until we reached the hotel.

***

The following year wasn't a good one for my father. His health rapidly deteriorated and for several months he was admitted to the Overton Brooks VA Medical Center in Shreveport, Louisiana.

When he finally came home in late 1989, his speech was somewhat slurred and he was confined to a wheelchair, but I still thought him mostly able-bodied.

Truth is, we never thought to treat him differently than from before.

The paper mill factory owners thought so, too. They saw no issue with him managing the plant floor from a wheelchair. But being the stubborn man that he was, my father quit rather than accept what he considered charity.

And it was around this time that he began to receive a great deal of mail from veterans' groups, anti-war groups, and also from veterans' anti-war groups.

Picking up and answering the mail was one of my self-assigned chores, so it wasn't unusual for me to open, sort, and, sometimes, answer the mail on his behalf. Usually my "answer" was to toss the letters into the fireplace, a habit I picked up from him. The anti-war groups urged my father to join so that their collective voices could tell the administration not to go to war with the Middle East.

Didn't they realize they were barking up the wrong tree?

So far he had shown no interest. If anything, I suspected the whole thing disgusted him while, at the same time, it held a tiny fraction of an appeal.

Did he miss the camaraderie he experienced while in uniform? The friendship?

Evelyn came into the living room, spied the envelope in my hands, and said, "Throw it out before he sees it, Willa."

My stepmother was working at the hospital again, but she could only get the night nurse shift. The night-care of my father fell again to my shoulders, as well as that of two-year-old Michael.

Other girls my age might balk at such responsibility, but I grew up taking care of my father, and Michael was so sweet and easygoing and used to a detached father, it was almost like he took care of himself.

At night, when I read a children's story to my brother, I also had the rapt attention of my father. Sitting in his over-sized wheelchair at the bedroom door, there was something child-like in him. Something innocent that he was trying to reclaim.

Maybe it was his way of not being alone, even though when I tried to bring him further into the room, or when I asked him to read the next chapter to his son, my father would rush away as if I scared him out of some dreamlike state.

Now, as I looked up at Evelyn—she was several inches taller—I opened a thick letter from a group based out of Dallas called the *War Resistance Federation*. They were planning an anti-war march in Austin, Texas.

"Daddy doesn't care about the mail, Evelyn. He says all these groups want to do is use him as a sock-puppet to further their own agendas, just like the government did when they shipped him off to Vietnam—*twice*—and ex-posed him to Agent Orange. And now that we're getting involved in the Middle East, he can't help but compare the situations."

My father didn't exactly say all of that to me, but I felt that I knew him well enough to say it to Evelyn, and these days I wasn't someone who shied away from speaking her mind. I knew what war did to men who escaped being placed in military caskets.

I didn't know my father *before* war, so I didn't know how different he might have been. Was he carefree? Funny? Was he a ladies' man? Would he have been a different type of father, the type who smiled and hugged his children? The type who seemed to enjoy living instead of waiting for death to catch up to him?

"You're a lot like Hale, Willa," Evelyn said in a tired voice as she tucked a stray hair behind her ear. We never argued. She was dressed for work and about to leave. She was good to my father, she adored Michael, and, in some small way, I believe she loved me, but I knew that by comparing me to my father, she wasn't complimenting me. "While you're at school, a man comes over and they talk in hushed tones. Every time I walk into the room, they stop abruptly, and wait for me to leave again. I think it's an attorney. Willa, he doesn't have much time left."

I shook my head. No, not my father.

"Daddy's on the mend. You must be imagining things."

She gave me an odd look, as if I was deceiving myself, and maybe I was. Evelyn was a nurse. She knew the medical side of things much better than I did, but *I* knew my father.

Or so I told myself.

Certainly I never put my father on a pedestal. He had too many issues, flaws, for me to think of him as perfect. But surely I would know if he was dying. Wouldn't he tell me?

Evelyn stepped closer to me.

"When he talks of those children's eyes, the ones who saw into his soul, they weren't alive anymore. When he screams out at night, he dreams of those children coming back to get him, to pull him into a dark abyss. What's worse is he *wants* them to. He wants them to exact their revenge. He saw the worst of himself, of humanity, and every day he swims to escape that concrete river."

I felt sick to my stomach and yet, I wasn't surprised. I just didn't want to believe that my father hurt anyone, but he must have. It was war. He was still fighting it, even now.

Concrete river. In everything except his physical body, my father was still stuck in Vietnam. In that concrete river. I wonder why I never made the connection until now. Deep down I probably always knew, I just needed to hear Evelyn's point of view first.

"What about Private Halverston?" I asked. "Daddy screams out his name at night, too. I have rubbed his name eight times and I have watched my father burn the flag from his grave every year since I was two."

Legal or not, I just wanted understand what my father was trying to *say*. Why did he burn the flags?

Evelyn's face fell. She didn't attend the gravesite with us.

She and Michael visited museums while I held my father when his legs went out from underneath him from standing so long in the cemetery. I fed him when his arms shook so bad he couldn't hold a fork, and I forced him to drink water with the pills he stubbornly refused to swallow.

"I asked, once," she said, taking the car keys from the half-moon table near the door. Only then did it occur to me that Evelyn appeared older than her age of twenty-six. "He never answered. Instead he cried, and when I tried to comfort him, it was like my skin burned him. Because I care about him, I no longer ask questions, Willa.

I don't know what Billy was to your father, but he must have loved him. No one names their children after someone they hate."

***

Two days before Christmas I turned fifteen and as a joint birthday-Christmas gift, I received a brand new Nikon FE2 camera.

Excitedly, I took so many pictures of random things—cracked sidewalks, my father's wheelchair when he wasn't in it, Evelyn's nurse shoes, and lots of photos of Michael as he ran around the house buck-naked—that I used up six rolls of film and only had one roll left for Christmas morning.

Earlier in the month I made up my mind that I wanted to study photography in college. While I didn't know that this conversation with my father and Evelyn would produce such a gift at Christmastime, I got the sense that my father was trying to make things right before he passed away.

I know now that I was in denial, but when spring came and he was diagnosed with pancreatic cancer, I couldn't ignore that he was in an incredible amount of pain and that he might...well...he might...

I couldn't finish the thought.

A girl of fifteen will always think that her father, no matter how *im*perfect, is immortal.

The year was 1990, Hale Schofield was forty-seven years old, and it was the first year we couldn't visit Private Halverston's grave.

My father was bald from chemotherapy treatments and his face was so pale his skin seemed translucent. When he smiled or laughed, neither of which was often, his teeth looked much too large for his face. I never knew his parents—my grandparents—so I didn't have a grandfather to compare his likeness to.

Spontaneously, I took a picture of him in front of the window.

It was early summer and he was dozing, but woke when the camera shuttered. The sun was behind him, casting his silhouette in a hazy, yellow glow, and I hoped that, when developed, he would look like an angel.

"Thanks Daddy."

I kissed him on the cheek. Evelyn and Michael were next door so my brother could play with another little boy. When I looked out the window from my father's perspective, I could see Michael chasing the neighbor's boy and having the time of his life.

I smiled when I realized that my father had fallen asleep watching his son play outside.

So he wasn't so cold or unfeeling. Or unloving.

He just didn't show it well. I looked into his face and in that moment I thought I could ask him anything. So I did.

"Tell me about Billy, Daddy."

He shocked me by answering me.

"Billy had no business in Vietnam. None of us did, Willa. At nineteen, Billy Halverston was so green I could see baby leaf sprouts growing out of his ears. He was tall, taller than me, and his hair was brown and wavy, like yours. He was assigned as a M113 driver in Company A. I was twenty-four and already on my second tour when I met him."

He paused and his brown eyes looked away from me.

I wanted to hear more about his first impression of Billy, to know more about how he lived before I learned about how he died. Because it was his death that affected my father the most. Or so I assumed.

"Did you love him, Daddy?"

"I—" He stopped suddenly and studied my face. What was he looking for there? Condemnation? Judgment? I hoped he read love and understanding. He cleared his throat. "I did, Willa. I was never a man of great emotion, but the day I met him something changed in me. It was like a dam opened up and I felt things I had never felt before."

"Did you tell him?"

His lips formed into a small smile. "Hell no. I punched him in the mouth right after I ordered him to get his ass in the armored personnel carrier."

I wrinkled my nose at him.

"That's not very romantic."

He made a sound that might have been laughter.

"Soon enough, Willa, you'll learn that love isn't this explosive thing that happens when two people meet. More times than not, one or both of you are fighting it, and before you know it fate has other plans and the choice has been taken away from you."

"So... Billy never knew how you felt?"

My father's eyes brightened. I could almost see the memory alive in his mind.

"Bill and I fought two wars in Vietnam. One against the enemy, and the one against each other. We fought it so much that it should have been obvious. But we were obnoxious kids."

He shrugged.

I wasn't fooled. "You didn't answer the question."

"Yes, Willa, he knew. Before he died we *both* knew. We never had time to make plans. A week later our armored personnel carrier hit a mine. Billy couldn't get out and I couldn't pull him out. I tried everything possible to pull him from the fire. I stayed with him until he stopped screaming. I can *still* hear him screaming my name ."

I looked at the hands in his lap. The burns that covered most of his arms took on a new meaning then.

"I'm sorry, Daddy." I was no longer hiding my tears.

"As soon as I healed, and as soon the Army discharged me, I went home and burned my uniform. My mother had a flag hanging off the porch. I grabbed that and burned it, too. I wanted to destroy *everything*, Willa." He coughed weakly and I helped him drink water. "I still do. Willa, will you do something for me?"

"Anything." I'd lasso the moon if he asked me to.

"When I die, burn the flag the army presents to your stepmother. Every time I see an American flag, it reminds me of Billy."

"Daddy, I don't know if I—"

"Promise me, Willa." He wouldn't rest until I promised and I didn't want Michael to see him in such an uneasy state. His hands found mine and squeezed.

"I promise, Daddy."

***

It's on my fifteenth visit to Arlington National Cemetery when I become the narrator and the owner of the rest of the story.

The previous owner now resides beneath his own headstone.

Hale Schofield, Sergeant, US Army, Vietnam, Jan 13 1943 to Jun 29 1990.

He was buried at the end of a long row, under a cherry blossom tree whose dark branches sheltered his gravesite from an early afternoon sun.

I liked the idea of his being protected from the elements.

I don't know if he wanted us to go through with the full military burial, but at least he's within walking distance of Billy. In a way, I wonder if he was preparing me for this moment every time he brought me here.

My father couldn't process Private Halverston's death anymore than he could accept my existence, not when he truthfully believed that *he* should have been the one who died in the war.

Near the end, his eyes seemed to ask himself: *Why did I get to extend my line when I extinguished the line of others*?

Because you were meant to live, Daddy.

Someone asked us to stand and the Honor Guard's riflemen completed the rifle volley before a lone soldier played Taps.

All the while my vision was full of the flag resting on top of his casket. The soldiers folded it into a perfect triangle, the white stars distinct against the blue fabric, and an officer presented it to Evelyn. She stared at it, unseeing, and just as my father used to do, she handed it to me.

"He never said it, Willa, but he loved you," Evelyn said.

This time I do not place it in a tie-dyed bag. I press it between Michael and me, and I hold my little brother tightly against my chest, as if I'm imprinting the best parts of my father into our souls.

There *was* good in him. I know it, even if he didn't.

The soldiers lowered his casket and for the longest time the only sound was that of the rustling branches of the cherry blossom tree.

"Daddy's no longer in the river," Michael said in a voice much more mature than that of a four-year old. He climbed onto Evelyn's lap.

My hands tested the weight of the flag. I traced the stars. I counted my tears as they fell on it.

I will mourn him the same way he mourned William Halverston. Forever.

"Willa," Evelyn said, her voice guarded. "What were your father's instructions about the flag? He asked you to burn it, didn't he? I won't stop you if you intend to honor his request."

Nineteen days ago the Supreme Court struck down the Flag Protection Act and affirmed that burning the American flag in protest was protected under the First Amendment.

"Yes, he wanted me to burn it. If he had his way, he'd want me to burn the ashes, too. But I won't. How can I burn something that symbolizes his military service, his sacrifice?"

Legal or not, the idea of burning the flag I held against my chest would be like lighting a match under my father and burning him alive. Looking at the flag made my father ill. It had the opposite effect on me.

My stepmother smiled. "In a way, you're protesting *his* protest. Why do I get the feeling Hale would approve?"

I smiled in return. Yes, he would approve. Instantly, I felt better about my decision. Michael stepped between us and hand in hand, we left Arlington National Cemetery.

Goodbye Daddy. Goodbye Billy. Every March I will return. I will visit my father as well as the man whom I was named after. A man my father loved very much.

And I will place flags on both their graves.

Kelly Washington is a former third-generation soldier who holds down a day job as a defense contractor working for the U.S. Army while moonlighting as an author. Her romance fiction typically centers on the military, including the novel series *Falling For Him* and stand-alone novel *Collide Into You*. She is also the

author of the four-book *Reclaimed Souls* series, a heart-pounding blend of romance, fantasy, science fiction, and adventure.
Her short fiction has appeared in the Fiction River anthologies
Recycled Pulp and *Hidden in Crime*. When not writing, she can
usually be found her hanging out at her website www.smallfic-
tion.com.

The Five-Dollar Dress: Mary Higgins Clark

First published in *Manhattan Mayhem*

It was a late August afternoon, and the sun was sending slanting shadows across Union Square in Manhattan. *It's a peculiar kind of day*, Jenny thought as she came up from the subway and turned east. This was the last day she needed to go to the apartment of her grandmother, who had died three weeks ago.

She had already cleaned out most of the apartment. The furniture and all of Gran's household goods, as well as her clothing, would be picked up at five o'clock by the diocese charity.

Her mother and father were both pediatricians in San Francisco and had intensely busy schedules. Having just passed the bar exam after graduating from Stanford Law School, Jenny was free to do the job. Next week, she would be starting as a deputy district attorney in
San Francisco.

At First Avenue, she looked up while waiting for the light to change. She could see the windows of her grandmother's apartment on the fourth floor of 415 East Fourteenth Street. Gran had been one of the first tenants to move there in 1949. *She and my grandfather moved to*

New Jersey when Mom was five, Jennie thought, *but she moved back after my grandfather died.* That was twenty years ago.

Filled with memories of the grandmother she had adored, Jenny didn't notice when the light turned green. *It's almost as though I'm seeing her in the window, watching for me the way she did when I'd visit her,* she reminisced. An impatient pedestrian brushed against her shoulder as he walked around her, and she realized the light was turning green again. She crossed the street and walked the short distance to the entrance of Gran's building. There, with increasingly reluctant steps, she entered the security code, opened the door, walked to the elevator, got in, and pushed the button.

On the fourth floor, she got off the elevator and slowly walked down the corridor to her grandmother's apartment. Tears came to her eyes as she thought of the countless times her grandmother had been waiting with the door open after having seen her cross the street. Swallowing the lump in her throat, Jenny turned the key in the lock and opened the door. She reminded herself that, at eighty-six, Gran had been ready to go. She had said that twenty years was a long time without her grandfather, and she wanted to be with him.

And she had started to drift into dementia, talking about someone named Sarah . . . how Barney didn't kill her . . . Vincent did . . . that someday she'd prove it.

If there's anything Gran wouldn't have wanted to live with, it's dementia, Jenny thought. Taking a deep breath, she looked around the room. The boxes she had packed were clustered together. The bookshelves were bare. The tabletops were empty. Yesterday she had wrapped and packed the Royal Doulton figurines that her grandmother had loved, and the framed family pictures that would be sent to California.

She only had one job left. It was to go through her grandmother's hope chest to see if there was anything else to keep.

The hope chest was special. She started to walk down the hallway to the small bedroom that Gran had turned into a den. Even though she had a sweater on, she felt chilled. She wondered if all apartments or homes felt like this after the person who had lived in them was gone.

Entering the room, she sat on the convertible couch that had been her bed there ever since she was eleven years old. That was the first time she had been allowed to fly alone from California and spend a month of the summer with her grandmother.

Jenny remembered how her grandmother used to open the chest and always take out a present for her whenever she was visiting. But she had never allowed her granddaughter to rummage through it. "There are some things I don't want to share, Jenny," she had said. "Maybe someday I'll let you look at them. Or a maybe I'll get rid of them. I don't know yet."

I wonder if Gran ever did get rid of whatever it was that was so secret? Jenny asked herself.

The hope chest now served as a coffee table in the den.

She sat on the couch, took a deep breath, and lifted the lid. She soon realized that most of the hope chest was filled with heavy blankets and quilts, the kind that had long since been replaced by lighter comforters.

Why did Gran keep all this stuff? Jenny wondered. Struggling to take the blankets out, she then stacked them into a discard pile on the floor. *Maybe someone can use them,* she decided. *They do look warm.*

Next were three linen tablecloth and napkin sets, the kind her grandmother had always joked about. "Almost nobody bothers with linen tablecloths and napkins anymore, unless it's Thanksgiving or

Christmas," she had said. "It's a wash-and-dry world."

When I get married, Gran, I'll use them in your memory on Thanksgiving and Christmas and special occasions, Jenny promised.

She was almost to the bottom of the trunk. A wedding album with a white leather cover, inscribed with *Our Wedding Day* in gold lettering, was the next item. Jenny opened it. The pictures were in black and white. The first one was of her grandmother in her wedding gown arriving at the church. Jennie gasped. *Gran showed this to me years ago, but I never realized how much I would grow to look like her.* They had the same high cheekbones, the same dark hair, the same features. *It's like looking in a mirror,* she thought.

She remembered that when Gran had shown her the album, she'd pointed out the people in it. "That was your father's best friend . . . That was my maid of honor, your great-aunt . . . And doesn't your grandfather look handsome? You were only five when he died, so of course you have no memory of him."

I do have some vague memories of him, Jenny thought. He would hug me and give me a big kiss and then recite a couple lines of a poem about someone named Jenny. I'll have to look it up someday.

There was a loose photograph after the last bound picture in the album. It was of her grandmother and another young woman wearing identical cocktail dresses. *Oh, how lovely,* Jenny thought. The dresses had a graceful boat neckline, long sleeves, a narrow waist, and a bouffant ankle-length skirt.

Prettier than anything on the market today, she thought.

She turned over the picture and read the typed note attached to it:

Sarah wore this dress in the fashion show at Klein's only hours before she was murdered in it. I'm wearing the other one. It was a backup in case the original became damaged. The designer, Vincent Cole, called it "The Five-Dollar Dress," because that's what they were going to charge for it. He said he would lose money on it, but that dress would make his name. It made a big hit at the show, and the buyer ordered thirty, but Cole wouldn't sell any after Sarah was found in it. He wanted me to return the sample he had given me, but I refused. I think the reason he wanted to get rid of the dress was because Sarah was wearing it when he killed her. If only there was some proof. I had suspected she was dating him on the sly.

Her hand shaking, Jenny put the picture back inside the album. In her delirium the day before she died, Gran had said those names: Sarah . . . Vincent . . . Barney . . . Or had it just been delirium?

A large manila envelope, its bright yellow color faded with time, was next. Opening it, she found it filled with three separate files of crumbling news clippings. *There's no place to read these here,* Jenny thought. With the manila envelope tucked under her arm, she walked into the dining area and settled at the table. Careful not to tear the clippings, she began to slide them from the envelope. Looking at the date on the top clipping of the three sets, she realized they had been filed chronologically.

"Murder in Union Square" was the first headline she read. It was dated June 8, 1949. The story followed:

The body of twenty-three-year-old Sarah Kimberley was found in the doorway of S. Klein Department Store on Union Square this morning. She had been stabbed in the back by person or persons unknown sometime during the hours of midnight and five a.m. . . .

Why did Gran keep all these clippings? Jenny asked herself. *Why didn't she ever tell me about it, especially when she knew I was planning to go into criminal law? I know she must not have talked with Mom about it. Mom would have told me.*

She spread out the other clippings on the table. In sequence by date, they told of the murder investigation from the beginning. In the late afternoon, Sarah Kimberley had been modeling the dress she was wearing when her body was found.

The autopsy revealed that Sarah was six weeks pregnant when she died.

Up-and-coming designer Vincent Cole had been questioned for hours. He was known to have been seeing Sarah on the side. But his fiancée, Nona Banks, an heiress to the Banks department store fortune, swore they had been together in her apartment all night.

What did my Grandmother do with the dress she had? Jenny wondered. *She said it was the prettiest dress she ever owned.*

Jenny's computer was on the table, and she decided to see what she could find out about Vincent Cole. What she discovered shocked her. Vincent Cole had changed his name to Vincenzia and was now a famous designer. *He's up there with Oscar de la Renta and Carolina Herrera,* she thought.

The next pile of clippings was about the arrest of Barney Dodd, a twenty-six-year-old man who liked to sit for hours in Union Square Park. Borderline mentally disabled, he lived at the YMCA and worked at a funeral home. One of his jobs was dressing the bodies of the deceased and placing them in the casket. At noon and after work he would head straight to the park, carrying a paper bag with his lunch or dinner. As Jenny read the accounts, it became clear why he had come under suspicion. The body of Sarah Kimberley had been laid out as though she was in a coffin. Her hands had been clasped. Her hair was in place, the wide collar of the dress carefully arranged.

According to the accounts, Barney was known to try to strike up a conversation if a pretty young woman was sitting near him. *That's not proof of anything*, Jenny thought. She realized that she was thinking like the deputy district attorney she would soon become.

The last clipping was a two-page article from the *Daily News*. It was called "Did Justice Triumph?" It was about "The Case of the Five-Dollar Dress," as the writer dubbed it. At a glance, she could see that long excerpts from the trial were included in the article.

Barney Dobbs had confessed. He signed a statement saying that he had been in Union Square at about midnight the night of the murder. It was chilly, so the park was deserted. He saw Sarah walking across Fourteenth Street. He followed her, and then, when she wouldn't kiss him, he killed her. He carried her body to the front door of Klein's and left it there. But he arranged it so that it looked nice, the way he did in the funeral parlor. He threw away the knife as well as the clothes he was wearing that night.

Too pat, Jenny thought scornfully. *It sounds to me like whoever got that confession was trying to cover every base. Talk about a rush to justice.* Barney certainly didn't get Sarah pregnant. Who was the father of the baby? Who was Sarah with that night? Why was she alone at midnight (or later) in Union Square?

It was obvious the judge also thought there was something fishy about the confession. He entered a plea of not guilty for Barney and assigned a public defender to his case.

Jenny read the accounts of the trial with increasing contempt. It seemed to her that although the public defender had done his best to defend Barney, he was obviously inexperienced. *He should never have put Barney on the stand*, she thought. The man kept contradicting himself. He admitted that he had confessed to killing Sarah, but only because he was hungry and the officers who were talking to him had promised him a ham and cheese sandwich and a Hershey bar if he would sign something.

That was good, she thought. *That should have made an impression on the jurors.*

Not enough of an impression, she decided as she continued reading. *Not compared to the district attorney trying the case.*

He had shown Barney a picture of Sarah's body taken at the scene of the crime. "Do you recognize this woman?"

"Yes. I used to see her sometimes in the park when she was having her lunch or walking home after work."

"Did you ever talk to her?"

"She didn't like to talk to me. But her friend was so nice. She was pretty, too. Her name was Catherine."

My grandmother, Jenny thought.

"Did you see Sarah Kimberley the night of the murder?"

"Was that the night I saw her lying in front of Klein's? Her hands were folded, but they weren't folded nice like they are in the picture. So I fixed them."

His attorney should have called a recess, should have told the judge that his client was obviously confused! Jenny raged.

But the defense lawyer had allowed the district attorney to continue the line of questioning, hammering at Barney. "You arranged her body?"

"No. Somebody else did. I only changed her hands."

There were only two defense witnesses. The first was the matron at the YMCA where Barney lived. "He'd never hurt a fly," she said. "If he tried to talk to someone and they didn't respond to him, he never approached them again. I certainly never saw him carry a knife. He doesn't have many changes of clothes. I know all of them, and nothing's missing."

The other witness was Catherine Reeves. She testified that Barney had never exhibited any animosity toward her friend Sarah Kimberley. "If we happened to be having lunch in the park and Sarah ignored Barney, he just talked to me for a minute or two. He never gave Sarah a second glance."

Barney was found guilty of murder in the first degree and sentenced to life without parole.

Jenny read the final paragraph of the article:

Barney Dodd died at age sixty-eight, having served forty years in prison for the murder of Sarah Kimberley. The case of the so-called Five-Dollar Dress Murder has been debated by experts for years. The identity of the father of Sarah's unborn baby is still unknown. She was wearing the dress she had modeled that day. It was a cocktail dress. Was she having a romantic date with an admirer? Whom did she meet and where did she go that evening? DID JUSTICE TRIUMPH?

I'd say, absolutely not, Jenny fumed. She looked up and realized that the shadows had lengthened.

At the end, Gran had ranted about Vincent Cole and the five-dollar dress. Was it because he couldn't bear the sight of it? Was he the father of Sarah's unborn child?

He must be in his mid-eighties now, Jenny thought. His first wife, Nona Hartman, was a department store heiress. One of the article clips was about her. In an interview in *Vogue* magazine in 1952, she said she had first suggested that Vincent Cole did not sound exotic enough for a designer, and she urged her husband to upgrade his image by changing his name to Vincenzia. Included was a picture of their over-the-top wedding at her grandfather's estate in Newport. It had taken place on August 10, 1949, a few weeks after Sarah was murdered.

The marriage lasted only two years. The complaint had been adultery.

I wonder . . . Jenny thought. She turned back to the computer. The file on Vincent Cole—Vincenzia—was still open. She began searching through the links until she found what she was looking for. Vincent Cole, then twenty-five years old, had been living two blocks from Union Square when Sarah Kimberley was murdered.

If only they had DNA in those days. Sarah lived on Avenue C, just a few blocks away. If she had been in his apartment that night and told him she was pregnant, he easily could have followed her and killed her. Cole probably knew about Barney, a character around Union Square. Could Vincent Cole have arranged the body to throw suspicion on Barney? Maybe he saw him sitting in the park that night?

We'll never know, Jenny thought. *But it's obvious that Gran was sure he was guilty.*

She got up from the chair and realized that she had been sitting for a long time. Her back felt cramped, and all she wanted to do was get out of the apartment and take a long walk.

The charity pick-up truck should be here in fifteen minutes. Let's be done with it, she thought, and went back into the den. Two boxes were left to open. The one with the Klein label was the first she investigated. Wrapped in blue tissue was the five-dollar dress she had seen in the picture.

She shook it out and held it up. *This must be the dress Gran talked about a couple years ago. I had bought a cocktail dress in this color. Gran told me that it reminded her of a dress she had when she was young. She said Grandpa didn't like to see her wearing it. "A girl I worked with was wearing one like it when she had an accident,"* she'd said, *"and he thought it was bad luck."*

The other box held a man's dark blue three-button suit. Why did it look familiar? She flipped open the wedding album. *I'm pretty sure that's what my grandfather wore at the wedding*, she thought. *No wonder Gran kept it. She could never talk about him without crying.* She thought about what her grandmother's old friends had told her at the wake: "Your grandfather was the handsomest man you'd ever want to see. While he was going to law school at night, he worked as a salesman at Klein's during the day. All the girls in the store were after him. But once he met your mother, it was love at first sight. We were all jealous of her."

Jenny smiled at the memory and began to go through the pockets of the suit, in case anything had been left in them. There was nothing in the trousers. She slipped her fingers through the pockets of the jacket. The pocket under the left sleeve was empty, but it seemed as though she could feel something under the smooth satin lining.

Maybe it has one of those secret inner pockets, she thought. *I had a suit with a hidden pocket like that.*

She was right. The slit to the inner pocket was almost indiscernible, but it was there.

She reached in and pulled out a folded sheet of paper. Opening it, she read the contents.

It was addressed to Miss Sarah Kimberley.

It was a medical report stating that the test had confirmed she was six weeks pregnant.

Mary Higgins Clark's books are worldwide bestsellers. In the United States alone, her books have sold over 100 million copies, and made her a #1 *New York Times* bestseller. She is an active member of Literacy Volunteers and the Mystery Writers of America. She is the author of thirty-five suspense novels, three collections of short stories, a historical novel, a memoir, and two children's books. She and her husband, John Conheeney, live in Saddle River, New Jersey. Her latest suspense novel, *The Melody Lingers on*, was published by Simon & Schuster in 2015.

Vanishings: Tananarive Due

First published in *Ghost Summer*

van-ish (v) 1: to pass quickly from sight: disappear
2: to pass completely from existence

THERE'S NO easy way to say this, ma'am, the memory of the highway patrolman's voice repeated in her head, a loop. *Your husband's vanished.*

Vanished.

Nidra shuddered. A year had passed, and no time at all. Frost clung to the windshield, so the wipers dragged and whined. She was almost driving blind. Visiting the place where Karl's truck had wrecked was dangerous in dawn's tricky light.

Nidra's skin vibrated when she approached the ramp to Interstate 285, where the curve grew sharp and a driver might spin and slide backward down a steep embankment, crashing into a stand of hardy Georgia pines. Like Karl. Nidra stopped a few yards before the exit, since it wasn't safe to linger near the curve. She parked on the shoulder with her flashers on. Her tiny Corolla shuddered when the semis thundered past with their urgent loads, spraying gravel from monstrous tires. The spot reeked of tragic endings.

Karl had been on his way back home. At least she knew that much.

Dead leaves made the grass so slick the Nidra nearly slipped as she made her way down the sharp grade. She wasn't sure she could find the exact place a year later, but the crumpled diet soda can winked from the bed of leaves, marking the spot. A large scrape remained across the thick-trunked tree where the Ford's rear fender had rested. The ugly white smear of exposed bark reminded Nidra of an open scab; no longer bleeding, not yet healed.

Nidra expected to find the truck waiting, an apparition. To find him. His voice. His face. Every shadow was Karl hiding in the shrubs; every rustle was Karl swinging from the tree branched. The Queen of Denial, her daughter Sharlene had called her last night.

That night, police had called Karl by all three of his names and asked if he was her husband. She said she'd rather they didn't come in, thank you, and waited to find out what the bail was. She knew the situation was bound to be bad, since they had come to the house instead of calling and used his full name like he was a serial killer. *We found his wallet in your pickup rolled off 285 near the Atlanta Road exit. There's no easy way to say this, but your husband's vanished.*

The officers had waited as if they expected her to cry or have a fit like on TV.

But they didn't know Karl. They didn't know about The Talk they'd had from Dr. Ross, Asia's pediatric oncologist, about their youngest daughter's white cell count. Karl might wish he's vanished, all right.

"He didn't vanish," she told the police. "He ran – I guarantee it."

Karl would come back. And when he did, he would wish he had never left. One year ago, this was where he had changed his mind and decided he wouldn't come home. Decided to flee to a secret life. To leave her and Sharlene to manage Asia's fevers and whimpers when it was time to go back to the doctors.

Nidra wiped away angry tears.

"Cowardly sonofabitch," she said to the tree.

Asia's school was a twenty-minute drive each way. In a rare moment of solidarity, Nidra and Karl had petitioned the county to pull Asia out of Glory Elementary around the corner because she'd come home crying every day from the teasing. The kids called her *Ghost* because she was so ill. They bumped into her in the hallways purposefully, pretending they could not see her as she passed them. Nidra had never seen Karl so mad. To keep him from doing something drastic and going to jail, they decided to find Asia a new school.

Spring Valley had better manners, smaller class sizes, and fresher paint. The only drawback was the long drive. When Karl's office shut down, he had been Asia's "designated driver," as he like to say, hardy har. In the months before Karl left, Asia often needed to come home from school early because she was weak or sick. They had spent entire days shuttling back and forth between Asia's school, her doctor, and the hospital. Or just the hospital.

But not today.

Asia say safely strapped on the passenger side, her bright red ski cap bent forward as she scribbled in her composition book. Asia had taken up drawing during her last long stay at Piedmont Children's. Asia was drawing Karl's profile again; his bushy mop of hair, the rounded tip of his nose, pronounced shading of his skin.

"Looks just like him," Nidra said. Down to the knot in her stomach.

Asia didn't answer, absorbed by her pencil's even strokes.

The school driveway was lit up in brake lights from waiting cars. Asia might still be marked tardy. Nidra wished she hadn't slipped out earlier to go to the interstate. The day had just started, and she was already behind.

A family of stick figures was pasted to the rear window of the SUV directly in front of Nidra's car, even a dog on the end. But a space stood empty between the tallest and third tallest. Nidra wondered who had vanished, and how. A parent? Had some poor soul been left alone with four children to raise? She only had two, but some mornings she dreaded getting out of bed. She wished she had a time machine to go back and stop Karl from getting in his truck. Or else jump in with him.

"Did you know black walnut trees have a poison so nothing else will grow near them?" Asia said. She learned a new thing about trees each week in third-grade science.

"Nope, didn't know that."

"Does every plant and animal do something special no one else does?"

"Maybe," Nidra said. "Probably, yes."

"What about me?" Asia said.

"Everything about you is special."

"No, really, Mom."

Asia's first teacher had advised Nidra to smile more, advice that was harder to remember each day. But she tried. "There."

"What? You're smiling?"

Nidra nodded and kissed the top of her cap. "Yep, you're the only one who can make me do that, pumpkin."

"Good one. Love you, Mom."

Asia sprang out of her door before Nidra could say *I love you, too.*

Nidra watched the easy bounce in her daughter's gait. Asia wasn't dragging like she used to before Karl left. She walked just like the other kids, her backpack swinging between her shoulders like the pendulum on a grandfather clock.

Still, Spring Valley's students and parents stared, heads slowly turning to watch her daughter as she walked up the stairs and into the school's freshly painted doors.

"Didn't anyone teach you manners?" she called out, too loudly. She sounded like Karl, nut she couldn't help it. Even Asia turned her head with the rest to see what the fuss was about.

Nidra waved at her daughter and drove away.

The sedan parked outside her house looked like an undercover police car: a dark blue Crown Victoria. Nidra's heart beat so quickly that the rush of blood dizzied her.

Karl had been in jail, that was all. Or on the run. Of course he was! He'd been a petty thief and a dealer in high school and promised he'd never stray again, so he'd been too ashamed to tell her and the girls. Nidra heard herself make a sound that was half laugh, half sob, an ecstatic rage.

But it was only Lenore Augustine waiting in the driver's seat, studying *Vogue* like it was contagious. Nidra was so disappointed to find Lenore that she nearly cried.

"Nidra!" Lenore said. "There you are. Have you seen that mess across the way? Hard to believe my brothers used to hunt squirrels and rabbits out here."

The nearby construction site hadn't seemed too bad when the foliage in Nidra's yard kept the new development hidden. Their house was built high atop a slope, so it had seemed like a tree house in the forest even though they lived only ten minutes from I-285 and five minutes from Publix. The builders' noise hadn't bothered Nidra as long as she could feel enfolded in the woods. But winder was coming, leaves were thinning, and the ugliness was in plain view.

"Answer's still no," Nidra said.

"Hear me out this time. It's almost a year. Next week is the anniversary."

"You don't have to tell me it's been a year," Nidra said.

Lenore came by every three months. She and Karl had both worked at the same Realty office before Clarkson/Myers shut down and everyone scattered for new jobs. Lenore had ended up in insurance, and Karl had ended up nowhere. Lenore and Karl had been close, hitting Happy Hour at Parkfield Lanes two or three times a month, that Nidra would have suspected them of an affair if Lenore hadn't been older than his mother. Right before Asia's diagnosis, Lenore had told Nidra they had married too young. *Nobody warns young people not to get married unless you can march into Hell side by side.*

When Lenore gave her car door a push, Nidra had to choice but to step back and let her out. Microscopic wrinkles painted a patchwork across Lenore's face, barely hidden by her caked makeup's false glow of youth. Had Karl showered with Lenore at cheap motels, run his fingers through her lifeless hair? Nidra couldn't quite see it, but she couldn't quite unsee it either.

"Do you know how hard it is to get a vanishing cert from the Georgia Highway Patrol?" Lenore said. "My client list would kill for your incident report – not to mention, my boss would kill me if he knew I was out here. In seven days, the insurance will be a much bigger fight. But you paid extra for the comp package, and Karl made me promise I'd look out for you."

"So he planned it," Nidra said. "With you. That's what you're saying." Karl was a con artist through and through. He's put on a hell of a show with his tears and carrying on before he'd driven off in the Ford.

"You know you don't mean that, Nidra. I'm saying to fill out the paperwork. The money is yours, and you should have it. You need it for Asia. For the medical bills."

Lenore's eyes reminded Nidra of the smug pity in Dr. Ross's face when he saw Asia waiting in his examination room, her cap bobbing as she swung her legs to and fro from the table's perch. *Can't you see how pale Asia is?* Sharlene had screamed during their fight last night. *You just don't want to look, Mom!*

But no. that couldn't be. Asia had three more weeks before her next doctor's appointment. Asia was symptom-free, without high temperatures, loss of appetite, or vomiting that had sent her and Karl to the emergency room with her bundled like a foundling night after night. Three weeks before Dr. Ross would test Asia's levels and start the next horror show ride.

"Asia is fine."

"Of course she's fine," Lenore said. "But you have bills-

"

"Cut the bullshit," Nidra said. "Just tell me where he is."

Lenore pursed her lips, a portrait of heartbreak.

"He's gone sugar," Lenore said. "That's what I keep trying to tell you. There are support groups, if that's what you need. Books I can give you. I went through it with my mom, so I know. I expect her to tap me on the shoulder every day. It's been hell. But read what the police said – no one could have walked away from that crash alive. I wish it wasn't true – I loved him like a baby brother – but Karl has vanished. He's gone."

Sharlene had seen Nidra with Devon last night. That was what started their fight.

Devon was Shar's high school geometry teacher. He's asked Nidra out for coffee after a parent conference three months before, as if to soften his report. The first night, they had only talked about Shar; how bright she was, how frustrating. They shared a common passion. Nidra sometimes went out to Devon's townhouse for a couple of hours three times a week now, usually after seven, when Asia was ready for bed and Shar was home for the night.

Nidra's agreement with Devon was firm. He could pick her up id he waited at the curb, but he had to take her straight to his place. The sex was great, like breathing again, but that was all it ever would be. She was a married woman, and she had to sort her family when Karl came back. Besides, dating had never led her anywhere except where she was.

Gawd, Mom, what do you SEE in him? Sharlene had wailed last night, and Nidra understood her point. Devon had braces at forty-five. He said he would wear the braces for "only" nine months, as if people in their forties had months to spare. Nidra was ten years younger than Devon, but his braces made her feel like his mother. He also had a weak chin and small frame. And Nidra loathes math, which she had yet to confess. But none of that mattered.

Devon was parked in his usual place, across the street in front of their neighbor's house. When she climbed in, she wondered if Karl felt as free as she did.

"Shar saw you drop me off last night," Nidra said.

Devon's hand lingered on the gearshift. "Meaning?"

"I need to start meeting you at your place."

The car almost trembled with his relief. They both knew she was looking for an excuse to remind him she was married. Even if she signed the paperwork and took the payout, certification from the Georgia Highway Patrol wouldn't change what would happen when Karl came home. How happy their daughters would be to see him. The light it would bring to Asia.

"I think this part makes it harder for her," Devon said. "The hiding."

"She's making a C in your class," Nidra said. "You're not her favorite person."

"You want me to raise her grade?" He sounded scandalized. "Because then I would have to sleep with every other kid's mother, and I don't think I have the stamina." He winked at her.

Nidra barked a laugh so loud that she covered her mouth. She felt a foreign, giddy impulse to lean over and kiss him. No kissing was another one of her rules.

Devon grew serious. "If the grade bothers her, she should stop gliding and engage. It's locus theorems, parallel lines, transformations. The rules don't change. She knows all of this."

Sharlene had screamed hateful things at Nidra last night – terrible words with claws, leaving them both gasping and sobbing. Thank goodness Asia had slept through it all.

"We fight about it," Nidra said, "so after tonight, I'll drive myself."

The silence was an escape for the first who grabbed the chance. Neither of them did.

"We need to stop at the corner market," Devon said. "I have a mango emergency."

Nidra had never known anyone else with mango emergencies. Devon had lived in the U.S. since he was fifteen, but Trinidad survived in his habits and his carefully modulated lilt.

"All right," Nidra said. "But just wait a hot minute."

Nidra didn't want to be seen in public with Devon, but she was a stranger at World Foods. The market was closer than Publix or Kroger, but the lighting was dim, the aisles were poorly marked, and she had trouble finding even simple foods. The store bustled with sure-footed Koreans, Jamaicans, Taiwanese, Mexicans, Cubans, and others like Devon looking for flavors of home. Nidra didn't recognize most of the fruit in the produce section. The rows were stuffed with odd shapes and colors, misshapen. Who are this angry red fruit shaped like a banana? Whose worlds bore these fruits?

Devon took forever choosing his mangoes, clucking over them like baby chicks. He bagged his ripened fruit one by one, careful not to bruise them. That done, he moved to dried dates. They were nearly as large as figs, mutants.

When Devon spoke to her, his voice was so low she might have imagined it.

"Sharlene is worried about her sister."

Nidra's stomach dropped. The floor dropped. The lighting seemed to brighten, then dim.

"She told you that?"

"Not me," Devon said. "But she talks to her friends, and they say she's deathly worried. Her sister is very ill, they say, and she isn't getting proper care. That's what she's telling them."

His voice was mere breath. So, so gentle a voice for such impaling words. Devon patted her hand and moved away to know his produce bags. They did not talk about Asia's illness: that was the first rule, the reason for the other rules. They did not talk about Asia, and they did not talk about Karl.

"I'll wait in the car," Nidra said.

Alone, she spent two minutes crying, two minutes drying her face and eyes. Devon opened his car door just as she snapped her purse shut.

"Do you still want to come with me?" Devon said.

Nidra shook her head. "Take me back, please."

Devon's anxiousness to find the right words filled the car with pained silence. "Nidra…"

"I left mac and cheese for Shar and Asia in my fridge," she said. "We can whip something together at my place."

Devon considered and nodded. Without a word, he drove her home.

"Eww," Shar said when she say Devon in the living room. She froze mid-step on the staircase, her face puckered. With her hair cut short, she looked like a willowy version of Karl; Nidra saw the resemblance most when Shar frowned. "What's Mr. Roy doing here?"

"Good to see you too, Sharlene."

"It's Shar," she said. "In my house, you call me Shar. And you can go now."

"Shar, don't," Nidra said. Her spontaneous plan had felt foolish as soon as she opened the door – indecent, really – but Shar had started downstairs before she could tell Devon she'd changed her mind. Shar stood halfway down the stairs, knuckles white on the railing, undecided.

When Nidra saw the living room through Devon's eyes, everything was crooked: the books, the rug, the sofa cushions, the photo frames. Everything.

"Did Asia finish her homework?" Nidra said.

Shar stared at Nidra with what looked like real loathing. "Yes, Mother. Anything else?"

"Are you done with yours?" Devon muttered, and Shar's eyes shot lasers at him.

"Yes, there's something else," Nidra said. "Devon's having dinner with us tonight. Is that all right with you?" She tried to sound casual. Like she wasn't begging.

Shar's lips shrank, tightening. "Is it all right if my archnemesis Mr. Roy, my geometry teacher drone, has dinner with us here in our house? At our table?"

"Yes, Shar. Is it all right?"

Shar still hadn't moved from the stairs. Nidra braced for the storm, in front of company this time. None came. "Your life," Shar said. "But he's a royal pain."

"Only during daylight hours," Devon said. "After dark, my true personality emerges."

He picked up the Christmas portrait Nidra and the girls had taken at Sears last year at her parents' insistence, their smiles so forced they looked manic.

"I'm sorry, Shar," Nidra said. "Hiding doesn't feel right. You said to stop pretending."

"It's nothing at all to you," Devon told Shar. "You're any other student, and your mother and I are friends."

Shar shrugged and went to the kitchen to get the dinner plates. Shar used to hide in her room to avoid her chores, but she never needed reminding since Karl left.

"Asia?" Nidra called upstairs.

"Right here, Mom."

The voice came from the stairs, but hung weightless in the corner shadows. Then, just as fast, Asia was midway down the stairs in a long black T-shirt. Asia's skin was the color of the stained teak-colored paneling on the wall behind her. Light from the foyer lamp shimmered, making her face seem to phase in and out against the wood's grains, like an optical illusion.

When Devon drew a hitched breath, Nidra realized she'd been holding her own since she heard *Right here, Mom* from thin air.

"Well," Devon said, sunshine in his voice. "It's good to meet you, Asia. Your mother has told me a great deal about you."

A lie, but a forgivable one for the way it made Asia's teeth gleam with a smile.

"This is my friend, Mr. Roy. He's –"

"I know," Asia said." I heard."

Nidra served the macaroni and cheese as they sat at the table. Devon silently said grace before he ate, a habit she had never noticed. Could it be they had never eaten together? She remembered the sound of his lungs hissing when he'd seen Asia.

Why had everyone seen how sick Asia was but her?

"My Daddy's vanished," Asia said to Devon.

Quickly, Nidra patted Asia's hand. "That's just what the police told us. We don't know."

Shar's stare was so pointed that Nidra had to fight the urge to hold her daughter's eyes.

"He's not coming back," Shar told Asia, and assurance, as if Nidra were a stranger who had just said something profane. Her stare held, daring Nidra to dispute her.

"No," Nidra said. "Probably not."

Packed molecules in the air seemed to drift clear of each other, making it easier to breathe. Karl would want them to have the insurance money. Both the girls needed new jackets instead of the old ones she's had to dig out of the coat closet. It was only late November, but it was cold.

Maybe Karl's truck had skidded in icy rain. Maybe that was how it had happened. He'd been on his way home. Maybe his last thoughts on this Earth had been of them.

"How do you like school?" Devon asked Asia.

Asia shook her head. "I hate it. Everybody looks at me because I'm sick."

Nidra tried to keep the panic she felt from her face.

"Yes, that's very rude," she head Devon say somewhere far beneath her. "It was that way for me, too, when my parents first moved us from my country. I was in a private school where no one had brown skin but me. They all stared. I ignored it."

"Yeah, screw them," Shar said.

"Who wants dessert?" Devon said, pulling out a produce bag.

Shar peered into the bag and blanched. "Do you know what those look like?"

"They're dates," he said.

Karl didn't like dates, so Nidra had gotten out of the habit of buying them by the time Shar was old enough to eat them. She could hardly remember who she had been when she was twenty, dropping out of Georgia State and marrying Karl because he had plans and made her laugh. Two months later she was pregnant with Sharlene, Asia. A life lived in a blur.

"I don't think they've ever tasted dates," Nidra said.

Devon cast Nidra a playful look. "Why are you depriving these girls?"

While Devon helped Asia choose the plumpest date, Shar peered over to study them.

"I'll try one," Shar said.

Asia squealed when she took her first bite. "It's so sweet! Like cake." She ate three more. She had a good appetite. Watching the fruit find Asia's mouth, Nidra remembered the bubbles in Asia's baby bottle when she drank, the way their dance had quieted Nidra's worries when Asia was small.

"Well?" Nidra said, watching Sharlene wrap her date pit in her napkin.

"It's okay." She scooted her chair. "It's time for Asia's bath."

"I'll take her up in a minute."

Shar stood and reached for Asia's hand the way she would at a busy intersection. "It's a school night, so the sooner the better. Come on, Asia."

After the polite good-nights, Devon watched as they walked away.

"You're so lucky," Devon said once he was alone at the table with Nidra.

"Which part?"

Devon slipped his hand over hers on the tabletop.

"Sharlene is such a big help to you," he said. "You have a lovely family."

The bathtub was full, the water crowned with bright white suds.

When Asia was two and Karl got a bonus at work, they'd used most of the check to refurbish the main bathroom upstairs. The floor, wall tiles, and bathtub were slick aquamarine, the color of the bathroom in her grandmother's house. The picture window overlooking the backyard was the biggest luxury of her lifetime.

Neighbors' lights twinkled in the dark like constellations. When the treetops were a full canopy, they never say lights at night. Now, even in the darkness, her backyard trees' steady shedding unmasked the lighted construction site down the hill: bare concrete walls half finished, machinery painted brightly in unnatural colors. She'd stopped noticing the view when it was pretty, and now it was gone. She could never catch hold of a moment.

Karl's good razor hung suspended in the toothbrush rack, coated with dust and powdery shaving cream residue. Nidra took the razor and almost put it in the drawer, but she buried it in her front pocket instead. It would still smell like his face.

"Asia?" Nidra called into the hall.

"I'm right here."

A splash echoed behind Nidra, from the bathtub. Suds parted at the foot of the tub as Asia sat up, a watery shadow against bathwater the color of the ocean. The bubbles clinging to Asia's hair and face framed her features. Nidra couldn't believe how pale Asia was since her last bath. Her bare skin was nearly invisible.

She would call Dr. Ross as soon as Asia was in bed. Nidra knew his cell phone number by heart. She wondered at her calm, but knew she was not calm anywhere except on the outside.

"You were hiding," Nidra said.

Asia giggled. "If I was a snake, I woulda bit you," she said, imitating Grandma.

Nidra sat on the rim of the tub and dunked Asia's washcloth into the warm water. "Here comes the snake," she said, slithering the cloth beneath the suds toward Asia's back. Asia pretended to scream, splashing to the other side of the tub. Nidra wanted to ask why Asia never told her she wasn't feeling well again, but she didn't have to. She probably had tried to say it, or expected Nidra to notice. As Asia's mother, after all. A mother should see first, not last.

Water splashed again, and a stream trickled from Asia's fingers. Asia played with the water for a long time. Nidra ran Dr. Ross's phone number through her head, sixes and threes.

"After your bath, you pick a story and I'll read it to you," Nidra said.

"Anansi, then."

However small, it was a plan. No mysterious or new tragedies waited in the next thirty minutes. A maw gnawing inside Nidra's stomach felt like a scream from her heart and womb, but Nidra enjoyed the sound of Asia splashing the water, playing unafraid.

"Look, Mom," Asia said in a hush, entranced. "I'm vanishing."

Crystalline threads twined Asia's fingers, blending her skin to the color of blue bathwater where her fading flesh rose and fell, rose and fell, across the liquid plane.

Tananarive Due is a former Cosby Chair in the Humanities at Spelman College (2012-2014), where she taught screenwriting, creative writing and journalism. She also teaches in the creative writing MFA program at Antioch University Los Angeles. The American Book Award winner and NAACP Image Award recipient is the author of twelve novels and a civil rights memoir. In 2010, she was inducted into the Medill School of Journalism's Hall of Achievement at Northwestern University. A leading voice in black speculative fiction Her novella "Ghost

Summer," published in the 2008 anthology *The Ancestors*, received the 2008 Kindred Award from the Carl Brandon Society, and her short fiction has appeared in best-of-the-year anthologies of science fiction and fantasy. Her first short story collection, *Ghost Summer*, was published by Prime Books in 2015. She collaborates on the Tennyson Hardwick mystery series with her husband, author Steven Barnes, in partnership with actor Blair Underwood. Due also wrote *The Black Rose* , a historical novel about the life of Madam C.J. Walker, based on the research of Alex Haley – and *Freedom in the Family: A Mother-Daughter Memoir of the Fight for Civil Rights* , which she co-authored with her mother, the late civil rights activist Patricia Stephens Due. In 2004, alongside such luminaries as Nobel Prize-winner Toni Morrison, she received the "New Voice in Literature Award" at the Yari Yari Pamberi conference co-sponsored by New York University's Institute of African-American Affairs and African Studies Program and the Organization of Women Writers of Africa. She has a B.S. in journalism from Northwestern University and an M.A. in English literature from the University of Leeds, England, where she specialized in Nigerian literature as a Rotary Foundation Scholar. In addition to VONA, Due has taught at the Hurston-Wright Foundation's Writers' Week and the Clarion Science Fiction and Fantasy Writers' Workshop. As a screenwriter, she is a member of the Writers' Guild of America (WGA). She lives in Southern California with her husband, science fiction author Steven Barnes, and their son, Jason.

Devil for a Witch: R.S. Brenner

First published in *Jewish Noir*

Whither? North is greed and South is blood;
Within, the coward, and without, the liar. Whither?
-W.E.B. Du Bois, "The Litany of Atlanta"

If you see the teeth of the lion
do not think that the lion is smiling at you.
-Al-Mutanabbi, Arab poet, 915-965 C.E.

The funeral for Leon Greenberg was graveside, the service short. As little as possible was said about the deceased. Nothing personal or elegiac. His death blotted out any cause for celebration of his life. If his existence had once been charmed, it was not mentioned. Star chemist, decorated Navy officer, brilliant raconteur, and once holding the enviable title of husband to a beautiful rich woman, no such attributions were uttered. Suicide was a willful negation of life. Out of confusion, sadness, spite, its legatees accepted that the dead man's last act overrode all others.

Across town at the reception, limos dropped the mourners at the Steiners' split-level wonder, a glass and steel extravaganza around the corner from the governor's mansion. It was Atlanta's most prestigious address even if the governor was a murderous bigot.

In the Steiners' living room, *shivah* was under heated discussion. "He's an atheist!" Irene Greenberg shouted.

"*Was*," Phil Steiner said.

"*Was! Was! Was!* I am his wife! I know what he wants!"

"He does not want *shivah*," she insisted. "When my father died, we sat *shivah* because he wanted it. We sat two nights until you went off to a golf tournament."

"He wasn't *my* father."

Irene shook her fist like an impotent human before the throne of God. "He gave you everything!"

"Stop it!" he croaked, holding her wrist and tightening his grip.

"My husband just killed himself! I'm permitted to completely lose my mind!"

"I'm sitting *shivah*," Marilyn Steiner, Irene's sister, said.

"Leon doesn't want it, but now that he's dead, he's helpless. He's in the clutched of Zionists!"

"Helpless!" Phil snorted. "Not with you as a defensive end."

"I loved Leon," Marilyn sighed.

"Everyone knows about that," Irene said.

"Shut up!" Phil ordered.

"Your husband wants me to tear my blouse because he knows I bought it on sale at Rich's. I don't wear Vera scarves and Charles Jourdan shoes like my sister. I can't afford to shop in New York." Irene twisted the end of Marilyn's scarf, shortening the loop like a noose. "Would you tear your precious scarf if Phil died?"

"Get a sedative!"

"Phil Steiner is a usurer!" Irene shouted. "Usurer! Usurer!"

Murmurs of sympathy followed as a phalanx of black maids lifted Irene off the ground and carried her to another wing of the house where Valium was forced under her uvula, her mouth clamped shut, and her neck stroked like a dog's. That was only after she broke Sarah Weiner's cane over Phil's arm while Sarah's hands were occupied with lox and deviled eggs. The cane splintered and caught Phil's shirt, ripping it open and scratching his chest. A tiny scratch but Phil agonized as if Irene had bitten his heart out, which she would have if she'd had the strength.

Later, when the pill wore off and she was home in bed, the recollection of the cane, it's percussive thwack, Phil's expression, the blood, his torn shirt, and the chaos and confusion that ensued were deeply satisfying. Irene laughed about it for years.

"Jesus, no!" he said although he didn't sound convincing. He sounded defensive.

When Stanley White reviewed the checks, he denied any knowledge of signing them. "Fakes," he said. He sounded extremely convincing.

"You know of outside agitators, union organizers, Communists, pinkos, those sorts of people on your payroll?"

"Of course not! Everyone who works here is happy!"

Phil slammed Leon's office door. "I lied to the FBI to save your goddamn ass! In case you forgot, that's a felony! Next time you're feeling goddamn charitable, use your own goddamn profits!"

"We don't have any profits."

"Whoever heard of a pauper giving away thousands of dollars?"

"Stories abound."

"Stories, Leon? Stories mean they didn't happen! You're out of your mind!"

"By my accounting, I took money that belonged to Irene."

"*Your* accounting! I pay overeducated accountants to manage my books. The entire time you worked there, you drew a paycheck and did nothing, Leon. Goddamn good-for-nothing, you listening?"

"Irene hasn't gotten her fair share."

"Irene? I thought you only cared about *shvartses* and commies."

For three years, the FBI had tracked Leon Greenberg's finances, marital difficulties, children's schools, taste in music, love affairs, drinking habits, and contributions to organizations under federal investigation. Agent Whipple unlocked a black attaché case and laid out checks forged by Leon Greenberf with Stanley White's signature.

Leon studied the checks. "I no longer work at Ace Linens."

"We are aware of your employment status," Whipple said grimly. "Nonetheless, we have proof you forged these checks."

"Is that what Phil Steiner told you?"

"We know about your links to Dr. King and Fidel Castro. We know you spent two weeks at a Mississippi Freedom School."

"Are you saying that's illegal?'

Agent Whipple smiled, showing a row of small amber teeth. "You know what's illegal, Mr. Greenberg. You'll soon be facing criminal charges and a long prison sentence."

Leon sat mulling over his Jim Beam. "Like how long?"

"Fraud, forgery, embezzlement are serious crimes."

Leon knew they were serious, serious by intent. He had acted according to conscience.

"In my defence, I can prove the funds were originally embezzled by my brother-in-law, Phil Steiner. Every penny belonged to my wife."

"We call that backpedaling, Mr. Greenberg. Backpedaling is something of an art."

Whipple painted a bleak picture of Leon's future. He had stolen, there was no doubt. He had distributed monies to suspicious causes. Certainly, he didn't believe a jury or judge in Georgia would be swayed by his pinko generosity.

Leon forced himself to stay sober. He considered his choices. *You trade the devil for a witch* was a country saying. Devil, he knew. Witch was unknown.

Suicide was not farfetched for a man in Leon's predicament. He had contemplated suicide. He'd read the existentialists and accepted suicide as an individual's ultimate act in a world where individuality was valued less and less. Under the ultimate threats of the Atomic Age, it functioned as a solace. A last resort. While it carried a stigma of shame, the stigma was one man's act of desperation rather than society's collective condemnation. Avoiding trial and prison meant there would be money for Irene and the kids. Money Leon couldn't otherwise provide.

The FBI would stage the suicide. That would pose no problem. They were adept at theatrics. At their meeting, Leon handed over suit, shirt, tie, socks, shoes, reading glasses, and wallet with ID. In exchange, he received a bus ticket to Louisville and identification of Dr. Leland Green with a CV that included published articles on the science of white superiority.

"You ready?" Whipple asked.

"How the hell could I be ready?"

"Ready to serve mankind."

"As a white bigot, that's always cause for celebration."

Agent Whipple laughed. "Instead of whimpering with liberal guilt, you can put your ass on the line."

Tears sprang to Leon's eyes. "What if..."

"You'll realize you made the right decision," Whipple sympathized.

"It wasn't a decision. You gave me no choice."

At the same hour, Leland Green boarded a bus at the Greyhound station, Leon Greenberg's car was locked inside a garage, its tail pipe stuffed with rags, its engine left running. Inside was the corpse of a Caucasian man of medium height with broad shoulders and a barrel chest, wearing Leon's best blue suit, pin-striped shirt, and gray knit tie. The man was the same blood type and shoe size as Leon and shared the same shade of thinning brown hair. Obviously, they weren't identical. Rather than take measures to destroy the body entirely and with it proof positive, the bureau decided to blow off enough of the stranger's face to turn it into pulp.

Leland's bus headed into the starry countryside. He pressed his nose against the window. The nose of a man who no longer existed. Or existed but no longer lived. The memories intact but the man gone. The inverse amnesia.

In Louisville, he read the hand-printed sign – DR. LELAND GREEN.

"Welcome," Hugh Martino said jovially. "Long ride?"

"An eternity," Leon mused.

Martino showed Leon his Buick with Oregon plates, his new driver's license and passport, a strongbox of cash and traveler's checks, a camera and telephoto lens, a first aid kit, and ice cooler, and a portfolio of articles.

"You think I can pull this off?" Leon asked.

"I don't think anything, that's why they keep me around. Here's your gun and ammo."

"Jesus, I don't know how to shoot. I never fired a shot in the whole goddamn war."

"They don't expect you to know what they know. You're thinking man, not a redneck. Hell, most of them can't read or write. Try to get in target practice. Squirrels, possums, cans. Go into the woods with your buddies. They know how to shoot. Anyway, woods is where talking gets done. It's trees that keep the secrets."

Phil Steiner whistled as he drove. He was an excellent whistler and was often asked at club or synagogue events to whistle a friend's favourite song. "Ebb Tide" was a spectacular tune to whistle. He parked his Lincoln next to the rundown apartment complex on Buford Highway. Constructed quickly after the war, the three-story buildings had not been well maintained. There were cracked windows, missing roof shingles, and greenways intended for playgrounds long overgrown with weeds and scattered trash.

Moshe Berger's apartment was on the second floor in building D. "Phil," he muttered, holding out his hands in European fashion and drawing Phil toward him in an affectionate hug.

"Moe," Phil said with genuine feeling.

Years ago when Moshe and his son first arrived from Europe as refugees, Phil Steiner had been their American sponsor. He'd found them the apartment on Buford Highway. he'd arranged for the synagogue to take up a collection of discarded furniture, kitchenware, and clothing to get them started. He'd given Moe a job driving a truck for Ace Linens.

Moe moved into the kitchenette for coffee and Sara Lee cheesecake, waving Phil to the living room sofa. "You look well," he said.

"Well enough. Are you teaching?" Phil nibbled on the cake.

"I'll be teaching until I drop dead," Moe laughed. He was on the history faculty at Spelman College. "You said on the phone?"

Phil had alluded to help. Spiritual help, Moe surmised. Whatever he could do, he would make himself available.

"We had an unexpected death in the family."

"I know about Leon. I used to bump into him on campus. Always brimming with life, wasn't he?"

"A nonbeliever but wonderful," Phil said begrudgingly. He'd not forgiven Leon for his humiliating encounter with the FBI. Phil's fingers clasped and unclasped. "It's difficult for me to speak."

"I know about difficult things," Moe said.

"That's why I came to you. Many times, I thought to come."

"Not to speak makes it worse."

"There's something I have to tell someone. You're the only one in the world."

Moe was taken aback. "I hope I won't disappoint you."

"Leon took his car into a garage and stuffed a rag in the tail pipe." Phil halted and started to weep.

"I'm sorry," Moe said softly, taking Phil's hand. His own wide and daughter had also been suffocated by gas.

"After the police found the garage, the car, and the body, they asked me to identify him. Of course, I agreed.

I was standing by for the task. His wide couldn't possibly do it. I was the obvious choice."

Countless times, Moshe had wished, dreamed and wished to have a single minute to gaze at the corpses of his wife and daughter. If only for an instant, Moe could have touched their lovely faces serenely composed like the dead often are.

"It was the hardest goddamn thing I ever did," Phil said in a sweat. "When I got to the morgue, they tried to prepare me. They told me I might be shocked. I didn't understand what they meant. It's true I'd only seen corpses in funeral homes, laid out and embalmed. I wasn't in the war. I never saw carnage, only photos and films." With the cuff of his shirt, Phil wiped his eyes. "They pulled Leon out of the freezer and uncovered him. I never told a soul, but I fainted."

There was silence while Phil composed himself.

"He'd blown his face off. Moe, you understand? A man goes to kill himself in a car with carbon monoxide and then shoots himself? What did this last message mean? I couldn't tell his wife he'd mutilated himself beyond recognition. I couldn't tell my wife. She was devoted to Leon. If I told anyone, it would have turned Leon into a freak. This face, it gives me nightmares. He must have been out of his mind. That's the only way to explain it."

The Natchez Trace is bordered by dense woods, rivers, pastures, and hills. It's a beautiful drive, but Leland Green failed to notice scenery. He was occupied with a temptation to abandon his new identity, steal the car, the cash, the passport and beeline over the border to Mexico. A romantic notion for a man without guilt. Equally occupying him was Leon the hero. Daniel heading into the pit. But he was incapable of ennobling his cause with romance or sainthood. Neither brave nor guiltless, not a Daniel or a Zygielbojm, he was penitent, tired, deflated, and by Jackson city limits, he'd shed any illusions of free will.

He checked into a downtown hotel. His preference was a new motel with a swimming pool, but the agency wanted him to present as bookish, indifferent to modern comforts, content with chintz bedspreads and dust ruffles, Gideon within arm's reach, and paintings of buggies and barns. After dinner in the hotel dining room, he strolled through the thick, stagnant air relieved by the occasional steamy gust over the river. Inside a phone booth, he took a fortifying swallow of Jack and inserted a dime. He gave his home phone number to the operator, hoping to hear his daughter's voice for a moment.

"What?" his wife hissed. "What? What? What? Can't you leave us alone?"

He'd disturbed her. Maybe, she was sleeping. There was no doubt she was mad. As mad as she'd been at the living Leon, she was likely madder at the dead man. Mad and relieved. His suicide had diminished her grievances. It would now appear *his* grievances overshadowed *hers*.

At the hotel, the clerk handed him a note in poorly printed letters: Meat 11 A.M. by stat U. Hairy B-E-R-G-S-T-A-D-T

"You read it okay, sir?" He asked timidly.

"How long you been working here?'

"Two nights, sir."

"You got to know how to spell to be a lawyer."

"Nigger lawyers know how to spell?"

Leon closed his eyes. He conjured Daddy King in his pulpit at Ebenezer Baptist. It was there he'd been introduced to *The Beloved Community* and called *brother*. There, he'd perceived what it meant to live an enemy. Only love conquers hate, King said.

"They spell right?' the clerk sneered.

"You better believe they do."

The next morning he walked to City Hall. He took a seat between the imposing bronze statue of Andrew Jackson and the antebellum building. At the appointed hour, a gentleman with a white standard poodle leisurely approached him. "Dr. Green?" he enquired.

Leon jumped up as Harry Bergstedt pumped his hand. "Meet Puss," Harry said.

Leon Green held out his biscuit-and-gravy fingers for Puss to lick. He found himself trembling.

Let them lead the conversation, Whipple instructed.

Bergstedt's smile brightened. "We've read your work with great admiration."

"Thank you," Leland whispered, unable to catch his breath.

For two years, the writings of "Hailstorm" had appeared in Klan publications and circulated in White Citizens Councils. Argent Whipple never divulged who wrote the articles or how the plot evolved. Leon suggested a local infiltrator was more sensible than an elaborate ruse, but they disagreed. With the country's international reputation at stake, they needed an intelligent outsider. Leon Greenberg put a man on their side who was capable of reasoning through information and responding with measured caution. He had the bonus of a personality that could win the confidence of both crackers and patricians. Violent crackers, the agency could identify. They were status quo. The planners and financiers remained clandestine. The agency wanted to know which bank president owned a white robe.

"I understand this is a research tour?"

"For a new book."

"And the subject, sir?"

"There's only one subject," Lee said, surprised by his resoluteness.

"In Jackson, you'll find many sympathizers. They've sent me out as welcome wagon to invite you to dinner. Meanwhile, what can I do to make you feel at home?"

"I already feel at home," Lee said, his left hand in spasm.

At seven o'clock, he stood stone sober on the doorstep of Harry Bergstedt's Belhaven home, it's façade as stately as Harry. Lifting the polished brass knocker, he tapped politely. The door was opened by an arthritic butler who ushered Lee to the parlor where Bergstedt immediately rose and hailed the guest of honour.

"To Dr. Leland Green, pioneer and preservationist."

Lee hesitated. Surely, he wasn't meant to dine with these men in this house. Surely, it was a scene from theater of the absurd. The butler was wrong, and he was wrong too. His will hung back, but his body swam into the room, shaking hands with seven men and one stunning woman.

"East Texas," Bergstedt said in lieu of a profession for Sally Shaw. "She owns it!"

She turned to Lee, fluffing the mound of tawny hair that fell loosely on her thin shoulders. "Can you tell?"

"Evidently, she owns Paris too!" Lee reposted, referring to her YSL frock, the black patent heels, the brimless horsehair hat, and an enormous diamond pendant.

Sally Shaw blushed with false modesty.

"What are you drinking, sir?" Harry asked.

Lee wavered, staring at Mrs. Shaw's gleaming russet eyes.

She held up a glass of Campari. "That's what I'm partaking of," she said.

"We might all be writing books if we didn't irrigate our cerebral cortex every night," Peter Smithson said. He was the local GM dealer.

Bergstedt handed over a crystal tumbler of carmine liquid. "Dr. Green has been out West too long."

"I once was a drinking man," Lee said.

Don't offer any personal information, Whipple instructed.

"But?" Sally Shaw grinned.

"It got away with me," he explained what would likely be his only truthful words all evening.

Her penciled eyebrows arched. "*Away* with you?"

They crossed they foyer to the dining room, the walls hung with oil paintings of men in uniform, each dated from a war, the uniforms more distinctive than the faces – 1812, 1862, 1898, 1917, 1942, and a recent portrait of a youth in garb of a Green Beret, Harry Bergstedt's son, Hank, serving in Vietnam.

Harry sat at the head of the oval mahogany table. At each place setting was a white gilded charger, an acid-greed porcelain plate, six pieces of festooned silver cutlery, an crystal goblet also gilded, two wine glasses, and individual crystal decanters of cucumber water.

"Dr. Green sir, will you kindly lead us in the blessing?"

Around the table, they linked hands. Lee had rehearsed such things, but he needed to sound unrehearsed. He paused to listen to the paddle fan overhead. Then, he began to paraphrase words of gratitude for the munificent bounty, remembering to ask the blessing in the name of Jesus Christ, Our Lord. An utterance that terminated Leon Greenberg. Again.

Dinner conversation was filled with complaints about business, weather, family, golf. Although Sally asked Leland questions, he resisted. He did well at redirecting. After dinner, Harry ushered them back to the parlor for Napoleon brandy, chicory coffee, cake, and contraband Cuban cigars.

"We like your point of view, sir. We like how you phrase things. That's what a good writer does."

"Thank you, sir," Lee said, forgetting for a few seconds that he was merely a good charlatan.

Never let your guard down, Whipple instructed emphatically.

"Jackson will be my base, but I want to roam around. I may even go as far as Texas."

"You talking my country," Sally said with gusto. "I got plenty of cotton pickers working in *peaceful equilibrium.*"

He noted with disappointment that Sally had read "Hailstorm."

"*Peaceful equilibrium* and *Compassionate Segregation* are slogans to propel a man to the mansion. Maybe, Harry wants to be gov'nor."

"I think we have a convincing case, sir," Harry's voice crescendoed. "What does counsel think?"

Billy Clarkson brayed, "Counsel thinks he'll never have another brandy."

"Our real concern isn't the Negra. Negrs, we know how to handle. We been handling Negras for hundreds of years. Feds don't worry me. Excuse me, Missus Shaw, feds don't know their bassackward from a hole in the ground. It's Jews who know the difference. Jews are putting their money on the black. If you're a roulette man, it's worrisome. Jews are funding the entire goddamn nigger insurrection.

Lee visibly shuddered.

"They're not as smart as you think!" Billy Clarkson exclaimed.

"They are! They're the smartest people in the world!"

Lee folded his arms. "I've met stupid Jews," he said, thinking of his college roommate.

"Not possible," Smithson interrupted.

Don't come across overly opinionated, Whipple instructed.

"There are stupid people everywhere," Lee blurted.

"If you got stupid Jews, maybe you got genius Negros," Sally Shaw reflected.

Harry winked theatrically. "Try to walk a straight line, a woman throws a curve every time."

Leland Green rented a carriage house in the Belhaven district and settled in with a portable Olivetti and a ream of paper. Except for Sunday church, he spent mornings at the library reading crime paperbacks. His favourites by Ian Fleming and Eric Ambler, the more vicious the better. Otherwise he wrote notes to Whipple or make feeble attempts to outline Hailstorm's new book. In the afternoon, he drove around the countryside, looking for signs of menace. Beside rail fences and at crossroad stores, he stopped to converse. It proved impossible to talk to frightened men. No one wanted a cold drink or a joke. No one except children let him take their picture. The Oregon license plate made him a foreigner.

Sally Shaw offered to escort him in her sporty Mercedes. To help him find "happy whites and happy coloreds," she said.

Colored surprised him. He considered it enlightened, but the car made him squeamish. In Atlanta, no Jews drove German cars except his sister-in-law, Marilyn Steiner. "I accept," he finally said despite the car and outfits that would feed the sharecropper's family for months.

She headed east toward Bienville, swung off the black-top at Morton, and bounced over a rutted dirt lane into the forest. The deepest ruts filled with chartreuse scum and mosquito larvae. She parked beside a small river under-neath a splendid white oak. Lee lifted the metal cooler from Sally's trunk, his eyes scanning her bare tan legs and sleeveless cotton dress dotted with violets. The dress came with a matching parasol she carried in one hand and in the other a dainty wicker picnic basket.

"This isn't much of a work mission," Lee said, chewing a drumstick and sipping a cold beer.

"My work mission," she lisped through her coruscating teeth.

"I'm not worth a mission, Mrs. Shaw," he laughed. In fact, he laughed freely.

"I thought I'd show you where *your* boys hand out."

"What do *my* boys do?"

"Boy things like drink, shoot at Coke bottles, hunt and fish. Who the hell knows? Chiggers are fierce so I stay over here and swim."

"You don't go for fish and game?"

"As uncouth as I am, I don't like killing. I eat it once it's dead, but I'm not a killer."

A quarter-mile from the river was a crude log construc-tion, a deep fire pit for trash, an outhouse, and an outdoor sink and shower fed by a rain barrel on the roof. Lee peered through a window, surprised by the shabbiness. Sally removed a bobby pin from her hair, twisted the wires, and stuck one end into the padlock.

"Y'all needing he'p?" a soft country voice called from the woods.

A man, ramrod straight and freshly shaven with bloody nicks on his neck, stepped forward. He stood with his hands in the pockets of well-worn overalls, soiled and busted canvas shoes, and on his head a faded shako whose provenance could have been the Napoleonic Age. He was a black Indian with Choctaw blood, his skin flushed red, his eyes different colors, one bright blue, the other muddy brown. He was called Hark although Hark was not his Indian name, Bending Willow, or baptised name, James Willie Johnson. It was a nickname bestowed by the plantation owner where his family used to sharecrop. Hark had lived near Bienville for eighty-six years. He was caretaker of Harry Bergstedt's clubhouse.

He lifted his hat from his hairless head and held it. "Missus Shaw, I saw yo' car over by the river."

Sally relaxed. The colored man made her feel as if she had every right to be there. "This is Dr. Green."

"Thought I'd fish but didn't bring my pole," Lee said.

"They got them plenty poled inside, Missus Shaw. They got them plenty everything you need, sir. I know the best place to dig for worms. Y'all wan' I can open up?"

Hark's gnarled fingers pulled a ring of keys from his pocket, dozens on a string with a rabbit's foot for good luck. He inserted a key in the padlock and another into the discus lock, then opened the door, moving aside to let Sally and the doctor pass into the hot, stuffy room that smelled of stale beer and sour terrycloth. Antlers hung on a wall, baseball bats and golf clubs leaned in a corner.

Lee noted the guns, including the Enfield 1917 rifle, the type that killed Medgar Evers. Hark reached for the rods and an aluminum case smaped with the Wheatley mark. "Unless y'all like flies, sir."

"They play golf?" Lee asked Sally.

"All talk in Mississippi divides according to class. Serfs debate the wonders of the combustion engine and gentry discuss golf. You'd think there wasn't another subject in the world except college football. So to speak, Ole Miss Rebels is common ground. Hark will back me up."

"Yes'm, I back Missus Shaw any day."

Leon complained to Whipple he was getting fat. Fat and useless. He was close to hating Leland Green and the vigilance required to mold him into a temperate, chaste Christian man. He certainly hated Whipple. Any discussion of timetable had been vague. Could the agency ask him to stay indefinitely? Yes, he thought they could. They could do whatever they wanted. He worked for them.

Then, there was the evening he felt himself crack.

You'll reach the point where you can't go on, but you'll push through, Whipple said.

"Of course, it happened," Lee shouted, socking his fist against his palm. "I was in the war, were you?"

"Not defending Jews."

Fuming, Lee rose. He walked out the front door and paces across the lawn.

Deep, slow breaths, Whipple instructed. *Once you get control of your breathing, you can think clearly.*

He composed himself and returned to the gathering. "It gives a good cause a bad mark to distort history," he said quietly.

Henry Bergstedt concurred. He supported Leland Green. He liked sound reasoning. "Dr. Green and I are on the same page about that. We can't depend on primitive emotions and ignorant falsehoods. That's over, gentlemen."

Randy McIntire didn't agree. He thought emotions and falsehoods were highly dependable. They'd served the cause very well. What didn't serve were pretentious theories.

In early November, Lee was invited to the country for hunting, drinking, and cards. As the weekend approached, he grew frightened. He might be asked to commit a crime. Whipple told him he was under no obligation to perform a violent act. If his loyalty to Harry's gang was tested, he wasn't sure how to refuse. He wondered if he should bring his gun. If cajoled into skinny dipping, his circumcised penis might become a topic of speculation. A joke or worse. Randy McIntire had planted the seed that Dr. Green was an apologist for Jews. Whatever was required, he was afraid he would fail.

On Friday night, he drove to Bienville beside the spectral towers of dead kudzu. There were no oncoming cars, no road lights, no moon or stars, only black sky and mammoth clouds. At the cabin's back entrance, Peter parked his Fleetwood Eldorado on a patch of flattened weeds beside two pickups. Five men stood nearby, smoking in the chilly dark under the pines, cigarettes glowing like fire-flies.

"Come on in, boys," Harry waved.

Lee felt his stomach lurch. He lifted the case of scotch from the trunk, truing to read the license plated on the trucks, heart pounding like a jackhammer, deafening as he bent down and scribbled the numbers on his calf. Harry lit the kerosene lanterns. Billy made a fire to drive out the cold and damp. The visitors took seats at the square, sturdy table. They looked average, Lee thought. Average Mississippi bigots – farmer, merchant, plumber, bartender, and sheriff's deputy. Mugs and a bottle of Cutty Sark were passed around. One of the strangers had a bushel of boiled peanuts. Harry and his boys were gar-rulous, almost giddy in contrast to the visitor's silence. None of them spoke. They were busy enjoying the luxury of scotch.

"Who's he?" Pawley asked. He was older than Harry, white-haired with wolf eyes and a nose like a baked yam.

"Dr. Green, y'all call him 'Lee'"

"Somebody needing a doctor?" Bee Jay asked. Bee Jay was Pawley's fifty-year-old nephew, bald with grubby cheeks, a drift in his left eye, a nickel wart on his chin.

"Only if we have to shoot y'all!" Billy said.

"Not funny when we doing yo' dirty work," Pawley groused.

"Doctor of religion," Harry said, stirring his drink with his finger. "You can get to be a doctor of anything."

"None of us got all night," Pawley said. He like the money but didn't care for the company. Harry Bergstedt and his men were arrogant. They acted as if they owned the world.

Peter Smithson unzipped his overnight bad, removed a map, and unfolded it on the table. Sloppy circles were drawn around Greenwood, Port Gibson, Vicksburg, Meridian, and the capital.

"Hear, hear! Meeting convened!"

Pawley ran his finger across the state, north to south. "Jackson?"

"Sure, why not?"

"You boys like the sound of that?"

"I don't go for Jackson," Bee Jay whispered.

"Can't hear you," Pawley snarled.

"Jackson got Yankees. No secrets in Jackson."

"What about Port Gibson?""

"Gemi-luth Chessed or however the hell y-all say it, it's a Jew house. I seen 'em."

"Fishin' good over there," Bee Jay said, worrying his wart, his hands skittish.

"Jew house got a dome on top just like goddamn commies in Russia."

"Town too goddamn small. Somebody notice us, for sure."

"I agree with Bee Jay," Bergstedt said. "I veto Jackson."

"You aiming to burn or bomb?"

"Fire's easier," Pawley said.

"Bomb makes an instant statement," Peter said. "With fire you gotta wait through an investigation. By time investigators finish with their rigamarole, it's old news. Nobody cares. Something else done stole the limelight."

"I prefer bombs as long as the building is empty," Harry said.

"Harry's got a soft heart," Bobby giggled.

"I don't happen to believe in random killing."

"Since when?"

Pawley took a swig from the bottle. "Since them Yankee niggers come down here with them white niggers, everything gone to hell. Nothing been the same."

"Murder isn't productive," Harry said. "Unless you can't help it."

"Murder means we're serious. It means they have to contend with a militia of self-defenders."

"What's doc say?" Pawley asked.

Lee's eyes were closed, his head sweaty, his bowels in turmoil.

The next afternoon, Lee drove with Harry to Forest, the county seat. They drove in Harry's new marlin blue two-door Eldorado as big as a ChrisCraft. The exact date had not been set, but the rabbi's house in Meridian and the synagogue in Greenville would be bombed on the same day. Code name, MARY PHAGA. Although Lee now had concrete information for Whipple, he didn't feel proud. He felt poisoned.

"You like those guys?"

Lee grunted.

"Pawley is something of a pyromaniac. I guess fire is an extra kick for him. That's why I insist on bombs. I don't want him sticking around to watch anything burn."

When the Temple in Atlantis was bombed, it was speculated the bomb was prompted by the rabbi's alliance with Dr. King. The next day the police surrounding the building, the rabbi invoked the vision of Jonah who tried to escape the difficult task that God demanded. HE spoke of the dual tides of living history and the impossibility of escaping what was right and what was wrong. It was the last time Leon Greenberg had been in synagogue.

Harry parked at the curb across from the post office. The sidewalks were crowded with farmers who'd come to town to shop. Black and white. Sometimes a black man stepped into the street. Stepped or was shoved.

Harry went to buy ice while Lee picked up a bucket of ribs and coleslaw. Harry put the ice in the trunk and climbed into the driver's seat. As he started the car, a child dashed across the street.

"Mr. Greenberg!" He cried, squatting beside the passenger window. "Member me?"

Leon shaded his face with his hand.

"You gave me my own book," the child said proudly.

Leon glared at the bright, wager eyes nearly level with his own.

"Boy, you're slobbering on my car!" Harry shooed. "Get on with you!"

The man next to the child dragged him upright. "What foolish talk are you talking now? Stepping into other people's business, making trouble." He boxed the boy's ears.

"Yeow-ow!" The child squealed. "Mr. Greenberg done come to my school."

When Hark was already dreaming, he heard an owl. From across the river, he heard it. A hoot, a yelp, a scream of predator or prey.

The next morning was Sunday. He sat in his rocker and read from Genesis, the book of Beginnings. The beginnings of paradise, sin, despair, hope, murder – brother against brother. At nine, he started for the clubhouse, following the path by his fields through the woods and over a plank bridge that crossed the small, meandering river. He was surprised to find the door locked, the yard empty, no cars or trucks, only muddy tracks.

He unlocked the door. The room was upside down. Smashed bottles, toppled chairs, the table and couch flipped on their side, bloodied cushions scattered on the floor. He circled the room, corner to corner, mumbling, "Lordy, Lordy, Lordy." He didn't stop mumbling as he set the furniture right and opened the windows to air out the alcohol and blood. In the outdoor sink, he soaked the stained cushions in vinegar and hydrogen peroxide. He swept aside the shards of glass. The golf clubs he picked up slowly because he was tired. One by one, he put them in the bag. He mopped the rough pine floor. As he worked, he felt worse and worse, remembering the hoot owl.

Tucked inside the screened porch was a generator and a large chest freezer. Mostly used in deer season,

Mister Harry occasionally put birds, squirrels, and possums in it. For big weekend parties, they stored white wine and vodka. A padlocked tow chain was wrapped around the sides, the handle, and the coil panel in back. Hark had never known Mister Harry to use a lock on the freezer, but he was sure he had a key. After a dozen mismatches, it opened. The chain was not so simple to unwind. It took all Hark's strength to wrestle with it. When he opened the heavy lid, he saw a man with a pillow over his head. He touched the body. Cool but not stone cold. He removed the pillow. The side Hark could see was drenched in blood. It was impossible to recognize a face, but he reeked of liquor. Hark stepped back to consider. He could leave the man. It wasn't his business. On the other hand, the man would probably die without his help. The death would be on Hark.

He went back inside the cabin. He gathered blankets and piled them on top of the man. He propped the locker open with golf clubs. He left the cabin and walked as quickly as he could manage. At home, there was no one. He wrote a message on a piece of rolling paper, stuffed it into a hollow tube, and opened the dovecote. He wrote, "Bring truck & boys." The message was for Estelle May, Hark's daughter, his seventh child and healer. He fastened the tube to Yoshi's leg, lifted his hands, and tossed the bird into the air.

"Hurry!" he cried.

Hark walked out to the blacktop. It was a cool, overcast day. Under his overalls, he wore a flannel shirt and sweater. He wore a skullcap. There were wintery under-currents in the air. The redbuds and sugar maples had turned red and gold. Id Estelle was home, he reckoned it would take an hour to get to him. An hour was optimistic. Optimism was part of Hark's nature. He believed things could get better. Even a nearly dead man in a freezer could get better.

From his overalls, Hark pulled out his pocketknife and a small piece of wood. He was not accustomed to idle-ness. If there was nothing else to do, he whittled. He didn't whittle with intention. He waited with childish antic-ipation to *see what might emerge*. A face, a flower, an angel, a pony. He was considerably skilled, and some-times others asked him to whittle them a talisman.

When Estelle arrived with the boys, he lifted himself into the cab. She leaned over and kissed her daddy's forehead.

"Clubhouse," he wheezed.

"If you messing in white people's crazy business, that make you crazy, too."

His blue eyes glowed. "We can bring him back."

"When they comes around to finish up their business, they gon' ask for you. You be the person they gon' ask. Where the man be? Where the man gon'? You ready?"

Estelle turned into the dirt lane that led to the back of the clubhouse. From the tracks, Hark could tell no one had come or gone. He pointed to the screened porch. Es-telle waddled after him. She peeked under the propped lid, pushing it back so it rested against the shed wall. She put her index finger on the man's neck crusted with blood.

"I got something." Her eyes glowed like Hark's. It was what he had counted on. Estelle May, seventh of seven in a line of three generations of sevens, born to heal.

She motioned to the teens, shrinking against the truck. "He ain't dead so you gotta lift him gentle." She raised the man's head. He moaned softly as each boy took the end of a limb like the four corner of a flag. He was broken, the white man. He'd been beaten everywhere.

Estelle drove slowly. It was bumpy until they reached the blacktop. Hark sat in the back of the truck with two of the boys. He held the man's head in his lap, speaking to him. He prayed over him and sang hymns. The boys held his legs to keep him steady. On the Bienville road, Hark covered him with a sheet. Estelle floored the accelerator until they reached the town limits. She pulled the truck behind her garage. The boys moved the man to the back of her washhouse. She ordered them to light the stoves, boil the kettles, bring basins and towels from the closet.

Estelle cut off his clothes and began to clean him. First with warm, soapy water, followed by a warm rinse. After the blood had been dabbed and wiped away, Hark recognized the man. It was Sally Shaw's friend. Estelle rubbed the man's chest and abdomen with lemon juice. For swelling on the arms and legs, she places compressed and comfrey, dandelion, horsetail. She girdled his cracked ribs in a mustard plaster. She splinted his ulna with strips of sheets and a garden stake. The leg, she stretched out and splinted with a crutch. The crushed thumbs, she set between popsicle sticks. The eye was nasty, but Estelle didn't flinch. Into his empty eye socket she squeezed lemon juice and laid a paste of turmeric and ginger over the hole.

When they turned him over, she saw sets of numbers written on the back of his calf. Two letters and four digits. She didn't know what they signified, maybe license plates. She wrote them down. She washed his back, his buttocks, his legs, erasing the numbers. Deep inside his trouser pocket, she found two more. By the ten digits, she thought they must be long distance with an area code outside Mississippi. Everyone inside Mississippi was 601. These were 404.

"Maybe, they ain't aiming to come back," Hark said.

"They aiming. They gon' dump him in the river. Or put him out for buzzards. The river's no problem if they dump good They trained to do that. They already know that's what they gotta do. What you plan to say if them boys swing by?"

"I plan to sleep in the fields."

"You gon' tell them you went there to make breakfast. Corncakes, like Mister Harry ask you. When you done found the mess, you say you done start to clean everything. Somebody come up the drive so you left. You didn't see nobody. You came on home. You don't know nothing."

Hark crossed his index and middle fingers. Whenever he lied, he crossed them like a child. Lying had never agreed with him. But lying was a strategy of survival. That was the fate of his life.

A month before Lee's outing to the clubhouse, Sally Shaw left Jackson to visit the Smokey Mountains. She left to go away from Harry after he declared he was willing to marry her. "*Willing?*" she cackled.

Six weeks later she returned, cold rain and wind had battered the countryside. From the Atlantic to the Mississippi, the land was sodden and bleak, the trees stripped bare, the fields filled with stubble, the shacks weathered to colorless wood, the empty lots piled with rusted machine parts, all of it streaked with red ferrous dirt.

While Sally was away, she didn't contact Leland Green. She resisted, hoping to enhance his expectations. On the outskirts of Jackson, she stopped at a phone booth and dialled his number. There was a buzz, then silence. After several tries, she asked the operator to check. The phone had been disconnected.

Her second call was to Harry. He dropped the receiver with excitement. "Sally Shaw! Where the dickens are you?"

At the hotel, Sally took a slow bath. She rubbed her body with African shea butter and her face with Clarins. She put her navy Pierre Cardin slacks, a cashmere sailor sweater, a collar of seed pearls, stacked Ferragamo heels, and a waxed cotton Barbour jacket.

At the curb, Harry and Puss waited under an umbrella. Harry had aged impressively. Distended bags under his eyes, unwashed hair, parched sallow cheeks, the smell of smoke on his clothes, signs of sleeplessness and neglect.

"Mrs. Shaw, you are a sight for sore eyes."

"Looks like you been weeping ever since I left."

Harry rubbed his poorly shaved chin." I do have bad news."

"Dr. Green?"

Harry sank into a chair. Sally Shaw was an uncanny creature.

"Hark died," he whimpered.

"Hark was old."

"Hark has been with me my whole life. He was my best friend."

"It was his time," she consoled.

"He was murdered."

"No!"

"Negras!" Harry muttered vacantly as if he'd had a stroke.

"Is that who killed him?"

"They gone insane. Killing an old man and burning everything."

"And Lee?" she winced.

"Same day Hark got killed, Dr. Green disappeared."

Sally gulped her whiskey and glanced out the window at the rain. "Well, surely?"

"They brought in Hark's daughters and grandsons. They brought in the Johnson boys. I guess Singlet Johnsons has most to gain if they acquire his land. River bottomed land, nothing more beautiful on Earth."

"And the funeral?"

"I bought the prettiest casket they make, lined with cream satin with genuine pewter handles. We finned the church with gladiolas."

Sally held up her glass for a refill. "Leland Green is quite the mystery. Where you suppose he went?"

"To hell," Harry said positively. "I doubt we'll ever see him again."

Leon lay in a room, curtains drawn, a small table and dim lamp beside the bed. His left arm and right leg in a cast, his thumbs in splints, his ribs wrapped so tightly he could barely breathe, his head bandaged, every part of him in pain. He wondered if he'd been kept alive only to be beaten again. His tormentors had wanted to know who sent him. They accused him of lying and spying. They said he could save himself if he confessed. Who stood behind him. Jews? Yankee niggers? Commies?

A small moth circled the lamp, occasionally leaving its orbit to glide over Leon's face. It was company, but visitor or visitation he wasn't sure. He reached out for it with his best working hand and felt a convulsion from his shoulder to his groin. He snatched the moth and enclosed it inside his weak fingers. Since commotion its wings made. Such life force. Like him, fighting to live.

"You woken up?"

Leon scrutinized what parts of Irwin's face he could see. African black with pebble-colored eyes. "You save me?"

"We nurse you. Estelle and Uncle Hark save you."

"Estelle?"

"Hark's girl brought you here three days ago Sunday."

"They almost killed me."

"They did kill you. They left you dead. Bleed out, suffocate, starve, all different ways you be dead. Or they come back to fetch you and throw you in the river. River filled with bones. You can't make me swim in no river."

"Hurts like hell," Leon patted the bandaged portion of his face. His skin itched beneath the gauze.

"Dr. Patterson came here. He want us to take you to the hospital. Hospital too dangerous. All of us in danger if you in hospital. Dr. Patterson stop over every night."

"What they done. Concussed me?"

Irwin stepped to the window and pulled the drape aside. "Your people come by," he said.

"What people?"

"Soon as you wake up, they plan to fly you out to Hawkins Field." He reached in his pocket and pulled out a card with a name, a number, and several hundred-dollar bills. John Whipple's card, taxpayers' money.

"We afraid to take it to the bank. We afraid to spend it. Everybody wanna know where we get money like this. They think we stole it."

"My people left it?"

"For medicine, doctor, extra for out trouble. They want us to swear we don't tell nobody. It told them I wasn't raised to swear."

"They ain't my people," Leon said gruffly. "They're swine." He'd been put out as chum worth a few hundred dollars.

Leon blinked at the white walls, the muted TV, the rain battering the window. He wished he could cry. He tried, but tears wouldn't come. Physiological or emotional, he wasn't sure. He leaned back on the hospital bed, awash with relief that the sham of Leland Green was behind him. Another version of himself was dead.

"You're a lucky man," Whipple said.

"To hell wit you."

"Once you're better..."

Leon yanked Whipple's sleeve. He would have pummeled him, but one sleeve was all he could manage. "I'll never walk right or see straight again. I fared better under the brunt of a world war than your shenanigans."

"Whenever doc says you're ready."

"You'll leave me alone?'

"After you choose a name, we'll get your papers ready."

"I can't think about a new name."

"What about 'Bar-do'?"

"Bardo?"

"Something you muttered. Something we tried to trace. No one by that name in Mississippi, but we found a town in Poland."

"It's a place in your head, Bardo."

"It doesn't sound real."

"Is that an ontological assessment?"

"Whatever you want to call it, that's your right."

"What about Bergstedt's thugs? They still have rights?"

"Peanuts," Whipple said.

"Peanuts kill same as anybody else."

"We can't arrest them until we catch them in the act."

Leon patted his head. "This act doesn't count?"

"We know nothing about it."

"I'd have told those boys anything. 'I love niggers' they made me say it. I was proud to say it."

"You did good, Leon. You've been a big help."

Whipple sipped the lukewarm coffee. It had been two harrowing weeks, but the screws had started to turn. Bergstedt, Smithson, and McIntire had been places under IRS investigation. Although impossible to get cooperation from local law enforcement, the agency had made in-roads in the governors' office. There were enough offences on Bergstedt's henchmen to harass them into good behaviour for a year or so.

"Won't they worry I'll talk?"

"We took care of Leland Green."

"What's that mean?"

"We made sure a body was found in the woods."

"Something you're actually good at."

"It was messed up, gnawed by animals and things."

Leon gagged. "I can't testify Pawley and Bee Jay killed me."

"You're dead, remember? Otherwise, we'd be ac-cused of entrapment."

"And Hark's family?"

"We're taking care of them, too."

"Is that called human sacrifice or quality control? What's the new term you use, collateral something?"

Later, Dr. Josephs visited Leon to discuss the new eye. "They do wonders with glass," he said. "It'll be a per-fect match."

Tears flowed down Leon's face onto the bed sheet. "I don't want a match," he cried. "I want the brightest blue you have."

R.S. Brenner is a literary pseudonym of Summer Brenner, the author of a dozen works that include short story collections, award-winning YA novels, noir thrillers, and the occasional essay. Her writings have appeared in dozens of anthologies and literary magazines. Performances of her work include *The Missing Lover*, a one-act play with staged readings directed by Peter Glazer; theatrical productions of *Richmond Tales, Lost Secrets of the Iron Triangle* and *Oakland Tales, Lost Secrets of The Town*; and recordings/performances with musical extravaganza, Arundo and Smooth Toad (Andy Dinsmoor, Bob Ernst, Hal Hughes, and GP Skratz). She has given scores of readings in the U.S., France, and Japan. She was raised in Atlanta, Georgia, and is a long-time resident of Berkeley, California.

Twisted Shikse: Jedidiah Ayers

First published in *Jewish Noir*

Eighty years after Charlie Birger kicked the Ku Klux Klan out of his corner of Southern Illinois I had the swastika tattoo on my chest artfully reworked into a rose. Or a vagina. Or whatever the fuck it was. It wasn't a swastika any longer. Pop told me once that I was named after the tough old Yid and it felt like a betrayal to have put that shit on my body in the first place. I'd been a scared kid just trying to stay alive when I did it and it seemed like a good idea. Never did fit in with the peckerwoods in Jefferson City, but I never had much trouble from them either. Originally I thought I'd have it refashioned into a six-pointed star when I got out, but I decided that was pushing it.

When Kate asked me what the blocky, ink design on my chest was, I told her "cubist." When I asked her why she'd pawned my bubbe's Kiddush cup to buy crank, she told me it was "obvious."

She sang for an outfit called The Taoist Cowboys who were a regular attraction at Carl's, the bar where I'd been working for five years. When they'd take the stage all eyes would be on Saint Kate as she shook her skinny, Scotch-Irish ass and tossed her hair in ropey, red braids to the shitkicker stylings of the band the RFT had once described as Aerosmith reincarnated as a cow-punk cult fronted by the banshee od Haley Mills.

Don't think about it too hard.

The first time I noticed how turned on she was by violence she was sucking blood out of my nose. Wasn't busted, but that third turd from the left outside Carl's had landed a lucky elbow before turning to run. I'd reeled back, pulled my pea-shooter, let it spit, and winged him as he was turning the corner. He gave a comical yelp and his retreating form canted to one side, but he didn't go down.

Kate had her own bruise from the skirmish rising among the freckles beneath her right eye, and at the Cowboy's next gig she looked at a raccoon dressed as Courtney Love for Halloween, but damn she didn't work it – compensating for the indistinction of the lyrics by forcing them through her puffy lips with gale force. The quartet of punks making a grab for the Cowboys' equipment outside Carl's hadn't expected the level of resistance Kate'd put up and all they got away with was a guitar. And a gram or three of amphetamines in the case.

"Whoa, whoa, whoa, nice shooting, Tex," she'd said, reaching for my pop-gun. "Lemme see that thing."

"Uh-uh," I snatched it away from her grasp.

"Well, I'd say you tried to miss him," she beamed, "but didn't quite. That was awesome. What do you pack?"

"Well, I'd say you tried to miss him," she beamed, "but didn't quite. That was awesome. What do you pack?"

"Well," I said, trying to tuck the damn thing away again, "it's no Desert Eagle great big ol' pistol, I mean .50 caliber."

She didn't miss a beat, "No, but you're still a badass Hebrew."

I did a double take at bother her recognition of the song and my tribe.

She stood on her toes, ran her hand between my legs and licked the blood trickling out of my nostril into my beard. "What kind of Jewboy likes country music, anyway?"

Her tongue in my orifice and hand on my crotch were equally exciting and off-putting. There was no denying the tightening of my pants, but I didn't entirely care for the implications. "What, you never heard of Kinky Friedman?"

That night she'd wrecked my bed. And in the morning kicked me in the head. Metaphorically. The Kiddush cup wasn't worth much to anybody else. I noticed it was gone about an hour after I noticed that she was."

But the cup held sentimental significance for me.

When I had gone own for selling crack to an undercover policeman, bubbe Malmon was the only family I had left. Mom slit when I was a kid, Dad had died when I was in high school, and bubbe had taken me in. She was an old-school conservative and a good woman, but her progeny had given her plenty of reason to be ashamed. She'd hired me a good lawyer who got me a short sentence, and she'd tried to visit me in Jeff City, taken a cab all the way from Delmar Garden retirement community she'd moved into when her health declined, but I wouldn't see her. I was too frightened of somebody else making more of my ethnic heritage than I ever had.

She wrote me letters. Prayed for me. Died a month before I was released. I didn't get to attend her funeral, but I'd had that Nazi abomination on my body obscured before I visited her grave. The cup was all that had survived of her, especially for me, and I walked out of the lawyer's office holding it—the entirety of my earthly estate. My spiritual one as well.

If I didn't suspect Kate would get off on it, I might've hit her. Instead I just said, "Show me where," and followed her directions to the pawn shop where I paid more to get it back than it was really worth.

At their next gig, I helped myself to an amplifier and nobody said shit. They'd just borrowed one from those Hooten Haller boys and knew better than to complain. Still—they worked a cover of "Choctaw Bingo" into their set that night, and Kate'd shot a finger pistol at me from the stage during our verse. I was angry all over again.

Of course that had me worked up enough to want another go at her, but that night she'd brought another date. Big guy with a spider web tattoo on his, I shit you not, neck. I seethed a bit, but steered clear, satisfied to post the amplifier on Craigslist and wash my hands of her.

Right.

She was leaning on my car when my shift ended. Neck Tattoo was heeled behind her. "Hey, Charlie Malmon, I think you've got something that belongs to me."

"That how you see it?"

Neck Tattoo straightened up and joined the adults' conversation.

"You want to give it back or shall I just take it?"

Before I could answer, he dropped a cinder block through the rear window and was reaching inside. He claimed the amp and stood holding it while Kate shot me with her finger gun again.

She backed out of my way while I fished the keys from my pocket and opened the driver's side door. She spoke to me in a self-satisfied, taunting voice. "Charlie, love, you still want to fuck me?"

Neck Tattoo's eyes pinballed in his skull.

I did. "I do."

Her eyebrows arched as she licked her fingertips and slipped them down the front of her jeans.

God damn it.

I grabbed the tire iron under the front seat and snapped the asshole's jaw with a single swipe. I opened the passenger side door and she climbed in. We left Neck Tattoo were he'd dropped next to the amplifier. They both looked broken.

Not gonna lie, it turned me on too, but I didn't take her back to my place.

She still liked it rough.

Agony separates itself from ecstasy pretty clearly with a few hours' remove, but her scrapes and bites and tiny fists beating on me felt indistinguishable from her kisses and licks and probes in the moment.

Ten miles north of us the local government was showing its ass to the world in the second act of a totalitarian

PRF clusterfuck as cops in full army drag maced and shot rubber bullets at citizens assembled to express shock, hurt and anger over the shooting of an unarmed black teenager by a white cop, but it wasn't anything we were paying attention to.

Instead I awoke several hours later on her futon surrounded by the case of *Walking Tall* looking like they'd run out of cousins to fuck. The leader of the pack, a six-foot, shiny-domed, cut-off sleeved Hazelwood hick with pickup truck testicles, I have no doubt, gave me the stink eye and asked if I'd been fucking his little sister.

"Sorry, were you not finished?"

I didn't even see the kick, I heard it. Right in the nose again. I hope that at least I got some blood on his boot.

Through blurry eyes I spotted Kate in the corner of the room clenching her hand between her thighs.

When her brother looked over, Kate stopped touching herself and straightened up. "What do you want Bryce?"

Bryce looked at me pointedly and acted cagey. Kate rolled her eyes, "What? Just say it, he's okay."

"I want you to go stay with Mom and Dad for a while."

"Well you can want in one hand and shit in the other."

Bryce wasn't hearing any of it. He told his crew to pack her some clothes and toiletries and they hopped to like good little toadies while Kate screamed at them that they'd better not touch any of her fucking stuff. Bryce grabbed her wrist and steered her into another room to talk in private. "You're going to. It's not a discussion. It's not safe in the city."

They were both yelling at each other within seconds and through the walls I picked up the broad stroke in Technicolor. Turns out the civil unrest of the night before had sparked a panic that the darkies were going to burn the city down, and every clear-eyed Christian should read the signs and flee to the southwestern borders of suburbia without looking back lest they be turned to salt.

"Are you fucking kidding me?" Kate said coming back into the room as I was pulling on my pants. Her refutation of the good sense her brother was preaching made me smile, which Bryce didn't like. He was right behind her and glared at me dressing in his sister's room. Kate looked in my eyes and addressed her brother with her back to him, "Be sure to tell Dad, I'm staying here 'cause I like kikes and niggers to eat my pussy."

Shit.

She had a thing, I guess, and getting me involved in violence seemed to be a big part of it. But fighting three big dudes at ten in the A.M. through a whiskey and cocaine hangover is a young man's pastime that I'd left behind in my twenties. To boot, as Bryce, or as I came to know him, Officer Schloegel, put it so succinctly, were I not to fuck off right the fuck then, I'd never fuck anything else ever again. The badge on his hip now visible and the butt of the Glock that his palm rested on inclined me to accept his plan.

I looked at Kate and said, "Let's not do this again," grabbed my shirt and walked barefoot to my car with the busted out back window and drove away, calling Kareem to come meet me before things could get worse.

"The hell happened to you?"

"I got laid," I said, wincing as I gingerly examined my once majestic, now probably broken nose.

"You got laid out."

"Yeah, well that's a damn fine hair to split."

My friend laughed, but his eyes were sad. "I think you're doing it wrong."

"I've been told that before."

I'd met him before he was a righteous ex-con activist cabbie. Back then he was just another backslid-Baptist, rock-slinging, Florissant-cracker named Brad. We both did our time at Missouri State Pen, but as he puts it, he came out belonging to something, part of a movement, and a friend of Allah while I was born with roots, ties to ancient traditions, a chosen people, threw it all away, and came out with nothing. Somewhere along the way Brad became Salami or Ali and I had to get that damn swastika wiped off my skin.

Somehow we're still friends.

Ahmed picked me up in his red cab at the garage where I left my Cavalier for repairs, and took me to the gyro place on South Grand for sustenance. Afterward he gave me his keys and wallet and we left his cab at his grandparents' house. Then he picked up the keys to their beige PT Cruiser and told them not to worry.

Overnight the eyes of the world were on our back yard, Palestinian activists on the other side of the world were Tweeting advice to St. Louis citizens for dealing with tear gas and police thugs—#Ferguson—and Abdul and his inam organized peaceful protests on the streets every night and staying on the lines through the chemical weaponry and skull-crackings, never raising a hand in violence or even defense and landing in jail anyway. My part was to drop him off at night and pick him up at the jail in the morning.

Part of me felt guilty each night for not being arrested right alongside my friend, but another part of me felt smart every morning for waking up in bed. I'd bring coffee and breakfast burritos and drive him back to his grandparents' home where he'd crash out for a few hours of sleep.

On our third time through this routine we caught a police tail leaving the station and the day after that there were strangers sitting in parked cars across the street from his grandparents' home in shifts. White=power activists started calling his job trying to get him fired, and harassed his family, following the elderly Baptists to the grocery store, to church and to bingo.

Hakeem quit staying there out of respect for the good people who'd raised him (though the intimidation tactics continued), and that's how my Tower Grove apartment became his new crash pad. Truth be told, I kinda hoped some of those "I am Darren Wilson" T-shirt wearing dipshits had the sand to set up camp on my block so I could stop by and say hi, but a daylight drive by was all they ever dared.

Till that night.

Kat was there. Of course. The *meshuge* cunt had just firebombed her own brother's house. That's the way the story was told anyhow. She'd shot a flare gun through the window panes of his kitchen window and it had started a fire that left some smoke damage, but was overall a pretty chickenshit little blaze. It wasn't the only attack on cops' homes in the area that week, but it was the only one that brought me any personal blowback.

She'd tried to burn his shit down while he was out upholding the Constitution and no on had been hurt, but a rag-tag group of self-appointed minutemen had been vigilant in their neighborhood watch and had followed her car all the way to my place.

I still can't decide if I think she knew.

She told me, she'd done it in retaliation for the coffee shop full of tired marchers the cops, her brother among them, had tear-gassed, forcing the panicked patrons into the blacked-out basement or out the back door into handcuffs. Shooting out her brother's window had gotten her pretty horny and she told me the story of her revolutionary actions in a feverish bout of reverse Taoist Cowgirl that chapped my hips.

I had the presence of mind to grab bubbe Malmon's Kiddush cup and secure it under a blanket with me before I passed out.

In the morning she was still there, and I felt a twinge of affection for the crazy bitch as she lay innocent in sleep. God knows it wasn't lust. I hadn't been this sore since the days of dry humping Reveka Weiss in junior high. Grinding on my crotch into her ample thighs until I'd orgasm in my underwear, I'd often wake in the morning to find scabs on my dick where I'd bloodied it against the zipper of my jeans. No, she wasn't getting to me through my poor abused genitals now. Must've been my poor abused brain.

When I picked up Faruq he looked damn near beat. I got him into the car and when I tried to hand him his coffee he ignored it and shut his eyes, clutching his kidneys. "Just let me get some sleep."

"Listen, man, why don't you take a night off? Let me go in your place tonight."

Saddam did something then that I'd never seen him do. And he wasn't weeping, but a tear escaped the outer corner of his left eye. I didn't say another word the whole trip. I opened the passenger side door for him and helped him out and he put his arm around me for the walk to my front door, but we didn't get there.

They hit us three feet from the curb and had bags over our heads before I even knew they were there.

They rang my bell pretty good and drove around with us on the floor of a van. Somebody's foot was resting on my head most of the time. When they took the hoods off us we were inside a parking garage and the side door of the vehicle slid back to reveal a cadre of grim, red-faced members of the Westboro Baptist farm team. Officer Schloegel front and center.

His eyes narrowed when he saw my face.

Toadie #1 noticed that. "You know this piece of shit?"

"Fuck yeah," Toadie #2 chimed in, "This guy knows his sister."

Toadie the First looked closer and recognition began to dawn.

The Grand Dragon spoke up. "What do you want us to do, Bryce? You want to have them arrested?"

Office Schloegel thought about it for a moment. "No. Not going to be worth trying to prosecute some bullshit arson charge. No fun anyway. I'm insured. But I don't ever want to see these two again, you hear me? Teach 'em a lesson for me, would you, fellas?"

I tried to speak in our defense, but it was on of the faculties I was bereft of.

Officer Schloegel got in his car and when the sound of his squeaky brakes faded out, the junior G-men went to work.

They didn't kill us, but I, for one, wished that they had a couple of times. I could get dentures I supposed, but I'd never play piano again. Hell, I might not manage picking my nose. Busted mitts, swollen testicles, incontinence, broken ribs and a knee that would never bend again, but there's nothing like the loss of an eye to get your attention. Not like it fell out of my skull, but it never worked again. The light just went out. It was like God saying, "No more of that, dickwad. Straighten up. Fly right."

And Brad. Shit, Brad. He was in a coma for three weeks. Brain damage. Paralysis. I never saw him again. I just asked after him. His grandparents and some members of their church were usually around, praying for him. Waiting by his bed for him to open his eyes.

It was a month before I walked again, and the limp was conspicuous. But I'd had time to think. Time to weigh things, I saw faces when I closed my eyes. Eye. Brad's, Kate's, bubbe Malmon's, my father's and even the smiling mug of ol' Charlie Birger on the way to the gallows.

Charlie was the last legally hanged man in the state of Illinois and he's buried in Chesterfield, a twenty-minute drive my father took me on once on the day he told me about my namesake. Charlie was accompanied up the gallows by a rabbi and insisted on wearing a black execution hood rather than white one so he'd bear no resemblance to a Klan member.

As much as I admired old Charlie's style, ours were not the same.

During the fall while the city, county and country held their breath for the grand jury to return with a decision on whether or not to indict a member of the power structure for performing his job with what some folks would say looked like a little too much enthusiasm, I bided my time, kept my head shaved to the scalp, and got a new tattoo.

Another swastika. On my neck.

I went to see the Taoist Cowboys one more time. Kate looked terrific, but I didn't. Nobody knew me. I'd cut all ties and was living off the pittance I made selling my possessions. Bubbe's Kiddush cup helped pay for the tattoo. And the grenades.

I started hanging around the shitkicker dives on the east side and deep South County until I spotted Toadie #1 one night at the Beaver Cleaver in Sauget. I got some information out of the bouncer and knew when to expect him the next week. Turned out his name was Charlie, too. Huh. We had some drinks and I threw the last of my money around and talk turned to the situation across the river and what troublemakers and thugs were gonna do when the grand jury decision came back not to prosecute.

We agreed, it was going to be bedlam.

I told him about my neighborhood watch initiative. Told him how I reported suspicious vehicles and neighbors all the damn time, but how the cops didn't seem to take me seriously. Nobody took a gimp with an eye patch seriously, I told him. He told me I ought to meet some friends of his and come out to their pre-Thanksgiving meeting, and I thought that sounded swell.

The next day I wrote two letters—one to Kate and one to Brad. I told Kate what her brothers had done. I figured if it meant anything to her then she'd probably do something pretty fucked up in retribution, but I also suggested that she seek some professional help for her whole life.

In Brad's letter I told him that he was my hero, the man I wished I could have been and he was right, I'd scorned my birthright and threw away every good thing I'd grown up with, but I that I finally had my own chosen people and that he was chief among them.

I threw both letters away.

Charlie picked me up where we'd agreed and he drove me out to a special meeting palce in a barn on somebody's farm way the hell out in Pevely. IT was a small group—six men in all. Bryce was not among them, but Toadie #2 and The Grand Dragon were both present, and after the Pledge of Allegiance and a prayer that I didn't know they took turns reporting their week's activities and observations.

When they came around the circle to my turn to contribute to the group, I struggled to stand on my gimp leg, but they waited for me respectfully. I told them that I was there on behalf of a friend of mine named Brad, only I used his Muslim name. I hope I got it right.

For a moment it was quiet enough in there to hear a pin drop.

All of them actually. I opened up my jacket and let the pins fall from the half dozen grenades I had strapped across my chest.

"*Shabbat Shalom,* motherfuckers."

Jedidiah Ayres lives in St. Louis, Missouri, and is the author of the novel *Peckerwood*, the novella *Fierce Bitches,* and the short story collection *A F*ckload of Shorts.* He also edited the anthologies *Noir at the Bar*, based on the reading series of the same name, and *D*CKED*, a dark fiction anthology inspired by none other than Dick Cheney. When not writing, he can usually be found haunting one of his three blogs: Hardboiled Wonderland, Noir at the Bar, and That'll Do, Pig.

The Color of Guilt: Annie Reed

First published in *Fiction River: Hidden in Crime*

Josef leaned heavily on his cane. His old bones did not fare well in the winter cold of Frankfurt, not even beneath the layers of his suit and heavy topcoat. His hand ached where the bones had been broken so many years ago, and his fingers, twisted and knotted with arthritis, felt stiff on the well-worn wood.

He stood alone in the cemetery, his breath puffing out before him in the late October air. A living ghost among the dead.

"You are being dramatic again," Elsa would have told him. "You are alive. The dead are dead. Let them rest in peace."

Elsa, his wife. Ever the pragmatist. If the ghosts of the past had haunted her, she had never told him.

The bare branches of the tall oaks near Elsa's grave creaked in a breeze that lifted Josef 's fine white hair from his scalp. In his youth his hair had been thick and black, and he had combed it with pride. He drank fine wine and smoked only the best cigarettes in the clubs he had gone to with his friends. His spine had been straight, his muscles firm, and his features striking. Many men had told him so, and he had believed them.

He had believed so many things in his youth.

Before the world had changed.

The dead grass crunched beneath his shoes as he shuffled his feet. He could not afford to stand still for long in the cold, not if he hoped to walk to the train that would take him south for the first time in fifty years.

The Berlin Wall had fallen the year before. Reunification was finally complete.

A man like Josef could travel again. Revisit the ghosts of his past.

Attempt to make atonement.

"I am here to say goodbye," he said to the simple marker on Elsa's grave. He heard the note of defiance in his voice as if he expected his wife, on this, the first anniversary of her death, to rise from the grave and tell him he was being a fool.

Perhaps he was.

"You were a good wife."

Far better than he had been a husband, but she had married him, and she had known what he was. Neither of them had pretended that theirs was a match born of love.

"I shall miss you," he said, surprised at the sudden pain the simple statement brought.

Had he come to love her after all? They had lived together for nearly half a century. She had kept him safe. Kept suspicious eyes from looking in his direction, and in return, he had ignored her dalliances, few as they were, with the women who sometimes stayed in their home. He had mourned his wife's passing, had missed her presence in their home, but the thoughts of her while he ate simple breakfasts alone had never brought him pain such as this.

With one bent-fingered hand, he patted his overcoat where it covered his heart. Where it covered the triangle he'd stitched on his suit coat the day before. The simple task had taken far longer than he'd expected. His fingers hadn't wanted to grip the needle, and his eyesight hadn't been good enough to let him slide the pink thread through the tiny hole in the thin steel on the first try.

Would his wife think him a foolish old man? After so many years of safe anonymity, to finally admit who he really was?

To say his true name?

"What does it matter?" she would say. "What can you change? The dead are dead. They do not blame you for living."

The dead might not, but he most certainly did.

As he had done every day for the last fifty years.

Josef couldn't catch his breath.

The boxcar felt like a tomb, cold and dark as a graveyard on a moonless winter night, and filled with quiet sounds made by people too terrified to scream. So many people, crowded so close together that to sit was to risk being trampled. The stench of unwashed bodies, urine, and vomit was so thick he felt like it coated his skin, and he gulped in huge lungfuls of air to convince himself he was still alive, but it wasn't enough.

The Gestapo had come for him a week ago. His name had been found in the address book of a man arrested as a criminal sexual deviant—a homosexual—and they had come for him.

Unlike many of the men he knew, Josef had kept himself hidden. He took precautions. He had destroyed everything he had ever received from any of his lovers. He had stopped going to the few clubs for homosexuals in Berlin that still existed. In a time when a simple look between men on the street could lead to arrest and imprisonment, he never smiled at any man in case the look might be misinterpreted.

None of that mattered. Josef had been identified as an associate of a known homosexual.

Josef had been thrown in prison, where he'd been beaten and abused by the guards until he had named other men he had loved and who had escaped into the west, while he had stayed, naively thinking himself safe from detection.

One of the other prisoners, an elderly queen he had seen in the city from time to time, had recognized Josef and tended to his wounds.

"If you find yourself on a train, dear boy," the man had said, "do not tell them what you are. It will only go worse for you."

Josef had expected to be put on trial for his crimes. He had been loaded on a train headed for the camp at Dachau instead.

He couldn't believe this was happening to him.

The woman crowded next to him held a small child in her arms. A girl, Josef thought. Although he couldn't see her clearly, he felt the brush of her long hair against his cheek. The woman hummed a quiet song—a lullaby per-haps—so softly Josef could barely hear it over the rhythmic sound of the train on the rails.

"Filthy queer," said the man on Josef's other side.

Josef held himself very still. No one could see the tri-angle sewn on his coat, the pink scrap of cloth that identified his crime. The car was too dark. No one could see. No one could see.

Oh, but they could.

The moon must have risen. Enough light filtered in through the cracks between the boards of the boxcar that he could see the face of the little girl next to him. She was watching him with large, dark eyes. Curious, but unafraid.

Time for fear would come soon enough.

Josef looked down at himself. The triangle on his coat looked as light as the two triangles that made up the six-pointed star on the little girl's dress.

Rough hands grabbed Josef from behind, jerking him off balance.

He fell awkwardly to the rough floor. He put a hand out to steady himself, and someone stepped on it.

He felt his bones snap beneath the hard boot.

Josef would have screamed but a hand covered his mouth as other hands pressed him to the floor.

He fought as best he could. Hot, red pain radiated up his arm from his broken fingers. Dust from the floorboards clogged his nose, and the taste of blood filled his mouth where his teeth had bitten into his own lips.

Blows rained down on his back. On his ribs. On the places still hurting from the beatings he'd received in prison, and Josef felt himself slipping away.

"Leave him alone."

A man's harsh voice cut through the crowd of bodies even though the words were no louder than a whisper.

"The guards will not care if we kill a queer."

"I will," said the man.

Different hands—hands as rough as the voice—pulled Josef to his feet. He found himself propelled backward again, the crowd parting for him, until his back hit the side of the boxcar.

The man who'd rescued him was taller than Josef, big-boned with a heavy forehead and thick, dark eyebrows. He was far too thin but still powerfully built. He wore a striped jacket and trousers marked with dark triangles. Josef could not see their true color in the gloom

Josef started to thank the man, but a large, callused hand clamped over Josef's mouth.

"I did you no favors." The man spoke so softly Josef had difficulty hearing him over the sounds of the rails. He nodded at Josef's coat. "You must rid yourself of that."

Josef remembered the old queen's warning. He had told no one of his crime, but the triangle he had been given did that for him.

"You must do it before we reach the camp," his rescuer said, removing his hand from Josef's mouth. "No one here will care how."

He cut his eyes to the side, and Josef followed his gaze. Josef could barely see the man huddled in the corner of the train car. He was the thinnest man Josef had ever seen, small and sickly, barely more than a walking skeleton. His shorn skull was covered with sores. The striped shirt he wore bore a triangle neither as dark as Josef's rescuer nor as light as Josef's own.

Not queer. Josef didn't know what color the man wore, but his crime was different than his own.

His rescuer's intent was clear.

"I can't," Josef said. He could not kill another man for his clothes.

"Then you will die."

His rescuer stepped away, turning his back on Josef as if he was no longer worth saving.

Josef's fingers throbbed. He held his hand tight against his chest and shivered. He told himself it was from the cold.

He was alone, as alone as a man could be in a boxcar crowded with people treated worse than cattle.

He would be killed at the camp in Dachau. If not by the SS, by other prisoners who'd been taught to hate queers just as those in power hated queers and Jews and Gypsies and anyone else who did not conform to the Aryan ideal. Or by the *kapos*, prisoners who oversaw other prisoners and who used and abused the weakest to the amusement of their SS overseers.

He would die because the clothes he wore identified who he truly was.

A laugh rose up in his throat, and he clamped his un-injured hand over his mouth in horror.

He had been attacked in this boxcar because his *clothes* identified him as queer. He had been able to hide who he was in Berlin. He had not dressed flamboyantly. He had not taken a lover in months. He had been *careful*, and now the pink triangle he wore would get him killed.

Josef did not want to die. He was only twenty-two.

He looked at the sickly man. Tremors wracked the man's body. Josef could see him trembling even in the poor light. He wondered if the man had lied to himself, believing that his tremors were only from the cold.

The man would die in the camp, and the salvation of-fered by his striped shirt, poor as it was, would be lost. Josef would be taken from the train by the SS and beaten, and still this man would die. Josef's thick, black hair would be shorn from his skull, his body would be abused, his spirit broken, and still this man would die.

He would die no matter what Josef did.

Those words repeated and repeated in Josef's mind until the hysterical laughter subsided and a numbness settled over him.

The words repeated as the moonlight faded, and dark-ness fell over the prisoners.

The words repeated as Josef felt his way along the wall of the boxcar, moving slowly and quietly to the corner where the sickly man stood shivering in the dark.

They were the only words Josef heard when the train finally stopped and the doors of the boxcar opened, and Josef, now wearing a striped shirt with a triangle of red, was herded along with the rest of the undesirables to the prison camp at Dachau.

The blonde-haired girl looked at Josef over her mother's shoulder. The West German countryside (German, Josef corrected himself; they were all one Germany again) blurred past the train's windows, but she stared at him, her large blue eyes gazing at him with such intensity that he thought surely she must see his crime.

He glanced down at his overcoat. The train was comfortably warm. Most travelers had removed their coats, but Josef still wore his. He needed it to hide the scrap of pink he'd sewn on his suit coat. He wanted anyone who looked at him to believe he was simply an old man riding a train. An old man who could not tolerate the cold German winter, even inside the warmth of the train.

He wanted to believe he was safe, but he knew better.

In the years he had spent hiding, pretending not to be who he truly was, Josef had studied the law that branded him and men like him criminals. Homosexuality had been a crime in Germany since the last century, when the Second Reich had declared sex between men as equally degenerate as sex between man and beast. The law had grown worse after Germany's defeat in the First World War, when the crime of homosexuality had been declared a felony, and the definition of homosexuality had been widened to include activities as harmless as kissing another man, or sending love letters to another man.

Or, as in Josef's case, merely by being a known associate of a homosexual man.

The train swayed slightly as it rounded a curve, and Josef turned his head away from the little girl and her mother. They reminded him too much of another little girl on another train. A little girl who had watched him more than fifty years ago as he'd removed the shirt of a man who had been too weak to stop Josef even as Josef dressed the man in his own clothes.

The last time Josef had seen this part of the German countryside, he had been fleeing with Elsa, newly forged Red Cross papers in their pockets that identified them as Martin and Ethel Lubetkin, a Jewish couple from Frankfurt returning home. The land had been blighted then, raw stumps of trees standing like silent sentinels guarding muddy battlefields ruined by the tread of tanks and the blood of countless dead. Now the land was covered with the first pristine snows of winter. The roads on which long lines of refugees had marched had been paved over, filled now with autos carrying a new generation of Germans who had not been alive during the war.

Josef and Elsa had lived their lives in Frankfurt among these new generations of Germans, but they had not been Josef and Elsa, the homosexual and the lesbian who had married out of safety and necessity. They had remained Martin and Ethel Lubetkin, non-practicing Jews, and Elsa's grave bore that assumed name. The deceit had protected Elsa, but even more, the deceit had been necessary to keep Josef from being returned to prison after the Allies defeated Germany.

The law that had sent Josef to prison before the war had not been repealed with the defeat of the Nazis. Homosexual men who had survived the horrors of Dachau and Auschwitz and Buchenwald were shipped back to prison to serve the remainder of their sentences for the crime of having simply looked with affection at another man. No time was deducted from their sentences for the years they had fought to survive in the camps.

Josef would have been sent back to prison if not for Elsa. If not for the forged papers she had obtained for them.

If not for the convicted criminal with the green triangle who'd saved him from a beating on the train that took him to Dachau.

If not for the man whose clothes he had stolen so that he would be identified as a political prisoner, not a homosexual.

The expansion of the law that had sent Josef to prison had been repealed in 1969, but homosexuality remained a crime even in this newly reunited Germany. What Josef planned to do could get him arrested, but the ghosts of his past—the man on the train, the men he'd named to keep the Gestapo from castrating him, all the queer men he'd seen beaten in Dachau while he hid behind his red triangle—the ghosts would not let him be until he did this.

He could not have taken this trip while Elsa was alive. He would not have jeopardized the careful life she had built in such a manner.

He hoped that she would forgive him now as he dishonored her memory in death.

Josef could not have said what he expected when he returned to Dachau, but it certainly wasn't the vastness.

Or the solitude.

Or the silence.

Josef was one of only a hundred or so men and women who walked through what was now known as the Dachau Memorial Site. They walked along the paths in this place where so many had perished in such a horrible fashion, their voices hushed as if they did not want to disturb the dead. Many had tears on their cheeks, but Josef 's eyes remained dry.

He felt numb.

This was not the camp he remembered.

Gone were the rows of long, narrow buildings that housed those not immediately sent to the crematory. Built at perfect right angles, a reflection of the Nazi obsession with order, the barracks had filled the huge space that was now filled only with long, narrow beds of crushed granite to show where the buildings had once stood.

Josef made his way to the spot where his barracks had once stood. Gravel crunched beneath his feet, and he wondered if it had been made from the rocks he had moved from one spot to the other and back again, backbreaking, meaningless work meant to break the minds of the prisoners as much as their bodies.

He closed his eyes. The pervasive smell of the dead and dying was gone. The memorial smelled no different than any other part of any other city surrounded by trees and grass and hedge-covered concrete walls.

It should be different here. People should remember. This place should make a difference.

But none of it did. The camp was simply a large piece of land tucked away behind trees and fences that people could ignore it if they chose to do so.

Or where those who had escaped its past could make foolish, worthless trips to visit.

He had removed his topcoat when he had stepped through the front gate, displaying the pink triangle on his suit coat for all to see.

And nothing had happened.

No guards had accosted him.

No police had arrested him.

The only one who had noticed was an old woman, as bent and white-haired as Josef. She had looked at him with rheumy, faded eyes, then looked quickly away.

Elsa had been right. The dead were dead. He could do nothing for the ghosts of his past.

He shivered in the afternoon chill. He should put his topcoat back on. No one here cared that one old queer had finally decided to quit hiding and show the world who he was.

The world simply did not care.

Josef made his way through the central corridor between the long rectangles of crushed granite to the rear of the memorial. Churches had been erected here as memorials to the dead, churches like none Josef had ever seen in his life.

Directly ahead lay the Catholic Church of the Mortal Agony of Christ, a circular stone cylinder open at the front that stood as tall as the oak trees that surrounded it. To his left where the disinfection hut had once stood was the Jewish memorial, a strange wedge-shaped building constructed of weathered, dark gray stone. At the far end of the building, a marble Menorah the color of the granite on which Josef stood marked the highest point of the wedge.

He watched as a few people, including the old, white-haired woman who had not wanted to look at him, shuffled down a ramp into the interior of the Jewish memorial, but Josef felt no desire to join them. The ramp was bordered by an iron fence that reminded Josef too much of the barbed wire that had surrounded the camp.

Instead, he turned toward the Protestant memorial, an odd-looking concrete building to the left of the Catholic church. Built like a layered spiral with tilted ceilings and surrounded by more rough gravel, the entrance to this memorial was below ground level, with widely angled stairs descending downward.

He had not intended to go inside, but he had gone inside none of the memorials he had seen. He already felt like an old fool for making such a worthless trip. The stairs were wide, and the way down proved easy even for an elderly man who needed a cane.

The floors inside the memorial were gently slanted, the walls more of the same unfinished gray concrete as the outside. The altar room had been simply furnished with four spare benches and a round concrete altar, with small concrete pillars on either side of the altar.

Josef found no solace here. He had never been a religious man. Not even in the dark of the barracks, when his hunger had been a living thing eating away his belly and he'd listened to the sobbing prayers of other men, did he turn to God for comfort. A

God who could let such evil exist in the world was not a God who would listen to the prayers of a man like Josef.

He could not say how long he stood in the altar room before he felt more than heard someone come up behind him.

His grip tightened on his cane. Would his arrest finally come here, in this house of a God he did not believe in?

"Are you looking for the triangle?" the man behind him asked.

Josef did not understand the question. For a moment he thought he had done such a poor job of sewing the triangle to his coat that it had fallen off. But no, it was still there, its hideous pink a sharp contrast to his black suit coat.

He turned to look at the young man standing behind him. Tall and well-nourished, his flaxen hair was cut close to his skull, his blue eyes clear and unexpectedly kind. He wore a tan-colored suit coat, dark trousers, a white shirt, and a narrow tie. His name tag identified him as a volunteer.

The man pointed to the pink triangle on Josef's coat. "I thought you might be looking for the memorial plaque," he said. "It is housed in the reading room. I can show you the way."

Understanding dawned, and Josef nodded his agreement. He had passed other plaques attached to the interior walls of the museum, but he had not stopped to read any of them. Perhaps in this odd place some small paragraph had been placed to memorialize the suffering of the queers in Dachau.

He was not prepared for the size of the pink granite triangle on display in the reading room. As wide as two men, the plaque replicated the scrap of pink cloth on his suit coat in flat, irrefutable stone.

Josef shuffled close to the plaque, his hands trembling on his cane. Words had been inscribed beneath the granite.

Words that brought tears to his eyes even as he read them.

BEATEN TO DEATH
KILLED AGAIN BY SILENCE
To the homosexual victims of National Socialism
The homosexual initiatives of Munich, 1985

Josef swiped at his eyes, suddenly angry with himself for surviving when so many had not. The silence had been his. His and so many like him, cowards all.

He had thought he could make up for decades of cowardice with one act of bravery. But how brave was the act when no one noticed?

The volunteer stayed in the room with him as he stood, head bowed, and tried to get control of himself. It took longer than Josef would have imagined possible, but the decades of guilt demanded their due.

When he finally lifted his head, the volunteer cleared his throat, and Josef turned to look at him. To his surprise, the man's eyes were shiny and deep with unshed tears.

"You are a survivor, yes?" the man asked him.

Josef nodded.

"And homosexual?"

Josef nodded again, his heart beating hard in his chest. It was the first time he had admitted that he was queer to anyone other than Elsa in the last fifty years.

"I am homosexual as well," the young man said. "I belong to a group who are working to obtain authority to move this memorial triangle to the official commemorative room at the front of the museum, but it is difficult. No one wants to acknowledge the suffering our people endured in the camps."

Our people.

The words struck a chord so deep inside Josef that he felt the kind of longing he hadn't experienced since the last time he had allowed himself to go to a club in Berlin. When he had been surrounded by men who loved other men. When he had last felt at home within his own skin.

But did he have a right to feel such longing when he had turned his back on who he was simply to survive?

Did a coward have a right to belong?

The young man tilted his head and seemed to consider Josef for a long moment before he spoke. "Perhaps," he said, clearly considering his words. "You would consider lending your support?"

"How?" Josef asked.

"By telling your story. There are those of us who are compiling histories—"

Shame flooded Josef's face, and he held up his hand. "Stop." He touched the pink triangle on his chest. "I did not wear this at Dachau. My experiences will not help you. There are those whose stories are more worthy than mine."

The young man did not seem surprised. "Then tell their stories," he said. "Tell yours. Each is equally as valid."

"I was a coward," Josef muttered.

"You are a survivor, and you came back." The young man held out his hand. "I do not know if I would be brave enough to do the same. I wish to know you better."

Josef had come here to expose himself for what he was. To atone to those who had suffered and died while he had hidden himself away behind a lie. He had thought simply wearing the pink triangle would be sufficient, but it had never been about that small scrap of cloth. It had been about who he really was.

Josef looked at the young man's hand, strong and capable, and took it with his arthritic one.

"My name is Josef Galen," he said. "I was arrested in Berlin in 1939 and taken by train to Dachau. And I am a homosexual."

Annie Reed's writing career began with a sale to the *Star Trek* anthology series *Strange New Worlds*, eventually appearing in three volumes before branching out into mystery and fantasy as well, selling stories to *Ellery Queen's Mystery Magazine*, and anthologies like *Time After Time*, *The Trouble with Heroes*, *Swordplay*, *Cosmic Cocktails*, *Hags, Sirens and Other Bad Girls of Fantasy*, *The Future We Wish We Had*, and *Wizards, Inc.* Her versatility led to her science fiction, fantasy, and mystery stories appearing in five of the seven volumes of Fiction River's inaugural year. She also received a Literary Fellowship award for her story "One Sun, No Waiting" from the Nevada Arts Council, and her novel *Pretty Little Horses* was a finalist in the Best First Private Eye Novel contest sponsored by St. Martin's Press and the Private Eye Writers of America. These days she divides her time between writing short fiction (her first love), appearing regularly in the *Fiction River* anthology series, *The Uncollected Anthology*, urban fantasy stories written quarterly on the same theme, and in *Ellery Queen Mystery Magazine*, and writing novels in whatever genre strikes her fancy. Her most popular fantasy stories, including her Diz and Dee fantasy detective stories, are set in a fictional version of Seattle called Moretown Bay. She has two mystery series: the Abby Maxon mysteries featuring Reno private detective and single mom Abby Maxon, and the Jill Jordan mysteries about rural Nevada Sheriff Jill Jordan. She;s also begun a third series, consisting of two crime novels, *A Death in Cumberland* and the upcoming *A Disappearance in Cumberland*.

Rusch & Helfers

The Heroism of Lieutenant Wills: Charles Todd

First published in *The Strand Magazine*, July/October 2015

Late June, 1916

"Where's Lieutenant Wills?" someone asked Banks as he boarded the transport in Portsmouth on his way back to the front.

The question irritated him. "Already on board, at a guess. I missed the early train down from London."

It had been a difficult farewell. Sally had heard rumors about a big push, and she was afraid.

"I wanted to see him off, and he wouldn't let me. He went to the railway station alone. He didn't want to watch me cry, he said. But I can't help crying when I know it might be the last time… You'll both come back? Promise me?"

"You know we will," he said, taking her hand. "Haven't we always?"

She smiled then, but he could still see the worry in her eyes. He had gone to her London house to say goodbye – against his better judgment. But then, when has better judgment prevailed over love?

"You'll keep him safe?" she asked, her voice trembling a little in spite of her resolve.

"I've kept him safe since we were nine years old," he reminded her. It was true." I give you my word, the Germans won't touch him."

She stood on her tiptoes and kissed his cheek. "Bless you," she said.

He fought the overwhelming urge to take her in his arms and tell her how much he loved her.

That would never do. He had no right.

"Where's Lieutenant Wills?" The officer at the port gates in France asked as he disembarked amid the chaos of off-loading guns and gear and men.

"I've been too seasick to care," he answered truthfully. It had been a hell of a rough crossing, trying to make headway in the teeth of the gale; he'd sat by the rail vomiting on and off for nearly six hours. His mouth still tasted of it, and he could smell it on the front of his trench coat. Rain was still coming down, cold for June, but it felt good on his face. He wanted to add that he wasn't his brother's keeper, but Wills wasn't his brother. He was – and he's been nearly their entire lives – his friend.

"Damned man has a stomach of iron," he added.

The officer chuckled. "Left you for dead, did he? He's probably gone ahead, then, to find his dinner."

Banks felt his gut wrench at the thought of food.

He remembered the first time he and Wills had set eyes on each other. They were nine years old and homesick, but trying not to show it. That hadn't stopped Wills from eating his own dinner and half of Banks' as well. Banks was the son of a small-town solicitor, and his grandfather – his dead mother's father – had paid his school fees.

"He'll grieve less if he stays busy. And there won't be any memories there to remind him. I'll pay, for Mary's sake."

His father said, "I'd rather keep him here. Rattling around this house without her or the boy – I'll go mad."

"No, you won't." his grandfather retorted. "You'll have your work, and there's your sister – she can keep house for you."

In the end, of course, his grandfather had won. Young Edward Montgomery Banks had been sent away to a strange school where he didn't know anyone until he met the thin, gangly Ronald Wills, whose parents were in Africa growing coffee and wanted their son to have a proper English education.

Banks heard Wills crying the first night, trying to stifle his sobs with the edge of his blanket. He'd thought it very brave to cry. He'd wanted to do the same, but hadn't had the courage, for fear the other lads would taunt him later.

They'd been inseperable since that first day.

He moved on, searching for his transport, and finally found the lorry well down the line, already crowded with the company of Welsh sappers. They were passing the time singing, their voices ringing out in that way they had: each man seeming to know his key by instinct, blending effortlessly with the other singers. It was chapel anthem, Banks thought, and bloody demoralizing with its emphasis on salvation. He climbed in the front with the driver and hoped they'd shut up as soon as the lorry had pulled away from the port. He was so tired his head was spinning, and he wanted nothing as much as a few hours of sleep. Trying to make himself comfortable in a seat never meant for comfort, he thought, *If the Germans are half as wretched as I am, they'll march back to Berlin forthwith.* Of course, the Germans never had to cross the English Channel, did they?

The driver was a stranger, thank God. Banks wasn't up to carrying on a conversation. He closed his eyes as the corporal patiently threaded his way through the chaos. Banks craved rest, knowing he'd be himself again if he could sleep. But Sally's face was waiting for him behind his lids.

From the moment he'd known Wills had done, he'd refused to dishonor himself or her by coveting her. Some things simply were not *done*. Yet, for all his good intention, he knew he would never stop loving her. *Damn Wills, damn him, damn him, damn him.* Because Banks had never quite been sure whether Wills had fallen in love with her too – or if he just wanted her because he knew Banks did. In all their years of friendship, Banks had never begrudged Wills anything. *Always the best for Wills, as if by divine right.* Banks had found that amusing – until it came to Sally. And this time, Wills had not so much as asked how Banks felt, or if he minded. For that matter, by the time Banks figured out which way the wind blew, Wills had already proposed. It had nearly destroyed him, the blithe announcement: *"Sally has made me the happiest man alive..."*

It was a three-hour drive to his sector, over bad roads that had been made worse by the mud churned up during the four days of rain. When the lorry lost a tire, he had to transfer to another vehicle heading north, and the new driver recognized him.

"Lieutenant, sir," the driver said cheerfully as Banks climbed into the seat beside him. "How was London?"

Crowded, he wanted to say. *Busy. A shortage of food, everyone in black.* Instead, he answered, "Much the same as ever." Because that's what those who weren't given leave wanted to hear.

"Thank God for small blessings! Where's Lieutenant Wills?"

"Gone ahead, I expect. I didn't see him on the transport." Banks answered, and added, "I caught the later train, and we sat for half an hour at a siding. I thought I'd miss my ship. Then I was seasick."

"Tweedledum and Tweedledee," the sergeant said, grinning. "That's what they call the two of you behind your backs. Did you know?"

Cheeky bastard, Banks thought. Aloud, he answered only, "I daresay." He and Wills had always been lumped together somehow. Even in school, they'd be mistaken for each other by masters who couldn't be bothered to learn the difference between them. Then in their first job, they'd been given desks side by side – although it was Banks who had wanted the position, and Wills had applied only for lack of a better idea. They seemed to have gone through life sharing everything. But not Sally. They had never shared Sally. And she'd had no trouble telling them apart, seeming in the beginning to not favor one above the other.

The sergeant, fighting the road, wasn't easily put off. "They think you bring them luck," he went on. "The men. It's meant as a compliment."

"Yes, I'm sure it's meant that way." As for luck, it had run out for Wills. He'd said as much two nights ago – or was it three? It was hard for Banks to remember now, his mind numb with fatigue.

"I always wanted to believe we were two sides of the same coin," Wills said. "But I expect that was wishful thinking. You have a darker side, and either I didn't want to see it or you were clever at concealing it. Maybe it was a little of both."

Banks answered, "Some men have all the luck. I'd hoped a little of yours would rub off on me. Perhaps if it had, there wouldn't be any darkness."

"Yes," Wills said, "Well, my luck's run out. All those battles you fought for me because you were bigger? I took them for granted, you know. As my due. Arrogant little bastard, wasn't I. I told myself your father served men like my father, and you served me. I said something to Sally about that, did you know? She laughed at me, called me a snob. Still, I thought it might weigh with her, if she came to make a choice."

"Did it?"

"I don't know, to tell you the truth. I did wonder if she chose me because I reminded her of her father." He smiled wryly. "Not that I'd have cared. It's just I never had much time for the man."

"Funny. He and I always got on."

That had been the end of the conversation. Later that evening, Banks had wondered why the two of them had ever been friends. Habit, he supposed. They'd faced bullies together at school, and that had been a bond, as had the fact that they were distantly related on their mother's sides. It had given them some comfort in the cold, unfriendly world od a public school they both loathed. Neither was particularly good at sports, and both were mediocre scholars. They'd had little in common with their classmates and nothing their masters wanted, not even great wealth or social prominence. They had envied the boys who had silver spoons or blue blood, excelled at cricket or rugby, or pleased their tutors with good minds. Si their stay at Harrow had been a matter of survival rather than a time either would look back on fondly. With some bravado, they'd called themselves The Outcasts. That and sheer tenacity had seen them through the worst of their five years of servitude. They were both too afraid to go home and tell the truth – not after the exorbitant fees that had been paid out.

Sally tested that bond. Banks had known she would the instant he'd laid eyes on her. Hair the color of sunlight, eyes a dark northern blue. She had loved them both. And it had been unbearable.

"You're Gemini, even sharing the same birthdate," she said laughing. "Imagine that, going odd to school and finding one's twin. Well, near enough. I adore both of you. How shall I ever choose between you?"

She meant the words lightly, but it had rankled all the same. And the first tiny crack in the friendship between two men took hold. It was barely visible then. No one had noticed, least of all him or Wills. But it was there, and it would grow wider, until Wills devastating betrayal finally made it shatter – at least where Banks was concerned.

He hadn't blamed Sally. He couldn't. Not even when Wills had the temerity to ask Banks to stand up with him. "After all, I've known you longer than anyone else," he said grinning. "Still, I asked Sally if she'd mind. She said she wouldn't." And Banks was struck speechless by the admission.

That was when he had begun to pray each night that he would survive long enough in the trenches to see Wills shot dead by a German before the wedding. God had for-saken him there. The marriage had gone forward, and Banks could do nothing about it. But Wills had seen his luck run out, hadn't he? Some men did oddly enough. Banks had expected Wills to be one of them, and in spite of his prayers, it had somehow shaken him.

Banks section was under heavy fire when he got through to the front lines and relieved his opposite num-ber, a harried, exhausted man already bleeding from several wounds and swaying on his feet.

"Where's Lieutenant Wills?" Captain Jordan asked.

"He's already here, isn't he?" Banks replied.

Captain Jordan was a thorough and capable officer. He didn't misplace men. He wiped his hand across his face. "God knows. It's been bedlam, all along the front. Wills' sector has been cut off for the last twelve hours. See if you can raise them, will you?"

But it had been impossible. All along the Rover Somme, communication was sketchy at best. The attack faltered, went forward, fell back, and struggled again for inches. It was a disaster, men dying by the hundreds, worse than anything Banks had experienced or expected. He had been on his feet for nearly thirty-seven hours when he and his men made a last valiant effort, succeeding somehow in pushing the tired Germans back a few hundred yards, far enough to reach the wounded caught in no man's land.

While searching in the last of light for a man calling out for water, Banks saw a dead officer – or what was left of him = in the shell crater. His jaw had been shot away and his body was a shambles. Around him lay a half-dozen German soldiers. Somehow the bloody fool had managed to take them with him before he died. Banks wondered if he'd gone berserk. Some men did, when fighting got too intense. A mad need to get it over with, whatever the cost.

He leaned closer.

"Anyone recognize him?" Banks called to his sergeant. But Norton had just come up the line a day before, and shook his head.

"Damned if I know who he is," he responded, watching his men furiously digging, using the German trench lines and stringing wire behind them. "Except he's an officer. Was. The boots."

It wouldn't be long before the Germans regrouped and came back to reclaim their lost ground, but Banks stared at the torn body, the hand still holding the empty revolver.

He finally said, "God help us Sergeant, I think it's Lieutenant Wills."

He knelt to search for some identification. If there had been any, he couldn't find it now. "Make a note will you, sergeant? I knew his family."

"Wills?" the sergeant repeated, peering at the remnants of a face. "Tweedledum? Isn't that what he was called? His own mother wouldn't know him now, would she? A crying shame." He shook his head. "I'd heard about him. A damned good man, from all accounts."

And that was to be Lieutenant Wills' epitaph. Minutes later, as the Germans counterattacked, Banks and his men were too busy trying to salvage the living to worry about the dead.

Three days later, they were rotated out of that hell, having held off the Germans until they were literally overrun. Banks looked down at his torn uniform, saw blood still oozing from cuts and scrapes, and thought "I'm alive." It was almost unbelievable.

He got his men out of there and to the nearest aid station. There wasn't a soldier among them who wasn't wounded, and he had the names of the dead on a scrap of paper in his pocket. An hour later, patched up, he was free to report his losses.

Banks gave the duty officer an account of the dead, the missing, including a description of Lieutenant Wills' mangled remains. "There was no hope of recovering the body," he went on, dropping his face into his filthy, bloodstained hands. "He was just married, you know. I can't think how I'm going to tell his wife. I promised her I'd keep him safe. Dear God."

The captain taking down the names nodded, "I knew him. Wills. A good man. Good officer." An echo of the sergeants' words. Banks made a mental note of them, to put them in the letter to Sally. The captain glanced up. "This will be a blow to morale. The two of you were something of a legend."

"Yes, sir. In my opinion, he deserves a medal. He was always fearless. There were eight German dead in that shell hole with him. *Eight*." He'd embroidered that by two Hun soldiers, but felt no guilt over it. "He must have held them off so that he men had time to get back to their own lines. That's all I could think of when I stood there looking down at him."

"You'll write to his family, then, will you? Captain Jordan's in a bad way. Septicemia, they're saying. You're the ranking officer now."

"Yes, all right, I'll see that it's done. And the others."

"Good." Captain Archer hesitated. "You're quite sure it was Wills? Even in that condition? We've lost thousands of men in the last few days, I'm hard pressed to keep up with all of them."

Banks raised his head. "Sergeant Norton was there. They're taking his leg off tonight. If he survives, he can confirm the identification. And the dead Germans."

"Then it's official. My sympathies, Lieutenant. You were close. It can't have been easy." Archer looked up, saw another officer standing outside the open tent flap, ready to report. "Get some rest, man, you're nearly dead on your feet."

Banks grimaced. He was. He made his way back to the rear and found an empty cot, collapsing into it. He lay there for a time then certain he was alone, he dug in his tunic pocket for the ring.

Sally would recognize it. She had given it to Wills as a keepsake when he went away to war. Banks had taken it from Wills' dead hand just before tumbling him into the River Thames – over a week ago now – his face battered beyond recognition. Long before his body surfaced somewhere south of London, Lieutenant Wills would be reported killed on the Somme. Dying for king and country. The detail of the eight dead Germans would see to it that he was mentioned in dispatches. There might even be a posthumous medal. The Army never got it wrong. This was a far kinder ending – for Sally – than having Wills declared a deserter, as he would surely have been.

The poor sod feeding the fish in the Thames would be buried in an unmarked pauper's grave. So much for divine right. And the remains of the unlucky young lieutenant – whom Wills had never arrived to replace and who died in that crater killing Germans – would be lost forever in the next surge of fighting.

It had all turned out rather well.

He'd taken a grave risk. He had no regrets. He could never marry Sally, of course, not with her husband's blood on his hands. But then, Wills no longer had her either. And that was the whole point.

As he drifted to sleep, he thought, *All I needed to get what I wanted was to keep my nerve. And what I wanted was to get even.*

It was an oddly comforting realization.

Charles and Caroline Todd are a bestselling mother-and-son writing team who live on the east coast of the United States. Caroline has a BA in English Literature and History, and a Masters in International Relations. Charles has a BA in Communication Studies with an emphasis on Business Management, and a culinary arts degree that means he can boil more than water. Their *New York Times*-bestselling historical series is set in post-World War I England and feature Ian Rutledge, a Scotland Yard detective struggling to put his life back together after the war. The series, which now spans eighteen volumes, has been critically lauded, and the first book, *A Test of Wills*, won the Barry Award and was named one of the 100 favorite mysteries if the 20th Century by the Independent Mystery Booksellers Association. More recent volumes have been nominated for the Anthony and Agatha Award, with the novel *A Question of Honor* winning the Agatha for Best Historical Mystery in 2013. The latest Rutledge novel is *No Shred of Evidence*. They also write a series about Bess Crawford, a nurse serving in France during World War I, and currently spans eight volumes, the most recent being *The Shattered Tree*.

Rusch & Helfers

Dr. Kirkbride's Moral Treatment Plan: Christina Milletti

First published in *Buffalo Noir*

If irony had a flavor, it would taste like steel. Oxidized. Unforgiving. My tongue is rusty from it when I phone my son on Saturday mornings. We get ten minutes. He won't give me five.

"Are you through, Mom?" he says when I tell him I love him.

He hangs up. Every week it's the same thing.

He hangs up. Every week it's the same thing.

A large metal door separates me from my children. Plexiglass. Fiber-optic cables. From the outside, the walls of the Richardson Complex look worn, the stone etched by snow and time. But the interior is scarred by a far worse erosion. The patients here roam halls eaten away by generations of rats. Joists rotting from seasonal ice dams. Our minds are as creaky as Ward E's floors. When I wake in the morning, plaster is rained down from the ceiling; a fine sand coats my sheets. Perhaps I'm just molting, my skin flaking away so that, one day, I can be someone else. Someone new.

Before I was sent here, there were rumors that mayor planned to shut the asylum's doors. Eject the so-called "moderate" cases outside the gates. Let the obdurate winds drive unwanted inmates downtown. To the empty warehouses and silos. Maybe into Lake Erie itself. The plan, I heard, was to reclaim the complex. Restore the bones of the building. Transform it. Maybe into a posh hotel.

Keep the form, but not the crazy content.

I don't blame the mayor. Its east to picture chandeliers in our grand foyer. The fourth-floor chapel made up as a ballroom. Even the signature towers – helmeted sentries above the patients inside – refitted as suits for political sponsors. Like all things in Buffalo, the plan had stalled. But it would get moving again. In six months. A year.

With better timing, a "moderate" case like me would have been left to myself. Tricked out with an anklet. At home.

My luck never changes.

From my therapist: *What do you make of that?*

Once again, the taste of rust swells, coats my tongue.

I close my eyes so see can't see me rolling them.

I thought that I'd left my problems behind, that I'd buried them in the many yards of many places I've called home since I met my husband. The dorm Ed and I filled with books, a futon, a used recliner. Later, a rented house with sloping floors. Then, when Ed joined Hampton, Payne, and Lynch, LLC, a tony, compact apartment seated off an upscale cul-de-sac not far from the Albright-Knox Art Gallery. We used to walk its mossy paths while Bobby, just a colicky infant then, howled shamelessly from his squeaky pram, much to the art lovers' dismay.

They glared. Ed laughed. His audacity once amused me.

Our last home was the farmhouse. Our Clarence farmhouse.

Now, we will never move into the home I imagined. The home Ed promised. The one thing I've always wanted. The one thing, it seems, I can never have.

If the past is the lens through which you observe the present, the one lesson I've learned – perhaps the only lesson I've ever learned – is that it's impossible to change your perspective. Only your eyesight changes. Which is to say: over time it gets worse.

Tell me your story, Dr. Kirjbrise now counsels. *Not his. Yours.*

The sun streams in lavishly through the barred windows. We should feel its heat the same way.

"My story, doctor?"

Call me Cheryl, she says.

Her linen skirt whispers against the Naugahyde chair, and I suddenly perceive a new sense to my words. Cheryl doesn't hear it. But then Ed often plants thoughts in my mind.

"Mystery, doctor?"

She makes a mark in her notepad.

"There's nothing mysterious about it," I say.

Meaning?

I just look at her. She knows precisely what I mean.

Write it all down, Jane, she says, handing me a paper and pencil.

I sign of trust.

So I do.

The past has a bit more give than we like to acknowledge. Like a fat man on a bus you squeeze by to get a free seat, it can make you wonder if the crush was worth the trouble. But if you exert your will, the past teeters a bit, makes an opening for you where before there was none. As for that unwelcome residue that gums up your clothing? Well, you might say it's the gooey evidence of what, in better times, I called desire. Now I simply reach for the hand sanitizer, and chalk up my chapped, antiseptic hands to the unpredictable pitch and heave of "desire's" obnoxious cousins: "change."

Bluster?

Cheryl has scrawled the word in the corner of my latest draft.

That's one word for it. When there's no other option, what else do you have?

Cheryl would no doubt say "the truth."

The truth that it's been almost a year since the rest of the world noticed Ed disappeared. What they don't know is that he took off long before that.

But no one believes me.

Why would anyone believe a wife who claims that, one day, her husband went to work on his book in his study. And he, quite simply, never came out?

Dr. Kirkbride once had the audacity to ask whether I was "aware" that getting "lost in a book," as she put it, is "just an expression."

To some questions there are no answers.

I've told her: I did not kill Ed. I have no idea where he is. I've told the police the same thing. I've explained to anyone who would listen: I have no idea what Ed was writing. Nor why. I've even admitted that every time I write my husband's name now – every time I try to account for our life and his disappearance – Ed seems to be standing behind me. Looking over my shoulder. His hot breath raising the hairs of my neck.

Right now I feel him. He wants me to stop.

Ed never left me at all.

The day my husband disappeared began much like any other. It was a school day. Ed was already hard at work on his book – he'd taken to sleeping on the couch in his study in order to, as he put it, "expedite his memory". So it was left to me to wake up our son, push him into the bathroom, then persuade Bobby to brush his teeth, wash his face, and wrestle his cowlick in place – all the while bracing the baby with my tender left tennis elbow. Then, down to the kitchen the tree of us went for breakfast, only twenty minutes to spare before the school bus was due to take Bobby to Harris Hill Elementary. With the exception of Ed's growing remoteness (which at that time struck me as not so very different from the absence of fathers who left for work before their children woke), our family that morning could have been any other in our neighborhood. The sun streamed in the windows. The smell of lawn pesticides lingered above the dew in the air. The baby drooled on the toy in her playpen. It was peaceful. It was boring. I'm sure I felt restless.

Now I miss those days the way an amputee misses a limb.

As usual, Bobby was running late, his book bag was only half packed, and he was wearing two different socks. But he was in a good mood. Ed roared at him from behind his office door as Bobby rocketed down the hallway.

Naturally, my son found it amusing.

"He's P.O.'d," Bobby grinned as he climbed into his chair.

It was one of Ed's pet phrases, one of those I'd always disliked. It made Ed sound peevish, like an old lady fussing over a pile of dog crap steaming on her front lawn. Maybe that's why when Bobby said it he made me smile – a boy channeling a father who was (in turn) impersonating a crabby octogenarian. In Bobby's squeaky adolescent pitch, I could hear Ed's voice. But because it was Bobby, not Ed, I'd laugh.

I put my hand over my smile (I didn't want to encourage him), as Bobby went to explain that his friend/nemesis Jimmy (it was hard to keep track) had been making trouble for him on the bus. But as syrup dripped from his chin, and he smacked his lips contentedly, I set my fears aside. There was nothing to worry about. He was high-strung and, like a monkey, tight and lean. Bobby could fend for himself, even if his heart was as impressionable as clay.

"Talk to your father," I advised, then flipped a pancake. A moment later, I slid it onto his plate.

Naturally, I knew Ed wouldn't answer a knock on his floor. He'd stopped answering knocks a month before.

Recently, he rarely showed up for dinner. I should have been more concerned. But, at the time, his absence was a relief.

I no longer had to negotiate his moods.

Bobby could have used Ed's help. My son was long-limbed and fast, but Jimmy Hammond – a bloated-face boy whose sweat smelled like onions – was fond of roughing kids up. Bully was in his future, everyone knew it. Everyone, that is, but his mother, Regina. A birdlike woman who held her shoulders like wings, she chirped at parties about her son's wit, while Jimmy's wiry, absent-minded father looked on in disbelief. How Regina gave birth to a brute like Jimmy is one of the mysteries of genetics... unless you believed a neighborhood rumor that Jimmy's egg rolled from an illegitimate nest. The current candidate was a strapping pool boy who stopped by Regina's home every Thursday while her husband was off at work.

Back then, I defended her. How young I once was.

"It's nice to see an independent woman get what she wants," I said, backing myself against Ed's crotch, knocking him off balance. He laughed, cuffed me away.

"Maybe later," he said.

As usual, later never came.

Now I wonder: was that the instant Regina appeared on his radar? Would this story have been completely different if I'd just kept my thoughts, my soft-boiled ass, to myself?

Of course, I wouldn't have had to look so hard for the piranha hiding within the school of sharks if Ed hadn't moved us north of the city to Clarence, to a so-called gateway development zone – an experimental neighborhood built by one of his clients, wedged between the muscular outer suburbs and the svelte inner exurbs, designed to appeal (so the pamphlet read) to "young, upwardly mobile homeowners looking for outer space and inner peace, for self-discovery and future fortune. Mean age: 38. No. of children: 1. No. of cars: 2. No. of homes: 1.5."

Ed's client had built the community on the homestead of an old barely estate. The original farmhouse itself was in good condition, and it stood at the heart of the neighborhood's newly built vistas where the development brochure still pictures (I'm told) a "community center anchored by an organic garden, kite shop, gallery space, and day spa." Ed whistled when he showed it to me. The new homes were a marvel, tricked out with solar panels, geothermal floors, whirlpools. Saunas, and media rooms. "We'll be at the center of all that," he said. "Not bad for a barley farm, right?"

True, the farmhouse was a steal. Sure, Ed was doing his wealthy client a favor. All that fresh air, meanwhile, was terrific for Bobby. But couldn't we have foreseen the effect our new-old home would have on us? Shouldn't we have known that moving into a farmhouse – no matter how quaintly maintained or historically fetching – surrounded by a dozen newly pointed minimansions was simply a bad idea? That our neighbors, high on the chemical outgas of new-home aroma, would begin to resent the mortality that our farmhouse – cast right in their sight line – stood for? All too soon, we'd feel under siege, all those eye on us, just waiting for the house to be razed.

It was all supposed to be temporary. "Just one year," Ed assured me. After that, his client was going to pay us a reasonable markup to move out, knock the farmhouse over, and build the spa in its place. The plans were on course. And then the Clarence Historical Society got wind of the scheme. Suddenly, the farmhouse was the county's "last emblem of pre-Fordian Agriculture and Animal Matrimonial Heritage." A legal intervention was filed and we weren't stuck, so much as waylaid, in a lawsuit against both Ed's client and Erie County. One year became three. Then Ed started writing. Quit his job. And once our credit tanked, well then we were stranded. So when Ed's tune about the farmhouse changed, I wasn't surprised. His new pitch was persuasive. "We're the cheapest house in an upscale neighborhood," he argued. "Moving?" He waved his hands about. "Why would we want to do that? When we sell we'll make a killing. Move farther out. To exurbs proper." We'd be set, he went on. Two middle-class kids would finally make good.

We wouldn't just nail the American dream to our doormat, he explained. We'd wipe our muddy shoes on it too.

"We'll show them," he said, pointing outside vaguely. At the time, I thought he meant our neighbors. The Historical Society staff. His former client. My mother.

Ed said it more firmly the second time: "We'll show them what's *what.*"

I must have sighed, because he wrapped my up in his arms. "Come on, Janey." He was so warm then. "Let's just see it through."

Ed wasn't just a lawyer. He was a salesman. All good lawyers are.

So I held my tongue. Dressed up our old girl of a home the way a retiree distracts from her sagging chin by plastering her cheeks with rogue. But our neighbors' front lawns were out front lines, and all that staring wore me down. Predawn joggers and postbreakfast strollers. Loose children and lost dogs. Midnight insomniacs and early risers. It wasn't looking itself that troubled me. Even I look in other people's windows. Sometimes intentionally. But our family made a subtle move from curiosity to *entertainment.* We were "them." The hothouse drama at center stage. We didn't belong. And it became more than evident as our neighbors sat on their porches sipping cocktails and nibbling overpriced cheese that they excused their bad behavior because they believed we were conditional. "Visitors" at best. "Interlopers" at worst. We'd be gone soon, they thought. So they lurked and peeped, scrutinized our dull program of getting to work, reprimanding our children, washing dishes, paying bills. How humdrum. Still they watched. Their hot eyes fixed on the backs of our necks.

Of all our neighbors, Regina Hammond seemed the most sincere. Which is to say, she craved sincerity the way a goldfish craves ocean – an idea out of her depth. I try to be kind to myself: How could I have known that she had her eye on Ed from the start? That she'd suck off my husband while I nursed in the next room? That by the time I'd fixed my hair, he'd fixed his fly.

The moral of the story is simple: the nicest neighbor behind your fence is malevolent once they walk through your gate.

Don't let their feet crush your grass. Stir up the brush.

Duck your head. Turn the hasp.

Don't let them see your fear.

On the day Ed disappeared, I was focused exclusively on getting Bobby to the bus on time with a hot meal in his stomach. My movements were economical from long experience. I signed a test, flipped a pancake, made myself a cup of coffee without moving more than two feet from any direction. I even spared a moment to coo to the baby who, sitting hunched like a frog in her playpen, was happily beating a wood spoon on the rail, making the kind of insistent, percussive music only in infant ears can love.

For a mother, I was at peak performance.

How little I once knew.

Bobby kept talking. I washed the dishes. The cat, meanwhile, had curled up at my feet. I had hold of a plate, a pan, a carton of milk. I barely listened as Bobby rambled on about his homework – something about polar bears and mortality rates – when I began to wash the boning knives as he did about salad forks: it was all the same to him.

My husband remains a peasant at heart. I always liked that about him.

I soaped the knife. There was a small stain on the handle that would not come off. As anyone might, I soaped it, rinsed it again. Raising the knife high in the sunlight, I turned it around to get a better look. The light glinted. I saw my face in the blade.

Then the knife wasn't in my hands. And Bobby's cat began to hiss.

What happened at that moment isn't so much a blur as a series of documented snapshots that remain bound together in my memory by virtue of my own disbelief. How, after all, could the knife have slipped from my hand with such force? Such fortuitous aim? Yet this one hadn't just slid from my hand but shot across the room and lodged itself in my son's left thigh. We stared at each other. Bobby was so surprised, he didn't cry out. Mouth agape, he simply stared at me, a wad of half-chewed pancake crammed in his left cheek, as the wound went white before the blood rushed back, welled up, began to drip between us on the floor. It was quiet. The cat stared. The baby watched. Outside, the landscapers put aside their edgers. Even the procession of morning traffic suddenly ceased its inevitable parade by our home. It wasn't until I heard Ed's Royal typewriter ring upstairs, in fact, that we began to move again, slowly, trying to assume the roles we'd once portrayed like the costumes I suddenly perceived they were. That's what I learned that day: a husband can become a monster; a son, a victim; a mother, a killer – in just an instant. That's all it takes for a new label to stick.

We are never quite who we think we are.

"Mom?" Bobby said. He was looking down at the knife hilt-deep in his skin, his leg like a ham hock being prepped for dinner. The knife wobbled tenderly as he panted tiny iridescent gasps. Then with a yank – I tried to stop him – he pulled the blade from his thigh.

Bobby has always been decisive. Just like his father.

"Stop!"

How long did it take me to move? Ten seconds? Twelve? Too long to rush to his side – to comfort him – to grab a batter-slick towel and bind his leg in a poor tourniquet that did little to abate the flow.

"Ed!" I'm sure I screamed. "For Christ's sake, Ed!"

There was no answer, and I had no time to coddle my reclusive husband from the half-light of his lair.

"Let's go," I said. Bobby stared at me blankly. "Your dad will meet us at the hospital."

What else did I say? I can't recall. I know I kept a steady rap going to keep us focused as I moved him from the chair toward the car, then ran back for the baby. "Take my hand, " I'm sure I told him as I pulled him upright. "That's good. Your arm on my waist. Now, all your weight on me." Finally we were hobbling toward the door. "That's just fine. You're doing great. Look how brave you are."

He was observing me with a singleness of attention that I hadn't felt since he was a tiny wrinkled pup curled in the crook of my arm.

"Mom?"

We were joined at the hip as we made our way to the car, but we were now also connected in a more profound fashion, as though the knife that had broken his skin had also penetrated other less permeable barriers – the ones between thoughts, between mother and son, between a child and himself.

"Mom," he was asking, "what happened there? Why did you hurt me, Mom? Did I do something wrong? Mom, why isn't Dad coming with us?"

In her car seat behind him, the baby burped, oblivious to the wreckage of her brother's leg or the pain in my lungs. I could not breathe. I could not answer even one of Bobby's questions.

After that, we never saw Ed again.

Before me, Dr. Kirkbride is rapt. Her hair is blond and looks as crisp as a dried corpse of cuttleweed. The urge to touch it is hard to resist.

It's not unusual for survivors of emotional violence to develop obstructive, often dangerous behaviors that inhibit, or preclude, emotional and physical intimacy, she says, her voice neutral, as she tilts her head. *Such patterns tend to get worse with age.* She pauses. *Were they a nuisance to your marriage?*

She asks the question so politely, I'm nearly disarmed. I fail to realize, for a moment, that she's referring to me, not Ed. But I pinch myself – hard – no doubt adding another bruise to my thighs.

"We had some troubles."

It's the nature of her occupation to mildly gloomy disclosures make her happy. A soothing, birdlike sound warbles in the back of her throat. Then, just as I think it's time to go – as I begin to gather my paper-thin housecoat and rise from my chair – she shoots off a final question, as though it's suddenly occurred to her.

Was Ed a good father?

She's smiling. She knows she's caught me off guard. Just as she intended.

"Of course. Ed loved his children."

My tone isn't defensive. But my qualifier undermines all my hard work. Every "I'm sure," "no doubt," and "of course," she's told me, augments uncertainty rather than diminishing it. The more convinced I seem, in short, the more skeptical she becomes. And she doesn't hide it.

On her wall, beneath her diplomas, Cheryl has hung a print of the Richardson Complex when it first opened: when its sandstone walls were surrounded by endless lawns and gardens and its tall windows weren't covered with grime.

When all the patients were bathed in light.

"What did they call your work back then?" I ask. "A moral treatment plan?"

Cheryl can't help looking pleased.

You know about my grandfather?

I shrug. During our mandated "library encounter time," I had skimmed a book about the building's design, and the first Dr. Kirkbride's – her grandfather's – revolutionary patient care "strategy."

"Do you think it works?"

She considers my question carefully. *Do you?*

I sigh. She is single-minded. "I did not kill Ed."

We stare at each other, like parents fighting when their children aren't far enough out of earshot. Dr. Kirkbride can project an uncanny silence when she chooses. I can't even hear her breathe.

As for me, the stress makes my eczema flare – my elbows start to itch, then the back of my neck. Even the inflames patch on my left hip.

She watched me squirm. A look, like sadness, in her eyes. There's no getting through to her.

Then our time is up, the session breaks. Out in the hall once again, an orderly at my side, I give in. By the time we negotiate our way down the curved hallway back to the female ward, my fingernails are wet with shredded skin and blood.

The orderly doesn't say a word. He just hands me a bandage. Then he's gone down the hall, the rubber soles of his orthopedic shoes squeaking softly on the old tiles. The sound is intolerable. It is comforting.

I am torn in so many ways.

Occasionally Regina calls on me. She waits in the visitors' center, legs neatly crossed at her ankles.

A year hasn't changed her. Two years haven't changed her.

I want to reach out and slap her face.

Dr. Kirkbride has encouraged these meetings. She's advised me to meet with my former neighbors, to *reconcile* (as she put it) *your memories. If not your stories.*

Regina is the person who called the police when Ed went missing, two weeks after Bobby's trip to the ER. Evidently, she expected Ed to check in each night. Me? I expected him to be writing his book.

"Regina," I said, as I opened the farmhouse door that day. Then, as the officers strolled up behind her: "You've brought friends."

Of course they weren't my friends. Regina wasn't my friend. Yet they allowed her to take Bobby to play in her yard while they asked me their questions. Regina has no shame.

"Someone has to look for Ed," she said as she turned to go. "You should have called the police days ago." She looked around, took in the curtains drawn over the windows. Then she was gone. And I was left with two officers in their sturdy square shoes weighing down my farmhouse floor.

"She's fucking my husband," I said, when they asked where Ed was, why he hadn't been heard from for days. When they said nothing, didn't register even a hint of surprise, I foolishly offered the truth.

"He's disappeared," I told them. "One day Ed was here, the next day he wasn't." I've repeated the same story ever since.

The officers asked other questions. Bobby's injury came up. I did my best to explain how the knife slipped. They nodded, took notes, then politely asked to look in Ed's office.

The light was shining in the east window as I opened the door to his study. Ed's typewriter sat idle on his desk, papers stacked in a neat pile beside it. A lone sharpened pencil lay on the blotter. His chair was tucked in. there were vacuum marks on the carpet.

Clearly, Ed hadn't been there all day.

The officers stared at the desk, taking it all in, before turning back to me. That's when their gaze drifted from me to the door itself, to the busted, scratched doorknob. Someone had obviously removed the knob, then reattached it.

Someone had broken in from the hall.

Shortly after, I was escorted away.

Now, when I see Regina across the laminate lunch table, I ask why she's come. Under the fluorescent lights in the visitors' center, even her delicate skin looks cantankerous. Yellow.

She feels a responsibility for me, she says. For what she did to my life. "To your children's lives." She pauses. "To Ed's" She always says the same thing. "It's the least I can do."

Finally: "Jane, I'm truly sorry."

My enemy is my last friend.

In this place I have no dreams. I thank Ed for that. Sometimes Cheryl. But mostly my friends Lithium, Lunesta, and Seroquel. After supper I dress for bed, except my Dixie cup dosage when the nurse stops in for bed check #1. I have one hour before she returns, one hour to write down my thoughts before the meds kick in. Right on schedule, she returns for bed check #2 and dims the lights. By then, I'm beginning to drift into the shadows, my mind closing down like a city shop door at dusk, eyelids growling for the floorboards. After that there's no going back. Eight hours later the lights creep back up, and so do I. There's no night anymore. The stars fail to align. I can't remember bed checks #3, 4, and 5. The nurses sidling in with their stale breath and rubber-soled shoes.

There are signs. My bathrobe has shifted on its chair. A small plant on the sill has been turned toward the light. The vent cover is awry on its half-stripped screws. I am not the first to hide keepsakes behind it: a ChapStick, a wad of soft tissues, a small red leaf carried in on Dr. Kirkbride's shoe.

The nurses keep track of our secrets. It is part of our therapy. We should have what they call "reasonable" secrets.

But we should not have dreams. Dreams lead to unreasonable secrets. Dr. Kirkbride doesn't need to tell me that.

If I can't dream at night, I will dream in the day. A dream that is common, simple, even true. A dream of everyday life. A dream at a window over cracked concrete. The staff's collection of rusty, dinged cars. Beyond, a scruff of young trees.

A dream of supermarkets and shoe stores. Banana peppers and crabgrass plots. Of post office clerks. Dental hygienists. Cavernous, slush-filled potholes cratering lost strip-mall parking lots. The places I once spent my time, trafficking clamshelled toys and canisters of apple juice. With the kids. Their noses in an unruly state of secretion. Demanding this toy. This treat. This ride.

This. Now. Please.

Where was Ed? Nowhere to be seen. My daydream accounts of this too.

The treeless plateau outside a big-box store was heaven then. The smell of tar rising from the pavement in summer. Hot gum on the soles of my sneakers. A squeaky, broken-wheeled cart. Bobby used to ride on the back. Handing on by one finger, hair in his eyes, he was a shoelaced peril, while the baby hiccupped and squirmed in her seat as I pushed. Her eyes on me. Always on me. Making sure I was there.

Back at the car, I strap them in. check all the latched and belts.

"Here," I tell Bobby. "This is for you. Because you are my first, my good boy. Because you are fierce, and my joy."

He rolls his eyes. Then takes the package from his hands.

In a moment, the plastic is in his teeth. He rips and tugs – his canines have evolved for this – and eventually peels from the transparent shell a remote-controlled plane. A car that talks. A BB gun. A bow and arrow. A puppy. A personal robot. A bounce house. A battery powered car. A rocket booster. A ray gun. My bright shining love.

The baby, meanwhile, chews on the ear of her new super-soft bunny.

Behind us, all the cars are gone. And so are the people. It's just the kids and me and a shopping cart with four new wheels on the perfectly repaved parking lot.

"Bobby," I say, looking at the cart, unbuckling him as though we've just arrived.

I don't need to say more. He's already by me, already sailing. Pumping his lean, strong legs, running and screeching and hopping on the front of the car as it flies, his T-shirt aloft. The strip mall, our island, in the vast dark sea around us.

A sound in the hall pulls me back to Ward E. Pulls me away from these children who no longer exist. They are older now, no longer know me.

They no longer want to know me.

Children never remember their parents' care. Our delicate footfalls. The stacks of warm washcloths. All the cool heads on fevered brows. It takes just a few years.

My children no longer remember my love.

Outside my window, a mown lawn. Trees. City houses. The lake.

On clear days, I can see all the way to Toronto. On days like today, when the sky falls and meets the gray water, I see only myself in the glass. Backlit. A smoky afternoon.

The clouds rolling up my eyes.

The halls are empty now. Many rooms are empty now. But I am here, still, roaming Ward E. A few like me remain because we cannot leave. We no longer have the will to leave. Desire takes too much energy.

I watch the construction begin. How the men shout. Repointing the sandstone. Resealing the floors. In the foyer, the table saws whine.

Ed is still with me. He won't leave me alone.

A marriage is always complete.

Christina Milletti's fiction has appeared in several journals and anthologies, such as *The Alaska Review*, *The Chicago Review*, and *The Greensboro Review*, as well as Harcourt's *Best New American Voices*, and Scribner's *Best of the Fiction Workshops*. Recently, novelist Paul West devoted a chapter to her fiction in his book *Master Class*. She's written a collection of short stories, *The Religious*, and is currently writing a novel, *Room in the Hotel America*. Her dissertation, "Innovative Ends: Gender and the Poetics of Transformation in Women's Experimental Fiction," examines the intersections of gender, performance, and speech act theory in the work of twentieth century women writers. Her teaching interests include: creative writing (fiction), theories of writing, hypertext and digital studies, twentieth century fiction, women's literature, feminist theory, and the history of the novel. She is the founder of and a Contributing Editor to BathHouse magazine, an on-line journal of cross-genre and interdisciplinary writing, as well as a former editor of The Little Magazine. She also teaches creative writing at the University at Buffalo in New York.

Amazonia: T. Jefferson Parker

First published in *The Strand Magazine,* July/Oct., 2015

My name is Austin Fodder and I am twenty-four years old. It seems like a lifetime ago when, fresh out of the University of California, Irvine, I applied for a job at Authentic Adventures Travel, which was located just a few miles from the campus. I had never seen myself as part of the hospitality industry. But the online job description for the travel agent trainee called for a four-year degree, computer and writing skills, and an "adventurous spirit." With dual majors in computer science and comparative literature, and a three-day cruise to my credit (Long Beach to Ensenada), I walked into AAT late that afternoon for an interview, my head held moderately high, believing I could do the job.

The agency was on the fifth floor of a mirrored tower in Newport Center. The elevator was swift and silent; the floor of the AAT lobby was red marble; the receptionist told me to have a seat. I did, and read through *Authentic Adventures*, a glossy magazine featuring new, classic, and future destinations. There were lots of pictures: placid-looking lagoons, jagged mountains, dense jungles abruptly ending at beaches on which colorful tribesmen stood. And quotes from happy travelers. According to my online research, AAT sent clients to properties all over the globe. None of the places were familiar. Many had names with exotic apostrophes, such as '*Atlotl-Ton or B'att* and all like that. The AAT slogan, which appeared on the cover under the title was: *RealWon'tWait*.

I was collected in the lobby by a very tall young woman who introduced herself as Ivy Slattery. We walked down a long hallway and she slowed her stride to match my average-length legs. She held a black tablet to her chest with both hands, reminding me of Jamie Frost in eighth grade, who held her backpack to her chest in the same way, in order to – I think, but will never know – hide her breasts. The hallway walls were hung with dramatically enlarged photographs similar to those in the magazine, with quotes from AAT clients superimposed on them. There were also oversized images of the satisfied travelers' faces. Everything was upscale and costly. Ivy's heels on the marble made an authoritative sound. I wanted the job.

"Don't let my father intimidate you," said Ivy. "And don't try to tell him anything but the truth. He's got a very keen ear for bullshit."

Ivan Slattery was a large man with long gray-black hair pulled back into a ponytail. His black suit hung shinily on his big frame. He had a wide nose with large pores visible even across the desk, and black, close-set eyes. He didn't look like he could be Ivy Slattery's father.

He confirmed that I had a current passport and was at least competent with a camera – not a phone camera, he insisted, but a real one with a decent zoom and fully waterproof. I felt as if opportunity's door had been opened because I did have a current passport (used once, on the Long-Beach-to-Ensenada cruise) and owned a waterproof camera (still in the box, grad gift from Mom and Dad, with note that encouraged me to "see this beautiful world"). When I told him I was competent with it, his back eyes bore into my face and I remembered what his daughter had told me about trying to fool him.

"We have a fam trip set for a very promising new destination," he said. Ivan Slattery had a rough, vast voice, almost a growl. "My last available agent has contracted some mystery ailment. Again. I can't do the fam trip myself. It's going to have to be you, Houston."

"It's Austin, sir. What is a fam trip?"

"A *familiarization trip*. It's them trying to impress us. If they do, we'll sell the destination. If they don't, we won't. Either way, you take the trip, see the heights, hear the pitch. They'll take good care of you, believe me. Be as demanding as you want. Act impressed but not overly. Your job is to document it all for me – and I mean thoroughly – and report back. Simple." He leaned back, folded his hands over his stomach, and smiled cagily. "I have a good feeling about this place. In fact, I have already instilled early interest in some of our more adventurous clients. That is how my business works. I'm always two steps ahead of the game."

"Great. What's it called?"

"Playa Amazonia."

"Very cool. What country is it in?"

Ivan tapped something on his tablet then raised a thick finger and stabbed one more key. "You figure it out. I just sent you all the information. You leave LAX tomorrow at six a.m. Don't forget the passport, and pack according to the instructions. Get a good night's sleep, Houston. I'm counting on you."

Ivy rode down in the elevator with me. It was just us. She held the tablet to her chest and smiled at me not only as if I'd accomplished something important, but as if she'd known I would. I looked up at her. She had a slender face, eager blue eyes, and her hair was honey-blond. "I'm very happy for you," she said. "And very proud." She hooked a falling wave of hair behind her ear, then offered that hand for me to shake. It was cool and small-boned and thrilling. My heart swelled with the spirit of adventure.

I arrived at the Playa Amazonia airstrip late the next night. A driver in a white van met me off the plane at the end of this (my third!) flight. There had been are-outing and long delays. My phone had failed hours earlier and the van driver spoke no English, so I knew neither the local time nor my specific location. I looked at the sky but the night was starless. The airstrip lights were smothered in mist, and the air was warm and humid and smelled of ocean. Tired, I loaded my heavy suitcase into the van while the driver sat smoking sullenly. Despite my fatigue—and with reluctance to admit it, since I myself have never been regarded as "easy on the eyes"—I couldn't help but notice that the man was unapologetically ugly. The last leg of the journey was a long ride on a white sand road so narrow that we would have had to pull over to let an oncoming vehicle pass. This did not happen. The headlights skittered across the dense greenery, but everything else was dark.

I woke in my room at the Playa Amazonia Hotel at 9:38 in the morning. The room was bight and clean, ground floor, with white walls and a salmon-colored tile floor and dark wood window frames and shutters. A small lizard stuck to the ceiling cocked his head and looked down at me. There was a vase of daisies on the table by the window and small native paintings of huts and beaches and jungle birds. Standing in a tall woven basket near the door were two umbrellas made of what looked to be local materials: handles of cane and canopies of thick braided palm fronds. I opened and closed one of them—smooth and well built.

I took pictures with the camera Mom and Dad had given me. I was happy to see the room service menu printed in both English and a language I didn't recognize, though the prices were high. Still dazed by some twenty-plus hours of travel and only a few hours' sleep, I did remember that my appointment with Mr. Troels was at two in the afternoon in the Playa Amazonia central square. My phone was still not working, even after charging while I slept. I stood on my porch and looked out at the unpeopled patio and pool, then to the wall of jungle rising beyond. Birds cawed and trilled from within, and small animals, perhaps monkeys, appeared briefly then vanished.

It was hot. I took more pictures, remembering Ivan Slattery's insistence on thorough documentation, and remembering Ivy's cool hand against mine.

I seated myself for lunch in the hotel café. Two local-looking men sat in a far corner, huddled up to a small table and talking intently. Again, I'm not one to throw stones, but I should note that both men were vastly overweight. My waiter was older and dark-skinned with short, straight gray hair.

"Coffee please," I said.

"Yes."

"Sir, what country are we in?"

"No."

Having been a waiter in a Mexican restaurant during my college years, I spoke just enough Spanish to confuse Spanish-speaking people. But it's the only other language I knew any of at all. *"En que pais estamos nosotros?"*

The waiter looked at me, puzzled.

"Estamos en Brazil o Columbia? O Peru?"

"No." He shrugged and left. Frustrated, I strode over to the two-top where the menu sat. They acknowledged me only after I'd stood there for a beat and I had the feeling they'd been discussing me.

"Good morning, gentlemen." They looked at each other, then back at me, with mild offense on their faces. "My name is Austin Fodder. Can you tell me, *please,* in what country is Playa Amazonia? *En que pais estamos nosotros?"*

"No."

"No."

One of them opened his hands in a sign of helplessness, his eyebrows rising. I noted that the men had thatch-topped umbrellas, which leaned in the corner behind them. They were smaller than the ones in my room, frayed with use. Back at my table, I wondered at the sudden rains that must fall here if the locals carried these rustic umbrellas even on such sunny days as this.

After a meal of grilled fish, brown rice, and toasted white bread, I walked into town. A few cars passed, all older though apparently well cared for, as you might find in Cuba. Playa Amazonia was set on a hillside behind a long sand beach. The town was small, but still larger than I'd imagined. Palm trees swayed over fragile-looking wooden buildings and the sidewalks rose and dipped with the sudden elevations and declines.

There were people out and about, mostly women but some men, too, all dressed in the older, more-formal fashions of poor but proud countries. Most were brown-skinned and dark-haired, but I saw fair blonds also. And all of them, young and old, moved briskly, as if in a hurry—heads up, alert, and often glancing toward the Playa Amazonia beach. I saw that nearly everyone carried a thatch-domed umbrella.

The only people not carrying them appeared to be the few tourists, such as myself. I looked up at the cloudless blue sky and wondered again at the swift storms that must hit Playa Amazonia virtually without warning. I also noticed that the signs here in town—there were only a few—

were all written in the same difficult language as the room-service menu back in my room. I stood outside a small market trying to make sense of the handwritten prices tackled over bins of produce: *Xysccl*—1.355 and *Lmj'ak*—2.116. Just outside the market's front door was a tall basket of native umbrellas: *Y'ap*—14.457.

The central square lay between the town and the beach. It was little more than dirt with benches around the perimeter and a stand of skimpy palm trees in the middle. It seemed to need a church or temple or something meaningful to complete it. There were trash cans and a water fountain and a few people hurrying through, each carrying a *y'ap*, but no one pausing or even slowing down. Again, I saw mostly women. Also some older men and boys. But the young-to-middle-aged men I saw were very few. And they were conspicuously challenged in obvious ways—some filthy, other obese or malnourished, others deformed or seemingly insane. But even these less fortunate souls were in some kind of purposeful hurry. I wondered if this country (whatever it was!) might be grindingly poor. It was possible that Playa Amazonia was the coastal capital of some destitute and forlorn country, and that these fast-moving people were the national equivalent of Manhattanites.

Mr. Troels was a short, slender man who appeared in the central square about the same time I did. He transferred his *y'ap* and we shook hands. His accent was heavy but his English was good. "I hope that your flights and accommodations were excellent."

"Flights bad, room good."

He smiled. Mr. Troels had a scruffy, thin beard and dark-brown hair that needed a trim. His accent sounded Dutch. "Come."

He led me down a street to a two-story wooden building and held open the door. The aroma engulfed me: a bakery. It was hot and powerfully fragrant and the racks of baked goods were picked over pretty well by then. Stout, flour-dusted women glanced at us. Mr. Troels waved me up the stairs and I followed him, the women watching me as I climbed.

His office was sparsely furnished and looked as if he was moving either in or out. On the desk between us sat a vintage landline telephone, black, with at tightly spiraled cord. There was also an older desktop computer, the kind with the bulbous monitor, white with ground-in dirt. Through the windows I could see the beach and the glittering silver ocean beyond.

"Mr. Troels, please keep me from feeling like a moron, but what country am I in?"

"Playa Amazonia, of course."

"I thought it was a town, a destination."

"Yes. Playa Amazonia is also the name of the capital. The nation itself has been a self-governing social democracy since 1894—the smallest on the continent. Once a Dutch colony. The language is a native one."

"Then we're in South America?"

He smiled and lit a cigarette. "Well, Mr. Fodder, where else *could* we be?"

I'm sure I blushed badly (lifetime curse). The thought crossed my mind that if Ivan Slattery could see me right now he'd fire me on the spot. And that Ivy's pride in me would vanish. I was their representative here. I took a deep breath and reminded myself of my dual degrees from the University of California, my "A" in Critical Theory 100, and my Long Beach-to Ensenada cruise, on which I'd helped to break up a casino fight and later won close to $200 (in ship credits) at blackjack. "Well," I forced a chuckle. "That's exactly what I'd *figured,* Mr. Troels, but I couldn't get one person to confirm it for me."

"The language, yes—impossible."

"Please impress me, Mr. Troels. Why should Authentic Adventures care about a country that takes twenty-odd hours to get to, has an unhelpful populace, and where—apparently—it rains so suddenly and heavily the locals carry wooden umbrellas even on the sunniest days?"

"Ah, good questions. For starters, we have the most beautiful beach on Earth. You will be more than impressed by it. The diving is without compare, the fishing superb—both deep sea and inshore. At exactly three o'clock each afternoon, the wind arises from the west and it blows very hard. As a result, this is the new kite-sailing capital of the world. Kite sailing, as you *probably* know, is the fastest-growing sport not only in America but in the world. Oh, Mr. Fodder, the hiking, gliding, birding, bungee-jumping, kayaking, and river running? Utterly superior to what your adventures have ever experienced! I have devised a slogan for Playa Amazonia: *The Best is Always Found Last.* Do you like it? By the time you leave here in five days, you will have had a taste of all these things. Just a taste." He put his fingers to his lips in a

French way (judging from movies). "In addition, our little capital of Playa Amazonia is in reality a very friendly place, once you settle into the native rhythms."

I tried to imagine what Ivan might say based on the half hour I had spent with him. "Facilities? I haven't seen one dive shop, or kite-sailing school, or fishing charter, or even a restaurant or bar with customers in it. A total of one hotel."

"What did you expect?"

"A destination!"

Mr. Troels sighed and slumped and finally spread his hands in the same helpless way that the man at the café had done an hour ago.

"I was very clear with Mr. Slattery that we are developing."

"Then I'm sure he told you that Authentic Adventures can't sell *developing*. That would be like a restaurant trying to sell only recipes."

Mr. Troels looked into the space above my head. "This has been a terrible misunderstanding. I was most very clear."

"Things don't always translate."

A very long silence followed. Then, "So long as you are here, you still must see the natural resources and beauties of Playa Amazonia."

I considered by wasn't really sure what to do. I *was* here. Maybe I should at least document the great potential that Mr. Troels saw in this place. The decision was Mr. Slattery's, not mine. "May I use your phone to call Mr. Slattery? My smartphone is useless."

"The desk phone doesn't work. It's a ... decoration."

"Then I will go home early."

He sat back, diminished. He cleared his throat quietly. "Perhaps since you are here you would at least see our beautiful and someday famous beach."

I felt badly for him, but more badly for myself and my failed mission. "I'll go see the beach while you find a way to make my travel arrangements. Please, this language is insurmountable for me."

"Take this *y'ap*. I bought it especially to welcome you to Playa Amazonia." He brought the thatch umbrella from the floor beside his desk, stood, and presented it to me with a sad sigh. It was larger than the one in my hotel room, and surprisingly heavy.

I walked the streets to the main boulevard leading down to the beach. The thoughtful gift umbrella was in my hand by my heart was heavy with the whole unnecessary mess. "*I have a good feeling about this place,*" I van had said. I took some pictures, as if this justified something. The boulevard was wide and covered in pavers and closed to cars. Pedestrians kept left and right like vehicles, most of them with *y'aps* (at least I felt more like a local now), heads up, looking often toward the beach where I was going.

The boulevard was long but as I finally came closer to the beach I saw that it was tawny sand, the color of a lion. From here, the beach stretched as far as I could see. There were dramatic outcroppings of dark rock along the shore, spires and arches and plateaus sculpted by centuries of wind and water. Beyond, the ocean was turquoise-blue and flat as a mirror. Above it sat puffy white clouds with flat bottoms, reminding me of the last few pastries in the bakery racks. I stepped out of my lane and stopped to macro-behold Playa Amazonia. Mr. Troels had been right: it really was the most beautiful beach I'd ever seen. I had seen Laguna Beach. And La Jolla Cove. And Pebble Beach. And the Mendocino Headlands. But this beach, even at a distance, had their world-famous features—all in one! I decided right then that I should stick to my original plan, stay the five nights, and see if any other of Mr. Troels' claims about Playa Amazonia, even if they were future-specific, might potentially be true.

Then the oncoming pedestrians were no longer just walking along, but running.

They broke rank, rushing past me on both sides, fumbling with their thatch umbrellas. Many of them were looking behind them, back at the beach. I dodged them and climbed onto a sidewalk bench for a better view of whatever had spooked them. From there I saw what looked like canoes landing on the beach, an entire flotilla of them! Fifty? A hundred? Figures sprang from the beaching craft, several per boat. Up the tan beach the charged, brandishing long slender spears. Even from here these people looked large. IT looked like an invasion of warriors of some kind. I felt paralyzed, not with fear but with fascination. The first wave of invaders was already halfway up the beach to the boulevard. The flood of Playa Amazonians continued past me toward town.

What followed happened faster than I could understand. First a flock of birds darkened the sky between the invaders and me. The frightened people of Playa Amazonia stopped and looked up toward the birds. In they sailed, slender and speedy. They dove gracefully in unison, hurtling with dizzying pace. The men and women and children all raised their *y'aps* toward the birds and huddled under their heavy thatch canopies. The birds whistled down, louder and louder. I scrambled off the bench and raised my *y'ap*, fell to my knees, and scrunched under it. Through a crack in the umbrella fronds I could see the skinny suicidal birds hitting everywhere at once, fast and close together, like raindrops in a thunderstorm—smacking into boulevard and sidewalks and against the thatch domes under which the people of Playa Amazonia and I had tucked ourselves. And I saw that these birds were not birds at all, but arrows. I held my camera up, just above the protective canopy of my *y'ap*, and used the motor drive option.

When the first storm of arrows had passed everyone stood up and ran for town again. You can bet that I did, too. We had made it maybe a hundred yards when a second wave of arrows began their deadly descent upon us. Again we fell to the ground and brought our knees to our chests and hunched our shoulders and brandished the *y'aps* at the arrows. I shot more pictures, randomly, camera held above the umbrella like a periscope. An arrow cracked into the thatch and I felt its power. This second deluge of arrows lasted longer than the first. Then, suddenly, like fish in a school darting together as one, we were up and running. We had only gone maybe fifty yards before we fell and covered up again. I could hear the archers' footsteps on the boulevard behind us. I was astonished to hear someone laugh.

The warriors were among us. I lay curled and trembling behind my *y'ap*, peering out through one of the small square openings in the thatch at the carnage likely to come. I thought of my mother and father, and my younger sister, Mary Ann, all back home in the greatest country in the world, in California no less. I told them I loved them. It was hard to get perspective through such a small aperture, or to see more than the condensed, hyper-zoomed images you might see in a badly filmed battle scene. But this is what I saw through the tiny square that jumped and shifted with every rapid beat of my heart: large bronze women; brief leather dresses; smoothly muscled legs and arms; hair pulled up high, spilling over like fountains; handsome faces elaborately and colorfully painted; wild eyes shining through; high cheekbones and straight teeth; knives and bows; scabbards on belts and quivers over shoulders; bare feet.

Suddenly a dark shin blotted out everything else, my *y'ap* was wrenched away, and I was left fatally positioned and looking up at my own certain death. From my lower elevation she seemed gigantic, a towering she-form glaring down at me. She held the knife—handmade flint, I saw—in her right hand. Her bow was slung over her left shoulder. Her eyes were dark and her expression, even through the vivid facial paint, was singular and unmistakable: she was looking for something. Her fountain of dark straight hair spilled forward as she looked down at me. Similar interviews seemed to be taking place all around but I was too afraid to take my eyes off her for fear she would run me through or slash my throat. She stared at me for long moment. I wanted nothing more than to understand what she wanted, and to give it to her. Then she crouched and offered me her free hand, which I took, and she helped me to my feet. My legs quaked and my knees quivered. To maintain eye contact I had to look up. I guessed her to be six-foot-three. In one of those daft inspirations that often overtake people under great stress, I said, "I'm Austin."

She set her hand on my shoulder and turned me around. I feared that knife. I had often read about terrified people losing control of their bowels and/or bladders but I did not. She had a smell that was musky but not offensive, like a patch of wild gourds. She continued turning me. When I came back face-to-face I saw that she had a questioning, analytical expression. As if she were measuring me. Or maybe trying to read my mind. Searching. She stepped back and made a circling motion with her knife and I turned around again on my own power, then, at her order, once again. When I came back to face her she grunted softly and a pained look crossed her bright, meticulously painted face. She put her knife-hand on my shoulder and eased me back to the ground. Then she trotted up-boulevard, toward town, through whole and broken arrows, where she joined her fellow warriors rousting Playa Amazonians, some of whom were standing and waiting for the procedure, while others still lay hunched behind their y'aps, bodies drawn up tight. I crawled under the sidewalk bench, pulled my umbrella closer to cover myself, and waited.

But not for long. A few minutes later the warrior women came flooding back down the boulevard toward the beach. They were trotting along, their bows over their shoulders, talking, laughing, making provocative gestures and sounds. Two of them clutched a young man by both his arms and he seemed to be struggling but not very hard. He appeared to be a tourist, like me. But unlike me he was a strong and very good-looking fellow. He looked alarmed but resigned as they rushed him past me toward their canoes on the beach.

I found Mr. Troels still hiding under his desk in his office. I dragged him up by his shirt, pulling so hard it ripped at the shoulder seam.

"You knew this could happen!"

"Don't be an ass, Mr. Fodder. How could I not?"

"They kidnapped a tourist!"

"Tourists are all they have left. They have already taken all the good young men from town. As I'm sure you noticed."

It struck me that I'd been passed over by the Amazons, found somehow lacking. I remembered the hard inspection that she gave me. Whatever that magnificent warrior woman was looking for, she did not find in me.

"Why?" I asked. "What will they do to him?"

"Whatever they want, I suppose. We assume they populate their nation in this way. And perhaps provide nutrition. We don't really know much about how they live. No man has ever returned."

"How often do they come?"

"The average is once every eighteen days."

"Amazons."

"Correct."

"Who you thought would be a good Authentic Adventures attraction?"

"No, no, Mr. Fodder. The Amazons are no more than local colors—ask anyone! Just nuisances, like feral cats or bears of the campground. It was always our beautiful beach that I believed in most. What did you think of it?"

I let go of him and went to the window and looked out. The canoes were disappearing into the flat silver horizon. The town seemed to be back to normal, except for the hundreds of arrows bristling from the sides and roofs of the buildings. I saw no blood and no injuries. Little groups of townspeople, most still holding their *y'aps*, had gathered on the street corners, looking back toward the beach and pointing, apparently recapping the events. A band of little boys raced through the streets, pulling arrows out of doors and walls, laughing, clutching thick handfuls of the stone-tipped weapons.

Turning back, I glared at Mr. Troels with a fury that was new to me. "*Get me out of here, Troels.*"

By the time I reached Caracas my phone was working. I used the layover to send photos and an email to Ivan. It seemed prudent to promptly share the horrors of Playa Amazonia on all my social networks—in case anyone on Earth might be considering a trip there—so I posted the better pictures and a detailed version of what had happened. It was as good and honest a description as I could write. I felt that it as Conradian. Without the pictures, my postings would have been unbelievable if not absurd, but Mom and Dad's camera had served me well. I thought how much Ivan would appreciate me saving his butt on Playa Amazonia. I imagined Ivy's beautiful face smiling down at me in gratitude for exposing the fraudulent Mr. Troels and surviving this ordeal. They would probably ask me to dinner in an expensive Newport Beach restaurant, where I could admire Ivy and hear about my next fam trip.

It took me twelve hours and two flights to get to LAX. I got into the very long US Customs line for citizens and checked my phone. The two texts from Ivan Slattery were brief and had been sent two hours apart.

One: *WHO TOLD YOU TO POST THAT SHIT, YOU WRETCHED SQUIRREL?*

Two: *IT'S VIRAL! GET TO AAT HQ IMMEDIATELY UPON RETURN. NO EXCUSES!*

I was too tired and wrung out to care. I said goodbye to the idea of a nice dinner with Ivan and Ivy, but really, I wasn't convinced it would really happen, then or ever. Strangely enough, I kept thinking about my rejection by the Amazon. What did she want that I didn't have?

Three long hours later, I walked into the Authentic Adventures lobby and the formerly neutral receptionist lit up with a huge smile. Ivy Slattery came bursting through the door with her arms out, Ivan was behind her, a hairy, dark blemish waddling across the red marble toward me. Ivy smothered me with hugs and cheek-kisses and all like that; Ivan threw his big arms around me and squeezed half my breath out.

"The bookings!" he yelled. "The bookings! The bookings!"

"They're coming in from men all over the *world*, Austin," said Ivy, with a very proud expression. It was the same expression she'd had after I'd impressed her father enough to get the job. "Thanks to you, we've got the Hotel Playa Amazonia booked for nearly six straight months. Solid!"

I felt my mouth actually hanging open. "But...what about the arrows? The Amazons?"

"You crack me up," said Ivan. "To visit a beautiful beach, be spared from murder, and then be kidnapped by tall women warriors? For God knows what purpose? Few men can resist! Mostly older gentlemen are booking, but that's fine—they can afford it. Now come in here, Houston. Ivy will show you how to book trips and get rich. When we're too tired to print any more money tonight, it's dinner at Villa Nova. On me!"

My rise through the ranks of AAT was swift. My computer science education helped with the everyday technology that often befuddled Ivan and even Ivy. And my degree in comparative literature helped, too: I took over the copy writing, from ads to catalogues to longer, more literary pieces that went out to men's magazines and directly to our more adventurous (prosperous) clients. After three months of AAT tourists going to and from Playa Amazonia, the only complaint we heard was: many called but few chosen. The Amazons turned out to be very discriminating about their men, which, weirdly—or perhaps predictably—made more and more men want to go. I'll admit that most of our clients were not particularly desirable, in the classic sense. On the coattails of our success in Playa Amazonia, most of our other destinations boomed too.

Of course the State Department got involved, what with the danger that we were sending citizens into. But our disclosure of risk were truthful, our contracts protected AAT from any responsibility for death or injury, and our lawyers were top-notch. After the men's outdoor magazine honeymoon (Playa Amazonia made two covers), the liberal media went after us, briefly, but we had no injuries other than turned ankles, dehydration, and minor arrow wounds. (We required our guests to carry *y'aps* at all times. Mr. Troels arranged to have "AAT" woven into the canopies with black-and-gold painted thatch). Of course the more people we sent to Playa Amazonia, the more "friendly" the media became. Our most satisfied customers—the rare few to be "chosen"—had not one bad thing to say about the destination at all, as no one ever saw them again. A class action suit was filed by men who had traveled to Playa Amazonia—some as many as four times—and been passed over by the Amazons without even a second look. I knew how they felt. A judge threw it out.

But like most overnight, blazing success stories, Playa Amazonia finally began to burn out. It was simple: the women had apparently gotten enough of what they wanted and stopped taking prisoners. Sensing the end, we at AAT raised our trip rates into the stratosphere, but the extravagant cost soon filled our junkets with rich techweenies (like me, but with billions), venal Wall Streeters, and other highly successful types who were really, sadly, not Amazon material. So the women stopped raiding altogether. You could hardly blame them.

Ivy and I were married at the height of the AAT bubble. Shortly after the wedding, Ivan foresaw the bust and sold the company for $28 million to a young, seriously buff hedge fund manager who had been passed over by the Amazons five times. I understood his need to somehow be accepted by these women, and wasn't surprised that after his cash buy-out, he spent an entire three months at Playa Amazonia—I mean right down there on the sane where the canoes might come up—living in a quickly constructed cinderblock "mansion," oiling up and lifting free weights on the beach every day, making deals on his satellite phone, hoping for the Amazons to come.

I felt for him. But I got mine.

T. Jefferson Parker was born in Los Angeles and has lived all his life in Southern California. His writing career began in 1978, with a job as a cub reporter on the weekly newspaper, *The Newport Ensign*. From there Parker moved on to the *Daily*

Pilot, where he won three Orange County Press Club awards. His first novel, *Laguna Heat*, was written on evenings and weekends while he worked as a reporter, and was published to rave reviews and made into an HBO movie starring Harry Hamlin, Jason Robards, and Rip Torn. His following novels were published to rave reviews and appeared on many bestseller lists, with two, *Silent Joe* and *California Girl*, each winning the Mystery Writers of America's Edgar Award for Best Mystery Novel. In 2008, "Skinhead" Central won Parker his third Edgar, this time for best short story. His last six crime novels—*L.A. Outlaws*, *The Renegades*, *Iron River*, *The Border Lords*, *The Jaguar*, and *The Famous and the Dead*—all feature Los Angeles County Sheriff's Deputy Charlie Hood, and deal with dangers along the U.S./Mexico border. Lionsgate has bought the rights to bring Charlie Hood to the big screen. His most recent novel is *Crazy Blood*, a novel set against the dangerous, competitive world of downhill skiing.

Play the Man: Dan Duval

First published in *Fiction River: Risk Takers*

Brenda, being six months pregnant, thought she looked hideous, huge and bloated, though I never thought so. However, being tied to a dining room chair with a ball gag strapped to her face did not help any.

Not that I looked much better, tied to another chair, without the gag.

We faced each other, in our own dining room, with only a corner of the dining table between us. I wished I could say something that would make her feel better, to slow the tears that trickled down her cheeks.

The only comfort I could give her came through my eyes. I tried to project calmness and patience. I couldn't think of anything else and there was nothing else I could do at the moment.

I didn't look at the chubby man that stood behind Brenda. His t-shirt did not quite make the turn around his belly to meet the top of the shorts that stopped at his knees. His socks weren't high enough to cover the tattoos on his legs: those were enough to identify him by themselves, so the ski mask over his head did little more than make him sweat.

The man behind me also wore a mask, but his dark pants, long-sleeved shirt and leather gloves did not leave any skin exposed at all. Brenda glanced at him once in a while.

The real problem in the room, though, sat on the other side of Brenda, opposite me at the table.

This third man did not wear a mask and I knew that he had no intention of leaving Brenda and I alive to testify against him. But then, a mask would not have disguised him from me, not with his high-pitched, whiny voice. I had heard it enough at one tournament table or another, while he used insults and just plain obnoxious chatter to try to tilt the other players.

Jason Blick was his name and poker was not his game. Oh, he often finished in the money but seldom at the final table. He barely knew how to play his cards and little more about playing the players.

"Nice house you have here, Billy Goat," Jason said.

I don't go by Billy or by Bill. My name is William Choat and I go by Will, having listened to that Billy Goat crap since grade school.

The dark bags under Jason's eyes and basset hound-jowls made him look like a tired old dog, but his eyes were never still and gave me the impression of the sneakiest member of the pack, number three or four in the pecking order with pretensions of becoming number one. Without the ability to even hold his own position, though, much less move up.

He waved a hand. "Pretty wife. Decent job, assistant manager at a bank. Nice life all the way around." He said it as if none of that was worth spit.

"And a baby on the way. How wonderful for you."

Brenda tensed up as if she were about to struggle again and I gave her the slightest shake of my head. Nothing she could do right now. Save her strength for when she might need it and could do something with it.

The good news for us was also the bad news: Jason was nowhere near as smart as he thought he was. People like that do not attract smart people, so these two thugs he brought along were probably not Nobel Prize prospects, either. But Jason wasn't stupid, either, so we would have to be careful to choose our moment.

"You've done pretty well by yourself after failing at poker," Jason said.

Few knew why I walked away. Jason sure as hell didn't.

"Terrible to feel old age creeping up on you, *idn't* it?"

I finally turned my head and looked at him.

"What do you want?"

"Oooh, stony. Same as the old days."

In my playing days I never had a real nickname, nothing beyond Billy Goat, and that only a few assholes used. The closest I came to having one stick was Iceman, because nothing ever seemed to bother me.

I've often wondered if I was some sort of sociopath, lacking the emotions that other people have, but Brenda showed me that I have the full set, love as well as anger, the most utter joy and loneliness like I never dreamed of even when I lived out of a suitcase in one hotel after another. Instead, I've found that I have feelings, I just don't let them out. A problem for a married man but I'm learning slowly.

I waited. Jason never could. He had to be *doing* something. If I could figure out some way to use that.

"Done very good for yourself, Billy Goat."

I waited.

"Well, I don't think you want to risk losing all of this just to protect that bank you work at, not when the government will make it all right."

"You want me to help you rob my bank?"

"Got it in one, Billy Goat."

"What's in it for me?"

"For you?" Jason acted surprised that I asked that. "You get to keep all of this." He waved his hands vaguely around the room."

He leaned over to touch Brenda on the shoulder and she shrank away from his touch as far as she could within the ropes they'd tied her with.

"You get to keep this."

Then he pointed at her bulge.

"And that."

As if.

If he had any intention of letting Brenda and I live, he would have sent someone else, someone I would not recognize the first time he opened his mouth. But Jason was here to rub my nose in it, to get the jollies from me now that he was never able to get at the table.

And what could I do?

I got home a few minutes before six, same as usual for a Friday evening, to find Brenda already trussed up, with Fatty holding a knife at her neck.

Our usual Friday was a quick dinner, then I was off to the Chamber of Commerce meeting. Friday was a bad night for meetings, but in our small town it was Kiwanis on Monday, Lions on Tuesday, VFW on Wednesday, and the new releases at our one movie theater on Thursday. Most of the business people in town belonged to more than one of these groups, so the Chamber ended up on Fridays.

When I didn't show at 7:30, my boss, Robert Lee (no relation) would wonder where I was and there was a good chance he would send our Chief of Police to check on me. After all, he had seen me at the bank just an hour before and I was perfectly fine and he would expect me to call if something had happened that would keep me from showing up.

All I had to do was wait Jason out.

"What I want from you is the security code for the alarm system. And the safety word in case your security company calls."

"You expect me to tell you."

Jason opened his arms wide. "Oh, no, not at all. Not the Iceman. We could beat on you all night and get nothing out of you but blood."

He nodded at the fat man, who pulled out his knife and touched the point to the side of Brenda's neck.

To her credit, she did not whimper when the knife pinked her, but I could see her trembling.

"Now her ...," Jason purred. "I bet you'll sing like an angel when we start carving pieces of her off." He leaned back in his chair. "Especially if we start digging in near her belly button and see how far in we get before that baby starts popping out."

At that, Brenda did whimper for a moment, before she took control of herself again.

I gave her a small smile. Nothing else I could do for her at that moment.

"But, of course, that means we have to go for blood right at the start and I think that will just make you more stubborn. So we'll have to increase the suspense a little. Play a little game. But first, we have a little chore for you."

He waved toward the skinny man behind me, who stepped into my field of vision, holding the cordless phone from the living room.

"We've been watching you for a while, Billy Goat. We know where you go and when, this tight little schedule you follow, week after week." Jason laughed.

Me, they had trussed up with duct tape. As the more dangerous captive, they gave me less room to wriggle than Brenda had. I would not be able to hold the phone myself.

"So, you are going to call your boss on his cell and tell him that you aren't coming tonight. Tell him that sweet Brenda is not feeling well and doesn't want to be alone tonight." Jason leaned forward and frowned at me.

"And you'll tell him that you'll be home all weekend, if he needs you. You see? We've been listening, too."

Smug bastard and wallowing in it.

If I had been hoping they would let one of my arms free to make the call, I would have been disappointed. As it was, I was not surprised when Skinny tapped in a number and held the phone near my ear—but not so near that he could not hear everything said.

"Hello," the voice said on the phone.

I cleared my throat. Fine time to get choked up. "Mr. Lee, this is Will Choat."

"Oh, hey, Will. What's up? You showing up tonight?"

"Probably not. Brenda isn't feeling well and doesn't want to be here alone."

"Heh. Always a bit more needy when they're pregnant, aren't they?"

I looked up. Brenda was looking at me and I stared directly in her eyes when I said, "The only thing I want in this world is to make her as happy as she can possibly be."

Expressing emotion around a ball gag when you are tied to a chair is not the easiest thing, but I think she got the message. She seemed to relax a little. Maybe there was a bit more glisten in her eyes.

I think so.

I'd be guessing.

"That's as it should be, Will. If anyone asks, I'll let them know."

Taking a breath is a tell, one of those little indicators of what you are thinking. But, if you don't breathe, you can't talk, so I took a breath and added, "I probably won't make the poker game at your house tomorrow night, either."

There was a pause at the other end, before Mr. Lee said slowly, "Okay."

"I might go in to the bank a little, but I think I'll just spend the weekend at home with my wife."

"Okay."

"So, my regards and regrets to the Chamber members."

Mr. Lee paused.

"Brenda is right there, isn't she?"

"Yep. Listening in on every word."

"Have to choose your words carefully when other people are listening in."

"Yes, sir."

Another pause. "Okay, Will. I'll take care of things on this end. You take care of Brenda and we'll see you on Monday, if not before."

"Yes, sir."

"And Will, stay safe, y'hear?"

"Yes, sir. Have a good night, Mr. Lee."

Skinny clicked the phone off and stepped back out of my vision.

Jason leaned forward over the table.

"What's this poker game crap?"

I didn't take a breath this time. "Monthly game at my boss' house."

"They do that last month?" Jason said, looking over my shoulder, apparently at Skinny.

"His mother-in-law was in town," I said, "so we didn't get together last month."

But his suspicion bone was aching, I could see it on his face.

"You gave up playing," Jason said. "Why would you play in some podunk nickel-and-dime game?"

The main reason I gave up professional poker was starting to throb in the back of my head. Too much strain, too much concentration, too much tension: headache, sometimes blinding. I had got to the point I was taking three extra strength aspirin before the session ever started, in anticipation of the headaches, more during the breaks. The longer I played, the worse it got. The older I got, the worse it got.

Brain scans and all sorts of tests didn't turn up anything the doctors could point their fingers at.

In the end, the only way to make them go away was to stop playing.

Hard to do when the money is so good and every greedy bastard in the world wants to push you forward to earn them another few bucks. I had people working for me who looked like I was stealing the food out their children's mouths when I talked about cutting back, much less quitting. Corporate reps begging to throw endorsement money at me if I would play just a few tournaments that they were sponsoring, maybe a few others, well, maybe a bunch of others.

If I hadn't met Brenda, I might still be playing. But blinding headaches and money were easy to leave behind when I walked away hand-in-hand with Brenda.

I shrugged as best I could with the duct tape wrappings. "The boss' game. I'm expected to show up."

"But now we have the whole weekend to ourselves."

I knew why Jason stopped playing. He always claimed the other man started it, by kicking him under the table. Maybe the punch to the side of the man's head could be excused, if the other man had started it. But beating the man on the floor with his own chair after knocking him out of it, that was a felony and a lifetime ban.

No doubt prison was where he met this crew.

Jason reached inside of his windbreaker and pulled out a pack of cards, which he placed on the table in front of him.

"I doubt that we can beat you or your lovely wife into submission, so let's play a game."

I wriggled my elbows, which did little more than make the tape bulge in a couple of places. "I can't hold any cards."

Jason smiled. "Of course you can't, so we'll play a game where you don't have to touch the cards at all."

Tapping the top card of the deck. "Let's ride the tiger with an old-fashioned game of Faro." Pulling his chair in Jason put his hands on the table, on either side of the deck. "Don't know how to play? An old master gambler like you?"

"No." No one played it anymore, much of anywhere, so why bother? Why not learn to play Whist? People still played that. A few.

"I'll tell you."

He flipped the top card off the deck and set it to his right. "Six is the winner." He flipped another and placed it on his left. "Jack is the loser."

He tapped the deck. "If this card is a six, you win. A jack, you lose."

Putting his hands back on the table, Jason smiled. "And what do you win?" He nodded to the skinny man.

Skinny grabbed my pinky finger, twisted it and gave it a jerk.

What's the point of trying to describe the pain? It drowned out my headache for a moment but it faded. In less than a minute, I was able to breathe again and the tears in my eyes cleared enough to see the new ones on Brenda's face.

"And what if you lose?" Jason flipped the top card and laid the nine of diamonds face up on the table.

"Huh," Jason said. "Nothing that time. Six cards give a result of fifty unknowns, 12% chance of something happening."

"Look at me, Billy Goat."

Jason waited until I looked him in the eye.

"If a jack comes up, my friend there will punch your wife in the stomach, as hard as he can. That's what you lose."

He rolled another card and placed the deuce of spades face up on top of the nine of diamonds.

"Now, in a real game, people would have bet on which cards they expected to come up before the winner or the loser, and get paid even money if it does, but we aren't using money here. We'll just keep flipping cards until you win or lose."

He turned up the seven of diamonds.

"Oh, close that time. Maybe one more."

Faro was a pure game of chance, no decisions to make beyond the guessing for the initial bets. No bluffing, no divining the other players' hands, nothing that made it more than just turning cards and hoping for the best.

A poker player, a real player, barely gave the slightest damn what his own cards were, only what he could make the other players *think* his cards were.

Ace of diamonds.

"Forty-seven cards left, with six result cards still to come up."

Between the throbbing in my hand and that in my head, I could barely concentrate, but I still had to think.

Jason was not the mastermind of this bank robbery. He might wish he was or maybe even think he was, but he couldn't hold a bunch of criminals together for any length of time, certainly not inspire them enough to try to pull off a harebrained theft like this.

Mine was a small-town bank. We had to order in extra cash to support the annual Kiwanis casino night. Certainly not enough money to warrant a full crew to open a time-locked vault.

The pay-off had to be in the safe deposit boxes but Jason had been in prison most of the last two years so where would he get information on what boxes were worth taking down?

There'd been a number of vault robberies across the country over the last year, all with the safe deposit boxes ripped apart and the contents scattered. Enough of them for the FBI to send out a flyer.

Opening the vault and defeating the cameras both had well-known procedures, from magnesium lances to micro-screens.

The hardest problems came in getting into the bank in the first place—*the external alarm system*—and staying in the bank—*the motion and heat detectors.*

Both of which ran to a security company that watched over both.

The gang hired Jason to get around that, to get the alarm codes and the security company password.

I might be his first assignment but I doubted it.

They would have wanted to try him out, possibly more than once, before they let him choose his target. I know I would and I knew him better than they did.

Jason flipped another card: queen of spades.

"Another close one. Good for Brenda."

That probably was the key.

Jason chose this place, chose me.

Robbery or not, this was his chance to beat me at last.

The deck he took out of his pocket.

Four of hearts.

Stacked, of course, because he wouldn't want the suspense to be over too soon.

The jacks would all be near the bottom of the pack because if they hurt Brenda, it was all over. Besides, as the deck grew shorter, I would know that time was running out, so if I were going to give in, it would be more likely as the number of unturned cards grew smaller and smaller.

There were still two more sixes in the deck, two more fingers I might have to sacrifice.

Ten of hearts.

The point of the sixes was the surprise value, so Jason would not have spaced them evenly in the deck—so I couldn't anticipate them—nor would they be all that close to each other, so that he and I could best savor the pain.

Six of spades.

Knowing it was coming did not help and Skinny broke my other pinky. There was nothing I could do to reduce the pain, nothing to do to ignore it.

Jason kept turning cards.

I knew where the last six would be, right above the three jacks, near the bottom of the deck.

There was no question of giving in.

The only question was when I would.

There was nothing to do but hope for that last minute miracle that would save both Brenda and me but she was the important one to save.

"You know," I said, "that you have to take me with you."

Jason shook his head. "No. I don't. You give me the codes and we leave." He waved at Brenda. "It will take her most of a day to get loose on her own and you sure as hell aren't getting out of all that tape by yourself. We'll be long gone. Just give us the codes and we're done. Save your last finger."

Jason sat back.

"C'mon, Billy Goat. Just give it up and we're out of here."

Ten or eleven cards left unturned in the deck. Once, I would have been able to say exactly, from across the room, but now I could not be certain. Too long away from the tables.

"No. You won't leave us here alone. One of your men will stay, to make sure we don't get loose, until you are done at the bank."

"Yeah, okay. True."

"We aren't safe until the rest of your team gets away and calls back to the man you leave on guard."

"So? What of it?"

"So, I have to make sure you get what you want and then get away clean. That's the only hope she has," I said, nodding at Brenda. I turned my head to look at Jason. "The only hope I have."

"You think we need to take you with us."

"Yes. The code words are a start but the security company expects me to answer the phone. They might recognize my voice, they might not, but the best chance you have to pull all of this off is if I'm the one to answer the phone when they call."

I kept talking. Maybe to keep my nerve up, maybe to try to keep Jason from thinking too much. I don't know.

"They *will* call. Whether it's a motion detector or a heat detector, they will call to check and they will expect to hear the same voice they hear every time I'm at work after hours."

I already knew Jason would not say yes or no. The purpose was to make me feel small, to make me hurt, so he was going to turn cards until that last six came up, no matter what he eventually decided.

He rolled the cards, one after the other.

If I gave in now, before that last six turned up, he would be robbed of some of the pleasure that he was depending upon, his game would be over. I had to hold out until that last "winner" card.

When it came up, there were only three cards un-turned, as I knew there would be.

Skinny broke the ring finger on my left hand.

If I lived through this, the doctors would have to cut my wedding ring off. There would be no other way to get it off the swollen finger.

Jason tried not to grin while I recovered from the pain but he couldn't keep his lips from twitching.

This was his moment, when he knew he had to win.

He didn't turn another card, just spread the rest of the deck, still faced down.

Three cards.

Jason lifted the corner of one of the three cards with his thumb.

"Well, we know what this is. Any last thing you want to say?"

What else was there to say?

"8-2-0-5."

Jason pulled a notebook and pen out of his jacket. "Let me write that down. Eight. Two. Oh. Five. That right?"

"Yes." No point in nodding. He wanted me to admit that I'd given in. He would make me say it.

"And the security code?"

"Peregrine."

"Like the bird?"

"Yes."

Jason tucked the notebook back in his jacket pocket and stood up.

"I guess we're done here."

He gathered up the cards, squared the deck, and stuffed it back into his pocket.

Unlike his two thugs, Jason had not worn gloves. It was hard to handle cards with gloves on. He pulled a large kerchief from his rear pocket and wiped down the surface and edge of the table near where he had sat. No pesky fingerprints.

He stepped out around the table and started for the door to the garage.

I felt my heart sink.

I'd guessed wrong and we were doomed.

I couldn't look Brenda in the eye.

"Bring him," Jason said, his back still to me.

I know Brenda died a little inside when Skinny cut me loose then wound more tape around my wrists and elbows.

And a little more still when Skinny led me away.

Getting Jason away from Brenda was the only victory I needed. Whether the fat man killed her or not, I could not control but I knew Jason would not have given her the slightest chance.

Now, at least, he would leave her alone as long as I was needed and apparently I had convinced him that my voice was needed on the phone when the security company called.

More time for that miracle to happen, for Brenda if not for me.

An odd thing about Brenda was that she liked her minivan. She liked it before she got pregnant and she liked it even more after, when she did not have to either climb up into it or down into it.

Jason apparently liked it also because we took her van and left my sedan in the garage.

What I liked the most when I was a professional gambler was the high I got while I was winning.

What I hated the most about it was the low that came after I won, after there was nothing left to do but go back to the hotel room and wait for a flight to the next tournament.

That was where Jason was now.

He'd be looking for something to bring him back up, to bring back the high he'd just gotten from his win.

I expected he was searching his mind for some way for me to give it to him.

I was hoping I could keep a low profile for a bit longer.

Jason sat next to me in the backseat and Skinny drove.

We eased slowly out of the driveway and puttered along, not too fast and not too slow, just three men on the way out for the evening. Nothing to attract any attention.

My town only has two large streets, which meet in the middle of town at one of our three traffic lights. One of those streets was the old highway, two lanes in each direction and we had barely turned on the old highway when we reached the middle of town and hit the light just as it turned red.

An SUV tooled through the intersection and stopped right in front of the van.

Red and blue lights started flashing from behind us.

Our police force only has the Chief, two officers, and two dispatchers.

They were all there, along with a county deputy and our local state trooper. They all had guns and they were all pointing those guns as they came up from behind the van and Skinny couldn't get his hands up fast enough. They had piled out of the three patrol cars that had snuck up behind the minivan with their lights off, after the SUV had blocked the van in front.

My boss, Robert Lee, climbed out of that SUV.

Like me, he had had a previous career before he ended up as a banker. His old job was as a police negotiator back East. He had to quit his high-pressure, adrenalin-fueled job when his sports betting got out of hand.

We met at Gamblers Anonymous. He was my sponsor. He helped me stay out of the poker rooms.

He also acted as a reserve officer in our local police department.

He sat with me and helped peel the duct tape off while we kept an eye on Skinny and Jason, both hand-cuffed in the minivan, while the rest of the police force headed for my house to overwhelm Fatty. I lost a lot of the hair on the back of my hands and it didn't help my swollen, broken fingers any.

The last man in town that would host a poker game was my boss and he was also the only man in town who knew that I dare not show up at one.

Information that Jason could not know.

Robert Lee didn't say anything to me. He didn't need to.

Only a few minutes passed before Mr. Lee's phone rang.

"She's safe," he said, as he tucked it back into his pocket.

He and I would have to talk later, when I came down off my high.

Dan C. Duval also got his start in the *Strange New Worlds* short story contest, winning the inaugural competition in 2005 with his story "Trek." Since then, his story stories have appeared in such varied anthologies as *Cosmic Cocktails*, the *Shadowrun* anthology *Spells and Chrome*, and several volumes of Fiction River, including *Risk Takers*, where this story first appeared, *Hidden in Crime*, and *Last Stands*. Calling himself a survivor of the corporate wars, he lives quietly on the Oregon Coast, where he turns out powerful stories like "Play the Man" on a disturbingly regular basis.

Rusch & Helfers

The Big Snip: Thomas Pluck

First published in *Dark City Lights*

When the new girl got in the can, all Sharon saw was a sunbaked skinny-ass white girl with chicken legs, and she wasn't sure how long she'd last. Probably couldn't lift more than fifty pounds, at least without complaining. She wore long sleeves and kept her nails trimmed to the quick, her dishwater hair tied back, tucked down the back of her shirt. Smelled like she'd just sneaked a cigarette.

Sharon gave her a week.

But she had lasted three, long enough for Sharon to call her by name.

"Good morning, Christina," she said, and climbed into the passenger side. She placed two boxes of syringes and vials of Telazol on the floor between her feet. "First stop's on Dyckman."

Christina had a driver's licence, and wasn't afraid to bully her way through traffic with the Neuter Scooter. They usually sent her fresh-faced girls from Queens or Long Island, who couldn't parallel park worth a damn. All pink and scrubbed and so full of love for animals that they'd eagerly serve three months spaying feral cats and snipping pit bull balls on the street before they were allowed to intern at the veterinary hospital.

True, in the operating rooms you had a sense of urgency, like on a medical TV show. Except instead of second-string Broadway actors playing the patients, you get pampered pets who probably ate better than you did.

The Neuter Scooter was a front lines, where you earned you bones at People Who Love Animals. Every morning, they drove the modified Econoline van to pet owners who'd signed up for an appointment to alter their dog or cat or cat at the PWLA (pronounced Poola) subsidized rate. You had to work quick and follow procedure, handle dogs that the owners barely knew, plenty of "outdoor" pets and friendly strays, and cats who'd nuzzle your hand and then flay your arm a moment later.

Sharon had just lost Lynndie, a plump powder-white Minnesota girl she'd trained into an op table warrior, to the hospital staff. Even though she's known all along that her protégé wanted to work inside – she was on her way to a vet degree – it stung of betrayal. They'd been a good team, had some laughs. It always hurt when the techs left. The unspoken words lingered like the stink of smoke on the new kid: if you worked in the van, it meant you were the B team.

When Fort Tryon Park loomed, Sharon pointed for Christina to cut right.

"I got it," she said.

Sharon didn't care for her driving. She hung in the far lane too long before a turn, and was a little too liberal with her use of the horn. But she couldn't complain; she was a lifelong New Yorker, and had avoided getting her licence first because there was no need, then out of stubbornness, and finally out of a strange sense of pride. She'd been born on Convent Avenue, a block downtown from the City College, in what was now called Hamilton Heights. The street crested a ridge on land once owned by Alexander Hamilton, whose house, now a museum, had been moved three times that Sharon knew about. Nearby St. Nicholas Park had a fine dog run, and she'd inherited her parents' building, living in one half and leasing the other to three white girls who'd been chased out of Williamsburg by hipster inflated rents. Girls that reminded her of Christina.

Their first patient was a gray bully mix named Tuco, a rambunctious boy whose ears and tale were intact. Christina double-parked and left the engine running. The Scooter had twin tanks to fuel the equipment.

"Tuke's not dog aggressive, but he humps just about anything in sight," his owner said. The sun lit up her natural puff of burnt-orange hair. "He's gonna break his lead and get himself killed one day, I know it."

"He'll settle down when we're done," Sharon told her. She ran the woman's credit card on a little gadget attached to an iPhone while Christina squatted down to play with the dog.

"Who's a good boy?"

He mounted her knee like it was the southbound end of a northbound Shih Tzu.

"Not you," Christina laughed. "Not you."

They carried him in the back and closed the doors. The van had an extended roof so they didn't have to hunch over. Tuco stood on the steel operating table, wagging his tail, breathing in the smells of hundreds of other dogs and cats who'd been there before him.

"Gimmie your paw," Sharon said. When Tuco obliged, she stuck him with a syringe of Telazol. He yipped and looked up like he'd done something wrong. Sharon rubbed his foreleg, easing the drug up the artery. "That's all, sweetie. That's all."

The wooziness hit his eyes, and Christina rolled him onto his back and strapped him to the table. Sharon checked his pulse, then gave Christina a nod.

"You're gonna end up doing it anyway," Christian said.

"If you don't practice, that's what we call a self-fulfilling prophecy."

Christina turned her head, but Sharon caught the eye roll. No one liked intubating when they first started. It was simple empathy, jamming a tube down a living creature's throat. They'd gag when they heard the slick and crunchy noises and felt the flesh resist. She held the dog's head as Christina unfurled the hoses hooked to the gas, and watched her angle of entry. "There it is. Ease it on it. You got it."

Christina bit her lip. Sharon gave her another try, then saw the confidence leave her hands. She took over. "Prep him," she said. "It's alright."

The tube went right in for Sharon; she'd done enough of them. It was like anything else: you needed the confidence to not be overly gentle, but not so cocky you didn't listen to your hands and wound up hurting them. She got the isoflurane flowing, and watched him breathe until she was satisfied.

Christina sighed and pulled a surgical drape over the dog. She took out a Bic razor and shaved a square of fur just above the testicles. "If I knew I'd be shaving balls when I made it to New York, I would've stayed home."

Sharon shook her head, then inflated the cuff on the endotracheal tube to hold it in place, so Tuco wouldn't vomit and aspirate during the procedure. "At least it's just dogs," she said. "Do they do men at those Brazilian places?"

Christina wet a gauze pad atop a blue gallon jug of chlorhexidine and scrubbed the square of pink-gray skin she'd shaved on Tuco's belly. "No," she said. "Far as I know, guys have to do that themselves."

"I don't know how you let someone down there," Sharon said. She could sign up for social security next year, but the flow of young vet techs kept her in the know. They talked about everything, including shaving their business.

"I don't," Christina said. "Couldn't afford to have someone else do it, even if I wanted them to." She squinted at the now-shiny patch of skin, and lifted up Tuco's genitals. "Fully descended. Ought to be a breeze."

When only one dropped, they called it a cryptorchid. The day Sharon told Christina that, she'd snorted like a wild hog. "You know a guy came up with that. Like they're a friggin' bouquet, or something. Hello, honey! Wanna put your tulips on my orchids?"

Sharon ran a gloved finger over the prepped area, then quickly made an inch-long cut. She held one orchid with the thumb and two fingers, like a tiny bowling ball, and squeezed it up its roomy sac until it popped out the incision she'd made. Then she closed the forceps around the vesicle so it wouldn't disappear back inside like a fleeing bait worm.

"Come on, do the snip," she told Christina.

Christina took the scalpel and leaned in.

"Just slice and go." On her granddad's farm the animals didn't even get anesthesia. Just cut and cauterize.

The razor severed the vesicle like overcooked spaghetti. "Now ligate." Christina tied it off and tucked it back inside.

Sharon tossed the freed testicle into the gut bucket. "Now number two. Come on, we got a long list."

The farm was one reason Sharon had headed for vet school. Seeing horses suffer from impaction colic, billy goats castrated with nothing but a clasp knife and a pair of pliers, and how the farmhands dealt with an explosion in the barn cat population. No, sweating in the back of an old van giving feral cats the Big Snip wasn't menial. For her it was a kind of penance.

She watched Christina perform the second removal, then closed the incision with a single stitch and a thin line of surgical glue. Christina cut the iso gas and removed the tube, and after he came to, they brought the sleepy pup, sans testicles, back to his owner.

"Plenty of water, keep him inside. He can go for a walk tomorrow, but no running for a couple of days. If he opens it up somehow, bring him in and we'll stitch him up."

They followed their clipboard nearly all the way up to Inwood. They snipped two toms, spayed a momma cat who'd littered twelve adoptees two weeks prior, then a yappy Chihuahua, and a fat black lab mix.

"Chryptorchid!" Christina called. She treated them like four leaf clovers.

On the ride back toward the clinic, a big bald man in a cardigan waved them down from the crosswalk.

"Pull over," Sharon said. It was Timothy, an actor who walked dogs down in Morningside Heights on his off time. He had two Afghans on leashes.

"Hey girl." Timothy was built like a football player, with a smile almost too big for his face. "How's the nut cutting biz?"

"You know," Sharon said. "Our job's never done. How about you? Who you got there?"

Timothy lifted one leash, then the other. "This is Tazi, and this is Karzai. They're dolls, but so prissy." Taiz put her paws on the side of the van and stuck her long nose in the window to lick Sharon's hand. "Oh, that thing you did? Worked like a charm. They never even noticed."

Sharon nodded, "Told you they wouldn't."

"Oh, and I have an audition for *Jersey Boys!*"

A cab honked behind them. "We'll see you later. You can give me those tickets you owe me."

Christina pulled back into traffic, and cut crosstown. She squeezed the van into a spot in front of a Jimbo's Hamburger Palace, and they washed up in back before breaking for a late lunch.

Jimbo's cooked their patties on the griddle, and finished them under a steel cup made for ice cream sundaes. It steamed them, and kept them tender. There were few things Sharon was nostalgic about, but her father taking her to the first Jimbo's open in Harlem was one of them, and their burger was the only one she'd eat.

They sat on Duct-taped red vinyl stools and waited for their burgers. Christina's with a Diet Coke, Sharon with black coffee.

"How's Alex doing?" Sharon asked.

"Alexie's good. Getting ready for pre-K already. I can't believe it."

"And Hester?"

"Kyle doesn't like her, but Lexie adores her. He even flushes her poops down the toilet." She thumbed through her phone, showed a photo of the little tow-headed Alexie hugging a plump tortoiseshell. Cute little thing. The cat hung limp with the tolerant mother's grin.

They ate their burgers, the Kaiser rolls soaked with grease and onions. A man ordering to go swept Sharon with his eyes. His hair and beard trimmed close, shot through with gray. She frowned at her burger and cut it in half with a wood-handled steak knife.

"What was your friend talking about?"

"Oh, just another snip."

Christina ducked and lowered her voice. "Remember what you said about guys shaving their junk? Kyle asked me to shave his, because he heard it would make him look bigger."

"Honey, no."

"One little nick, and that was the end of that," Christina said, with a snort. "I didn't have all this practice then."

Sharon shook her head. She'd heard on NPR that the popularity of shaved genitals had put the existence of crab lice in jeopardy. No loss, that.

"The snip job for Timothy was on the sly," she said. "This couple he knew, theater patrons. You'd know their name. Big dog they brought home from Italy, where they were married."

He was a Neapolitan mastiff named Otto, the size of a large black panther or a small bear, and the owners kept him intact. The woman wanted him neutered, but the husband wouldn't allow it. He was a good dog, but they couldn't control him, and he got dog aggressive. Timothy got his hand cut up, trying to break him off another dog.

"They paid him and the other dog's owner off, to keep Otto off the vicious list. I met Timothy walking him in St. Nicholas, where the big dog run is. I had Caesar with me, and he put that Otto in his place with one look, no balls or not."

Caesar was her boy, a big white whale of a boxer mix with one brown eye and one ice blue.

"He told me about the disagreement between Otto's owners, and I suggested a solution."

"What did you do?"

"Neuticles," Sharon said. "You know. Those prosthetics." Some owners preferred their dogs to look intact. They'd crop the ears and the tail, but wanted two balls swinging around back there. "So we didn't shave him, I did the incisions, kept it real clean. Squeezed those fake nuts in there, like I was putting pits back inside a plum."

"No way?"

"Yup. Glued him up and you couldn't tell the difference, not even up close. And he settled down soon enough. He's still a spoiled, hyperactive dog, just like his owners. Hell, Timothy brings him to the dog park by car service. That dog gets a cab faster than he does."

The gray-bearded man stopped by Sharon's shoulder. "I could put a smile on that face."

Sharon set her burger down. "You know what'd make me smile? Not getting told to smile all the time."

His grin twisted into a sneer. "Well you don't have to be a bitch."

"Go on, now." Sharon wagged her steak knife, the teeth gristly with red. "I worked really hard all day in the back of a hot ban snipping off dog balls, I can cut one more pair."

Christina covered her mouth not to laugh. She looked over her shoulder as the man slammed the door.

"Can't even eat my lunch," Sharon said, and wiped the shreds of meat offer her knife with a napkin.

Tuesday was TNR day at the shelter uptown. Trap Neuter Release. They drove up to assist with the cats the shelter had caught. Feral things with matted coats and crusty eyes. Interns gave them shots and shaved the snarls of their fur. One tom yowled in protest, his voice roughened like a seasoned smoker's. It took three interns to hold him down and inject the sedative.

Sharon put Christina on prep and intubation.

"I don't know," she said. "You always end up doing it."

"This assembly line's just what you need to get over that hump."

The shelter was an old building with a lean to it, and no air conditioning except a few overworked window units. Sharon peeled off her lab coat and worked in a tank top. Christina wore her long sleeves and wiped her brow between motions.

"Why don't you take that off?"

"Don't want to get scratched."

Sharon shrugged. The cats were sedated already. She was a firm believer that once an adult, a person had already decided whether or not they were going to be happy or miserable.

She'd found happiness early in life, then lost it to her own pigheadedness; in the years that followed, happiness seemed difficult to find and harder to hold onto, and she slowly embraced the adage that if you wanted devotion, a dog was a sure bet, while people of either sex could only be counted on until they saw the next best thing.

She didn't care whether Christina was comfortable, but she did mind if she learned to intubate. Sharon kept on her back until she worked through her hesitation. It took a few tries and some guidance, but five cats later she was doing it. Maybe not like a machine, but with enough confidence to keep things running. She had one slip of the cuff, and a pink and gray female regurgitated. The vomit smelled like fermented fish heads.

Christina gagged. "It smells like garbage bags in Chinatown!"

To her credit, she fixed the cuff before running for the sink.

A goateed intern brought her a pair of clean scrubs to change into.

"Nice ink," he said, eyeing her lean forearms.

Sharon looked over while she glues up a scrawny female's belly. Christina's arms were covered in tattoos. The artwork showed talent, and her pale skin made for a good canvas. Swirls and autumn leaves and symbols. Over the inside of one elbow, a sailor's heart tattoo with her boy Alexie's name and birthdate in engraver script. Sharon didn't understand why anyone would want one tattoo, much less that many, but it wasn't the art that bothered her.

She put it aside and got back to work. There were always more ferals that they could snip in one shift, and today was no exception.

The shelter provided lunch in the form of cheap greasy pizza from the dollar a slice joint around the corner. They washed up and ate outside, where it was cooler, leaned against the brick.

Christina held out her arm and ran a finger over a track mark. The silver pocks showed through the ink. "These are from a long time ago," she said. "I'm a sponsor now."

"That's good," Sharon said. She tossed the spongy crust of her pizza toward a trio of pigeons. "See you inside."

After work, Sharon walked and fed Caesar, and took a blue train downtown to the Cubby. She drank Stoli and Seven; the fizz lingered on the tip of her tongue. A napkin around her drink absorbed the sweat, and the glass didn't touch the bar until she'd finished it.

She had lost her eldest brother to heroin when she was a little girl. She asked her mother: why would anyone give themselves a needle? Her mother had no answer, and in the fifty-two years since, Sharon couldn't find one. We all dealt with pain in different ways, even animals.

It always amused her, that adage about veterinarians being the best doctors, because the patient couldn't tell them what hurt. You couldn't tell, maybe you had no business being a doctor. At least animals were honest about pain, and growled or snapped. People, they liked to bury it, in all sorts of ways.

The clinic had been broken into several times over the years, for syringes and sedatives. But more often, half used vials of ketamine went missing. Her previous tech, Lynndie, had put herself through vet school by tending bar; she told Sharon that ketamine was called Special K, and it was used both recreationally and as a date rape drug. There were bars where if you wanted to remember the rest of your night, you finished your drink without it ever leaving your hands.

But it wasn't Christina's track marks that had bothered her. Like the tattoos, it was something you got used to seeing. There'd been something else just as familiar, around the wrists and forearms.

A woman half her age with close-cropped hair and a beauty mark beneath her left eye bought Sharon's next drink. They talked about the music and the weather and dogs, and Sharon forgot what it was she'd noticed until the next morning, when the young woman pulled a shirt over her tattooed shoulders, petted Caesar on the head, and let herself out of the apartment.

Bruises beneath the inkwork, on the insides of the wrists. Right where you'd hold someone's hands when you had them up against the wall, nose to nose. Thumb-print smudges between the radius and ulna, some yellowed and faded, others red rimmed, fresh, and purple.

She thought Christina was smarter. But over the years, she'd learned that if a horse wanted water, it found the corral on its own, and leading them to it often engendered more resentment than gratitude.

She'd been kicked enough to know.

They were busy enough that Sharon stopped noticing when new bruises joined the old, and she was thankful she'd minded her own business. For all she knew, the marks could be from anything. Maybe Christina took judo, or like being held down as a kink.

Christina's sense of humor didn't waver. Fridays, when the other techs on the shift went around the corner for a drink, she always bowed out, saying she had to pick up her son from his grandparents. And as her skills improved, she showed no inclination to abandon van duty for a cushier gig in the clinic.

The show of loyalty softened Sharon's view of her.

The last snip on the clipboard was a bull mastiff female on Riverside Drive by the tennis courts. The owner was a little man who had half his hair pulled back in a little po- nytail knot, leaving silver locks framing his face. Plaid shirt with sleeves rolled, revealing nice strong arms. The kind of man who looked like a sculptor or Buddhist priest, but usually turned out to be a financial planner or a hand model.

"Jonquil's in heat," he said, rubbing her immense fore- head. "Will that be a problem?" Jonquil was one hundred- and-ninety pounds of black-and-tan jowl and slobber, sit- ting spread-legged on the sidewalk, her pudenda swollen and red.

"There's a greater chance of bleeding," Sharon said. "I usually recommend waiting until she'd out of her cycle."

"This guy at the park's got a Doberman he can't han- dle, he's all over her."

Christina raked her nails over the dog's back, and Jon- quil butted her head into her, begging for more.

"You should bring her to the clinic."

"I can't really get away, is the problem. I've got clients all day, during you hours. And weekends, you're booked for months. I called."

He squatted and kissed Jonquil on her wet coal nose. "I just don't think Jonny girl wants puppies."

It took them both to lift Jonquil onto the table after the Telazol kicked in. Christina intubated her like a pro, and Sharon strapped her down and crossed her paws.

"Jesus," Christina said, as she shaved the belly. "She's red as a baboon's ass."

"Get her prepped," Sharon said. Usually she appreciated the sense of humor, but the lack of urgency set her off.

She made the cut with care, but blood welled immediately. Christina soaked it up with gauze and Sharon quickly inserted a spay hook, and fish out the first horn of the uterus. She extracted the grape-bunch of ovarian follicles, clamped it at both ends, and cut them at the bud.

Blood formed like red beads of sweat, then pooled. The dog's belly heaved beneath the surgical sheet. Christina inhaled sharply.

"More iso," Sharon said. "Quarter turn."

Christina adjusted the flow of gas and Jonquil's breathing settled. Sharon sponged the blood and ligated the uterus with three quick loops of surgical thread. She kneaded the flesh, leaning in close to see, but no blood appeared.

Sharon followed the pink worm of the uterus to the second horn and squeezed it out. "You can see why we don't go for hot dogs much," she said.

Christina let out a breath of relief, and shook her head with a little eye-roll. Her fingers clawed for a cigarette.

Sharon repeated the cut, this time ready for the blood. She moved slow and smooth with practiced motions, cinched tight little stitches, and checked for bleeding several times before tucking everything back inside Jonquil's belly.

"Ease up on the iso," she said, as she finished tying up the knots to close the abdomen. "Let's get things cleaned up. Detube her."

"I'm too jittery," Christina said, her face flushed.

"She'll be alright. She's just got a big old heart."

Sharon flinched as Christina stepped in to give her a hug. Her hair smelled of strawberries and stale smoke.

Sharon patted her shoulder. "Your first scare?"

"Yeah." She rubbed her nose then looked away, cleaning up the operating table.

"I'll bandage her up," Sharon said. "Go have a puff."

"Thanks."

As Sharon bent to get the adhesive tape, she saw Christina squeeze toward the front of the van. Her hand went into the pocket of her scrubs, and came out empty.

Outside she gave Jonquil's owner the papers for post-operative care.

"Doesn't she have to wear a cone?"

"No, just keep an eye on it. If it gets dark red, like her cookie, bring her in. and keep her out of the park for a few days, let her rest. She'll still be in heat for a day or two, it'll take a while to get the hormones out of her system.

He handed them both a folded twenty, before walking sleepy Jonquil slowly up the stoop.

In the van, Sharon waited for the doors to close, then turned off the ignition.

"What-"

"What's in your pocket? That's the only question," Sharon said, clutching the keys in her palm.

"My cigarettes, what are you talking about?"

"Don't insult me now. Don't." The pleasant mask melted from her face, into the look she'd inherited from her mother.

Christina reached into her pocked and removed a pair of Neuticles. The expensive ones, soft as breast implant. The largest size, like the ones Sharon had put in Otto the mastiff.

"What, you selling them?" Sharon said. "They cost a few hundred, wholesale. Am I gonna have to inventory the whole truck?"

Christina's lower lip trembled, and she mashed her palms into her eye sockets. She kicked the floorboards and rocked with silent sobs.

Sharon drove them to a shady spot in Riverside park. Christina gripped the cracked beige dashboard the whole way. After they parked, she hiked her scrubs. Leopard spot bruises between her ribs.

"He likes to jam his thumb in there," Christina said. "Don't say it. I'd leave if I could. But he'll get custody. His parents, they say it every time they can. 'Oh we just *love* having little Alex over. Wouldn't you like to live here all the time, instead of your tiny apartment?' His name's *Alexie*, bitch!"

Sharon felt cold around the edges, like she'd barged into a house where the heat had been turned off. "If you need a lawyer, I know a few."

"It won't matter." Christina held out her arm, ran a finger over the track marks. "Kyle says they'll use my record against me. I'm clean five years, I'm not even on fucking methadone."

"Then why are you stealing, if you don't want a lawyer?"

Christina lit a cigarette, rolled down the window. The cherry ember bobbed as she laughed out an exhale.

"Well, that's where I ask a big favor."

Besides the Neuticles, Christina had palmed a syringe and a fresh vial of Telazol. Needle, a scalpel blade, surgical glue, and thread.

Sharon told her she was out of her mind.

"Well then Alexie goes to Kyle's parents, or protective services. My parents ain't worth a damn, so don't even ask. I can't take this anymore."

"Does he hit…"

"No, he just takes it out on me and the cat, for now. The last straw was when Alexie started talking. He uses the same condescending voice on him, when he gets mad. Next thing, he'll stand there smoking in the door of his bedroom while he sleeps." She looked out the window. "Looking at him like he's less than shit."

There was more. On the drive back, she learned where the bruises came from. When she said no.

She listened without comment, until Christina told her the plan. Then she laughed.

"You need the gas to keep him under," Sharon said. "He would've woken up with you down there, screaming and bleeding, then you'll really lose your boy. Pretty sure there'd be jail time."

No, this was a van job. And she would need a partner. A smart one.

Sharon took the spare set of keys to the Neuter Scooter home Friday night. Kyle's favourite bar was one of those new speakeasy types out in Bushwick, where the only thing bigger than the ice cubes was the check. It smelled of old wood and music blared from cheap speakers, muffling any attempt at conversation.

Sharon wore a short dress that she sometimes took to Cubby's, or a hunting ground uptown when the mood struck her. She kept the makeup light, like a neighborhood holdout enjoying herself, someone who refused to let the trust fund kids take over.

It wasn't a difficult role to play. Gentrification had begun its creep into Hamilton Heights. She enjoyed the restaurants, but not the accompanying shift in neighborhood tone forced by increases in rent. You could always take trains to try new places, but home was home.

Here the barflies were uniformly young, and mostly white. A couple had a stroller with their conked-out child, but most were singles out hunting. The kind of bar Lynndie had warned her about.

Sharon played with her phone until a spot opened at the bar near Kyle and his group, and ordered a Vodka Seven. They didn't have 7 Up, so she nursed a Moscow Mule instead.

Kyle wore a checked shirt and a knit bow tie, a long but near beard, and those stretched horn rims that everyone seemed to wear. He was tall but not built, and dominated conversation among his friends with sweeping gestures reminiscent of a stage magician.

A young man cozied to the spot beside her and tried his game. Perhaps he felt it was his duty to talk to her, alone as they were in the crowd. He bought her a drink, and she bought him one, to let him know where they stood, while he pouted, she used his body as a shield to spritz an entire vial of ketamine into Kyle's Rock & Rye.

She hugged her would-be friend goodbye and told him he was sweet, then cleared her bill with the bartender, as Kyle's friends slowly drifted off in pairs. He gripped the mahogany for purchase. She turned, brushing him with her hip.

"Oh hello there," Kyle said, with a gleam of eye teeth. "How'd I miss you?"

"I could be your grandmother," she said. His great-grandmother, maybe. She'd been the first to break the streak of motherhood by sixteen on her mother's side.

"No way," Kyle said. "Well, know what they say. Black don't crack."

She feigned a smile and sipped her drink. She saw why Christina had once liked him, he put on a good show. But there was a layer of demanding beneath the ready smile, a hunger for attention, that Alexie's sudden appearance must have offended. Her own father had it, but he'd been pleased to have a captive audience in his children. He may have pouted when they complained of

hearing a story for the thousandth time, but he never became petulant. It was their mother who'd driven them
away, one by one.

She let Kyle talk, as the K and alcohol loosened his
rivets. When she suggested he might like to go home, he
assumed she meant hers and leaned in to whisper. As
she pushed him away, she thumbed the empty vial of Ketamine into his jeans pocket.

She checked her phone. Christina would have Alexie
in bed by now. She let Kyle snake an arm around her
waist, and guided him out the front door onto the dimly lit,
crooked sidewalks.

Down the block, Christina would be waiting in the van.

But Kyle would never make it there. The dose of ketamine was surely fatal, and that was the only way. Sharon
had tried to explain, that dogs are one thing, and people
were another.

And besides, it wasn't the balls that were the problem.
It was the brain.

Thomas Pluck is the author of *Blade of Dishonor*, *Steel Heart:
10 Tales of Crime and Suspense*, and is the editor of the Lost
Children charity anthologies *Protectors* and *Protectors 2*, which
benefit PROTECT: The National Association to Protect Children. He hosts Noir at the Bar in Manhattan, writes regular
columns for *Criminal Element*, and is the Social Media Editor
for PROTECT. He lives with his wife and their two cats. When
not writing he like to hike, and has been known to consume the

occasional beer. His work has appeared in *The Utne Reader*, *Beat to a Pulp*, *[PANK] Magazine*, *Burnt Bridge*, *Spinetingler*, *McSweeney's*, *Pulp Modern*, *Crimespree Magazine* and elsewhere.

The Purslow Particle: Neil Schofield

First published in *Alfred Hitchcock's Mystery Magazine, December 2015*

The detective inspector was in late and in a bad temper. He had a hell of a time getting through the rush-hour traffic. He made the mistake of coming across London Bridge. It just seemed to get worse and worse. How could so many people cram themselves into one city every day? It was like ants. No, it was worse than ants. He had a vision of a silo. They went off, bang, didn't they, silos? When the concentration of stuff in the air reached a critical point and the temperature reached *its* critical point, one grain of flour or whatever decided it was too hot and under too much pressure burst into flames. And that was that. Bang.

He was relieved when the station custody sergeant pushed open his office door to interrupt this depressing train of thought.

"All right?"

The D.I. nodded. "I've had a look at him, Norm. Just put my head around the door. Doesn't look like much, does he? Seems like your ordinary suburban sort of bloke."

The custody sergeant nodded.

"Just goes to show, doesn't it? It's always the quiet ones you have to watch."

The D.I. said, "There's no doubt, I suppose? I mean, before we go in and take it all down? It was him and it was deliberate?"

"We've got three witnesses. Could have had ten if we wanted, but these three were the nearest. No doubt it was him. They saw him push the other bloke, clear as anything. They were right next to him. And it was deliberate. He waited around for the lads to arrive. Could easily have had it away in all that bollocks. You know what it's like down there when someone goes under a train."

The D.I. nodded. He knew what it was like.

"Not him. He waited for the lads and then said he wanted to confess. To murder. So they bring him in. he's been sitting nice as pie, just waiting."

"Right", said the D.I., "I'll take Beebe in with me. We'll see what we've got here."

"Want to take a mug of tea in with you?"

"No, don't bother. If it's as cut and dried as you say, this isn't going to take long. What's his name again?"

He had thought: All right, let's get a few things straight Gordon Purslow, what do those words actually mean? I mean, what is their true inner meaning? Is it a definition or simply a label? Because if it is a definition, then hiding somewhere in those words is what I am, the *me*. But if it's just a label, then it doesn't matter what I'm called, because Gordon Purslow doesn't define, it merely indicates a something that just happens, for our present and purely temporary purposes, to be called a Gordon Purslow. And what does *called* mean, anyway?

He was standing on a traffic island, crammed in among dozens of others, waiting for the lights to change so he could cross the road to join the crowds of people streaming along on the other side.

He thought: Now, if Gordon Purslow is a definition, then it must somehow define someone first of all who are fifty-three years old, of medium height, of medium build, of moderate looks, nothing fancy, pleasant enough but nothing to write home about. It must also define someone whose wife left him a year ago because she couldn't stand the boredom, the nothing, the void that had been their life together, or so she had said viciously packing her cases before viciously slamming the door. And finally it must also define someone who just lost his job in an economic restructuring, as they prettily called it. And at fifty-three, after thirty or so years at the same job, could Unemployed Gordon Purslow really be a definition? Because for thirty or so years the definition of Gordon Purslow had included the precondition that he was married and employed. If he was not married or employed, he could no longer be described as Gordon Purslow. But you can't just change the definition of something, just like that. Can you?

He was standing stock still on the edge of the pavement, thinking all this. These were the first coherent thoughts that had gone through his head since leaving the office after the awful, the *dreadful* interview with Frank

Pawson, the personal director. He preferred not to think about that interview because really, amid all the pabulum, all the anodyne phrases about departmental fusion and corporate imperatives, the weasel words like downsizing, all that came out of it, the bottom line, was that for thirty years or so, Gordon Purslow really hadn't made a difference. To anyone, or anything. The world had rolled around thousands and thousands of times and it would have rolled round just the same if he hadn't existed.

And isn't that essentially what Marjorie had been saying when she left. But it wasn't true. Was it? Surely everyone made a difference. Everyone counted. If not, what was the point? Or perhaps, oh, God, just perhaps, that was the dreadful point. There *was* no point.

He stepped suddenly off the pavement, and was suddenly hoicked back by a strong arm which pulled him out of the path of a double-decker hurtling toward Piccadilly Circus. The wind of its passage gave him an extra little push.

"You want to watch yourself, you do," said a cheerful voice. Gordon turned and looked at his savior, a large man in a horrible brown mock-leather jacket. "Kill yourself if you like, but try to do it in private," said the man.

Gordon didn't know what to say.

"Wasn't thinking."

"Yes, well, a Number 93 can stop you thinking for good, squire. Turn you into a smear on the tarmac," said the man over his shoulder as, with the little man now green, he crossed the road briskly and disappeared into the flood of pedestrians.

Gordon crossed the road and turned down a side street. At the end, the canopy of the Palladium was brightly lit with garish colored bulbs. He stopped for a moment to look at the giant photograph outside. Some musical he had never heard of, involving seminude, featured showgirls and sequined showboys with odiously synthetic smiles. Next door there was a pub. Gordon realized that this is he wanted: a nice quiet drink in a quiet side-street pub. He pushed his way in.

Unfortunately, this was a matinee day and the pub was packed with coachloads of Northern retirees, who had evidently just completed an act of joyous communion with the feathered showgirls and slithy showboys next door. He pushed his way out again.

But the next pub he came to, opposite the Marlborough Street Magistrate's Court, was nearly empty. It was half past four, just too early for a quick drink after the office and just too late for the heavy lunchers to be still there.

There were two solitary drinkers in the far corner, three characters at the bar fighting over who was going to pay for the next round, and that was it. The barman sauntered over to Gordon, with an air of might as well, he had nothing much else on at the moment.

Gordon ordered a beer, a lager, then changed his mind and asked for a large scotch. He added a splash of soda from the syphon on the bar and took it to the corner table, where the lighting was agreeably dim. The argument at the bar had ended amicably, it seemed, because now the barman had sauntered over to the trio and there was a lot of argy-bargy about who was going to have what.

"I," said the payer, "will have a large brandy. Your very best, if you please, Gervase. And Henry here wants a scotch, of the large persuasion, if you'd be so good. And Gordon here wants a large dry martini with two olives in it. Right, Gordon?"

"Right," said the Gordon here, who also had his hands in his pockets. He was rocking from side to side.

"And last but not least, one for your good self, Gervase, seeing as how you've had to courtesy to serve us."

"Thanks," said the barman joylessly, "I'll take a half of cider."

"Whatever suits you suits me, Gervase."

Gordon Purslow wondered if the barman's label actually said Gervase, decided that it probably didn't and that it didn't matter, and that Gervase didn't care what they called him.

"Now," said the large man, handing over a ten-pound note without looking, and continuing a conversation about the ordering of drinks and evidently interrupted, "the point is, Gordon, the point is that you can't put up with that sort of thing. Henry here knows that, don't you Henry?"

Henry nodded judiciously, pursing his lips.

"Henry here went through the very same sort of palaver only last year, when those half-wits over in White Plains started playing silly buggers with the quotas."

"Right," said Henry.

"Absolutely," said Gordon.

Gordon Purslow took a drink and then took out the packet of cigarettes from his pocket. It was the first packet he had bought in twenty years and he still didn't know why. He wondered whether it was worth getting up and going outside to smoke one. What would the sensation be like?

A sensation of – what? Nothing very much probably. A bit of a light-headedness, probably. Nothing to get excited about. Nothing very much at all, really.

"I mean," the large man was saying, "if you let 'em get away with that, what are you, in the end of the day? You're nothing, that's what you are, nothing."

"Less than the dust beneath our chariot wheels," said Henry.

"Right," said the large man. "Yes. Right. Less than the dust. And treated as such."

Dust, thought Gordon. Dust particles. He's right, is Henry. That's what we are. He had a sudden image of a hundred, a thousand, a million conversations like this going on all over the city. A million conversations going nowhere, deciding nothing, signifying nothing. And he had a picture of a million people like him, sitting drinking solitary drinks, going out into the dark to smoke solitary cigarettes without the slightest idea of why, of what they were or why.

Then the idea came to him equally suddenly. No, not dust. *Brownian Movement*. At school in the third form, that had always caused a laugh. Just the mentions of Brownian Movement had been enough to cause an unquenchable outbreak of sniggering. Brownian Movement. First observed by Robert Brown in 1827. He could remember writing that word for word in the end of term physics paper. The definition: *When colloidal particles are suspended in a fluid medium, they are subjected to impacts from the molecules of the medium and are in continuous random motion.*

Robert Brown had said nothing about colloidal particles sitting drinking large scotches in half empty bars, but there might as well have been. Especially colloidal particles which had been subjected to a number of impacts from the molecules of the medium. Like losing your job. Like losing your wife. Like suddenly losing all idea of who you are or who you are supposed to be.

Except, in fact, old Robert hadn't know the half of it, had he? Because today we're up to our knees in particles, aren't we? Robert was talking about things he could see under a microscope. now, all you hear is madness, particles, particles. some that might exist, might not, you couldn't make hear=d or tail of it all. The God Particle, for instance, what was that all about, then?

He had finished his scotch. He really ought to go and catch his train. What for? What was waiting for him in the semidetached house in Ruislip? And that was another thing. The house he had bought three years after their marriage with a massive mortgage. He could remember the Building Society manager smiling at him and recommending that he take out an endowment insurance policy. Part of the premiums, he said, would pay the interest, and the rest would be invested. So, at the end of the term, the invested capital would pay off the mortgage and leave him with a nice lump sum into the bargain. Good scheme. Except, with the fully declared depression, the price of the property wasn't worth thinking about. If he sold the house now, he'd be selling at a loss, just enough to pay off the rest of the mortgage with next to nothing left over. So there was nothing there. Nothing. He had a sudden attack of vertigo at the thought of leaving the bar, opening the door, and looking into nothing, endless Black Nothing.

Gordon stood up and walked to the bar. He ordered a second large scotch and went back to his table. There was something terribly important on the edge, on the very edge, of his mind, a thought that he simply had to capture because if he didn't it would escape him forever.

You see, that was what it all was. Millions, billions, of particles cannoning about in a completely random fashion. That was what it was all about. That was *all* it was. And if you were a particle, you could pretend that it had meaning. You could go through the motions: get a job, get married, have children, go on holiday to Ibiza, take up philately or weight training, believe in God or organic foods or in Scientology, whatever pleased you. But in the end, all that had no point, no meaning. You were just there to *be* there. You were a particle. And if one particle wasn't there, another would be. Another, completely indistinguishable from the first, with just as much point, making just as much or as little difference.

And that wasn't fair. That couldn't be fair. That couldn't be what it was all for. Or perhaps it was, and the joke was on us.

The conversation at the bar had stopped. He looked across at the three men, and saw they were staring at him. He realized that he had just laughed. Laughed out loud, right there, all alone at his table. He wondered just how long he had been immobile, not drinking, simply staring in front of him. It might have been the second scotch, but suddenly Gordon felt stifled. He had a tight feeling in his chest, and there was a ringing in his ears. He put the cigarettes in his briefcase, stood up, picked up his umbrella, and walked unsteadily to the door.

"Take care, my friend," the large man turned from the other two and called after him. "Don't let the bastards grind you down."

Gordon paused before opening the bar door to leave, with that dreadful vision of the Nothing on the other side, then pushed through the doors into the street. It was all right. Everything was still there. It was night now. He took a deep breath of cold air and felt better. And there you are, he said to himself. The street was filling up now, with office workers streaming out of the blocks, filling the sidewalks, crossing the street, going in all directions at once. There they are, the particles, millions, billions of them. Going nowhere, for no reason. Continuous random motion.

He began walking toward the tube station at Oxford Circus. All at once the thought of coming to rest somewhere had an appeal. He joined the stream of particles filling the pavements, wandering from side to side, sometimes cannoning into other particles who were streaming equally aimlessly in the other direction. At the top of Carnaby Street, there were at least three streams, four even, crossing each other, the number of impacts, he saw, was considerable. It was ridiculous. Pointless. He found himself saying so out loud, and getting some worried looks from other particles for his trouble.

Down in the underground station it was chaos. There must be thousands, he thought, cramming themselves into this underground chamber. He wondered idly if you crammed enough particles into a small enough space whether you could create a critical mass, and if so, what would happen. And whether whatever it was that happened would make any difference.

On the platform the press was appalling. There was no room for movement, Brownian or otherwise, just an immobile mass, standing face front, waiting for the train. Gordon thought, but you could make a difference, you see. Particles aren't just there to receive impacts. Even a particle has an impact, and the impact must create a difference, a change. If particle impacts particle, change must occur. Even in Robert Brown's day, even now.

And what would happen if there was a God Particle among them? He smiled slightly.

He began to push through toward the edge of the platform. Other particles became agitated, and there were light impacts, and some insignificant reaction, which he ignored. He had his eye on a particle at the edge of the platform, one very much like him, in his fifties, slightly balding crown, carrying a briefcase and an umbrella, gazing in front of him, waiting for, listening for the train.

There was a whisper in the tunnel, a movement of air, that ruffled hair and made faces turn. Gordon was now behind his fellow particle.

He eased himself to the other's side. The press of bodies behind him was going to make this easy. We can all make a difference, especially me. I *have* to. If not, what else is there for a God Particle to do? Gordon maneuvered himself just behind the other, until he was poised, ready to give a slight but firm shove. Particle impacts particle, he thought, as the train cleared the tunnel, and the squeal of the brakes filled his ears. Particle impacts on particle and make a difference.

The D.I. was watching D.C. Beebe putting the statement into the word processor. He sighed.

"Thanks," he said to the custody sergeant, taking the mug of tea. "Well, that didn't take long."

"He's coughed then?"

"Oh, he's coughed. I had a job getting him to stop. And he's given us a beautifully reasoned account of the whys and wherefores."

"So what's his story then?"

The D.I. squeezed the bridge of his nose between thumb and forefinger. "Oh, lots of reasons, really. A real rabbit's stew of things, lot of financial and domestic and work problems, no point to anything. And then there's a lot of really odd-the-wall stuff about everything and everybody being meaningless. Particles, bollocks like that. You can read it all for yourself if you've got the stomach for it. Or the patience. But I'll tell you something for nothing. The first thing the beak's going to do is ask for a shrink's report."

The custody sergeant nodded and said, "He was laughing to himself earlier. Before you came in. He's next door to being off his onion, you ask me. Got to be. Pushing a complete stranger under a train. And he nearly got the bloke next to *him* as well."

"Well, he's not laughing now. I'd still like to know if there's really no link between him and the bloke he pushed in front of that train. And, in fact, what have we got on the victim?"

The sergeant grimaced.

"Young Dawson got a hold of his briefcase. It was lying on the platform. The rest can wait."

The D.I. made a face. Yes, let the rest wait for the pathologists.

"From the stuff in his case, he sounds almost like a clone of him in there. Fifty three years old, office worker, perfectly ordinary bloke, nothing known. Lives – sorry *lived*, poor bastard – down in Ruislip. His name's Purslow, Gordon Purslow. Nice way to end a day, going home minding your own business, doing no harm to anybody, and a nutcase pushes you under a tube train. What a way to go."

The D.I. didn't seem to be listening. HE sipped his tea and stared out of the window, down at the flocks, the crowds, the unending streams of people crowding through the streets.

Then he said, "That's the fourth one we've had in two weeks, isn't it?"

"What, blokes going under trains? Yes, it must be the season for it."

The D.I. said, "Yes, could be. Perhaps it's started."

The sergeant stared at him.

"*What's* started?"

The D.I. went on staring down at the street for a moment, then shook his head to rid himself of a worrying and slightly ridiculous thought.

"Oh," he said, "oh, nothing."

Neil Schofield is an Englishman born in Yorkshire. For the past two decades, he's been living in Normandy, France, with his partner and live-in French person, Mimi. He's also been writing short mystery fiction for the past fourteen years, after spending ten years in theatre lighting, first as a production electrician and touring chief, and then edging into lighting design. From there, he became a writer and producer of conventions, sales conferences, product launches, et al. In the 1990s, he graduated to writing "Tourist Rides" for attractions around the world in France, Singapore, Australia, Berlin, and even London. In 2000, now relocated to France, he started writing crime and mystery stories, and soon selling them regularly to *Ellery Queen's Mystery Magazine* and *Alfred Hitchcock's Mystery Magazine*. He's been a Reader's Award finalist, as well as made the Barry Award shortlist for a story co-written with Melody Johnson Howe.

The Rites of Zosimos: Angela Penrose

First published in *Fiction River: Alchemy and Steam*

The body lay sprawled upon the stable midden amid reeking dung and acrid straw. Someone had dumped a barrow load on top of it before realizing what was there; the overturned barrow lay to one side in the hardpacked dirt beside the grey-weathered fence that divided the rear stable yard from the lane.

Sir Peter Estridge squatted down to take a closer look at the corpse's skin, most of which was visible. The entire body from feet to face shone in the late morning sun under a coating of escaped humors—mainly phlegm and blood it would seem from the blend of clear, viscous substance smeared with red. It was a nauseating sight, coupled with a lingering meaty scent, and he controlled his stomach with some effort. A reeking mess to one side proved some earlier witness, likely a stablehand, had failed to do the same.

"Burned," he said. "Poor bugger."

"Boiled." The correction came from Lady Catherine Morwood, Dean of the Ionian School within the Universita Hermetica, who had invited herself along when news of a dead man behind the university stable had come into the administrative offices.

Sir Peter clenched his jaw on a protest that, of course, that was what he'd meant, and only replied, "As you say."

He stood and looked around to where the stable master lingered in the rear doorway of the building, two younger men peering past his shoulders in wide-eyed horror.

"Do we know who he is?" Peter asked. "One of yours?"

"No, sir, not ours," said the stable master. The others shook their heads.

"You're sure?" The way the corpse lay, the face was visible to one side, but the distortion would make identification difficult.

"I sent Tommy round to everyone and he eyeballed all what work here," said the stable master, who apparently had some common sense. "That one be none of ours."

"I would say a student," said Lady Catherine. "Or a young master. Somewhat advanced, more prideful than justified, and impatient. And unfortunately, likely to be from my side of the yard."

Peter watched as she stepped forward, careful of her skirts about the mess. She was swathed in black, veiled and gloved. Peter had never seen her dressed differently, save for the veil, even at dinners. It was an eccentricity shared by a few old women in society. Lady Catherine had little to do with society outside of the academic world, but she'd been the Ionian Dean since before he came to school as an eager teenager; he guessed she was a contemporary of his grandmother, and that she was too vain to show wrinkled, spotted skin.

She used her ivory headed cane to tip the body's head slightly upward and studied the face.

"I don't recognize him," she said, "but I likely know him. Stupid boy." She stepped back and turned to the stable master. "Have him brought up to the frigidarium. We'll keep him there until we find out who he is, and send him back to his people."

The man clearly wanted to object, but he just nodded and said, "Of course, m'lady," and sent the two men off to fetch some canvas to carry the body on.

"Thank you for your assistance," she said to Peter. "You may tell Dean Everard that I'll look into the matter, and inform him if anything further requires his attention."

Peter doubted very much that Anthony Everard would step gracefully aside, and not only because of the traditional rivalry between Lady Catherine's Ionian School and Dean Everard's Newtonian School. Modern practicality might squabble with the more traditional spirituality, but such a ghastly murder needed to be investigated, not merely contemplated.

It wasn't his place to contradict Lady Catherine, however, so he only said, "I will convey your message," and bowed.

Something about the tilt of her head gave Peter the impression she was smiling at him, but it was only a fleeting sense. She nodded and walked out of the stable yard, her step firm and spry.

Peter glanced back at the naked, boiled man lying on a dung heap before following her.

***

When Peter returned to Dean Everard's office suite, a slightly musty set of rooms paneled in dark oak, lit by a combination of diamond-paned windows and luminous ether lamps, he sent out an order to have a roll taken of all the students and masters of the school. He didn't mention to anyone getting the idea from the stable master; the dean had a strong sense of hierarchy and Peter decided not to give him a reason to find fault with the notion. But however sure Lady Catherine might be that the dead man was one of hers, Peter preferred surety to supposition.

Notes began to show up by mid-afternoon, when the Dean came thumping back through the office. He was a burly, florid man, with a bushy mustache and thinning hair under his hat. Large hands bore the scars of heat and metal. He'd spent the early part of the day in a series of meetings, the latest with the university bursar. Peter didn't expect him to be in a jolly mood, and wasn't disappointed.

"Estridge! What happened with the dead man? Some drunken stable hand, I imagine, fell out of a window and broke his neck?"

"No, sir," said Peter. "I'm afraid not. We've yet to identify the man, but I have inquiries being made. The body is difficult to identify, however. He seems to have been boiled to death."

"Boiled? Damnation! Are *you* drunk?"

"No, sir," said Peter with all patience. The dean was a practical man and rarely reacted well when things turned odd. "Lady Catherine accompanied me. She seems sure it was one of the Ionians."

"They're boiling each other now?" The dean stopped in mid-rant and stared at the floor for a few moments. Then he huffed and said, "Some young idiot took the Zosiman dream texts as literal. Usually they have the brains to ask about it first."

"Err, Zosiman?" asked Peter.

The dean scowled at him. "Fourth century Greek alchemist, one of the fathers of hermetics. In my day, we never granted a degree to a student who didn't have a decent knowledge of the history of our art. Useful practice is one thing, but you can hardly be called an educated hermeticist if you've not read Zosimos. At any rate, it's all allegory. He dreamed of being distilled and refined, the art applied to man. It's a spiritual metaphor, and anyone with an ounce of brains realizes it. Apparently our dead man lacked an ounce of brains." He waved a hand at Peter and said, "Let me know if it turns out to be one of ours. And find out who he was working with—that one needs expelling."

"Yes, sir!" Peter called to the dean's retreating back. Of course, there had to be an accomplice. There was no vessel large enough to boil a man anywhere near the stable yard, and the dead man hadn't walked out to the dung heap and flung himself upon it. The dean might be a blunt and abrupt man, but he had considerably more than an ounce of brains in his head.

An undergraduate hurried in with a note—two more masters had accounted for all of their students and staff.

If this was really all about refining the body as one refined gold or steel, Peter doubted the dead man could be one of theirs. The Newtonian school focused on the practical, laboratory application of the art. Their students, those who didn't stay to teach, had made their marks in the modern world, and some had gotten rich as well—the university had some fat endowments from students who'd gone on to success.

A Newtonian had worked out the distillation of liquid fire that allowed locomotives to move people and goods all over England, Europe and America. Another Newtonian had further refined the fire into a gas and, collaborating with an engineering mechanic, had developed a safe airship. Flights crossed the Atlantic four times per week, without a single explosion since 1818—almost thirty years, now.

Newtonians were practical people. Hopping into a boiling vat was a piece of idiocy, and Peter'd wager his new reverberatory furnace that the dead fellow was one of those wool-headed Ionians. Even Lady Catherine thought so.

Which meant, of course, that it was a Newtonian.

Word came half way through dinner, from Master Blanchard who supervised Dee House. William Tarrant hadn't been seen since the previous day, and a phlegmatic mate of his had agreed to take a look at the body. It seemed to be young Master Tarrant, so far as his friend could tell. Inquiries went on, but Tarrant was a man of regular habits, and missing three meals with no word left was enough to set his friends to talking and searching.

Tarrant's body was sent home to his parents, his demise noted down as an accident (the idiocy involved kept out of official records for the sake of the family) and the university president made an announcement at dinner to the effect that the Zosiman Rites were not to be attempted by anyone who hadn't prepared for longer than any of the undergraduates had been alive, and unsupervised by a senior Ionian master. Applicants were to present themselves to Lady Catherine.

Peter thought the word spreading of Tarrant having been boiled to death would be enough of a deterrent, but forms had to be followed.

***

The business of the university proceeded apace for the next four weeks. No word came from Lady Catherine's office about an accomplice or accomplices of Master Tarrant. Peter hoped anyone involved had learned a hard lesson, and turned his attention to organizing the schedule of lectures for the upcoming term. He was nearly done when word came of another boiled body found on the dung heap.

"This is quite enough," said Lady Catherine. She'd come to

Dean Everard's offices, down the corridor and a world away from her own, and stood leaning on her cane in his doorway, her back to Peter's desk in the reception room.

They'd discovered that the dead man was another New-tonian, and that fact seemed to upset Lady Catherine above the mere fact of a boiled corpse.

"What does a Newtonian even want with the Zosiman purification process?" she asked. "Assuming any of you even believe in it—which I can only assume Master Tar-rant and now Lord Nathan did—what possible use would you find in it? Help me understand, Everard, because I am at a loss."

Peter heard his Dean huff out a sigh. "I've no idea," he said. "Anyone who's interested in your philosophical, mystic botheration becomes an Ionian. There *is* no use to it that I can see."

"Well, someone is convincing your boys that there's a benefit to them in trying it," she said. "At first I thought it had to be one of mine, impatient to get on with it. The Rites of Zosimos take long years of study and prepara-tion, and at that most don't care to chance it."

Everard made a skeptical sound that would not be ac-ceptable in a lady's drawing room. "And the last person to actually try was, what, four or five centuries ago?"

"Not that long, no, although long enough. It's the cul-mination of a lifetime of spiritual study and illumination. Certainly the young pups who've been trying it could not have been ready, even if they'd been on my side of the yard."

"No, I'm sure not," said Everard. "Back in the nine-teenth century, we've obviously got a group of idiots who need a good kicking."

"I agree," she said. "May I borrow your secretary? He has a strong stomach and young legs, and I think we'll have need of both."

"Certainly," said Everard, "confiscate him for as long as you need." He raised his voice and called, "Estridge? Are you out there?"

"Here, sir," said Peter, trying to catch up with events. Were the two of them actually cooperating?

"Excellent. Help Lady Catherine sort this mess. I'll have Billbury shuffle your papers in the mean while."

Peter winced, but said, "Of course, sir."

"We'll be off, then," said Lady Catherine, and she strode out, Peter following in her wake.

As soon as they were clear of the door, she said, "I want to speak with that boy who identified Tarrant's body, Avery Oxhill. He should be in Master Blanchard's laboratory at this time of day, I believe."

"I believe you're correct, ma'am."

They crossed the quad with barely three minutes to notice the fine day. Spring buds put a fresh green on trees and shrubs, and a brisk breeze blew through the archways and down the walks running between the tall, gabled granite buildings.

Master Blanchard's laboratory occupied a favored corner location, overlooking both a hedge knot and a playing field. The large room rose a full two stories high, with windows letting in the spring sun to glitter on copper piping, steel vats and a myriad of shapes of glassware.

Half a dozen students, five young men and a young woman, worked among the crowded benches. Peter looked about, then called, "Oxhill? You in here?"

"Oy!" called a voice from the far side of the room next to a towering boiler. Peter led Lady Catherine through the maze of apparatus, following the sound of a pumping steam bellows. Oxhill, a thin young man with hunched shoulders and a permanent scowl, had one hand on a rotary stopper while watching a hogshead-sized vessel made of thick glass. Several tubes penetrated through the top, one of which was connected to the bellows. Peter recognized the sublimation rig; the bellows was pumping air out of the vessel to produce a vacuum, necessary to the process.

He waited for Oxhill to come to a decent stopping point; Lady Catherine waited with equal patience. When Oxhill finally turned his attention to them, he straightened, startled, and gave her a bow.

"Lady Catherine, apologies."

"It's no matter, Oxhill. You were occupied. Even Ionians are familiar with laboratory procedures."

"Of course, ma'am. Ah, can I help you with something?"

"You identified Master Tarrant's body," she said.

"Ah, yes, I did. Nasty business, that." He looked away and swallowed hard.

"You were a friend of his, then. Who else did he go about with?"

"Well, just about everyone knew him," said Oxhill. "That is, he was friendly enough, been around a while, did some laboratory work, gave some lectures to the pups."

"Let's not waste time, boy. You know what he tried, and now Lord Nathan as well. Someone must have put them up to it, put the idea in their head. Most Newtonians your age have never heard of Zosimos. Who's been talking about it?"

"Ah..." Oxhill glanced at Peter, but Peter just stared at him. "That is, I never heard the name until the president's speech, ma'am. I've not heard anyone talking about it before that."

"Perhaps they didn't mention Zosimos by name. Any whispers about purifying the body? Any ideas about improving one's understanding of the work by perfecting the worker through the art?"

"No, ma'am!" Oxhill shook his head so hard his pomaded hair flopped loose. "Nothing of the sort, I promise."

"Hmm." She studied him for a few moments, but he didn't crack. Finally she said, "Very well. Contact me, or Estridge here, in your dean's office, if you do hear anything. Understand?"

"Yes, ma'am. Of course." He bowed again and she turned away in a rustle of black skirts.

They left the room and Lady Catherine said, "I'm not sure he was telling the truth, but we'll get no more out of him at the moment. Onward."

She led him about, through four more laboratories, three classrooms and the library. She spoke with various friends, roommates and students of both Master Tarrant and Lord Nathan. Peter occasionally helped her find someone, but other than that lent nothing to the proceedings save his presence.

No one would admit to hearing about anyone pursuing the Zosiman Rites, or anything that might sound like them.

When Peter and Lady Catherine exited to the quad once more, the sun sat somewhat lower in the sky than it had been when they started. They paused under a statue of John Dee, and Lady Catherine consulted an ornate brass pocket watch.

"Some seeds planted," she said. "I've a meeting I can't miss. Come to my office tomorrow at three. Between now and then, I want you to hunt for the apparatus that killed those boys. Find me a pot large enough to boil a man, and we can perhaps find out who's been using it. And notify me if anyone we spoke with contacts you."

"Yes, ma'am," he said.

She nodded and strode off.

It was nearly two hours until dinner, so Peter started back through the laboratories. Unfortunately, the Newtonian studies tended toward processes applicable to industry and commerce, which meant eventually scaling things up. The glass vessel Oxhill'd been working with was large enough, actually. Oxhill was gone by the time Peter got back around to his laboratory, but he rummaged through the notebooks on a nearby bench and found a log of usage for the sublimation rig.

It'd been running experiments both nights, when Tarrant died and again when Lord Nathan died. Peter hadn't really thought it would be this one; the vessel was large enough but it would have to be moved to a place where heat could be applied.

That was true of several of the large vessels he found, and most of the others had been processing one thing or another on one or both of the nights in question. He found undergraduates and junior masters who'd been monitoring the processes in most cases, and tables of data showing that the equipment had been occupied by something other than water and bodies in all cases.

There might be deception somewhere, but it would involve considerable time and effort.

He quit that evening with barely enough time to change for dinner, then started up again in the morning.

By the next afternoon, he'd turned up nothing that stood out as suspicious, and he went back to the administration building to meet Lady Catherine. On his way he made a quick pass through the office—wincing at the mess Billbury had made of Peter's organization already— to find that someone had left him a note while Billbury's back was turned. "No idea who it was," said Billbury. He was about Peter's age, in his mid-thirties, with a receding hairline and an earnest manner. He meant well, and had a great understanding of principles and precepts, but his grasp of details was weak at best. He handed Peter a sealed note with his name on it.

Peter broke the seal, a blob of plain wax with no impression, and read:

Sir Peter,

I've been told you're making inquiries into recent go-ings-on. There is a small group attempting the purification of man. Word is that completion of the process will grant perfect understanding of all hermetic principles. I've heard that the man organizing things has gone through the process himself, successfully. I don't believe it, but some do. I don't know his name, no one will say. I over-heard some voices, all male, talking about "the rite" some weeks ago at the back of the library, second floor near the arched window in the evening, a bit after eight. They were a row over and I didn't see who it was, and didn't think it was important at the time.

The note was unsigned. Peter turned it over thinking it must continue, but there was nothing.

He presented himself in Lady Catherine's office a minute later and reported his lack of success in searching for the deadly apparatus. He also showed her the note.

"I expected no more," she said, speaking of his failure while perusing the note, "but methodical is best for this sort of thing." She paused, turned the note over as he had, then reread it, then looked up and asked, "What do you make of this?"

"I was thinking whoever wrote it is afraid to say more. They don't say so, but there must be some threats going around. Why else remain anonymous, especially since they didn't tell us much of any use?"

"I agree. This is getting sinister."

"I rather thought it was sinister from the start," Peter ventured.

"I thought it was idiocy from the start," she said. "Idiocy is always more likely than villainy. There might well be some villainy involved, however. If you've nothing pressing the next few evenings, I'd like you to spend some time near the arched window in the library, say between quarter of eight and half after. Who knows, it might be a regular meeting place. For now, we'll search on." She tucked the note into a pocket and stood. "If you've checked all the laboratories, then we'll check other places. Come with me."

She led and he followed. Lady Catherine had keys to doors Peter had never seen unlocked, which made sense. She likely had keys even Master Blanchard had never seen, since she was a generation his elder and had been at the university that much longer. She led Peter through attics and cellars and utility rooms—the entire university had steam heat, and hot and cold tap water, so it made sense that of course there were boilers and pumps that served the university itself, outside of the laboratories. Peter'd simply never thought of it before.

It was in one of the utility rooms where they paused. She looked around, then pointed to one side.

"There," she said. "Over there. When I was an undergraduate, we came down here to drink beer and talk about things we didn't want the masters overhearing."

Then she had him shift several barrels with rusty pipes sticking out, like twigs in a vase, from where they sat all dusty and be-webbed between two huge boilers. He noticed, while flailing at the webbing, that it was stuck to the pipes and the barrels, but not between the two barrels, nor between the barrels and the boilers. As if the barrels were moved regularly, but not cleaned off.

Behind was a narrow door with a big, old-fashioned keyhole. Lady Catherine fished up a big, old-fashioned key on one of the several key rings she'd brought in a pocket, and with an application of mineral oil, she unlocked the door.

The passage behind was narrow and dark, but clear. An old-style oil lamp hung just beyond the doorway; Peter lit it with a lucifer from his jacket pocket and walked ahead, carrying the lamp. A pair of fat pipes the size of a man's thigh ran on either wall up near the ceiling, with smaller pipes down the walls. The passage ran straight on, with narrower cross-passages running to either side periodically. The smaller pipes followed the branches, but the two large pipes went straight on.

After passing the third cross passage, Peter stopped, trying to picture in his head where they were. He turned around, looking past Lady Catherine in the direction they'd come, then around again.

"This... we're under the quad," he said. "Those side passages run to the buildings on either side. We started underneath the Great Hall, and we're heading toward Bacon Hall."

"Very good," said Lady Catherine. "It's most efficient for every building to have a boiler in its basement, but when this was first built, they had the notion that one great boiler could serve all. In actuality, it takes far too long to heat, and ridiculous amounts of fuel to keep hot, even in the middle of the day when no one is bathing. It was disconnected and abandoned before you were born."

Peter nodded and resumed walking. Another hundred feet or so and the passage opened out into a broad, low room, lined with grey brick. The two large pipes, which Peter had assumed originated at the two boilers in the first cellar, led to a much larger pipe which itself ran out of the largest boiler he'd ever seen. Black iron, the lot of it, encircled with rusting bands. A dozen men clasping hands couldn't have encompassed it around. It had to be lined with something, lead or ceramic, something that wouldn't corrode, or it'd be a pile of rust by now. Beside it was a wooden vat set up on a platform of smooth wood with brass fittings. A short flight of stairs led up to the platform so one could walk round the vat, and a pair of narrow catwalks, railed only on the two outer sides, ran across the top from one side of the vat to the other.

"What's the vat for?" he asked, his voice hushed. "I mean, what was it built for?" He was sure this was where Tarrant and Lord Nathan had died.

"Outflow. To control pressure if things got out of hand. As I said, it was early days for this sort of thing and it's not terribly efficient." She walked over and studied the boiler and its controls. "There've been changes made here, I'm sure of it. It's been a long time since I've seen this place, but I don't recall it being this complex. And no one made this style of knob then, and the lettering on these dials..."

Peter went up the steps and peered into the vat, half expecting to see another boiled corpse. It was empty, or mostly so, he was relieved to find. "It's been used," he said. "There's a bit of water left in the vat, down around the pipes. If this rig was disconnected generations ago, it should be dry as an old bone."

"Pipes?" She climbed up and stood next to him to look in at the lead pipes crisscrossing the bottom of the vat, beneath a screen of expanded copper. "Hmm. Come help me pry this cover off—I want to see what's what here."

Peter said, "Yes, ma'am," then after a pause, "It's nearly time for dinner. We could come back later?"

She shook her head. "Tell anyone who inquires that I'll not be at dinner. This is much more interesting. You help me with this cover and then run along."

"I can stay and help you," he offered. "I'm not very hungry."

"Thank you, but no. It's been a while since I had a chance to tinker. I know young people are always hungry, so you go on off."

Peter had to stifle a smirk—she obviously had mature men lumped in with growing boys—but said, "Yes, ma'am. And I'll go to the library after dinner, see if anyone turns up."

"If you like," she said. "But we know where they come now, and we know when they'll be here."

"We do?" Peter felt like he'd missed something.

"Of course. Last night was the dark of the moon, as it was four weeks earlier when Tarrant died. Whoever's running this circus thinks the phase of the moon has anything to do with the rite. Or perhaps is just using it for show-manship. At any rate, we've nearly a month before anyone is likely to do anything we can expel them for."

"If someone is... is doing this deliberately, then it's murder," Peter pointed out. "Expelling hardly comes into it."

"We have to expel them before they hang, dear."

He couldn't really argue with that.

***

Another thing he couldn't argue with was that a whole parade to the vat room on the night would tip off the people they were trying to catch, likely scattering them forever. Lady Catherine wanted to settle the matter herself, and would allow Peter to accompany her, but no one else. Under orders not to mention anything to anyone, he waited.

Approximately a month later, Peter and Lady Catherine made their excuses after dinner and went down to the vat room. Peter had argued for going earlier, but Lady Catherine insisted there was no rush.

"They'll be doing this at or near midnight, mark me," she said. "For the drama of it."

They moved to a dark corner of the room and prepared themselves to wait. Lady Catherine sat down on the floor, cross-legged, all but invisible in a huge poof of black skirts and settled herself with an air of meditation. Peter hadn't meditated since he was a pup newly at university, before he'd chosen the Newtonian path, so he sat next to her, with her camouflaging darkness between him and the vat, and leaned against the wall to nap.

He awoke to a great clatter of feet and echoing voices, roused himself and stood, Lady Catherine beside him, peering out of their dark corner. Eight figures in black robes marched in, chanting something in a version of ancient Greek he didn't quite recognize. Six of them worked stoking a fire in an enormous firebox around the far side of the boiler. One of the figures busied itself in front of the control panel; Peter heard bellows pumping, and machinery groan and chuff.

The eighth figure climbed to the platform beside the vat, removed the robe and draped it over the railing, then lay down flat on the wood. Once the firebox was going, the six came back and surrounded the supine figure, three on either side, their chanting low and monotonous.

Peter heard a hissing sound coming out of the vat. Steam from the pipes along the bottom, to keep the water hot? He shrank in on himself at the thought of plunging in. The vat was deeper than he was tall; there'd be no climbing out before one scalded to death.

The chanting faded away and the figure at the control panel said, "Witness all here, that you might see the truth of the Rite!"

He pushed a lever and a great rush of steaming water poured into the vat, surely enough to fill it near to the top. Peter heard the water bubbling and saw the man in charge climb the steps to the platform. He shucked his robe; he was naked underneath.

He lay down a few paces from the other supine figure, who hadn't moved. "A minute of meditation is all I require," he said.

Peter couldn't see what he was doing, surrounded as he was by his robed followers, but they ran through two iterations of their chant, then all squatted down by him.

One of them said, "One, two, three, up!" and they all stood, lifting the leader on their hands.

Lady Catherine gave a light snort beside him. "I'll wager they each have only two fingers under his body," she whispered. "We did that when I was at boarding school, when the house mistress thought we were asleep. It's pseudo-spiritual rubbish."

The six robed figures carried their leader over the top of the vat, three of them on each catwalk, his body suspended between them. The anonymous voice repeated, "One, two, three, go!" and they dropped him.

Peter jerked forward but Lady Catherine's surprisingly strong grip on his wrist kept him back, and another hand closed over the shout that wanted to come bursting from his lips.

"The leader is successful, remember?" she whispered.

Peter stood frozen for a moment, then nodded until she released him.

The six followers chanted louder, peering down through the steam at their leader, who was presumably not boiling to death. The pump wheezed and the bellows heaved, the fire roared and the gears turned, clicking.

Peter estimated no more than two minutes had gone by when there was a louder click, then a sluicegate opened and steaming water poured out of the vat, rushing away down a pipe that had to lead to the sewers. A timer of some sort? Although safety seemed ludicrous at that point. The naked leader stood, lifted his arms in the air, and the six followers oohed and ahhed. One clapped until a companion smacked him on the arm.

"The Rite purifies the body and gives it dominion over the elements and processes," said the leader. He led them in another obscure Greek-ish chant, then descended the steps and put his robe back on. "We will allow Brother Parker twenty more minutes of meditation," he said, then he turned back to the control panel.

"What the hell was that?" whispered Peter. "No one can dip himself in boiling water, much less take a leisurely immersion, and walk out whole and healthy."

"That one certainly can't," Lady Catherine whispered back. "Therefore it was a trick."

Twenty minutes later, a rush of boiling water poured into the vat. The six robed followers lined up on either side of Brother Parker.

The leader, standing at Parker's head, looked down and intoned, "Art thou prepared?"

Parker apparently nodded or the equivalent, because the six did their one-two-three-lift trick and started for the catwalk.

Lady Catherine strode out into the dim light and said, "All right, that's enough."

There were several yelps of startlement. The robes dropped Brother Parker, luckily onto the decking beside the vat, and three of them took off.

"*Stay* right there!" she snapped. Her voice echoed off the stone ceiling like a thunderclap. Everyone stood stock-still, including Peter.

She circled around to the step side of the vat and herded the near-fled men up before her. Peter followed, and they all gathered on the platform.

"Hoods off, right now," she ordered. Everyone obeyed except the leader. She gave him a hard stare and said, "Don't bother hiding, Lane. I recognized your voice. What exactly do you think you're doing?"

Lane straightened and glared back. "I've discovered the secret of the Rite. Our Newtonian brothers can make great use of it, so I—"

"You're a fraud," she said. "With hot water and bubbles through pipes. Care to jump into the water now that it's actually boiling?" She gestured toward the steaming, boiling vat. Lane stood still, but stiffened as though resisting a retreat.

"I've already immersed myself. I prove my mastery at each Rite."

She herded him with her body right up next to the vat, then removed a glove. She took Lane's wrist and held it over the boiling water. "Let's try together."

"It's not necessary," he babbled. "I've already—no, wait—" She plunged both their hands into the water and he screamed.

Lane was a husky man, but no matter how he struggled he couldn't get away from Lady Catherine. He twisted and jerked, pummeled her with fist and knees, but she shrugged it all off like an adult ignoring a toddler's tantrum. It was a good half minute before she brought their hands out. She dropped Lane's swollen, blistered and oozing hand from her own smooth, pristine one. The only bumps on her hand were water droplets, and they ran—and steamed—away.

"You're a fraud," she repeated. "And a murderer."

"Data," he gasped. "I was studying the Rite..."

"You're an arrogant child who uses people like rats. I'll come to your hanging." She turned to stare at the others, who were all huddled together. Parker had retrieved his robe at some point.

"You're all idiots," she said. "I know who you are. I'll give your names to Dean Everard. He'll decide whether to expel you. Get out of here."

They tripped over each other to get down the steps and out the door.

Peter picked up her black glove and handed it to her, silent.

"Thank you, dear." She pulled it on over her smooth hand. Her smooth metallic hand. Not metallic like gold or silver or copper, but if flesh were a metal, refined and pure.

She smoothed the glove down and descended the steps. Peter hauled Lane to his feet and followed her, still silent, out of the room.

Angela Penrose has been an SF fan since the original *Star Trek*, and got into fantasy not too long after. She was a history major, and thought "The Rites of Zosimos," first published in *Fiction River: Alchemy & Steam,* was a great opportunity to pull SF, fantasy and history all together. She writes romance under another name, but fantasy and science fiction has always been her fictional home. Recent stories have appeared in *Fiction River* volumes *How to Save the World* and *Reycled Pulp*, as well as a story in the shared-world anthology *Crucible: All New Tales of Valdemar*, edited by Mercedes Lackey.

Rusch & Helfers

The Girl Who Loved Shonen Knife: Carrie Vaughn

First published in *Hanzai Japan*

I only want one thing in the whole world: for my band, Flying Jelly Attack, the world's greatest Shonen Knife cover band, to play at Cherry Blossom High School's Spring Dance. Two things stand in my way:

     1) Lizard Blood, a Lolita death metal band, out bitter rivals
     2) The end of the world

Lizard Blood isn't a real band. They only care about going viral and how many hits they can get on UltraPluz. They never really learned to play their instruments. Instead, they use synthesizers plugged into programmable neuromuscular implants, upload whatever song they want to play, and play it – or "play" it, rather. They even have their implants synced to they can play together – not that that really matters when it's death metal.

Lizard blood's fake lead singer and fake lead guitarist, Yuki Niamori, is very rich – or at least her family is – and she can have anything she wants. What she wants is to be lead singer in a Lolita death metal band that will play at Cherry Blossom High School's Spring Dance.

She must be stopped.

As for the end of the world, I'm, not really paying attention. It's got something to do with cyber attacks on big banks draining all the money out of their systems – not transferring it, not stealing it, just deleting it as if it never existed. The banks are shutting down and the government can't stop it. Experts are saying to change your online passwords and stuff, but that doesn't help because the hackers fix the system so it doesn't need passwords at all. Change your passwords and biometric logins all you want, doesn't matter. The hackers still delete everything you have.

It's not like I have that much money anyway, since I spend everything on guitar strings and upgrading my amps. And we still have to go to school, even though half the teachers haven't shown up all week and the other half are threatening to strike if they don't get paid soon. Our parents are making us go because they think it's safe – Cherry Blossom High School's security guards are still here when the actual police have fled the city. It's all very complicated, but I'm working too hard to get the cord progression right on "Brown Mushrooms" to notice. If we don't go play at the Spring Dance, nothing else will matter.

The big audition for who gets to play at the Spring Dance is in three days. Only two bands have signed up: Flying Jelly Attack and Lizard Blood. Attrition – we scared everybody off. Yuki possibly made threats – at least, she's made them to us.

Miki, my bass player, says out best course of action is to avoid Yuki and her girls entirely. Ru, my drummer, goes into a murderous rage whenever we mention Yuki or Lizard Blood. She's prone to murderous rages, where all her hair stands on end and her eyes go wide and she bares her teeth like some kind of demon. Miki and I both have to hold her back to keep her from doing damage. It's this kind of thing that makes her a great drummer.

Trouble is, we can't avoid our enemy entirely when our enemy seems bent on searching us out.

There we are, just hanging out between classes – or these days, just hanging out until we find out whether we'll be even *having* classes. Miki, hair in ponytail, her wire-rimmed glasses slipping down her nose, hunches over her deck doing something online – because she's *always* doing something online when she isn't playing – while Ru and I discuss what we should wear to the audition. Modern art mini-dresses or jeans and leather jackets? Cute or vintage rebellious? Whatever would make us the most different from Lizard Blood, is my opinion. Ripped jeans and anger.

"I don't really care, you pick," Ru says. When she isn't angry, her hair lies flat in a pixie cut. Really, I don't even know why I'm asking her – she doesn't have any fashion sense at all. Me or Miki pick out all her clothes. If we didn't have school uniforms she might not wear anything at all.

"I just want you to pick one, skirt or jeans?"

"Kit, look!" Ru points down the hallway and I swear the lights dim and a mysterious wind begins howling past us. Even Miki looks up from her deck.

Lizard Blood appears standing together, glaring a challenge at us: Yuki, with Azumi and Hana flanking her like acolytes. Between all of them, their poofed-out skirts fill the corridor. They have dyed their hair three different shades of pink: hot, bubblegum, and rose.

We get to our feet and it's like an Old West standoff.

"Hello, Yuki," I say. "What are you doing here. Shouldn't you be *practicing*?"

"You can't win," Yuki says. Her arms are at her sides, her hands in fists. She's wearing a black and white striped dress trimmed in lace and a little derby hat the size of an apple. She is above school uniforms, as she has often informed us. Just think, if she spent as much time practicing guitar as she did dressing, she could actually learn to play. "Why don't you give up?"

"We'll let the judges decide." I cross my arms. I'm not afraid of her. "It's only fair."

"I'm trying to save you the humiliation of losing."

"That's very kind of you, I'm sure."

She studies a manicured, black-painted nail. "I don't know why I bother. You're too stupid to listen to *anyone*."

At that, Ru roars and launches herself as a mad battering ram at the trio across from us. Miki and I grab her just in time, hooking our arms across her body and holding fast.

Predictably, Yuki laughs. Her henchthings start in a second later, and stop after she does. Throwing a last glare at us, they turn on their high-heel patent-leather Mary Janes and march away.

"I hate her *so much!*" Ru hisses, slumping in our arms out of exhaustion.

"Our best revenge is to win the audition and play at the dance," I say. "We'll practice tonight, right after school."

"I may be late," Miki says, her expression scrunched up in apology. "I have ... a *thing.*"

"A thing? What *thing*?"

"Just. It's. I'll explain later."

She turns and runs, bumping up against a boy standing at the end of the corridor. It's like he just appeared. He glances briefly at Miki, then stares at us, and I wonder how long he's been standing there. Did he see the whole confrontation with Lizard Blood?

This guy, he's *cute.* He's in a pale suit with a blue shirt and a thin tie. The jacket sleeves are rolled up and his hands are in his pockets. His dark hair flops perfectly over his forehead, framing his very mysterious gray eyes.

"Who is *that*?"

"I think it's the new boy," Ru says. "Just transferred in."

I can't look away, but I have nothing to say to him. Then, with a final dismissive glance, he turns and is gone.

Seriously, this is not the time to be distracted by such things as new boys at school.

I try to find out everything I can about the New Guy, but it's not a lot. He transferred in from New Tokyo Poly-technic, but I don't know anyone from there I could ask for gossip. He's taking a normal roster of classes, but rarely speaks. Even though he's collected a gaggle of girls and a few boys following him wherever he goes, he ignores his admirers completely.

"I bet he's a secret agent," Ru says. "He's spying."

"On what?"

"I don't know. Just on something."

What can there possibly be to spy on at Cherry Blossom High School?

"Or an undercover cop, like in the movies. He's going to make a drug bust and set the whole school in an uproar."

"As long as he waits to do it after the Spring Dance."

The guy stands in the doorway of the lunchroom and just... watches. I'm not thinking it's drugs because with the city falling apart and the police on strike, would they really send someone to bust drugs at a high school? This has to be bigger than that, which means he's a government agent. There's and international spy ring made up of teachers. Or a secret cavern under the school with a den of giant monsters.

I bet the school is home to a secret laboratory creating superheroes," I say, and Miki and Ru just stare at me. I keep going. "You know, like some of out fellow students may in face be superheroes in disguise, with a strange mental or physical powers. There's a secret high-tech gymnasium under the real gymnasium where they do their training."

Miki says, "If there are any secret superheroes, why don't they do something to save the city?"

That is a very good question.

Finally, school ends and we can get to work. Despite saying she would be late, Miki's already at out practice space in a second music room behind the school's auditorium's stage. She's finally put her deck away. Ru and I hurry to get our instruments and tune up. We have the space for an hour and have to make the most of it.

We've spent months working on our set: "Twist Barbie," "It's a New Find," "Banana Chips," and of course our signature "Flying Jelly Attack." This is for a dance – we have to get people dancing first thing or we're doomed. But Shonen Knife makes it easy to dance. Their music is all about dancing and being happy. How can we not win the audition, when Lizard Blood is all about death and fashion? Of course, times being what they are, maybe people are in the mood for death.

We practice and we start to feel better.

Besides the dancing and expressing happiness, another reason I started a Shonen Knife cover band is that the lyrics are pretty easy to learn.

"Naaaa na na na naaaaa na na na naaaa na na naaaa na na naaa –"

This is music in its very purest form, I think.

Everything's coming together, we're rocking , and I start to think maybe we should back off, save our strength to ensure that we don't peak before the audition. But then Miki biffs a cord. I'm about to yell, but she's staring at the door. We all look.

And there he is, studying us with this little frown and a narrowed gaze, like he's on some kind of treasure hunt.

The New Guy, in his perfectly starched suit and his very cool manner. Is he following us around? What does he want with us?

"Hey!" I yell. "This is a private rehearsal, can't you read the sign?" I'd taped a handwritten sign to the outside of the door to discourage gawkers.

He glances at the sign, then back at us, and his lips press into a thin, uninterpretable line. Why doesn't he *say* something? Then I have a terrible thought: is he spying for Lizard Blood, so they can learn our strategy for winning the audition?

Before I can yell at him again, he walks away. Only one thing to do: I unsling my guitar, gently set it down, and charge after him.

"Kit, wait!" Miki yells, as Ru shouts, "That's not a good idea!"

"I have to do something," I shout back. "He can't just lurk in doorways and get away with it!"

Miki turns panicked. "But he could be dangerous!"

He's far too handsome to be dangerous. Mysterious yes, but not dangerous. At least not a bad dangerous. Heroic dangerous, maybe. He looks like a hero.

"Hey!" I yell, and what do you know, he actually turns around.

"What?" he asks. His voice is soft but somehow compelling – authoritative and full of secrets. The voice totally goes with that suit.

"I want to know what you're doing here! You're not really a student, are you?"

His gaze is appraising. Smoldering, and appraising. He has better eyelashes than I do.

Finally, with a curt, dismissive nod he says, "It's best you don't know. Don't pay any attention to me. Go back to your friends." He walks on, turning the corner ahead.

When I chase him around the corner, he's gone.

Disaster.

Principal Jono is trying to cancel the band auditions for the Spring Dance. I argue with him, explaining that the auditions are a necessary distraction from the current tragic events and that hearing us perform would raise morale among the students.

"But Kit," he says sadly. He's a large, balding man with a thin comb-over and drooping face. "I don't think we'll be able to even hold the Spring Dance. Band auditions seem just a little ... pointless right now."

I declare, "What lesson are you teaching us with that kind of attitude? Are you saying we should give up? Are you telling us that perseverance in the face of adversity is not a good quality to have? Of course not! We must show that we are better than the evil that lurks in the rest of the world! Cherry Blossom High School and the Spring Dance will not be defeated!"

He relents, but I think only to make me go away.

Another reason I started a Shonen Knife cover band is the clothes. Basically, we can wear whatever we want, as long as we match. We can wear surf T-shirts or white tunics or leather jackets or bell-bottoms or miniskirts. And no matter what, we're *cute*, spreading brightly colored happiness wherever we go. Lizard Blood, with their fancy corsets and big crinolines and just bitty hats and velvet boots and too much makeup – it's like a uniform with them. Baby-doll fascists. It's sad, really.

I would spy on Lizard Blood – do they plan on playing a lot of screechy thrash or are they actually going to go with a set list that people can dance to? Because if they expect to win the audition they have to play stuff that people can dance to. Unless Yuki has paid off all the judges. This is an angle I haven't considered, and it leaves me thoughtful, because even with all the banks shut down, her family is so rich that she still has money. She keeps telling everyone she still has money, anyway.

If she's paying off judges, what can I do to compete? Nothing. Unless I can somehow expose her bribery plot. Maybe, just maybe, the New Guy is here to investigate Yuki. That would be helpful.

After the banks lost all their money, a bunch of people started looting grocery stores and things because pretty soon they wouldn't be able to buy anything. Some people tried to keep going to work and pretending everything was normal, convinced that their money would return and they'd get paid and the police would arrest all the looters and everything would be fine.

But then the water stopped. The hackers broke into the computer systems handling the city's water treatment and distribution plants and deleted the software. Water flowing through pipes stopped. No more showers, no more drinking. The hoarding of bottled water began. People fled, and the streets and trains out of the city became impassible.

Everyone says it will only be a matter of time before the hackers destroy the power grid as well. I don't think they'll go that far since they need the power grid and computer networks functional in order to do all that hacking in the first place. Nevertheless, just in case, I acquire a gas-powered electric generator for our instruments. Even if the city goes completely dark, we will still be able to audition for the Spring Dance. If I'm truly lucky, Lizard Blood will not have an electric generator, but since Yuki is rich I'm not counting on it. She has everything. If we're going to defeat her, we need to rely on our immense talent, the fact that we are good guys, and the sheer uplifting power of the music of Shonen Knife.

The dance will be in the gymnasium, the biggest room in the school, with polished wood floors, a high ceiling, and one wall full of windows looking over the city's downtown skyscrapers and monorail tracks. The monorail isn't running anymore because the hackers corrupted the system's software. A couple of trains crashed before the authorities shut it down.

Miki and Ru come with me to scout out the area where we'll be playing for auditions tomorrow. Well, Ru and I scout, and Miki sits in a corner and works on her deck: headphones on, eyes on screen like there's nothing else in the world. It's weird.

"What are you doing on your deck all day? You can't possibly have that much homework." The teachers who still bother showing up have stopped assigning home-work in favor of teaching us survival techniques like starting fires, collecting dew for drinking water, and spin-ning wool into yarn. Who knew they're all survivalists? It's almost comforting.

"Nothing. Never mind. It's a secret."

Like that isn't suspicious.

And then when I turn around – there he is again. New Guy. Watching us from yet another doorway. *Staring*, like some creep. A very handsome creep in a nice suit, but still.

I'm about to yell, but he slips away as if he hadn't been there at all. Miki and Ru also look after him.

"That's it," I mutter.

"You said it," Ru mutters with me. Her hair starts to get messy, which means she's about to rage out.

"Don't worry. We'll find out what this is all about. I have an idea."

Here's how we set a trap for New Guy. First, we sched-ule another impromptu practice. Technically, we don't have the practice room reserved, but since no one else at the school is playing any music and most classes have been canceled, no one stops us. The trick is, we have to catch him as soon as he shows up. No delay, no time for him to figure out anything's wrong. Just boom, captured, and then we can shine a bright light on him and demand that he spill the beans.

But Miki isn't there. We get the practice room at the right time, have our ropes and a flashlight and everything ready to go, and she's not there. How are we going to fool New Guy into thinking this is a legitimate practice if Miki isn't here?

"This isn't going to work." Ru looks despondent.

"No, it will. The plan doesn't change."

We wait in ambush, standing on either side of the doorway, each of us holding a can of Silly String. I plug my phone into speakers and play a concert bootleg of "Redd Kross." Maybe it won't fool him – maybe he'll know it's actually Shonen Knife on a recording and not us – but I'm willing to take that risk.

We hold our breaths and wait, wait... At our other practice, this was about the time New Guy appeared in the doorway. Sure enough, listening hard past the beat and the bass line, I hear footsteps, a careful approach of expensive loafers. Fu and I exchange a glance.

New Guy peeks in, looking confused for a moment when he doesn't see anyone. That's when we attack.

Silly String is a really good weapon because it's totally shocking and totally nonlethal. We cover him in instant rubbery spaghetti. Futilely, he puts up his hands to fend off the swarm of plastic, but it's no good – he's covered. When he stumbles back, trying to turn and get a good look at his attackers, he trips over the rope we slung across the floor. He goes down with a crash and lies prone. We stand over him, empty cans held out like guns. Ru is growling.

"What are you *doing*?" he exclaims, picking Silly String from his face, blinking at us. His thin frown might be curled into a snarl.

"Why are you following us?" I demand. "What do you want with us? Are you spying on us for Yuki? Are you working for Lizard Blood?"

"What are you talking about?" he says with admirable calm, given that he's lying on the floor covered in yellow, orange, green, and blue Silly String. He starts to sit up. The plastic bits come off him in one giant sheet.

"Don't move!" Ru shouts. Her eyes are red and her teeth are bared like a wolf's. If she could grow fangs, she would. He doesn't move.

"It's all right," I say to her, lowering my now-empty cans of string. "I think he's safe."

He regards us both. "Where is your friend? Your bass player?"

My heart gives a little jump knowing that he pays attention enough to know who plays what instrument and that he knows the difference between a bass and a guitar. Not everyone does.

"She's out. Why do you care?"

He looks at us so calmly, speaks so evenly, you'd never know he'd just been attacked with Silly String. "Because it's true. I am spying on you."

"What?" Ru yells, and I have to grab her arm before she starts clawing at him.

"Why?" I say. "Who are you working for?"

"May I ask you a question?"

He totally isn't a student. He's not even trying to pass for one anymore, not that he ever did. He stands, scraping off the rest of the string. "Do you know what your friend Miki does on her deck all day?"

Ru and I look over at each other. I say, "Homework, I think."

New Guy is very serious now. "We've traced the cyber attacks on the national banks and water system to this school. We believe one of the students here at Cherry Blossom is the hacker."

"You... you don't think it's Miki, do you? It can't possibly be Miki!"

"Why not?"

"Because she's a good guy! Because she knows all about Shonen Knife! Because I trust her!"

He presses those skeptical lips together. I almost cry.

"If you trust her, then help me clear her. Find out what she's doing with her deck. But don't tell her I'm investigating her."

"We can't spy on our friend!" Ru says. But of course, we can. We have to, and New Guy knows it.

"If you'll excuse me." He adjusts the cuffs on his jacket and leaves the room like nothing happened.

Half an hour later, Miki shows up with her base. And her deck. Ru and I haven't had the heart to start playing without her.

"Sorry I'm late, I got held up. They're rationing water now, you know that? I'm trying to find a way to sneak bottles out of the kitchen – hey, what's wrong?"

I stare, stricken. Miki, dear sweet Miki, hacking the city infrastructure to destroy it? I don't believe it, not for a minute."

"We're depressed," Ru says, which is true enough.

"You can't be depressed, auditions are tomorrow! We have to practice!" Miki says.

I feel grim. "I think we've practiced as much as we possibly can."

"You mean-"

I nod. "We're ready. It's time to face Lizard Blood."

This is it. The most important day of my life. will I be allowed to spread the message of true pop rock through the universe, or will I be defeated? I feel sick to my stomach.

We decide on wearing A-line tunics and pants in primary colors to better channel Shonen Knife, and to separate ourselves from the frilly bleakness of Lizard Blood. Sure enough, they show up in black and white with double crinolines and corsets, the curly purple wigs and giant eyelashes dashed with glitter. They carry their instruments proudly, and their neural implants gleam along their arms and foreheads. Like they think they can't lose.

All we have are calluses on our fingers.

Everyone's there. At least, everyone who is left is there" Principal Jono and the remaining survivalist teachers, clipboards in hand and pencils raised, ready to judge our worthiness to play at the Spring Dance. A crowd of students gathers in the back of the gym, thrumming with eagerness. This is going to be the fight of the century.

The stage waits, bare.

I hate this, waiting, my guitar slung over my shoulder, plinking the strings. They make weak little ringing sounds, since the instrument's not plugged in yet. It's the same sound my hear will make if it breaks, if we lose. Ru holds her fists over her eyes, like she can't even watch, her drumsticks sticking out of them like antennae.

But even right before the audition, Miki sits on the floor, working on her deck.

I glare at her. "What are you doing? You're always on your deck. I'm worried about you."

"What? Oh – it's a secret. But you'll like it. I promise."

Off to the side, New Guy watches us closely. What if he's right? What if Miki is behind the destruction of the city?

What would Shonen Knife do? They would trust each other, and they would play. That's all we can do.

Principal Jono will flip a coin to see who goes first. He announces: "Flying Jelly Attack is heads, Lizard Blood is tails. Whichever side lands up will get to choose whether they go first or last."

Yuki and I stand on either side of Principal Jono, seething. Soon, it will all be over. The coin spins, glinting in the light coming in through the windows. It seems to spin forever before falling like a bullet into Principal Jono's hand. He slaps it on the back of his other hand, looks at us both, and finally reveals the outcome.

"Heads!"

I should have thought more about what would be best: play first and get it over with, play last to leave the final impression with the judges, play first to show how great we are at warming up a crowd, play last so we could respond to Lizard Blood's strategy –

Miki taps me on the shoulder. "Let Lizard Blood play first."

She seems very confident, hiding something behind her big brown eyes and glasses. Okay, then. Shonen Knife trusts each other, so I trust her.

"Lizard Blood will go first," I say and step aside.

It takes them a stupidly long amount of time to set up because they have to plug in their instruments, warm up their neural implants, synch all their systems, and I figure this will be a black mark against them because the longer they take the more restless everyone gets. But I know them, I've heard them, and once they start playing, they'll cast some kind of weird headbanger spell that will overpower the crowd with a wall of death metal. They'll burn out everyone's hearing before we even get onstage.

But then something happens. Something *amazing*.

Yuki starts to strum a chord - that is, her uploaded programming directs her arm to play a cord. And nothing happens. Her hand goes limp and splats over the frets, and her other hand tangles in the strings instead of strumming. Azumi does a little better, getting her bass to play a couple of chords, but they're *bad* chords, out of tune and wavering. The drumsticks fall clean out of Hana's hands. When she scrambles to pick them up, she falls off her stool.

It's like they're not in control of their own bodies. It's like something has gone wrong with their neural implant programming.

I look at Miki, who nods with satisfaction. "That's what I've been doing with my deck – hacking the implant software Lizard Blood uses to play their instruments. It was tough because they had massive protection on their system. Military-grade firewalls. Best money can buy – you know Yuki. But I got through, you know?"

I stare at her with really big eyes. "You. Are. A. *Genius.*"

She's my new hero. I could kiss her, but I have to go back to watching Yuki and Lizard Blood fumble around, trying to figure out what to do with their instruments without the software to guide them.

New Guy arrives in time to hear the explanation. "Ah. That clarifies much," he says. "That only leaves one suspect in the bank-hacking case. Thank you, girls."

"What?" I blink at him.

He approaches the stage and draws a badge from his pocket. Yuki and the others finally go still.

"I am Detective Fukaya, and you, Yuki Niamori, are under arrest for destroying the city through the cybernetic network."

Well, who expected *that*?

Yuki should deny it, but she doesn't. She throws down her guitar and clenches her fists. Even Azumi and Hana look surprised, so they must not know anything about it.

At the edge of the stage, Yuki looks over us all, green eyes filled with rage.

"You think this is just an act!" she shouts. "You never respected me because you think all this is fake!" She gives her frilly skirt a tug. "It's not an act! It's *anarchy*! Yes,

I destroyed the city's banking and water infrastructure! I want everything to *burn!*" She throws horns with both hands and screams, "ANARCHY!"

I have to admit, I finally sort of respect Yuki a little because she seems very honest about her mission.

She jumps off the stage and shoves Detective Fukaya aside. He's so surprised he doesn't go after her right away – I mean, who expects Yuki to do anything that smacks of effort? So she runs and we all think she's going to get away, but then Ru trips her. Just sticks out her foot, and Yuki goes sailing, purple curls flying and tiny hat spinning off toward the ceiling. It's great. Detective Fukaya arrests Yuki. Azumi cries while Hana leads her away, arm around her shoulders to comfort her. And that's that.

It turned out Miki had such a hard time hacking Lizard Blood's system because all of Yuki's neural interfaces and military-grade firewalls were a cover for her high-level hacking activities. Lizard Blood really was a fake band. Who knew?

So, that's how Flying Jelly Attack triumphed and won the chance to play at the Cherry Blossom High School Spring Dance. We auditioned with our signature song, "Flying Jelly Attack," and we sounded triumphant. That just goes to show that Rock and Roll Will Never Die.

Unfortunately, by the time of the Spring Dance the power had indeed gone out all over the city. But that doesn't matter because we have a generator, and we insist that the Spring Dance go on as planned for the sake of good morale. We decorate the gym and fill it with students. It seems like a miracle that everybody comes, but I know I'm right: times like these, everybody just wants to dance. So we play for them. Outside the windows, far away in the city, mobs riot at bank headquarters and government buildings for not doing more to stop the economic collapse. A couple of skyscrapers are on fire and helicopters buzz around them, recording footage for the news. The city really is falling apart, but I don't care, because my dream has come true: my band is playing at the Spring Dance. The Cherry Blossom High School gym is the safest place in the city. Hundreds of students surge screaming at the stage, and me and my girls have our instruments plugged into amps, ready to go. I look at Miki and Ru, meet their gazes, and they nod back at me. Their hands are poised to begin. Nothing else matters.

I turn to the microphone and call, "One two three four-!"

Carrie Vaughn is the *New York Times*-bestselling author of close to twenty novels and over seventy short stories. She's best known for the Kitty Norville urban fantasy series—currently includes thirteen novels and a collection of short stories—about a werewolf who hosts a talk radio advice show for supernatural beings, and the superhero novels in the Golden Age saga. She also writes the Harry and Marlowe steampunk short stories about an alternate nineteenth century that makes use of alien technology. She has a Master's degree in English literature, graduated from the Odyssey Fantasy Writing Workshop in 1998, and returned to the workshop as Writer in Residence in 2009. She has been nominated for the Hugo Award, various RT Reviewer Choice Awards—winning for Best First Mystery for *Kitty and The Midnight Hour*— and won the 2011 WSFA Small Press award for best short story for "Amaryllis." A bona fide Air Force brat (her father served on a B-52 flight crew during the Vietnam War), Carrie grew up all over the U.S., but put down roots in the Boulder, Colorado area, where she pursuers an endlessly growing list of hobbies and enjoys the outdoors as much as she can. She is fiercely guarded by a miniature American Eskimo dog named Lily.

Parkside: SJ Rozan

First published in *Buffalo Noir*

Frankie was watching through the window then the police came to the Wisnewski''s. He spent a lot of free time at the window anyway, making scary monster faces and claws, growling, snarling, pretending he was about to jump across the air shaft, sometimes pulling his pants down and mooning until Petey Wisnewski finally had a tantrum. Then Petey's mom would come wallop him. By that time Frankie was out of sight, and old lady Wisnewski never knew what set Petey off.

It wasn't the first time he saw the cops come to the Wisnewski's. The dad was always beating on the mom, and both of them smacked the kids around, and some-times the yelling and screaming was so loud the neighbors called the cops. They'd come and pretend to be reasonable, but you could see from their shoulders and the way they were kind of twitchy that they were really saying without using words that they'd throw the mom and dad in jail and take the kids away if they didn't cool it. So the parents would cool it for a while, and then something would happen, and everyone was thumping on everyone else again.

Eddie O'Brian said Frankie should let up on Petey. He said it wasn't Petey's fault that Frankie's mom made him let Petey tag along wherever he went just because they were some stupid kind of cousin, and it wasn't Petey's fault anyway that he was only five. Eddie had like twenty brothers and sisters, on maybe just ten, but whatever, he didn't give a shit if little kids were climbing all over him all the time. But for Frankie, since his dad left it was just his mom and hum, and his mom worked all day out at Wegmans. He liked to do what he liked to do and it pissed him off to have Petey stuck to him everywhere. And he wasn't so sure it wasn't Petey's fault. Petey had that mean kind of smile, like his dad's, when Frankie told his mom no but his mom said yes and made him go to the Wisnewski's and take Petey someplace. Frankie figured going to school and doing his homework was enough, and his mom should've been happy with that. Eddie didn't even always do that. What Frankie did, him and Eddie and the guys, after school or weekends when there wasn't Little League or Pop Warner, that should've been his business. Shit, he even went to church with her most Sundays, why couldn't she leave him alone after that?

But no. Say, if Frankie wanted to go up to Parkside Candy for some fudge. That was a great expedition. You had to take the bus up Hertel, and once you got up near the Parkside you could jump on the metro was only underground sometimes, and sometimes in a cut like a tunnel with no roof. Frankie's dad said that was Buffalo right there, you think you're in the sunshine but you're still in a hole. But Frankie liked it because you could close your eyes and pretend you were riding a real subway, in New York or Chicago or someplace, not Buffalo, not all shabby low buildings and thought, wasn't just the detour metro ride. It was still Buffalo when you came back, but inside the candy store, the wood gleamed and the mirrors were polished and it was quiet, like everything was slower. Like it was a different Buffalo. His mom said that was the old Buffalo, from a long time ago when everyone had a lot of money. Frankie asked if his dad had a lot of money then too, but she said it was much longer ago than that. Frankie wasn't sure what that meant but he loved to go to the Parkside.

Actually, having Petey along was okay for a while. The first time they went there, the lady gave Frankie extra fudge because she said his little brother was so cute, carrying his teddy bear, holding onto Frankie's shirt. Frankie started to scowl and say, *He's not my brother, he's just my stupid cousin, and besides he has snot all over his face,* but Eddie was there that time and poked him in the ribs. Frankie got what Eddie meant – Eddie was smart – and stopped himself just in time, and the lady smiled and slipped them the extra couple pieces. Him and Eddie even gave Petey some, and they told him he really, *really* had to never tell anyone they came all the way here, because of course it was way past where they were allowed to go without grown-ups.

That first time worked out fine, so a couple more times Frankie told his mom he was going out to play, his mom told him to take Petey to give Petey's mom a break, and Frankie said, *Yeah, yeah,* and they hiked it over to the bus stop, Frankie galloping just a little faster than Petey could go and then turning around to yell at the kid to move it.

The fourth time was the trouble. Petey left the damn teddy bear in the store. What a jerk! They had to go back for it, because Petey wouldn't stop howling. Everyone on the bus was staring at them. They got home late, but it still would've been okay except that little baby Petey started crying when he saw his mommy and told her about almost losing the fucking teddy bear.

That night Frankie's mom beat his butt something fierce.

He was grounded, but even though she wasn't home until suppertime she knew if he went out because he had to go over every hour and check in with old lady Wisnew-ski, but if she wasn't a witch sure looked like one and she smelled bad. He thought she might be drunk enough that she wouldn't notice if he checked in or not, but he wasn't sure so he kept doing it.

Still, a couple of those one-hour times, Frankie raced to the bus and the metro and took a short ride anyway. He couldn't go all the way to the Parkside but instead of imagining he was riding under Chicago he was on a real train, not the metro, on a long trip West to find his dad. Out West they had horses and deserts, and he wasn't sure but he thought it didn't snow. That would be as awe-some as skyscrapers.

The only good part was, as long as Frankie was grounded, stupid little Petey was stuck too. His sister and brothers wouldn't take him with them anyplace, when pissed Frankie off because the brat was much more their job than Frankie's.

Eddie said he should just chill and play with his Wii or something until his mom got tired of the whole grounding thing. But Frankie didn't have a Wii. His mom said they couldn't afford it, which Frankie didn't get because it was only a little thing you held in your hand and pointed at the TV, so how much could it cost? But anyway, he didn't have one, so while he was grounded and thinking about Eddie and the guys running and smashing into each other on the football field without him, it was either watch TV, which was pretty stupid, or make Petey cry, which was fun.

Frankie ducked back once more as the cop looked out the Wisnewski's open window again. He was good at ducking back, from all those times old lady Wisnowski came to see what Petey was yowling about before she smacked him. Now she wasn't smacking anybody, just crying, and she didn't say anything when the cop seemed to be asking her why the window was open on a cold day like this. She kept crying and he shook his head. He was one of the cops who'd come before, and he gave his partner the kind of look that said he knew something like this would happen. They always thought they were so smart, cops. Jerk. He didn't look for a second at the rope that ran between the two buildings. Even if he had, he wouldn't have seen anything on it, but if he was so smart he should have looked, and then he should have said, *That's not a clothesline, who'd hang clothes to dry in a stupid dark, air shaft like this?*

When the cops left they took old lady Wisnewski with them, and one of Petey's brothers who was home. Frankie couldn't see the door shut but he heard it because the window was open. He realized: now he could go out. What could his mom say? Old lady Wisnewski wasn't there to check in with. He could even say he'd tried, which was going to be a lie, because he was headed out to the football field right now. Well, almost right now. He checked the kitchen clock. He had plenty of time. First he's go to the bus and then to the metro and ride a few stops, and then, when he was someplace else, he was going to stuff Petey's stupid teddy bear in the metro station garbage pail. That's what Petey opened the window to try to get, after Frankie had made a noose and hung it from the rope. There it was, dangling, with Frankie putting his hands around his own throat and making a cross-eyed, choking face. Petey had howled and cried, and slammed his fists, and snot ran out of his nose, but Frankie had just laughed and made the choking face again. So Petey opened the window and stood on the sill and reached too far, and then had fallen, which is why the cops came.

Frankie decided he'd better wait to go out until the ambulance guys and cops own there stopped taking photos and measuring things, and finally covered Petey all up and took him out of the courtyard. He'd seen it on TV, that that's how it went with bodies. Then he'd gunplay football, smash and slam and pound with the other guys. But on the way, after he got rid of the stupid bear, he'd go up to the Parkside. He didn't have much money, but that was okay. The lady there would give him extra fudge for his cute little brother, who couldn't come with him today.

SJ Rozan's work has won multiple awards, including the Edgar, Shamus, Anthony, Nero, Macavity, and Japanese Maltese Falcon. She's published fifteen books and four-dozen short stories under her own name, primarily featuring the detecting duo of Lydia Chin and Bill Smith, as well as two books, *Blood of the Lamb* and *Skin of the Wolf*, with Carlos Dews as the writing team of Sam Cabot. She's served on the National Boards of Mystery Writers of America and Sisters in Crime, and is ex-President of the Private Eye Writers of America. Born in the Bronx, she now lives in lower Manhattan. *Bronx Noir*, a short story anthology she edited, was chosen by the New Atlantic Independent Booksellers Association as its "Notable Book of the Year." Along with writing, she speaks, lectures, and teaches, and runs a summer fiction writing workshop in Assisi, Italy.

Gun Accident: An Investigation: Joyce Carol Oates

First published in _Ellery Queen's Mystery Magazine,_ July 2015

Do you recall the sequence of events. They asked me.

But I could not reply coherently. Because I could not remember coherently. _The gun was fired close beside my head. The explosion was so loud I could not hear and I could not see and when I realized where I was, the right side of my head had struck the hardwood floor just beyond the rug and that was where I was lying but I could not move. On the floor it came to me that I was shot, and (maybe) I was dead because I did not feel anything or hear anything._

For a long time then I did not move for (maybe) I was dead. It was a thought a clever child would have—if I did not try to move, and did not fail to move, then I would not know (maybe) if I was dead or if I was still alive.

2.

I am begging him _No! Go away._

It is still the time when he is alive. Before the bullet enters his chest, and his heart explodes.

Travis is alive and he is on his feet but he does not hear me. He is alive but he is laughing at me and so he does not hear me. And I realize that my throat is shut up tight and the words are trapped inside my head. *Go away go away! Please go away!*— I am begging him.

It is that time he cannot realize— he is still alive. He is laughing and his face is bright-glaring with happiness because he is alive and cannot imagine any time when he will be not-alive for (it is said) no animal can comprehend its own death.

There is Travis, and there is the other who is older than Travis. Instinctively I know that I must not look at his face. I must not lift my eyes to his face. I must not give him any reason to believe that I might identify him.

It is inborn, such cunning. It is as natural as trying to shield your face with your arms, doubling over to protect your belly and groin. It is purely instinct, this desperation to be spared harm.

And so, I do not look at the other. *The other* is the one at whom I do not look. It is my cousin Travis from whom I cannot turn away because it is my cousin Travis who has grabbed hold of me and it is my cousin Travis who has the gun.

3.

In dreams sometimes it is like this. I am lying very still, my arms and legs are numb or paralyzed. There is a medical term— *peripheral neuropathy*. A tingling sensation in fingers and toes that moves upward bringing with it a loss of feeling, a spreading numbness, a kind of am-nesia of the body.

No I do not "believe" in dreams and would not bore or exasperate anyone with the idiocy of most dreams but this is not a dream exactly—for I am not asleep, though I am paralyzed as in sleep.

There is an explanation for why we are "paralyzed" in sleep: A part of the brain shuts down so that when we dream of running, for instance, we don't actually run—we are prevented from moving our muscles, and waking our-selves.

Except of course sleepwalkers do "walk"—and remain asleep.

At such times I am very frightened and yet calm-seem-ing for it is crucial never to show fear. If there are witnesses who might laugh at you, or bring harm to you. As I knew my cousin Travis Reidl and the boy or young man who'd been with him—(whose face I never saw but whose voice I heard, and it was not a voice I recog-nized)—would laugh at me, and hurt me. And I was thinking *If I don't move I will not have to know if I am alive or not-alive. It is better not to move.*

It is a delicious paralysis like floating in water so icy-cold, there is no sensation at all.

Until one of the children wakes me, pulling at my shoulder.

"Mom-my! Mom-*my!*"—for children do not like to see their mother lying beneath bedcovers tense and tight as a clenched fist.

"Mom, *wake up*"—my daughter Ellen cries in her sharp, furious child-voice that pierces the deepest sleep.

And so within seconds I am awake, and I am sitting up, and I am Mommy again. And I laugh at the children, who appear frightened, to assure them that yes of course, Mommy is fine.

It is the morning of our yearly trip to visit the children's grandparents in Sparta, three hundred fifty miles away in upstate New York in the foothills of the Adirondack Mountains.

4.

Do you recall the gun, I was asked.

And the answer was *No— not the gun but the deafening gunshot, I recall. Not the gun (which I never saw clearly, my eyes were blinded with tears) but the consequences of the gunshot.*

In the *Sparta Journal* the handgun would be identified as a double-action .38-caliber Colt revolver. It was the property of Gordon McClelland of 46 Drumlin Avenue, Sparta, who'd had a homeowner's permit for it issued several years before, in 1958.

A homeowner's permit means that the gun owner must keep his gun on the premises. It is not legal to remove the gun from the house, to carry it in a pocket or in a vehicle as a "concealed weapon."

Mr. McClelland also owned hunting guns—two deer rifles, a shotgun. These were locked in a cabinet in his home office that my cousin and his accomplice-friend could not open.

When the gun went off close beside my head I could not think.

I did not know what had happened—I did not know if I had been hit. I did not know if my cousin had knocked me down onto the floor—

I'd been pushed, or shot.

I did not know if anyone had been shot. I did not know if the shot had been deliberate or an accident.

Twenty-six years later! No one asks me any longer but the truth is, I still do not know.

5.

Here is a surprise: The McClelland house is still standing at 46 Drumlin Avenue as if it were an ordinary house in which no one had died.

This is not a pleasant surprise. It is a surprise that grips me each time I return to Sparta, like a claw.

If I am with others, for instance my children, in this car, I never indicate that I am upset, or even distracted—usually I continue driving past 46 Drumlin without another glance.

For why have I come here, when there is no need? *Why?*—my fourteen-year-old self might shout at me.

"That house—an old teacher of mine used to live here . . ."

I hear myself speak in a faltering voice more to myself than to my daughterin the passenger's seat beside me, and to my son in the backseat.

How strange, and how misleading. To refer to Mrs. McClelland as *an old teacher*. In fact, I remember Gladys McClelland as anything but *old*.

Yet *former* seems too deliberate, too formal. In speaking to my children I speak an unadorned language which is the language of maternal affection. I don't want to impress my children, or even to teach them vocabulary words—I want them to trust me.

So they will think that their mother is someone like them, an adult but essentially a friend, whom they can trust as they can't trust other adults.

For I remember vividly, when I was a little girl, understanding that the loyalty of adults is to other adults, not to children. You dare not tell a parent your innermost thoughts. You dare not betray *secrets*.

My daughter Ellen asks what kind of teacher was Mrs. McClelland.

For a moment I am struck by *was*. I know that the McClellands moved away from Sparta a long time ago but I have no idea if they are still living—probably yes, since they were only just middle-aged in 1961.

"'What kind of teacher'?—a very good teacher. An excellent teacher. We all loved Mrs. McClelland. . . ."

"What did she *teach*, Mom?"

"Mrs. McClelland taught 'social studies.' And she was my ninth-grade home-room teacher also."

Was. Impossible to avoid *was*.

You might expect Ellen to ask something more—why did I love my ninth-grade teacher, what was so special about Mrs. McClelland, and what became of Mrs. McClelland—but she has lost interest; it is an effort for even a courteous eleven-year-old to care about a mother's memory of an old teacher. In the backseat, eight-year-old Lanny is peering out the window at something that intrigues him, in the opposite direction, as indifferent to his mother's chatter as if it were the droning of a radio voice.

"She was—Mrs. McClelland—someone special. In my life . . ."

I am gripping the steering wheel with both hands. I am staring at the dignified old colonial with its soft-red aged brick looking just slightly weatherworn, and dark green shutters in need of repainting, and steep shingled roof with an antique weather vane at one of the peaks, the figure of a leaping deer. Has anything changed? *Is* this really the house? Each time I visit Sparta, each time I drive past this house, my senses are aroused as if with a whiplash to my bare back.

Only you, Hanna. No one else.

I don't think that I need to tell you—do not bring anyone else to this house. Do not let anyone else inside.

Of course strangers live at 46 Drumlin Avenue now. If I were to ask my mother who lives here, which I would never do, she would likely stare at me, and say, with a hurt, defensive little laugh, "Who lives there? I have no idea."

Within a few months of the shooting the McClellands moved out. At school it was known that Gladys McClelland could not bear to live in a house in which a "young person" had died.

Do you promise, Hanna?

Yes. I promise.

At my parents' house on Quarry Street in a very different neighborhood of smaller houses and smaller lots I turn my car into the familiar driveway with a flood of relief. But then the flood keeps coming, a rising pressure inside my head.

The children rush from the car, eager to run into their grandparents' house after the tedium of the long drive. But I am feeling too weak to move—leaning against the steering wheel weak-armed, dazed. Waiting for the pressure in my brain to subside. Waiting for the sensation of terrifying fullness to subside.

It had to be, what happened. There was no choice.

"Hanna? Dear, is something wrong?"

Someone has opened the car door, and is shaking me. My mother, leaning over me. Her anxious face is too near, like an unmoored sun. And behind her, my father looking grayer-haired than I recall.

My parents are concerned that I'd turned into the driveway—braked the car—the children ran inside the house—but that I'd remained in the car.

They'd hurried outside to see where I was and found me at the wheel—"Looking like you were asleep, but with your eyes open."

But I am all right now, I tell them. I am out of the car, and hugging my parents, and it is true, I am fully recovered from whatever it was that had gripped me fleetingly but terribly.

"Hanna, so good to see you! Welcome home."

6.

Helping out. Both my mother and I were proud of the fact that, during her husband's hospitalization in Syracuse, I'd been asked to *help out* my teacher Mrs. McClelland.

My responsibilities were to drop by the McClelland house once a day after school to bring in the mail and newspaper, to feed Mrs. McClelland's cat, and to water her plants as needed—"Of course I will pay you, Hanna."

When Mrs. McClelland told me what she would pay for each hour I spent in her house, I was stunned—nearly twice as much as babysitting rates.

It was an emergency situation. The McClellands had not known that Mr. McClelland would require surgery so suddenly, and Mrs. McClelland would be away from Sparta for several days at least, staying in a hotel in Syracuse, near the University Medical Center fifty miles away. A substitute teacher would take her place. And Mrs. McClelland was hoping that I could *help out.*

It was April 1961. I was fourteen years old and in ninth grade and in love with my homeroom and social studies teacher Mrs. McClelland who seemed often to favor me—at least, I was one of a number of students whom Mrs. McClelland seemed to particularly like.

Gladys McClelland was a strikingly attractive woman of an indeterminate age—she might have been in her early forties but she seemed to us much younger, of a generation distinct from our mothers' generation, as her clothing, hairstyle, intelligence, and zestful personality set her apart from other teachers at our school. She wore her shoulder-length blond hair in a "pageboy"—wavy, shiny, turned under; her face was glamorously made-up, like a face on a fashion-magazine cover; her shoes were high-heeled, and her stockings were sheer, often dark-tinted. Her girl students had memorized most of her clothing— cashmere sweaters, pleated skirts, tight-cinched belts; we knew her rings, jewelry; we knew several coats, of which the most elegant was dark wool that fell nearly to her ankles, with a collar that might have been mink. Her figure wasn't what one would call slender but rather "shapely"—hips, breasts. She reminded some of us of the Hollywood actress Jeanne Crain—a beautiful woman who was yet *nice*.

It was known that Mrs. McClelland lived with her husband in a large, attractive house in Sparta's most prestigious residential neighborhood. It was known that Mrs. McClelland's husband was someone important—a World War II war hero, a retired army officer. He was a businessman, or a professional man—lawyer, banker. As Gladys McClelland resembled Jeanne Crain, Mr. McClelland resembled darkly handsome Robert Taylor.

Why did we love Mrs. McClelland? She wasn't an easy grader—she made us work—but she was sympathetic with us, and patient. She was often very funny. Her teaching manner was a combination of wit, humor, and seriousness; we laughed a good deal in Mrs. McClelland's classes, though what we laughed at was difficult to explain or to repeat to others. Mrs. McClelland had a way—almost, it was flirtatious; certainly, it was affectionate—of calling upon students who were reluctant to volunteer answers, and initiating with even the shyest or most awkward a kind of dialogue; one day, I would learn that this was the Socratic method—questions following questions in rapid-fire succession.

Mrs. McClelland's philosophy was: We all knew much more than we knew that we knew. The teacher's job was to draw such knowledge out of us—"Like poking through a grating with a big pronged fork, seeing what's there and hauling it up." (Was this one of Mrs. McClelland's clever remarks? We laughed to hear it.)

Boys were mesmerized by Mrs. McClelland, we knew. Some boys.

Others, sulky older boys who disliked school and shrugged off poor grades, biding time until at the age of sixteen they could quit school forever, said things about Mrs. McClelland that were not so nice, we knew.

By ninth grade a girl has been made to know that she is, in the eyes of (most) boys, her body. *Tits, ass.* And nastier words, some of us tried never to hear.

(It was rumored that, sometimes, these words were scrawled on Mrs. McClelland's car in whitewash, or spray paint. And that as a consequence Mrs. McClelland was allowed to park her new-model yellow Buick in the area of the administrators' parking places, visible from the office windows.)

In Mrs. McClelland's warmly musical voice our names acquired a special distinction. I would remember the morning in our homeroom when Mrs. McClelland lightly touched my shoulder saying, "Hanna, may I speak with you?"—indicating that I should follow her out into the corridor.

I felt my face heat with blood at this unexpected request. I felt the keenness with which my friends observed me, hurrying after Mrs. McClelland in high-heeled black leather shoes rimmed with ornamental red stitching.

There was no more alarming prospect, being asked to speak with a teacher in the corridor out of earshot of classmates. Like hearing your name over the loudspeaker, the dreaded commandment *Come at once to the main office.*

In such ways were hapless students informed of family emergencies, sudden deaths. Rarely such interruptions of routine brought good news.

It was not like Mrs. McClelland to betray unease or edginess. Even now, though she was clearly anxious, she smiled at me, and spoke calmly to me; she knew that I felt uncomfortable by being singled out for attention. She told me about the sudden "family emergency"—her husband had to have surgery in Syracuse the next morning.

"It isn't major surgery," Mrs. McClelland said carefully. "Gordon will be all right. It's just that—we weren't prepared for—so suddenly—tomorrow morning at seven o'clock . . ."

Could I *help her out?*—Mrs. McClelland was asking.

Of course, I said *yes.* I was touched that Gladys McClelland would select me for such a responsible task. Often in homeroom I assisted her in various small ways, passing out papers to classmates, watering and trimming her house-plants, which grew profusely on the window sills—spider plants, philodendron, cacti. When Mrs. McClelland sprained her ankle in a skiing accident, and came to school hobbling on crutches, I was one of those who helped her get around, carried things for her which she couldn't easily carry for herself. *Girls! Thanks so much. What would I do without you . . .*

Mrs. McClelland had swiped at her eyes, she'd been so moved. Some of us had brought her flowers for her homeroom desk: roses, carnations, and a *Get Well* card in the shape of a fluffy white cat.

I knew that my mother would not disapprove of my "helping out" my teacher in her emergency. My mother was often jealous on my behalf when other people's daughters seemed to be surpassing her daughter, and she was always eager to hear about my teachers' interest in me, as if such interest reflected well upon herself, who'd been born in rural Beechum County in a ram-shackle farmhouse, and had dropped out of school in ninth grade.

The McClellands lived only a few blocks from our house, which was on a narrow street literally below Drumlin Avenue, winding along the edge of an ancient glacial hill. Often I babysat for neighbors, but I did not think that the McClellands had children.

I was a quiet, diminutive girl for my age, who wore my sand-colored hair in a way that partly covered the left side of my face, to hide a birthmark on my cheek. The birthmark was of the size and hue of a small strawberry and had something of a strawberry's texture—slightly raised, distinctive to the touch. To me, nothing was more defacing or ugly than this birthmark. As a young child I'd been tormented over the birthmark, mercilessly; even my friends had never let me entirely forget it. And even at fourteen I was sometimes singled out for mockery by crude boys. In any mirror my gaze moved involuntarily *there*—to check if the strawberry birthmark still existed, or had disappeared miraculously.

Is it a sign from God? But—why?

In my dreams even now, decades later, when the erasure of the old birth-mark would make not the slightest difference in my life, still I find myself anxious to check my mirror reflection, staring into a cloudy glass as if my very life were at stake. Often in such dreams I am being harassed. Someone is shouting at me in derision, and laughing. But I am not able to see even my face in the dream mirror, let alone the little birthmark. Helplessly I think—*How foolish is vanity. How futile.*

I remember myself as a plain girl of no particular distinction, except for the birthmark. Yet, photographs of me taken at this time show a moderately attractive girl—when smiling, I might have been called pretty. I'd felt unpopular, friendless—though in fact I had many friends in school, among them several of the most popular girls in my class. I'd been elected vice-president of our eighth-grade class and would be again elected vice-president of our junior class in high school. I was involved in numerous "activities" and was always an honors student—but high grades seemed to me a kind of embarrassment, the consequence of hard work as hard work seemed but the consequence of desperation.

Nothing that I'd accomplished seemed of particular significance, since it had been accomplished by *me.*

And so it was wonderful, that Mrs. McClelland liked me enough to entrust me with visiting her house while she was away. This was enormously thrilling to me, I could have wept with gratitude.

When I returned to my homeroom desk several girls asked me what Mrs. McClelland had wanted with me? — but I couldn't tell them, just yet. My heart was filled to bursting with a secret so delicious, just to impart it too quickly was to risk diluting its wonder.

After school that day Mrs. McClelland walked me through the rooms of the large colonial house on Drumlin Avenue, which previously I had only seen from the street.

The McClellands' house was one of a number of handsome old houses on Drumlin Avenue with which residents of Sparta were all familiar. Dreamily you bicycled past such houses in which important citizens lived. In other neighborhoods in the small city (population twelve thousand) people were often viewed in their driveways, on front walks and front lawns; often, they were viewed working on their lawns. But never the residents of Drumlin Avenue, who hired others to do their lawn work. And if they appeared out of doors it was at the rear of their large houses, hidden from view.

Even in adulthood you would go out of your way to drive past such distinguished old residences, wondering at the secret lives within even as, with the shrinkage of time, you are apt to know that happiness does not require such houses, and that inhabiting such houses guarantees nothing.

How strange to me, at fourteen, to be so suddenly— so *easily*

—inside this Drumlin Avenue house! And how strange to be alone with my teacher Mrs. McClelland in this private place.

It was rare for me to be alone with any adult not my parents or a close relative.

And Mrs. McClelland was not quite the same person whom I knew from school. On the eve of her husband's surgery she was visibly agitated. The witty, composed, and self-assured teacher had vanished and in her place was a distracted woman of my mother's age, not much taller than I was. Though she was wearing her teacher's clothing of that day—red wool jacket with brass buttons, pleated red-plaid skirt, dark-hued stockings, and black leather shoes—she did not exude an air of glamour. Her hair was brushed back behind her ears and her lipstick was worn off. Her usually lustrous, playful-alert eyes were red-rimmed and damp with worry. In a brave voice Mrs. McClelland told me that her husband had been brought by a private car to Syracuse that afternoon, to check into the hospital attached to the medical school; she would make the drive early the next morning, hoping to arrive at the hospital at about the time her husband's surgery was scheduled to begin. She explained that he was having "minor surgery"—"nothing to worry about"—adding then, with a breathless little laugh, "Except of course any sort of surgery requiring anesthetic is not *minor.*"

And several times she insisted: "It's important, Hanna—don't let anyone else in the house while you're here. Only your mother, if she wants to come with you, but—no one else. Do you promise?"

Gravely I promised *Yes.*

Soon after our conversation that morning in school Mrs. McClelland telephoned my mother. It had not occurred to me that she might telephone my mother at all. It would not have occurred to me that my teacher would require permission from my mother to hire me for this task of "helping out"—but of course Mrs. McClelland had acted properly, and graciously.

Mrs. McClelland was telling me that the upstairs rooms would all be shut:

"No need to go upstairs at all. And my husband's home office—at the end of the hall, here—will be locked. When you bring in mail for 'Gordon McClelland' just put it with the other mail, on the dining-room table."

Mrs. McClelland spoke quickly, with an air of distraction, leading me through the downstairs rooms of the beautifully furnished house. I had never seen such interesting furniture—a large, sinuously shaped coffee table seemingly made of a single piece of smoothed and polished red-brown wood, like the interior of a tree; a miniature piano, made of some sort of white wood—was this a harpsichord? I did not dare ask for I was too shy, and I sensed that Mrs. McClelland would be impatient with idle questions. Her instructions for helping out were more elaborate than I would have expected: I was to take care of the cat, and tend to the plants; bring in the mail and newspaper and anything that might be tossed onto the front steps; switch on lights in several rooms, raise and lower the blinds each evening in a different way, turn on the TV—to suggest that someone was in the house. "Try to spend at least an hour here, if you can. So that Sasha doesn't feel totally abandoned. You could do homework, on the sofa here. You could watch TV. You are welcome to eat anything you find in the refrigerator or the freezer but—of course—just *you*. No one else."

Mrs. McClelland spoke rapidly without uttering my name, as if in the exigency of the moment, her eyes darting about, the fingers of one hand nervously turning her platinum-gold wrist watch around her wrist, she'd forgotten who I was.

One end of the elegant dining room had been extended into a sunroom with ceiling-to-floor plate-glass windows and a skylight and in this space were potted plants of various sizes and shapes. Some were spectacularly beautiful—a large Boston fern, in a hanging basket; a row of African violets in clay pots; a five-foot Chinese evergreen. These plants required far more complicated care than the relatively simple plants Mrs. McClelland kept in her homeroom which were mostly cacti and jade plants, that could go without watering for long periods;

fortunately I'd brought along my notebook, so that like the good-girl student I was, I could take notes.

Mrs. McClelland instructed me to water the ferns sparingly—"Enough to moisten the soil. You can judge how dry the soil is by touching it. *Don't over-water.*" No water for the "snake plant"—an ugly, tough-looking plant with tall spearlike leaves; no water for the enormous jade plant, which looked like a living creature with myriad, twisted arms; no water for the orchids, which looked impossibly exotic and fragile. There were English ivy and grape ivy, philodendron with flowing leaves, spider plants, and peperomia—all of which would require watering / spraying in two or three days. Several African violet plants with small delicate petals required the most complicated care.

"If a leaf turns yellow, pinch it off. And don't move any of the plants, of course, each is in its optimum position for sunshine. Remember to test with your finger, to see if the soil is dry. And remember—*don't overwater.* Any more than you would want to drown, no plant wants to be drowned."

It was the sort of offhanded, wry remark Mrs. McClelland might make in school, with a smile that indicated she meant to be funny, and so we might laugh; but here in her house Mrs. McClelland did not smile, and so I knew she did not mean to be funny, and I was not meant to laugh.

She would leave the sprayer and the green enamel watering can on the floor by the plants, she said. There would be water in both, at room temperature; when I replenished the water, I should make sure that it was not too cold, or too hot.

All this while, a sleekly beautiful silver-blue Siamese cat was observing us at a distance, following us from room to room but never crossing a threshold. The cat's eyes were a startling blue. Her ears were much larger and more angular shaped than the ears of an ordinary cat and her chocolate-tipped tail was switching with obvious unease or annoyance. I had never seen such a striking animal up close. Mrs. McClelland said that she hoped I might "make friends" with Sasha, but the prospect did not seem likely; the cat continued to keep her distance from us, even as Mrs. McClelland tried to entice her with a cat treat that resembled a handful of cereal.

"Sasha! Sasha, come here. Kit-*ty*."

Each day I was to open a fresh can of cat food for Sasha, Mrs. McClelland said, as well as provide her with dry food and fresh water. Sasha would be upset at being left alone, and so possibly she wouldn't eat—at first; but even if she hadn't finished her food from the previous day, I was to wash out the bowl and dry it with a paper towel and open a new can. I was to "vary" the cans—tuna fish, salmon, chicken, beef—in that order; each day I was to change the water bowl. Mrs. McClelland showed me Sasha's litter box which was kept in a corner of a large utility room off the kitchen, and this litter box was to be changed at least every other day—"Before it gets seriously dirty, or Sasha will refuse to use it."

Refuse! I had to smile thinking of our family cats who were forcibly put outside if they balked in freezing weather and who had not the privilege of any sort of refusal.

"Sasha, come here and meet your new friend! No one will hurt you."

The silver-blue Siamese kept a wary distance. Her icy eyes betrayed no more recognition of the devoted mistress who called to her in a cajoling voice than of her "new friend."

"You must not let Sasha slip outside—she may try to, when you open the door. She can be devious! But a Siamese is strictly an indoor cat and could not long survive outdoors."

Could not long survive outdoors. I wondered if this strangely phrased statement could be true. If the pure-bred Siamese would not soon adapt to a new environment, like any cat, and become a feral creature.

I assured Mrs. McClelland that I would not let Sasha slip outside.

At this moment the phone rang. Mrs. McClelland gave a little cry of pure fright and for a moment looked terrified. I was embarrassed to see my teacher fumbling for the phone, and looked away as Mrs. McClelland murmured evasively, "Yes, thank you! I'm fine. I will be driving to the hospital tomorrow. I've asked one of my very dependable ninth-grade girls to look in on the house while I'm away. . . . Yes, of course I trust her!" Mrs. McClelland shot me a squinting smile as if to reassure me.

As Mrs. McClelland spoke on the phone to this person to whom she clearly did not wish to speak at this time, I drifted away so that I wouldn't overhear. Dropping to my knees, whispering, "Sasha! Kit-ty!"—trying without success to entice the sleekly beautiful Siamese to approach me.

It was disconcerting—it was shocking—to see our admired teacher in this state and to realize that this was the true Gladys McClelland, emotionally dependent upon a man, a husband; not so very different from my mother and my female relatives. The other, our glamorous teacher at Sparta Middle School, was a performer of a kind, who'd captivated our attention but who was not real.

Not until years later when I was a young married woman would I understand why Mrs. McClelland was so frightened. I would understand the blunt, terrible truth—*A career is not a life. Only a family is a life.*

Before we left the house Mrs. McClelland had me practice opening the door with her key—not the front door but the kitchen door, which was the door she wanted me to use; she gave me a typed list of instructions and telephone numbers; and she gave me several twenty-dollar bills—"In case you need emergency money."

Sixty dollars? I could barely speak. This was more than I might have fantasized earning if I'd helped out Mrs. McClelland for weeks.

Though I told Mrs. McClelland that I was perfectly able to walk the short distance home, she insisted upon driving me. I understood—(this was evident from Mrs. McClelland's classroom personality as well)—that once Mrs. McClelland had made a decision, she would not change it; she knew what should be done, and would do it.

"It's dark. It's cold. Of course I'm not going to let you walk home, Hanna."

Hanna. The sound of my name in Mrs. McClelland's voice suffused me with warmth.

In the November twilight, that comes early, and darkens to night by six P.M., I was grateful that my parents' small asphalt-sided house on narrow Quarry Street wasn't clearly defined and I was grateful that my mother had no idea that Gladys McClelland had pulled up to the curb in front of the house in her canary-yellow Buick—as in a teenager's nightmare, my mother might well have run outside to invite her in.

That evening my mother interrogated me about the visit. What sort of house the McClellands lived in, what my duties would be. My mother was pleased and excited for me—(she'd already begun to boast about my *helping out* my teacher to relatives)—but she was apprehensive too: If something happened to the McClellands' house, would her daughter be blamed?

Mrs. McClelland had told my mother how much she intended to pay me but my mother could have no idea that Mrs. McClelland had already paid me, several times more than the sum she'd promised. I considered whether to tell my mother about the sixty dollars, and when—but not just yet.

I felt a stab of rebellion, resentment. My mother would take most of the money from me, if she knew. But she didn't have to know how much money there was.

It's my money. I am earning it.

Like most of the adults of my acquaintance, my mother was not given to extravagant praise. Generosity of spirit was not typical of either of my parents' families, who'd grown up on small, unprosperous farms in the area, adults who'd lived through what came to be called the Great Depression. If my mother and her female relatives spoke well of anyone, however it might be deserved, there was invariably a pause in their conversation, and a qualifying rejoinder—*Of course, look where she came from. That family.*

And so when my mother spoke positively of Mrs. McClelland—"gracious"—"kind"—"a real lady"—I waited to hear what she would add; but all she could think to say was, thoughtfully, "They don't have children, her and her husband. I wonder whose fault it was."

7.

"Hello? Hello . . ."

So nervous and excited the following afternoon when I first entered the McClelland house I couldn't resist calling out in this way as if I half expected someone to be home.

But the house was empty of course. Except for a murmurous sound, a muted cry, a rapid scurrying of cat claws on a hardwood floor—the silver-blue Siamese fled from view as soon as she realized a stranger had arrived.

"Sasha! Kit-*ty.*"

I saw that a few things were not as I'd expected. Mrs. McClelland hadn't left the sprayer and the watering can on the dining-room floor; these were in the kitchen. In the sink, breakfast dishes were soaking as if she'd departed hastily. On a kitchen counter, scattered pages of the previous day's *Sparta Journal*. A hall closet with door ajar, and a bare light bulb burning inside.

I remembered how distracted Mrs. McClelland had been the previous afternoon. How frightened she'd been when the phone rang—as if she'd feared the worst.

We are sorry to say—bad news....Your husband has died.

Later, I would discover that several of the upstairs rooms hadn't been closed as Mrs. McClelland had planned—that is, their doors hadn't been shut. After some anguished deliberation I would close these doors, reasoning that if Mrs. McClelland believed she'd closed the doors, to discover them open would be a shock; naturally she would think that I'd been prowling in a part of the house forbidden to me.

Thinking *It might a test, how honest I am.*

But this was not likely: Mrs. McClelland already trusted me. Mrs. McClelland liked me.

Mrs. McClelland is my friend.

I'd brought in mail and newspapers and left these on the dining-room table where Mrs. McClelland had indicated. There were several letters for *Mr. Gordon C. McClelland* that appeared to be business letters or bills and just one letter for *Mrs. Gordon C. McClelland* that did not look especially interesting.

All this while I'd been calling for Sasha in a light airy voice. To my disappointment Sasha ignored me.

Deftly I removed yesterday's (partly eaten) cat food from the cat's plastic bowl, and opened a new can—tuna. The pungent odor of tuna fish filled the kitchen. Fresh dry food, and fresh water. It did look as if the lonely cat had eaten something, and when I checked her litter box in the storage room, that too had been used, if sparingly.

But where was Sasha? Keeping her distance.

Back in the kitchen, I washed and dried the dishes in the sink. Here too I was concerned that when Mrs. McClelland returned she might think that her student helper had left the dishes soaking, and not her.

I thought—*Mrs. McClelland will see how clean the house is! Mrs. McClelland will be impressed.*

With the same fastidious care I dealt with the house-plants. I was determined not to make any blunders, and disappoint my teacher who had such faith in me.

At close range I examined the orchids—so fragile, and so beautiful! These were native to Mexico and South America, Mrs. McClelland had said. Their flowers were so subtly colored, I could not have described them: silvery pink, pearly lavender. And the petals were so finely marked, like Japanese or Chinese calligraphy I'd seen re-produced in books.

I thought—*Someday I will have orchids like these. A house like this.*

I'd intended to examine some of the many books in the McClellands' bookshelves which had been built floor-to-ceiling in a library like room adjacent to the living room—but I didn't feel at ease in this room; nor did I feel at ease turning on the McClellands' floor-model television, which was so much larger and more beautiful than my parents' small black-and-white television. For what if something happened to the television set when I turned it on? I had a dread of being blamed.

Next to the TV room was Mr. McClelland's "home office"—which Mrs. McClelland had locked, she'd said. I did not try this door for I could imagine Mrs. McClelland observing me, frowning.

Somewhere behind me—or upstairs—there came a sound, like harsh breathing. My heart leapt in my chest like a frightened little toad.

"Hello? Hello . . ."

There was no one—of course. (Was there? No one?)

This house was so much larger than my parents' house! I had not even any idea how many rooms.

Suddenly, I had to leave. Had to get out of this house.

Though I had not been here for twenty minutes and had not executed all of the tasks Mrs. McClelland expected of me. Though the lonely Sasha must have been waiting for me to approach her, and plead with her to eat.

Hurriedly I switched off lights, and fled to Quarry Street to my own house. Not a thing had happened—and yet I felt shaken, and exhausted.

Seeing that I seemed distraught, my mother questioned me about the visit. Had something gone wrong?

No! Not a thing had gone wrong.

"But is the house all right? Is the house as Mrs. McClelland left it?"

This was an odd question. All I could stammer was, "I think—it is. Everything is all right."

413

"She called me today. From Syracuse."

"Called you? Mrs. McClelland?"—this was confusing to me, I wasn't sure that I had heard correctly. "What—what did she say?"

"Gladys called to ask about the house, and you. I don't think she cares to talk about her husband, whatever it is that's wrong with him. She's a very private person and I can understand that—I'm exactly the same way. 'Minor surgery'—could be anything." My mother spoke casually yet with an air of pride. "It's like we're old friends, Gladys McClelland and me—over this emergency. I mean, the way she called upon you to help her out. She said you are a 'very thoughtful'—'very trustworthy'—girl. I guess she doesn't remember, but we've met once or twice, in town. I didn't try to remind her because it might have embarrassed her not to remember me."

This report of my mother's was astonishing to me. Mrs. McClelland and my mother, talking on the phone!—talking, at least in part, about me.

It was disconcerting to imagine Mrs. McClelland befriending my mother, for the "friendship" would be very one-sided. I dreaded the prospect of hearing my mother innocently boasting of her friendship with a woman who lived on Drumlin Avenue, and the relatives listening resentfully, and mocking my mother behind her back.

Who does she think she is! Making herself ridiculous.

My mother volunteered to accompany me to the McClellands' house, next time I went. Quickly I said no for Mrs. McClelland had expressly told me not to bring anyone with me.

"I don't think that Mrs. McClelland would mind, if you brought me," my mother said, hurt; and I said, "But I promised. I can't break my promise."

The second evening at the house I was determined to do everything Mrs. McClelland had requested. Mail, newspaper. Fresh cat food, water, and litter box. Houseplants.

This time the lonely Siamese cat appeared in the kitchen doorway staring at me with icy blue eyes.

I spoke to Sasha in a gentle, cajoling voice as Mrs. McClelland had, but Sasha made no response, as if I were invisible. Unless I was imagining it, the cat seemed to have lost weight already; I had never seen so sinewy-thin an animal, with such stark, staring eyes.

When I tried to approach her, submissively on my heels, Sasha crouched against the floor as if about to bolt, her chocolate-tipped tail switching violently. A low, strangulated growl issued from her throat. She hissed, and then she mewed plaintively. She could neither come forward to be petted, nor could she run away to hide.

Futile to plead with a cat, yet I heard myself pleading. "Sasha! I'm your friend. You can trust *me*."

But Sasha would not trust me. With the cunning of the feral animal who has been only partly domesticated, she kept her distance.

It was nearing dark. And then it was dark. Again I wanted badly to flee to the comfort of my home.

I felt foolish lowering blinds in certain of the downstairs rooms—then, a little later, raising them again. (Or was I supposed to keep the blinds lowered overnight, and raise them the following night? I couldn't recall.) I'd switched on lights in all the rooms—too many lights?—while I tried to do geometry homework sitting on Mrs. McClelland's leather couch, that wasn't very comfortable, as the floor lamp behind my head cast shadows that made it difficult to read.

Yet, since Mrs. McClelland had gestured toward the leather sofa for me to use while doing homework, I felt obliged to sit there; I might have sat in another chair in the living room, or at the kitchen table beneath a brighter light, but somehow could not force myself.

Also, I could not seem to read coherently. I was distracted by my surroundings. The house that was so beautifully furnished seemed hostile and cold to me, like the interior of an expensive store; the living room was so large, it seemed to me that the farther walls dissolved in shadow. Cars passing on Drumlin Avenue cast the glare of their headlights against the walls and ceiling, though the house was set back a considerable distance from the street. From time to time somewhere in the house the lonely Siamese cat erupted in a high-pitched, piteous yowl, a cry of utter desolation and misery that chilled my blood, as if I had been torturing her, and was to blame for her suffering.

At last, to demonstrate to myself that I was not afraid and that I could behave as a normal teenager might in such circumstances, I switched on the television set. The screen glared with softly bright colors. Voices shouted at me out of an advertisement for detergent. Close up, the screen was too large for my eyes to focus on and when I tried to switch channels, the same advertisement, or one near identical to it, appeared.

It was 7:15 P.M. when the phone rang. I was terrified, for a moment I could scarcely breathe. Then, I staggered to pick up the receiver, and a woman's voice was saying

Hello? Hello? Hello?—it was Mrs. McClelland, sounding very unlike herself.

"Yes? Hello? This is . . ."

"Hanna! How are you? How is the house?"

"The house is—all right. I've done everything you told me . . ."

"And how is poor Sasha?"

"Sasha has been eating. She is still a little scared of me but—I think she will be making friends with me soon . . ."

Mrs. McClelland asked again about the house. She seemed anxious to know about the mail, and if the phone had rung while I'd been there. (This was in an era before voice mail. A phone simply rang and rang in an empty house, with no way of recording a lost call.) She asked about "my substitute" at school and seemed gratified to hear that the substitute wasn't at all sharp-witted or much fun, and didn't seem to be comfortable in the classroom—"We all miss you, Mrs. McClelland. Everyone is asking when you will be back."

"Soon! Next week, I'm sure I will be back."

I asked about Mr. McClelland and Mrs. McClelland said in a bright brave voice that he was doing well—though there were "complications" following surgery—"fever"—"infection."

I did not know what to say to this. Awkwardly I repeated that Mrs. McClelland's students all missed her and hoped she would be back soon.

"Thank you!"—Mrs. McClelland may have intended to add something witty and reassuring but her voice simply ended, as if a switch had been thrown. Soon after this painful telephone call I switched off the lights and fled home "Hanna. Han-*na*!"

The voice was singsong, just slightly mocking. At a little distance you would mistake it for playful.

That was what I thought—a playful voice. A friend of mine who'd learned somehow that I was inside the McClelland house, and had come to visit me.

It was 6:20 P.M. The evening of my third—and final—visit.

This time, I was resolved to spend at least an hour in the house, as Mrs. McClelland had requested. This time, the lonely cat seemed to be waiting for me in the kitchen, and fled only after she saw that I was not Mrs. McClelland.

As I cleaned out the cat's dishes, and set out fresh food, I saw that Sasha had returned, tentatively.

Though Sasha still distrusted me, and would have bolted if I'd made any move toward her, she began to rub her lean, sinuous silvery-blue body against the doorframe; she was mewing, not as an ordinary cat mews, but in the hoarse, throaty, interrogative way of the Siamese, that sounds almost human. It was touching to see the beautiful cat behaving in this way, desperate to show affection but not daring to come closer to me, or to allow me to approach her.

This was very encouraging! I would have something to report to Mrs. McClelland.

Unfortunately then, the doorbell rang. In the silent house the sound was jarringly loud.

Was someone at the front door? At first I was too startled to comprehend what the sound meant.

Immediately, Sasha panicked and fled.

My instinct was to hide—to pretend that I wasn't in the house—for only my parents knew that I was here, at this time.

Thinking *It must be someone who knows the McClellands. It would not be anyone who knows me.*

Not a delivery, at this time of evening. No one whom Mrs. McClelland would have expected.

If friends of the McClellands had planned to visit, they'd have called beforehand. Houses on Drumlin Avenue were not the sort of houses you dropped in upon casually, happening to be in the neighborhood.

Whoever was ringing the bell would reason that no one was home and give up after a few minutes, I thought.

Except: Several of the downstairs rooms were lighted, as Mrs. McClelland had instructed.

And now I realized what a bad idea it had been, to switch on lights in the house! For whoever saw so many lighted rooms in any house would naturally suppose that someone was home.

In the living room, which was a long room with a row of windows facing the street, the blinds were drawn so that no one could look in. That, at least, was a good thing.

Yet, the individual at the front door rang the bell again. And again. And so I knew, this was not natural. This was something else.

I was in the hallway by this time, looking toward the front door. Though the hall was darkened, the adjacent living room was lighted with a single chandelier I'd switched on when I had entered the house.

By the way the bell was being made to ring-ring-ring several times in rapid and rude succession, I knew that this was no friend of the McClellands. "Hanna. Han-*na!*"— it was a male voice, singsong.

At first, I wanted to think that the voice was playful. A voice out of my childhood past—

Hanna! Come out and play.

Quickly I calculated who this might be. Must be.

My cousin Travis Reidl. It could be no one else.

But how could Travis know that I was here? I had told no one except my parents.

And then it came to me—my mother must have told one of the relatives, boasting about my *helping out* my teacher this week—and this person told my aunt Louise Reidl, an older half-sister from whom my mother was estranged, who lived nine miles north of Sparta in rural Beechum County. And Louise Reidl was the mother of my cousin Travis.

It was a shock to me. It was exciting, and it was a shock. My cousin Travis Reidl whom I had not seen in possibly a year. At the McClelland house, of all inappropriate places.

How like Travis, to show up where he wasn't wanted. Where he did not belong. Pressing his finger insolently against the doorbell, peering through the glass panel into the foyer which must have seemed to him absurdly elegant, like a foyer in an expensive hotel—in mock-playful tones calling, "Han-na! We know you're in there, baby-girl. C'mon! It's cold out here."

As if Travis had roughly tickled me, I began to laugh. But then, I began to tremble. How awful this was! I felt a stab of sheer dismay—shame—if Mrs.

McClelland should learn of this . . .

"Han-*na*! Trick or treat!"

Travis began to strike the door with its knocker as if he wanted to break it.

"Open the damn door, Hanna, or we're gonna break it down."

We. I could see more clearly, there was a second person with Travis standing on the front stoop. Both were wearing hoods to obscure their faces.

My cousin Travis was my "rogue" cousin—so I thought of him, though I had never told him of course; Travis would have been flattered at first, then offended. All of the Reidls were quick to take offense if they suspected you were being condescending to them, or critical.

It was sobering to think that Travis must now be seventeen—when we were children, that would have seemed *old*. As a boy he'd been a sort of artist, or cartoonist—he'd drawn crude, funny, colorful pictures in emulation of comic strips and comic books; he'd wanted to be a musician, like Bob Dylan, and acquired a secondhand guitar when he was twelve, which he taught himself to play surprisingly well. (Eventually, the guitar was broken or stolen. Travis had been devastated.) Now Travis had become a high-school dropout who'd been arrested (as my mother had told me) on suspicion of vandalism, break-ins, and theft, with another, older boy named Weitzel who also lived in rural Beechum County; they'd received only suspended sentences and probation, not incarceration (as my mother believed they deserved).

My parents spoke disapprovingly of the Reidls—a large sprawling family to whom my mother was related through her half-sister Louise. These were relatives who lived in the country, in old farmhouses, or in trailers, on what remained of farmland property, sold off over the decades. Rural Beechum County was surpassingly beautiful, in the steep glacial hills of the Adirondacks, but I would not have wanted to live there—everyone seemed to be poor, and being poor had hardened their hearts.

My aunt Louise had been married and divorced at least twice—three times?—and had had at least five children who'd "given her trouble" and of whom Travis was the youngest, and had once been the most promising.

Yet, I was Travis's "special" cousin. I know that he thought of me in that way, as I thought of him.

When I'd been a little girl and my mother had still been on friendly terms with her half-sister Louise, she'd often brought me with her to visit my aunt, who'd lived in a ram-shackle old farmhouse near the Black Snake River. Though I was three years younger than Travis, my mother left me to play with him. My favorite times were when we drew pictures together with Crayolas on strips of paper. My drawings were of chickens and cats while Travis's were likely to be Viking warriors on horseback wielding swords and decapitating their enemies. At the age of eleven Travis created his own comic book—a vampire saga with white-skinned, bloody-mouthed creatures whose dark thick-lashed eyes bore an uncanny resemblance to his own. When he was older, Travis created a remarkable series of comic books relating the bloody apocalyptic adventures of "Black Snake Avenger"—a white-skinned Samurai warrior with a magical sword who inhabited a fairy-tale American city.

At unpredictable times Travis would suddenly lose interest in what he was doing and turn on me, teasing and bullying me as his older brothers teased and bullied him. He was easily excitable, moody and quick-tempered. Only when I began to cry he relented—"Hanna, hey! Don't cry. I don't mean it."

So suddenly it would seem, my cousin Travis was begging me not to cry, and speaking tenderly to me. Once we'd been running together and I'd tripped and fallen—(in fact, Travis might've tripped me)—and when my skinned knee began to bleed Travis washed the wound and found a Band-Aid to put on it. He told me not to tell my mother—"She won't let us play together if you do." Of course, I didn't tell my mother.

As we got older, Travis became moodier. His older brothers were brutal with him, and his mother's men friends treated him badly. Exactly when my mother stopped visiting my aunt, I don't know; it seemed to have happened abruptly, but may have been gradual. As the change in Travis must have been gradual.

Still, at the thought of Travis I felt a complex, pained emotion—a kind of love, but laced with apprehension.

I did not truly believe that my cousin would hurt *me*. But I did not trust him not to hurt others, or not to damage property or get in trouble with the law.

This past year we'd only seen each other a few times, by accident in town or at the mall. At a little distance Travis would wave at me, even blow a kiss—meaning to be funny. "Hiya there, Hanna! How's my sweetie!"—but he was with his friends and had no time for his young girl-cousin. He was in trouble for underage drinking, and for drugs. Though his grades at Sparta High were B's and C's he quit school at the age of sixteen after being suspended from school for fighting in the parking lot. (Though it was known that Travis had been defending himself against older boys, everyone involved in the fight was punished equally.)

I'd thought that my cousin had been treated unfairly by school authorities. Adults seemed fearful of him since he'd grown tall, and did not trust him. He'd cut classes, and was a "disruptive" presence in certain of his classes—male teachers were particularly threatened by him.

I remembered how he'd frightened me once with an elaborate fantasy about "committing a massacre"—his classmates and teachers at school, strangers at the mall, his own family.

He would wear a mask, he said—"No one would know it was *me*."

The perfect crime was murdering his own family in their sleep, Travis said. He would kill them one by one, with a knife; he would wash the knife thoroughly; he would return the knife where it belonged. He would take all the money he could find and hide it in his special hiding place in the old hay barn. Then, he would break a window on the first floor of the house so that glass fell inside—cops always checked for break-ins. He would tell the police that he'd run away into the woods when the killing started, and that he had not seen who the killers were. He spoke with an air of childish glee, seeing how his fantasy discomforted me.

"Why would you want to kill your family? Your *mom*?"

Travis grinned and shrugged. Why not?

By the age of seventeen Travis had grown nearly six feet tall. He was whippet-thin. His eyebrows were heavy, coarse. His eyes were light-colored and sly. Often he blinked as if he had a twitch or a tic—you thought of fish moving erratically in dark water. Often his jaws were covered in stubble. His wavy-dark hair was parted in the center of his head, shoulder-length and straggly. He wore headbands, baseball caps, hoodies. He wore a black leather jacket, jeans, and boots. His forearms were tattooed with eagles, screaming skulls. The back of each finger was tattooed with a miniature dagger. He worked at minimum-wage jobs—busboy at Wendy's, loading dock at Walmart. County road maintenance and snow removal, tree-service crew. He quit these jobs, or was fired. He smoked dope. He dealt drugs. He was suspected of breaking into houses. He no longer lived at home and none of the relatives seemed to know where he lived, or with whom. The last time my mother spoke with Aunt Louise, who'd called her to ask bluntly why my mother seemed to be avoiding her, my aunt complained of Travis that he was "out of control" and there were times she was "scared as hell of him" and thinking of getting a court injunction so he couldn't step foot on the property— "Except if I do, I'd be afraid how he'd react. Travis might really get violent, then."

Louise had laughed, and her laughter became a fit of coughing. My mother was shocked and had no idea how to reply.

I knew that there were girls in the high school, and girls who'd graduated, who were attracted to my cousin Travis despite his bad reputation, and I felt a stab of jealousy. Thinking—

Travis will be mean to them. They will be sorry.

"Hanna? Hey, Hanna? C'mon, be a good girl. Let us in."

Travis was striking the door with the iron knocker, pleading and braying. I had the idea that he was drunk, or high on drugs—I hoped it wasn't amphetamines, which I knew to be dangerous. I didn't dare come to the door to shout at him to go away—that would only provoke him.

I reasoned that Travis couldn't know that I was in the house. He could not actually know that anyone was inside. I told myself—*They will go away in a few minutes. They will not hurt anything. If I don't provoke them.* After what seemed like a long time, but may have been only five or six minutes, the loud, rude knocking at the front door ceased. The ringing of the doorbell ceased. And my cousin's mocking singsong Han-*na!* ceased.

They'd given up and gone away. I thought.

Cautiously I approached the front door. There appeared to be no one on the front stoop, or on the sidewalk. In the living room I peered out a window where I saw nothing, no one—the McClellands' front lawn, the five-foot wrought-iron fence indistinct in light from Drumlin Avenue.

I was faint with relief. I didn't truly think that Travis wanted to harass or harm me. Nor would he want to steal from the McClellands—he'd be too readily caught. He liked me, he wouldn't want me to get into trouble—unless he resented me, as the Reidls resented my family.

Yet, I loved my cousin Travis. I did not want to see him—especially not tonight, in the McClellands' house—but I loved him, at a distance.

Thinking of how, after a storm, electric wires lay on the ground, lethal if you touch or step on them. Sometimes the wires are literally crackling with electricity, throwing off sparks.

Live wire. Travis Reidl was one of these—lethal if you come too close.

Seeing that Travis and his companion were gone, I was eager to be gone from the McClelland house myself.

There was no romance in lingering here. The glamour of the house had faded, now I felt so vulnerable. I would switch off lights, raise blinds. Quickly I watered and sprayed the plants—concerned that several of the African violet leaves were looking yellow. Badly I regretted that poor Sasha had been frightened by the doorbell ringing and had run away to hide somewhere—very likely in her cat-brain, she was blaming me.

I returned to the kitchen, which was brightly lit. I was preparing to leave when I heard voices and muffled laughter at the kitchen door.

"Han-na! Got you, girl."

To my horror the doorknob was being roughly turned—but the door had locked automatically when I'd shut it. Travis's face appeared at the window, livid with anger and mouthing ugly words: "*Let me in! Let—me—fuckin'—IN.*" Before I could scream for him to stop, Travis struck the window with his fist, broke the glass pane which flew into the kitchen and shattered on the floor like sleet.

Now, Travis reached inside to turn the doorknob and open the door. Must've cut himself on jagged glass since there would be blood splotches on the door, and on the linoleum floor, but he seemed scarcely to notice.

Outside, Travis's friend balked at following him into the kitchen.

It seemed he hadn't expected Travis to behave so recklessly. "What the hell? What're you doing?"—I could hear him cursing Travis, as Travis was cursing him. If this was Weitzel, he was a stocky, heavy-jawed young man of about twenty with a fattish face, partly obscured by a gray jersey hood drawn tight over his head.

He and Travis were arguing. Then he walked away. Travis called furiously after him, "Go to hell, asshole!"

While the young men were arguing just outside the kitchen door I might have run through the house and out the front door, screaming for help. I might have run into the street, to stop a passing vehicle—or across the street, to a neighbor's house. But I did not do this—(I would try to explain afterward, faltering and shamed)—instead I stood vague and blinking as if my legs had turned to lead; standing in broken glass wanting to think that my cousin Travis was just being playful, and had not meant to actually break a window, and force his way into the McClelland house. *Travis would not do anything bad to me! Travis is my friend.*

No matter that the window had been shattered, Travis shut the door behind him, hard.

Travis seized me, and shook me like a rag doll.

"Why didn't you let us in! Goddamn, Hanna, this's all your fault."

I tried to push Travis away but his grip on my arm was tight, and painful. I could smell his breath, which was fierce with fumes like gasoline. And I could see his eyes, blackly dilated. Travis was "high"—crazed. Travis was in the most excitable mood I'd ever seen him in, and had to be dangerous. Yet still I wanted to believe that my cousin would not hurt me.

I begged Travis to leave. I tried to explain that my homeroom teacher lived in this house and that I was *helping her out* while her husband was in the hospital—except I didn't say that he was in Syracuse, hoping that Travis wouldn't have this information; possibly, Travis could be led to believe that Mr. McClelland was in the small Sparta hospital, and not thirty miles away.

"Don't worry, Han-han, nobody's going to hurt this stinking millionaire house. And nobody's going to hurt you. Except—don't you try to call the cops, or make a run for it. Try anything like that, girl, you will regret it."

Was Travis joking? In our games as children, he'd sometimes talk like this—threatening, mean-sounding. If I gave in immediately, he would not usually continue; he would not shove me around, or hit me; if I cried, he would relent at once and say he'd just been kidding. But now, though tears shone in my eyes, and Travis could see that I was frightened and upset, he was not placated.

He was laughing, though he was angry. He was angry, though laughing. He had not expected that his friend would abandon him and several times looked out the window as if he might see him outside—"Damn asshole. *Coward.*"

When I dared to pull at Travis's arm, and pleaded for him to go away, he shoved me with the palm of his hand flat against my chest—"Don't mess with me, Hanna. I'll go when I'm finished here."

"Neighbors might have heard you break in, Travis. Somebody might have called the police . . ."

"Fuck anybody heard anything! These millionaire houses, built so far apart, nobody hears anything and doesn't give a shit anyway."

Travis was exploring the kitchen, which was certainly the largest kitchen he'd ever seen. With cries of mock admiration he flung open cupboard doors, yanked out drawers, snatched up a silver ladle to strike shining copper pans that were hanging from an overhead beam like a manic drummer striking drums—"This is like—what? 'kettle drums'?" I was terrified that Travis would smash crystal glasses and expensive china out of sheer meanness. I was terrified that Travis would grab items out of the refrigerator—milk, fruit juices, jams, leftovers in plastic containers—and toss them about randomly. But his attention was drawn to a glass breakfront cabinet where he discovered a lavish store of wine and liquor bottles— here, he seized a bottle of Scotch whiskey with a hoot of triumph. He was very warm, feverish. He was laughing, muttering to himself, cursing under his breath. Suddenly feeling hot, he yanked down the hood of his cheap jacket, then struggled to free himself of the jacket, and flung it onto the floor. Beneath, he was wearing a black T-shirt cut at the shoulders, soiled work pants without a belt. It was shocking to see that Travis's hair, that had once been so wavy, and beautiful, was matted and stiff with dirt now, as if he hadn't washed it in weeks. Shocking to see that his skin was sallow, and blemished. There was something vulturelike about him, his narrow face, skinny and slightly concave torso, jerky motions—I would realize afterward that my cousin was a drug addict, a "junkie"—this is what junkies look like.

"Time for a drink! Celebrate!—gettin' together again. Ain't you been missin' me, Han-na? Ain't I your 'favorite' cousin?"

Travis poured whiskey into two glasses, and insisted that I drink with him. I told him no, I could not—but Travis forced the glass against my mouth, and forced my teeth apart, so that some of the liquid ran down my chin but a little remained in my mouth, so that I had to swallow; the liquor burned and stung with a medicinal pungency, and caused me to cough. Travis laughed at me, and pulled me after him into the hallway, and down the hallway to the first room, which was the TV room; here, Travis whistled through his teeth seeing the console-model television, which was surely the largest and most expensive television set he had ever seen. He switched it on, and switched through the channels so roughly I thought the knob might come off in his hand.

The TV screen glared bright-colored. Travis was too restless to watch anything for more than a few seconds. The volume was high, and so I thought—(but it could not have been a serious thought)—that neighbors might hear the unusual sound in the McClellands' house, and come to investigate. But this was my desperation, and not my common sense.

Travis muttered that he'd be coming back to take this TV—he'd need a damn truck to haul it. Music blared up from the TV, the buoyant and brainless music of advertising, and Travis took hold of me in a pretense of dancing, clumsy, panting, laughing at the look in my face that must have been a mixture of horror, dread, embarrassment, shame—"What's the matter, Han-na, think you're too good for me? Your cousin from Black Snake River you're too good for?" He was belligerent, bemused.

Travis insisted that I swallow another mouthful of whiskey. Another time much of it dribbled onto my clothing, and some of it down my throat. Travis was gripping my hand at the wrist, hard. He joked how he could snap my "sparrow arm" any time he wanted.

I was beginning to feel sickish, lightheaded.

"All your family, you think you're too good for the Reidls. But I have news for you."

Travis drank more whiskey. To force me to drink, he slid his arm around the nape of my neck, held me tight, and pressed the glass against my mouth. I struggled, but he was too strong.

Thinking desperately—*He will stop, soon. He will go away. He does not want to hurt me....*

It was uncomfortable, the way Travis held me. He'd hardly looked at me before—his eyes had leapt about, blinking—but now he was looking at me, close up. I could see his blemished skin, the fine broken capillaries in his eyes. I could smell his breath, and the odor of his body.

"What're you afraid of, girl? You lookin' like you don't know me."

I tried to ease away, laughing. I did manage to ease away from Travis's tight grip but dared not run from him, for I knew this would be insulting to him.

He said, as if thoughtfully, recalling something amusing, "You know, you're an 'accident'—just like me."

"I am not."

"You are! My mother says so. Your mother told my mother, she says 'Hanna is our accident.' And my mother said, 'Travis is *my* accident. I think you got the good deal, Esther.' "

I was stunned by this. The offhandedness of the remark. But knowing it could not be true, for my mother would never say anything like that. Especially, never to her half-sister Louise.

I thought—*He's just teasing. Travis likes to tease.*

I hated Travis suddenly. I wished that Travis was away somewhere—in the juvenile facility at Carthage, or farther away—like one of his older brothers who'd joined the U.S. Army—in the war in Vietnam.

I did not wish that Travis was dead, though. I would never wish that Travis was dead, I would miss him so.

Though I continued to beg him to leave, Travis dragged me with him into the dining room. Here he mock-marveled at the "fancy glass chandelier" and the "plant jungle." He had nothing but scorn for the many potted and hanging plants. "What's this? *Orchids*?" He seemed both offended and amused by the beautiful flowers. He stooped to sniff at the odorless orchids and African violets. As I looked on in horror, he broke off a purple striated orchid flower, which he tried to stick behind his ear, but it fell to the floor.

"Travis! Please stop. Please just go away."

"Go away *where*? This is where I am."

Next Travis tormented me by threatening to urinate into one of the potted plants. And then, to my horror, that was what he did—unzipped his pants, and urinated into the jade plant.

Seeing what he was doing, I backed away hiding my eyes.

Heard myself laughing. A high-pitched shriek of a laugh, like one who has been tickled hard. Like one who has been killed.

"That's how we do in Black River. Nothin' to surprise *you*."

Travis was enjoying this, tormenting his good-girl cousin. Wanting me to laugh with him. Almost, I felt a longing to join him in his bad, childish behavior in this house beautiful as a house in a magazine—except this was Mrs. McClelland's house, and I would never do anything to hurt or upset my teacher.

The whiskey was making me dizzy, lightheaded. I had swallowed only a small amount, but it had gone to my head.

There was the watering can. I picked it up, and poured water into the jade plant, thinking to dilute the toxic urine. Belatedly I remembered, Mrs. McClelland had said *No water for the jade plant.*

This was very funny, for some reason. I began laughing, and then I was choking, and vomiting—spitting up hot liquid, as Travis laughed at me.

Wanting to go to the kitchen, or into a bathroom, to rinse my mouth. Nothing so disgusting as the taste of bile.

But Travis forbade me to leave his side—he didn't trust me not to run away.

Travis was helping himself to fistfuls of silverware out of a breakfront cabinet. Seeing the look in my face he sneered. "All this fancy shit they got here, nobody's going to miss. Some folks got too much, and some folks too little."

So careless, some of the silverware fell to the floor. Travis gave it a kick.

"Travis, please go home. I won't tell anyone if—if you go home now . . ."

"Damn right you're not going to tell anyone, sweetheart. If you do, your whole face is going to look like that 'birthmark'—real red, and real ugly."

This hurt. This was malicious. I could not believe that Travis meant to say anything so cruel to me, knowing how I felt about the birthmark.

I stammered, saying when the McClellands returned, and saw that things were missing, I would have to tell them who'd taken them; and Travis said coldly, without his simpering grin, "I doubt you will do that, Hanna. You will regret it if you do."

I knew that this was so. I would not tell anyone what happened here—what was happening, that I was helpless to prevent—what Travis did, or said. I would have to invent a story—as a frightened and guilty child invents a story stammered to adults who will wish to believe her, no matter how preposterous her words.

For I remember vividly, many years after I left the small city of my childhood to live hundreds of miles away, how

I'd rarely confided in my mother, still more rarely my father, as a girl. So many secrets, that had seemed shameful to me then but were surely trivial, commonplace—the secrets of early adolescence. What drifted through my head like sinuous undulating water snakes in Wolf 's Head Lake, in the rushes where we'd catch sight of them sometimes, screaming with exaggerated horror.

Though I can remember crying and being comforted by both my parents, mostly I remember shielding from them, or keeping to myself, those things that must not be told to anyone.

10.

I did not see the face of the other person. He was wearing a hoodie like Travis but he did not lower the hood. But I could tell he was older than Travis—he was not someone I knew. I did not recognize his voice.

There was no time. From the moment they broke into the house and began taking things until they went into Mr. McClelland's home office and found his gun and the gun went off—everything happened too fast.

Because he was older than Travis, I think. Because they were both "high." Because Travis wanted to impress him. Because Travis had always had that weakness—teasing younger children, because he had been teased himself by older boys. And wanting to impress the older boys.

And so Travis did the hurtful things with the gun, to me. To make his friend laugh. Except his friend stopped laughing. His friend said for Travis to stop. And Travis would not stop. So his friend shoved Travis, and tried to pull the gun away, and the gun went off, beside my head. And Travis fell down. And I was on the floor, and I could not move in terror that I had died. And I could not think, for the ringing in my ears. And a black pit opened, and I fell inside.

11.

Begging my cousin Travis to leave the McClellands' house but he will not leave. His face glows like a bulb. Like a deranged sun / comet. Like the white face of a Samurai as the warrior lifts his sword to swing and decapitate in a single terrible motion.

Dragging me with him through the rooms. Laughing at my misery. Opening the door to Mr. McClelland's "home office"—which had not been locked, as Mrs. McClelland said it would be.

And this too is a betrayal—

Mrs. McClelland had said she would lock this door.

Boldly Travis Reidl steps inside this room. Because there is nothing and no one to prevent him.

Travis whistles through his teeth, impressed by the floor-to-ceiling mahogany bookshelves filled with books. Fireplace, enormous antique desk. "So many fuckin' books! Nobody ever read so many books." It is the resentment of one who might once have wished to read such books, but knows himself lost to them now.

Jeering, Travis examines the items on Mr. McClelland's desk. Ledger-sized appointment book, black fountain pen, silver lead pencil. Silver! Travis shoves this

in a pocket. There is a calendar inset in a leather frame—
"Lookit this goddamn thing!"—that seems particularly to
enrage him.

Grunting, Travis pulls out drawers in the large mahogany desk. Most are filled with files. I am grateful that he
isn't yanking the drawers out of the desk and spilling their
contents on the floor. In the lowermost drawer, he has
discovered something—he whistles through his teeth. It
is a gun. He lifts the gun in his hand, and his eyes narrow
with excitement.

"Jesus! Just what I need."

I am very frightened. I did not know there was a gun in
the house. I had no way of knowing. Why did Mrs. McClelland forget to lock the door!

I want to run away, to run out into the street and call
for help, but I know that my cousin Travis will punish me
terribly if I try. He will shoot at me—he will shoot one of
my legs, to bring me down. And he will laugh at me on the
floor screaming in agony. *Didn't I warn you, Han-na! You
disobeyed.*

Somberly Travis examines the gun, turning the chambers. Is the gun loaded? Travis asks me if I know what
Russian roulette is?

No. I tell Travis no.

I do not know what Russian roulette is. (Of course I
know what Russian roulette is.)

I am trying not to cry. Still I am thinking *Travis likes me!
He will not hurt me.*

It is like prayers in church. *Heavenly Father who gives
us all blessings. All blessings are from You.* Begging God

to be good to you because your terror is that God will not be good to you. And so I am begging my cousin Travis though I do not dare beg aloud.

Remembering how Travis had said in a dreamy voice he'd have liked to bring a gun to school. Remembering the "massacre" comics. There were no guns in his mother's house, for an older brother had fired an air rifle at Travis when he'd been a little boy, hitting him in the back, and his mother had taken the gun away from the brother, and threw it in the Black Snake River. And Travis had not been allowed to have a gun. He'd said, When I'm old enough I can buy my own guns. I won't be living here. I don't need anybody telling me what to do.

Now he has Mr. McClelland's gun, which is like a gift to him. If you believe in fate, or destiny—this is not an "accident" that the gun has come into Travis's hands. And so gravely he examines it. He turns the cylinder, peering into it. He is transfixed, there is a strange radiant smile on his face. Despite the sallow skin and dirty, matted hair I can see that my cousin is a beautiful boy. A beautiful ruin of a boy. A young-old boy, with bruised and bloodshot eyes. I am afraid of Travis but yet, I am drawn to Travis. His eyes lifting from the gun to mine, rapidly blinking as if the sight of the gun is dazzling and he is part blinded.

"Did you ever hear of a suicide pact? I think it would be the test of love."

It is very strange to hear the word *love* uttered in Travis's scratchy voice.

But quickly I shake my head—*no.*

Though thinking, to be found dead, in a boy's arms—this is a haunting thought.

There was a couple in the high school who'd died together. But it was believed that the boy had killed his girlfriend, driven his car into a lake, through ice, so that they'd drowned together.

Like an actor in a film Travis positions himself in front of a mirror above the fireplace mantel. To my horror he presses the muzzle of the barrel against his head. He smiles at himself in the mirror, winks; brushes a strand of ratty hair out of his eyes. Then as if he has only just thought of it he lowers the revolver, carefully shakes bullets out of the cylinder, drops them into a pocket. Slyly he looks at me, who has been standing all this while a few yards away, unable to move.

"See? The gun isn't all loaded. There is a chance."

"Travis, no. Please—put the gun away."

"'Russian roulette.' Just one bullet left. It's cool."

Fascinated by what he sees, Travis continues to stare at himself in the mirror. His posture is straight as a soldier's. He seems to have forgotten me. He poses holding the muzzle of the barrel against his forehead as a dreamy look comes into his eyes. It appears that he is about to pull the trigger, then he whirls like a gunfighter in a Western, with bent knees, aims the muzzle at me instead, and pulls the trigger. There is a *click!*—on an empty chamber.

I am so frightened, I have wetted my underwear. My heart is pounding. Sweat breaks out in my underarms. But Travis just laughs at me.

"Try another time? Hey?"—he points the barrel at me and I crouch, shielding my head. As if this would stop a bullet.

Begging, "No, please. No—please. Travis . . ."

Travis laughs. He is excited, elated. He has me powerless. I am his captive. His vassal. He is the Black Snake Avenger, about to execute a hapless captive.

"I told you, there's just one bullet in the cylinder. There's a chance."

I am too terrified to respond to my teasing cousin.

Travis says, "Kneel down."

"No, Travis. No, please."

Travis rubs the muzzle of the gun against the side of my face which I try to keep hidden—the ugly red birthmark beneath my left eye. Cruelly teasing— "Hey. Want me to shoot this off?" He thrusts the barrel into my mouth. I am choking, terrified. He would not pull the trigger and murder me—would he? The muzzle strikes against my teeth, a pain so intense it registers as numbness. I am trying not to cry uncontrollably. I am trying to obey Travis so that he will pity me, and have mercy on me as he used to do when we were children. Telling myself he would not kill me, for he loves me. Yet, Travis is laughing meanly. That sniggering laughter of boys who have found someone weak to torment, who cannot hurt them in return.

And now Travis does something I would not believe he would do—he tears open my sweater and pushes the gun muzzle against my breasts—the puckered, terrified flesh inside my small white-cotton 32-A brassiere. The gun muzzle is damp from my saliva but still cold and I am shivering and shuddering and so frightened, I have wetted myself—again. And Travis shoves the gun barrel down inside the waistband of my corduroy pants—as if he wants to "tickle" my stomach—and farther down, between my legs—and I am screaming now with pain, and squirming—Travis is grunting and laughing quick as if out of breath from running—flush-faced, telling me that I will have to be punished for wetting myself for I am a dirty disgusting girl.

I am crying helplessly now. Travis has mercy on me, but it is the mercy of disgust. With his booted foot he shoves me away. He drops the gun onto the leather chair as if it has been defiled by the wetness in my underwear.

"Stop crying! Nobody has hurt you—yet. Walk—on your knees. Walk, and you can save yourself."

I am on my knees, close beside the chair. Desperately, clumsily I reach for the gun—the gun Travis has let drop—it is a miracle that I have the gun in my hand—in both hands. The gun is heavy—heavier than I would expect. The barrel is long, and hard to keep lifted—it wants to lower itself, like a dowsing rod. Seeing me with the gun in my hands Travis cries, "Hey! Goddamn you—" as I pull the trigger—try to pull the trigger; it is not easy, and at first the trigger doesn't move—and then it moves, with a *click!* on an empty chamber. Travis is furious now, swooping to snatch the gun from me, and I pull the trigger again and this time there is no *click!* but a deafening explosion, and Travis is jolted back—Travis is shot in the chest—the look of fury fading from his face as he falls to the floor. Like a terrified animal I am crawling away—trying to crawl away—on my hands and knees. I am desperate to escape Travis who (I am sure) will lay his hands on me and hurt me very badly for having disobeyed him. The gun has fallen from my hands. The gun is too heavy to hold. The gun is on the floor, close by Travis who is lying in front of the fireplace groaning and thrashing. Though I can see blood spilling from Travis's chest none of this is real to me—I cannot believe that Travis has actually *been shot*— it is clear that Travis is teasing me, and in another moment will leap to his feet, to punish me. Yet, the gun has fired—I can feel the impact of the shot, a quivering sensation in my hands and wrists. The sound was deafening, there is a roaring in my ears so loud I can't hear, and I can't think.

Except—*It was an accident. The gun fired by itself.*

12.

It was an accident—I think. Travis had the gun and his friend tried to take it from him and—the gun went off.

I did not see his face. I did not recognize his voice. When he and Travis broke into the kitchen I knew not to look at him for I was in fear of my life.

On the floor for a long time I could not move.

There was a pressure inside my head like a balloon being blown to bursting. I knew of cerebral hemorrhage, *I had looked the words up in the dictionary and had frightened myself.*

How long it was, after Travis's friend ran out of the house, I don't know. And then, there was the doorbell ringing but so far away, I could barely hear it.

And then, the neighbor came to the back door. And saw the window had been broken and saw the bright-lit kitchen and no one in it and called Hello? Hello?

Is someone here?—and came into the hall and into the room where Travis had fallen, and I had fallen, and saw that Travis had been shot and believed that I had been shot as well where I was lying unconscious on the floor, my head just off the rug and onto the hardwood floor where it had struck hard but it appeared that I was breathing, and so he knew I was alive.

13.

Gun Accident at Drumlin Ave. Residence
Burglary Accomplices Quarrel, Gun Fires Killing Area Teen

As if the gun had fired by itself, and the bullet had lodged in the seventeen-year-old Travis Reidl's chest totally by chance, perforating his heart. The aorta was torn, within minutes Travis bled to death. Travis Reidl whom those who'd known him since childhood would call *troubled, difficult, school dropout, suspect in recent break-ins in Beechum County.* Of whom it was said that his mother had spoken of getting an injunction from the county court to keep him away from the family home—*Not a bad boy in his heart but involved with drugs and drug dealers and it is no surprise, one of those bastards killed him.* In the

Sparta Journal it would be reported that the individual who'd fired the gun, the "accomplice" of Travis Reidl, had not yet been apprehended by Sparta police.

14.

It is twenty-six years later. I have been staring out the window at the dark, dripping November sky. Downstairs, my mother and children are in the kitchen. A smell of fresh-baked banana bread wafts up the stairs. I am expected to join them, and I am eager to join them, except— my legs are weak, the pulses in my head are still beating.

Outside there is something urgent in the sky. The swirl of the sky of early winter. The way life is sucked into a whirlpool, spinning faster and faster, until it disappears into a point. The wind has risen, the windows are drafty. Blackbirds are flocking in the tall trees that surround my parents' house, a storm of blackbirds, so many it is astonishing—almost, it is frightening. A welter of wings against the window, broken-off cries in midair. Hundreds of black-feathered wings—thousands?—preparing to migrate south. I feel a powerful yearning, impossible to describe. *I want to go with you. Where are you going, don't leave us.*

I am thinking of how I was questioned by sympathetic Sparta police officers and by other adults who cared for me, and did not wish to upset me further. For I was dazed and mute from what had been done to me and would not recover for a long time. And would not be "normal" for a long time. The story that I would try to tell over and over

was a confused and incoherent story for I had been trau-
matized by what had been done to me by my own cousin
Travis Reidl. Chipped tooth and bleeding lips from the
gun muzzle shoved into my mouth, red welts on my
breasts and belly, bruises in the "genital area"—in the
newspapers, these shameful details would not be revealed.

Who was your cousin's accomplice? I was asked.

And all I could say was that I had not seen his face. I
had not recognized his voice.

Did he threaten you, if you told? If you identified him?

Did he say that he would come back and kill you,
Hanna?

I could not speak. I could not speak aloud, the men
listening and taking notes.

But whispering to the woman police officer who was so
sympathetic, when he'd opened his pants to urinate in
Mrs. McClelland's jade plant, because he was drunk and
he was high on drugs, I had quickly shut my eyes and
turned away.

What is his name, could you describe him, could you
identify him, but I said that I could not for it would be a
terrible thing to mistakenly involve an innocent person in
the death of my cousin.

Police questioned the Drumlin Avenue neighbor who'd
called them. Police questioned other neighbors who
claimed to have heard a car's doors being slammed shut,
men's voices outside, and a girl's scream and a single
gunshot at 7:10 P.M. but no one could identify the vehicle,
still less the accomplice of the slain boy.

Several times police brought twenty-two-year-old Steve Weitzel into headquarters for questioning. They were certain that Weitzel was the person who'd accidentally shot his friend Travis Reidl in a break-in / burglary that had gone wrong but each time they'd had to release Weitzel for there was not enough evidence to arrest him.

If Weitzel had been my cousin's accomplice he would have known that he had not shot Travis and just possibly, he could have guessed who had shot Travis. But Weitzel could not have claimed that someone not himself had shot Travis for to have claimed this would be to acknowledge that he'd participated in the break-in with Travis, but had run away before anything had happened.

Instead, Weitzel claimed that he knew nothing about the break-in on Drumlin Avenue, nothing about Travis Reidl that evening. He'd last seen Travis days before, he would claim.

It was not an era in which small-city police detectives knew to secure a crime scene carefully. Fingerprints on the weapon used to shoot Travis Reidl at close range were said to be "smudged." No fingerprints were taken from me.

The gun was returned soon to Gordon McClelland, for it was Mr. McClelland's lawful property.

Those weeks, months of ninth grade when I carried myself like glass that might shatter into pieces at any moment. Treated like a convalescent by my friends, as by my teachers. Seeing pity in their eyes, and a kind of repugnance. For whatever had been done to me, they did not wish to know.

In those days there were no words like *sexual abuse, molestation*. *Rape* would not be uttered aloud, nor would *rape* be printed in a family newspaper like the *Sparta Journal*.

And so, no one knew exactly what had happened to me, even the doctor who examined me, and wrote his report for the police. Nor could I have been expected to explain, who lacked the vocabulary also, and who lapsed into heart-pounding panic and spells of muteness if questioned too closely.

The neighbor who'd dared to come into the McClelland house would tell of having found the bodies—the shaggy-haired boy "like a biker" shot in the chest, the girl who'd looked scarcely older than twelve or thirteen collapsed and scarcely breathing, he had thought had been shot also.

He had knelt over the girl, and tried to revive her. He saw that her clothing had been torn. Her skin was deathly white. Her eyes were rolled back up into her head like the eyes of a doll that has been shaken hard and her bleeding mouth was open and slack with saliva but—she was alive.

The following week, Gordon McClelland was discharged from the medical center in Syracuse and returned to his home but the McClellands would not live in the house on Drumlin Avenue for long. Their house had been defiled, Mrs. McClelland said. The beautiful old colonial would be sold at below its market price to a couple moving to Sparta who knew little of the "gun accident" and did not wish to know more.

Mrs. McClelland returned to our homeroom and to teaching social studies for the remainder of the school year but was not so buoyant as she'd been. Often she seemed distracted. She did not always listen to the answers to questions she herself had asked, which made us restless, and uneasy.

No longer did she take time to make up her face as she'd done before. The glamorous pageboy hairstyle had vanished, often she merely brushed her hair behind her ears, or fashioned it into a knot at the nape of her neck. No one would have said that she resembled Jeanne Crain. Though she wore many of the same clothes they were no longer so striking on her.

The McClellands would move from Sparta soon after their house was sold.

After the initial period of police questioning no one spoke to me about what had happened to me that night. There would be the rumor, that Hanna Godden had been *hurt*. By her own, older cousin—*hurt*.

In the (unspeakable, shameful) way in which a girl can be *hurt* by a boy or a man.

Yet, this was not so. I knew that this was not so. A terrible thing happened in my presence but it did not happen to me.

The early 1960s was not a time in which children or adolescents who had suffered "traumas" were brought to therapists. In fact, there were few therapists in Sparta. In fact, the term "trauma" was not in common usage. Like other adults of the era my parents believed that healing was a matter of *not dwelling* upon the past.

Mrs. McClelland did not blame me for anything. She understood that I had not invited my cousin Travis into the house, and that I had begged him to leave. She said to my mother, "Poor Hanna! It was my fault to entrust someone so young with such a responsibility" and my mother said, flattered, "Oh no—Hanna was happy to help out. It was an accident, the terrible thing that happened."

My mother might have thought to blame herself. Of course, she did not.

When I spoke with Mrs. McClelland I was stricken with shyness. I understood that my teacher did not like me so much any longer—she did not feel comfortable with me. And all I dared to ask her was how Sasha was?—and Mrs. McClelland said, with a sudden smile, "Sasha is well. Sasha is amazingly well recovered, and sleeps with us now almost every night."

In all that she told people Mrs. McClelland never failed to speak of me as a very good girl, one of her best students. What a tragedy it had been, those criminal intruders had forced their way inside the house. Mrs. McClelland knew who Travis Reidl was—he'd been a student of hers several years before. She'd thought that Travis was surprisingly bright and promising for a boy from rural Beechum County but she had not trusted him. Travis was the kind of student you would not dare to turn your back on, to write on the blackboard, for fear that he would make the class laugh by gesturing comically / obscenely behind your back. Mrs. McClelland said of Travis that he was a "disaster waiting to happen."

Only when I return to Sparta, and spend some time with my mother, will it be revealed that my aunt Louise had confided in my mother that she felt "sick and guilty" about what Travis had done to me. My aunt had not denounced her son to the police or to any strangers but she told my mother that she was sorry and ashamed, how Travis had behaved. "He was so fond of Hanna, that's a fact. Hanna was his favorite cousin. He'd never have wanted to hurt her if he'd been in his right mind. I hope you know that, and Hanna knows that."

My mother had said yes, we knew. And we appreciated Louise telling us.

Startling me out of my reverie at the window comes the call—*Han-na?*

Where are you?

They are waiting for me downstairs. Soon, I will join them.

My children know nothing of Travis Reidl, of course. My children have only the vaguest knowledge of who their mother is, and was. For who would tell them? The adults who surround them will protect them from the harm of too much knowledge.

Visiting Sparta, only a few times in twenty-six years have I encountered or even glimpsed Steve Weitzel. Once at the mall behind Sears, another time in a 7-Eleven store. Each time the encounter was uncanny, unsettling. We did not know each other when we were young; I'm sure that Steve Weitzel hadn't known my name though he'd have learned my name after the shooting. When we see each other as adults, Steve Weitzel stops in his tracks and stares at me as if he is trying to summon back a memory of me, with the effort of one trying to drag a heavy weight out of deep, black water, that is entangled with seaweed.

This is the visit when, another time, by accident, I will encounter Steve Weitzel. With my daughter Ellen crossing the parking lot behind the bank and there is a middle-aged man staring at me. He is wearing a soiled windbreaker and soiled work pants. His face looks as if it had been roughly swabbed with a wire brush. There are broken capillaries in his eyes like tiny worms. Steve Weitzel has become a thick-bodied man with badly thinning hair, a blunt brute face, sullen eyes. The kind of man who doesn't stand aside for you if you are entering a building as he is exiting it and who doesn't allow you to go first in line, though you have arrived first. Yet, seeing me, and glancing at the eleven-year-old girl beside me, Steve Weitzel hesitates, as if he is about to speak.

But I do not want this coarse-looking man to recognize me. With the polite but fleeting smile of a woman who has been away from Sparta for much of her adult life and who is no longer certain whom she should remember—(former classmate? neighbor?)—and who is a stranger, I am about to continue walking past Steve Weitzel, gripping my daughter's hand, when he says, in a voice that sounds as if it has not been used in a while, "Hanna, hello. Thought that was you."

Joyce Carol Oates is, quite simply, a master of the written word. Author of more than forty novels and hundreds of short stories, as well as poems, plays, book reviews, she published her first work, the short story collection *By the North Gate*, in 1963, and followed that with her first novel, *With Shuddering Fall*, and has published at least one volume every year, whether it be a novel, collection of short stories, poems, plays, or essays, all while teaching full time at Princeton from 1978 to 2015. Her body of work has been lauded around the world, been translated into countless foreign editions, short and feature films, and received many awards, including The O. Henry Award, the Pushcart Prize, the National Book Award, the Stoker Award, the World Fantasy Award. She has also received honorary degrees from Mount Holyoke College and the University of Pennsylvania. Her work has been nominated for the Pulitzer Prize five times, and she is a continuing favorite to win the Nobel Prize for Literature. With her first husband, Raymond, J. Smith, she founded the literary magazine *The Ontario Review* in 1974, with the goal of publishing the best art and fiction from the U.S. and Canada; it was published until 2008. Currently she lives with her husband and writes in Princeton, New Jersey.

Year's Best Crime & Mystery

Damage Control: Thomas H. Cook

First published in *Manhattan Mayham*

She'd been found in the dilapidated Bronx apartment where she'd lived for the past seventeen months. It was a basement apartment and had only a couple small windows, but she'd made it darker still by drawing the curtains. It was so dim inside that the first cop to arrive had stumbled about, looking for a light switch. He'd finally found one only to discover that she'd unscrewed all the light bulbs, even the ones in the ceiling and the fluorescent ones on either side of the bathroom mirror.

Neighbors later told police that they hadn't seen a single sliver of light coming from her apartment for well over a month. It was as if the terrible capacity for destruction that I'd glimpsed in her so many years before had at last grown strong enough to consume her entirely.

A Detective O'Brien had related the grim details over the phone, the deteriorated condition of her body being the most graphic, the fact that the smell had alerted the neighbors. Then he'd asked me to meet him at the police station nearest my home. "Just following standard procedure," he'd assured me, "Nothing to worry about."

We'd agreed on a time and date, and so now here I was, dealing with Maddox again, just as I'd done so often before.

"So, tell me, what was your relationship with this young woman?" Detective O'Brien asked immediately after we'd exchanged greeting s and I'd taken a seat in the metal chair beside his desk. His tone was casual enough, but there was an implication of something illicit in the word *relationship*.

"We took her in when she was a little girl," I told him.

"How little?"

"She was ten when she came to live with us."

That had been twenty-four years earlier. My family and I had lived in Hell's Kitchen when there'd still been some hell left in it; sex shops and hot-sheet hotels, burnt-out prostitutes offering themselves on the corner of Forty-Sixth and Eighth. Now it was all theaters and restaurants, chartered buses unloading well-heeled senior citizens from

Connecticut and New Jersey. Once it had been a neighborhood, bad though it was. Now it was an attraction.

"Us?" Detective O'Brien asked, still with a hint of probing for something unseemly. Had I abused this child? Is that why she'd embraced the darkness? Luckily, I knew that nothing could be further from the truth.

"With my wife and me, and our daughter Lana, who was just a year younger than Maddox," I told him. "She stayed with us for almost a year. We'd planned for her to stay with us indefinitely. Lana had always wanted a sister.

But as it turned out, we just weren't prepared to keep a girl like that."

"Like what?"

I avoided the word that occurred to me: *dangerous.*

"Difficult," I said. "Very difficult."

And so I'd sent her back to her single mother and her riotous older brother, hardly giving her a thought since. But now this bad penny had returned, spectacularly.

"How did she come to live with you in the first place?" O'Brien asked.

"Her mother was an old friend of ours," I answered. "So was her father, but he died when Maddox was two years old. Anyway, her mother had lost her job. We were doing well, my wife and I, so we offered to bring Maddox to New York, pay for the private school our daughter also attended. The hope was to give her a better life."

O'Brien's expression said everything: *But instead . . .*

But instead, Maddox had ended up in the morgue.

"Did you know she was in New York?" the detective asked.

I shook my head. "Her mother remarried and moved to California.

After that, we lost touch. The last I heard, Maddox was in the Midwest somewhere. After that, we had no idea where she was or what she was doing. What was she doing, by the way?"

"She'd been working as a cashier at a diner on Gun Hill Road,"

O'Brien told me.

"Maddox was very smart," I said. "She could have . . . done anything."

The detective's eyes told me that he'd heard a story like this one before; a smart kid who'd gotten a great chance but blown it.

I couldn't keep from asking the question. "How did she die? On the phone, you just said her body had been found."

"From the looks of it, malnutrition," O'Brien answered. "No sign of drugs or any kind of violence." He asked a few more questions, wanted to know if I'd heard from Maddox over the last few months, whether I knew the whereabouts of any family members, questions he called "routine." I answered him truthfully, of course, and he appeared to accept my answers.

After a few minutes, he got to his feet. "Well, thanks for coming in,

Mr. Gordon," he said. "Like I said when I asked you to come down to the station, it's just that your name came up during the course of the investigation."

"Yes, you said that. But you didn't tell me how my name happened to come up."

"She'd evidently mentioned you from time to time," O'Brien explained with a polite smile. "Sorry for the inconvenience," he added as he offered his hand. "I'm sure you understand."

"Of course," I said, and then I rose and headed for the door, sorry that Maddox's life had ended so early and so badly but also reminding myself that, in regard to my finally pulling the plug on the effort I'd made to help her, she'd truly given me no choice.

At that thought, her image appeared vividly in my mind: a little girl in the rain, waiting for the taxi that would take us to the airport, the way she'd glanced back at me an hour or so later as she headed toward the boarding ramp, her lips silently mouthing the last word she would say to me: *"Sorry."*

But sorry for what? I'd asked myself at that moment, for by then she'd had so much to confess.

———— · — · — · ————

"Did you see her body?"

I shook my head. "There was no need. The building super had already identified her."

"Odd that your name came up at all," Janice said. "That she'd . . . talked about you."

My wife and I sat with our evening glasses of wine, peering down onto a Forty-Second Street that looked nothing at all as it had when Maddox lived with us. Night was falling, and below our twelfth-floor balcony, people were on their way to Broadway, among them a few families with small children, some no doubt headed for *The Lion King.*

"So, she came back to New York," Janice said in that meditative way of hers, like a philosopher working with an idea. After a moment, a dark notion seemed to strike her. "Jack?"

I turned to face her.

"Do you think she ever . . . watched us?"

"Of course not," I said, then took a sip of my wine and eased back, trying to relax. But I found my wife's mention of the possibility that Maddox might, in fact, have stationed herself somewhere near the building where we'd all once lived, and where Janice and I still lived, surprisingly unnerving. Could it be that after all these years, she'd returned to New York with some sort of vengeful plan in mind? Had she never stopped thinking of how I'd sent her back? As her life spiraled downward, had she come to blame me for that very spiral?

"It's sort of creepy to think of her slinking around the neighborhood," Janice said.

"There's no evidence she ever did that," I said in a tone that made me sound convinced by this lack of evidence. And yet, I suddenly imagined Maddox watching me from some secret position, a ghostly, ghastly face hatefully staring at me from behind a potted palm.

Janice took a sip from her glass and softly closed her eyes. "Lana called, by the way. I told her about Maddox."

Lana was now married, living on the Upper West Side. Our two grandsons went to the same fiercely expensive private school that both Lana and Maddox had attended; Lana with little difficulty, Maddox with a full repertoire of problems, accused of stealing, cheating, lying.

"Lana and I are having dinner while you're in Houston," I said.

Janice smiled. "A nice little father–daughter outing. Good for you."

She drew in one of her long, peaceful breaths, a woman who'd had remarkably few worries in her life, who liked her job and got along well with our daughter, and whose marriage had been as unruffled as could have been expected.

With a wife like that, I decided, the less she knew about the one time all that had been jeopardized, the better.

"Lana took it harder than I thought she would," Janice said. "She'd wanted a sister, remember? And, of course, she'd thought Maddox might be that sister."

"Lana's done fine as an only child," I said, careful not to add a far darker truth, that my daughter was, in fact, lucky to be alive, that the year Maddox had lived with us had been, particularly for Lana, a year of living dangerously, indeed.

"We were very naive to have brought Maddox to live with us," Janice said. "To think that we could take a little girl away from her mother, her neighborhood, her school, and that she'd simply adjust to all that." Her gaze drifted over toward the Hudson. "How could we have expected her just to be grateful?"

This was true, as I well knew. During the first nine years of her life, Maddox had known nothing but hardship, uncertainty, disruption. How could we have expected her not to bring all that dreadful disequilibrium with her?

"You're right, of course," I said softly, draining my glass. And with that simple gesture, I tried to dismiss the notion that she'd come to

New York with some psychopathic dream of striking at me from behind a curtain, smiling maniacally as she raised a long, sharp knife.

———— · — · — · ————

And so, yes, I tried to dismiss my own quavering dread as a paranoid response to a young woman who'd no doubt come to New York because she was at the end of her tether, and the city offered itself as some sort of deranged answer to a life that had obviously become increasingly disordered. I tried to position my memory of her as simply a distressing episode in all of our lives, with repeated visits to Falcon Academy, always followed by stern warnings to Maddox that if she didn't "clean up her act," she would almost certainly be expelled. "Do you want that?" I'd asked after one of these lectures. She'd only shrugged. "I just cause trouble," she said. And God knows she had, and would no doubt have caused more, a fact I remained quite certain about.

And so, yes, I might well have put her out of my mind at the end of that short yet disquieting conversation with Janice that evening as the sun set over the Hudson, my memory of Maddox destined to become increasingly distant until she was but one of that great body of unpleasant memories each of us accumulates as we move through life.

Then, out of the blue, a little envelope arrived. It had come from the Bronx, and inside I found a note that read: *Maddox wanted you to have something.* It was signed by someone named Theo, who offered to deliver whatever Maddox had left me. If I wanted to "know more," I was to call this Theo and arrange a meeting.

I met him in a neighborhood wine bar three days later, and I have to admit that I'd expected one of those guys who muscled up in prison gyms, cut his initials in his hair, or had enough studs in his lips and tongue and eyebrows to set off airport metal detectors. Such had been my vision of the criminal sort toward which Maddox would have gravitated, she forever the Bonnie of some misbegotten Clyde. Instead, I found myself talking to a well-spoken young man whose tone was quietly informative.

"Maddox was a tenant in my building," he told me after I'd identified myself.

"You're the super who found her?"

"No, I own the building," Theo said.

For a moment, I wondered if I was about to be hit up for Maddox's unpaid rent.

"Sometimes Maddox and I talked," he said. "She usually didn't have much to say, but a few times, when she was in the hallway or walking through the courtyard, I'd stop to chat." He paused before adding: "She'd paid her rent a few months in advance and told the super that she was going away for a while. He assumed she'd done exactly that, just gone away for a while, so he didn't think anything of it when he stopped seeing her around."

"She planned it, you mean," I said. "Her death."

"It seems that way," Theo answered.

So, I thought, *she'd murdered someone at last.*

Theo placed a refrigerator magnet on the table and slid it over to me. "This is what she wanted you to have."

"*Beauty and the Beast*," I said quietly, surprised that Maddox had held on to such a relic—and certainly surprised that, for some bizarre reason, she'd wanted me to have it. "I took her and my daughter to that show."

"I know," Theo said. "It was the happiest day of Maddox's life. She remembered how you bought the magnet for her and put it in her hand and curled her fingers around it. It was tender, the way you did it, she said, very loving."

I gave the magnet a quick glance but didn't touch it. "Obviously, she told you that she lived with us a while."

He nodded.

"Unfortunately, I had to send her back to her mother," I told him bluntly, picking up the magnet and turning it slowly in my fingers. "She told lies," I added. "She cheated on tests, or, at least, she tried to. She stole."

And that was not the worst of it, I thought.

All this appeared to surprise Theo, so I suspected he'd been taken in by Maddox, fallen for whatever character she'd created in order to manipulate him. She'd tried to do the same with me, but by then I'd seen how dangerous she was and had acted accordingly.

"And so I sent her back," I said. "I'm sure that's what she wanted all along."

Theo was silent for a moment before he said, "No, she wanted to stay."

Perhaps at the very end, Maddox truly had wanted to stay with us, I thought. But if so, that only meant she'd have done whatever she had to do to accomplish that goal. In fact, I decided, that might well have been the reason she'd done what she'd done that night in the subway station.

"She was capable of anything," I told Theo resolutely.

At that point, I actually considered telling Theo the whole story, but then found that I couldn't.

After a moment, Theo nodded toward the refrigerator magnet. "Anyway," he said, "It's yours now."

———— · — · — · ————

"What are you supposed to do with it?" Janice asked when I showed her the *Beauty and the Beast* refrigerator magnet. She made her well-known and purposely exaggerated trembling notion. "It feels like some kind of . . . accusation."

Suddenly it all became clear. "It's Maddox's way of giving me the finger just one last time," I said. "Making me feel guilty for sending her back. But she was the one who made it impossible for her to become a part of our family." I shook my head vehemently. "So, I'm just going to stop thinking about her."

I wanted to do just that, but I couldn't.

Why? Because for me, it had never been "to be or not to be, that is the question." It was what a human being learned or failed to learn while on this earth. For that reason, I couldn't help but wonder if Maddox had ever acknowledged in the least what I'd hoped to do for her by bringing her into my family, or if she had accepted the slightest responsibility for the fact that I'd had to abandon that effort. With Maddox dead, how could I pursue such an inquiry? Where could I look for clues? The answer was bleak but simple, and so the very next day I took the train up to the Bronx.

Maddox had lived in one of the older buildings on the Grand Concourse. I'd gotten the address from Detective O'Brien, who'd clearly had more important things on his mind, a girl who'd starved herself to death no longer of much note.

Theo was in the courtyard when I arrived. He was clearly surprised to see me.

"Have you rented out Maddox's apartment yet?" I asked.

He shook his head.

"Would you mind letting me see it?"

"No," Theo answered casually.

He snapped a key from the dangling mass that hung on a metal ring from his belt. "They're coming to clear out her stuff tomorrow."

"Did she have a diary, anything like that? Letters?"

He shook his head. "Maddox didn't have much of anything."

This was certainly true. She'd lived sparely, to say the least. In fact, from the drab hand-me-down nature of the furnishings, I gathered that she'd picked up most of what she owned from the street. In the kitchen I found chipped plates. In the bedroom I found a mattress without a bed, along with a sprawl of sheets and towels. When she'd lived with us, she'd been something of a slob, and I could see that nothing in that part of her personality had changed.

"That day you told me about," I said to Theo after my short visit to Maddox's apartment, "the day we all went to see *Beauty and the Beast*. Did she say why she thought that was the happiest day of her life?"

Theo shook his head. "No, but it was clear that it meant a great deal to her, that day."

I remembered "that day" very well, and on the subway back to Manhattan, I recalled it again and again.

It wasn't just that day that returned to me. I also recalled the many difficult weeks that had preceded it, causing a steady erosion in my earlier confidence that Maddox would adjust well to New York, that she would succeed at Falcon Academy and, from there, go on to a fine college, her road to a happy life as free of obstacles as Lana's.

At first, Maddox had been on her best behavior, though in ways that later struck me as transparently manipulative. She'd complimented Janice on her cooking, Lana on her hair, me on my skill at playing Monopoly. On the first day of school, she'd appeared eager to do well; she had even seemed proud of her uniform. "It makes me feel special," she'd said that morning, and then she flashed her beaming smile, the one she used on all such occasions, as I was soon to learn, and that I'd taken to be genuine, though it wasn't. But the dawning of this dark recognition had come slowly, and so, as I'd walked Maddox and Lana to their bus that first school day, then stood waving cheerfully as it pulled away, I'd felt certain that I now had two daughters, and that both of them were good

———— · — · — · ————

Janice was still at work when I returned home after making my bleak tour of Maddox's apartment. I was already on the balcony with my glass of wine when she came through the door. By then the sun had set, and so she found me sitting in the dark

"I went up to the Bronx today," I told her. "To Maddox's apartment."

She looked at me with considerable sympathy. "You shouldn't feel like you failed her, Jack," she said quietly.

With that, she turned and headed for the bedroom. From my place in the shadows, I could hear her undressing, kicking off her dressy heels, putting away her jewelry, and then the sound of her sandaled feet as she came back onto the balcony, now with her own glass of wine.

"So, why did you go there?" she asked.

I'd never told anyone about that day, and I saw no reason to do so now. "I was just curious, I suppose," I said.

"About what?"

"About Maddox," I answered, "Whether she ever . . . " I stopped because the words themselves seemed silly. Even so, I couldn't find more precise ones. " . . . ever became a better person."

Janice looked puzzled. "Maddox was just a child when she left us, Jack," she said. "It wasn't like she was . . . formed."

But she hadn't just "left us," to use Janice's words. I'd sent her back, and I couldn't help but feel that Maddox must have known why, must have understood what had become so clear to me *that day*.

It had come at the end of a harrowing eight months of difficulty, and even as I'd bought the tickets for *Beauty and the Beast*, I'd suspected that my options were becoming fewer and fewer with regard to Maddox staying with us.

There'd been the continually escalating problems at Falcon Academy, where Maddox had repeatedly made excuses for the accusations hurled against her. She'd never intended to steal Mary Logan's fancy Mont Blanc pen; she had simply picked it up to give it a closer look, then mistakenly dropped it into her own backpack, rather than into Mary's. And, after all, didn't those two bags look similar, and hadn't they been lying side-by-side in the school cafeteria?

Nor had she lied about how she'd gotten hold of Ms. Gilbreath's answer sheet for an upcoming history test, because it really had fallen out of the teacher's pocket, and she'd seen that happen and meant to give it back immediately, but she was already a long way down the hall, and so, well, wasn't it only natural that she tucked it into the pocket of her skirt so that she could give it back to her at the end of the school day? And anyway . . .

Maddox had manufactured explanations for everything that came her way, most of them vaguely plausible, as she must have realized, a fact that increasingly worked against her in my mind. It wasn't just that she lied and stole and cheated; it was that she did it so cleverly that, in every case, the charge against her emerged with that fabled Scottish verdict: "Not Proven." For was it not possible that an answer sheet might fall from a teacher's notebook . . . and all the rest? Listening to her exculpatory narratives, I began to feel like Gimpel the Fool in I. B. Singer's famous story. Was I, like Gimpel, a man who endlessly could have the wool pulled over his eyes? In secret, did Maddox laugh at my credulity in the same cruel way that the villagers mocked Gimpel?

I'd been in the throes of just that kind of searing analysis of Maddox's character as I'd stood in line at the box office. But there was an added element as well. Maddox and Lana had lately begun to quarrel. A room that once seemed plenty big enough for two young girls to share had become, over the past few months, an increasingly heated cauldron of mutual discontent. There were arguments over where things, particularly underwear, were dropped or left to dangle. Crumbs were an issue, as were empty bottles; Lana the neatnik, Maddox the slob. I'd endured shouting and crying from Lana, sullenness from Maddox, but at each boiling over I'd refused to intervene. "Work it out, you two," I'd snapped at one point, and I expected them to do exactly that.

Then, suddenly, and for the first time, our home life was rocked by violence.

It was a slap, and it occurred as the culminating act of a long period of building animosity between Lana and Maddox. The shouting matches had devolved into sinister whispered asides at the breakfast and dinner tables, little digs that I simply refused to acknowledge but that, over time, produced a steady white noise of nasty banter. Gone were the days when Maddox complimented Lana's hair or when Lana even remotely pretended that she considered Maddox her sister.

And yet, in many ways, as Janice sometimes pointed out, they were behaving exactly like a great many sisters do. My wife had never gotten along with her older sister, and I knew that the same could be said of countless other siblings. Still, I had wanted harmony in my household, and the fact that the relationship between Maddox and Lana had become anything but harmonious produced a steady ache in my mind. The truth is that, on that day, as I stood in line waiting to buy those tickets, I felt wounded, perhaps even a tad martyred by the conflict between Maddox and Lana. After all, was I not a man who had selflessly taken in another person's child and who, rather than gaining a spiritual pat on the back for the effort, reaped a daily whirlwind that was tearing my home apart? And that, just the night before, had finally erupted in an act of violence?

Had I not heard that slap, I might never have known that it happened. But as soon as did I hear it, all notion vanished of my no longer intervening in the disintegration of my family life.

The door to their room was open. They were now sitting on their respective beds, Maddox with both feet on the floor, Lana lying facedown, her head pressed deep into her pillow.

When she raised it, I saw the fiery red mark that Maddox's hand had left on her cheek.

"What happened?" I asked from my position in the doorway.

Neither girl answered.

"I won't leave this room until I know what happened," I said.

I walked over to Lana's bed, sat down on it, and lifted her face to see the mark more clearly.

Then I stared hotly at Maddox. "We *do not* strike each other in this family," I snapped. "Do you understand me?"

Maddox nodded silently.

"We do not!" I cried.

Maddox whispered something I couldn't understand. Her head was down. She wouldn't look at me.

"No matter what the reason," I added angrily.

She lifted her head. Her eyes were glistening. "I mess everything up," she said softly.

Suddenly, I found that I couldn't buy one bit of it, neither her tears nor her weepy self-accusation, which, however vaguely, had the ring of an apology. *No,* I decided, *you have fooled me all along,* and with that grim realization, I abruptly believed that all the accusations against her were true, all her explanations false. She had played me as a con artist plays a mark. I was her pet fool.

And yet, despite all that, I knew I would not send her back.

No, there had to be a way to help Maddox.

Besides, there was plenty of time.

And so, in an effort to reset everything, I decided that we should all take a deep breath, give it another go, do something together, something that spoke of sweetness and kindness and the power of a human being to look beyond outward appearances.

That was when I thought of *Beauty and the Beast*.

———— · — · — · ————

Lana was already seated at a small corner table when I arrived at the restaurant. She was dressed to the nines, as usual, with every hair in place. Her life had gone very well. She had a good job and a good marriage, with two nice little boys who appeared to adore their parents. From childhood down to this very moment, I told myself as I sat down, she'd gotten everything she'd ever wanted.

Except a sister.

It was a thought that immediately brought me back to Maddox, to how right I'd been in removing her from the circle of our family.

I brought up none of this latest news, of course, and we chatted about the usual topics during our dinner: how her work was going, how the boys were doing, upcoming plans of one sort or another. We'd already ordered our end-of-meal coffees when she said, "Mom told me you've been thinking about Maddox."

I nodded. "I suppose I have."

"Me, too," Lana said. "Especially that day."

"The day we went to *Beauty and the Beast*?" I asked.

Lana looked puzzled. "Why would that day be special?"

I shrugged. "Okay, what day do you mean, then?"

"The day Maddox hit me."

"Oh," I said. "That day."

"The thing is, I provoked her," Lana said. "I was just a kid, and kids can be cruel. I see it in the boys. The things they say to each other."

Tentatively, I asked, "What did you say to her?"

"I told her that she was here because nobody wanted her," Lana said. "Her mother didn't want her. Her brother didn't want her. I told her that even you didn't want her." She paused and then added, "That's when she slapped me." She lifted a slow, ghostly hand to that long vanished wound. "And I deserved it."

I wondered if Lana had come to blame herself for my decision to send back Maddox. If so, she couldn't have been more wrong. It wasn't anything Lana had done that decided the issue. The blame had always lain with Maddox.

"Maddox had to go," I said starkly, still too appalled by the evil I'd seen in the subway station to reveal what had truly convinced me to send Maddox back.

The thing that struck me as most odd now, while Lana sipped nonchalantly at her coffee, was the sweetness that had preceded that terrible moment. *Beauty and the Beast* had come to its heartbreaking conclusion, and, along with the rest of the audience, we were on our way out of the theater, Lana on my right, Maddox on my left. As we approached the front doors, Lana suddenly bolted ahead to where items associated with the show were on sale. Maddox, however, remained at my side.

"I liked it," she said softly, and with those words, she took my hand in hers and held it tenderly. "Thank you."

I smiled. "You're welcome," I said as my heart softened toward her, and I once again harbored the hope that all would be well. Lifted by that desire, I stepped over to the counter and bought two refrigerator magnets. I gave one to Lana, who seemed much more interested in the T-shirts, and the other one to Maddox.

"Thank you," she said softly. "I will always keep it."

She turned toward a couple who were exiting the theater. They had a little girl in tow, each holding on to one of the child's hands.

"That's what I want," she said in that odd way she sometimes said things, looking off into the middle distance, speaking, as it seemed, only to herself. "I want to be an only child."

By then, Lana had made her way to the theater's front door. "Can we go to Jake's, Dad?" she asked when we reached her.

Jake's was a pizza place in the Village where we tended to have dinner on those days that we found ourselves downtown and didn't want to rush home to cook.

I looked at Maddox.

"Jake's okay with you?" I asked happily.

She smiled that sweet smile of hers. "Sure" was all she said.

The subway was only a few blocks away. We walked to it amid the usual Times Square crowd, at that time a curious mixture of vaguely criminal low-life and dazzled tourists.

On the train, I sat with Maddox on one side and Lana on the other, a formation that continued as we exited the train and made our way to the restaurant. During the meal, Lana spoke in a very animated way about *Beauty and the Beast,* while Maddox remained quiet, eating her slice of pizza slowly, sipping her drink slowly, her gaze curiously inward and intense, like one hatching a plot.

We were done within half an hour. The restaurant was near Washington Square, and so, before returning home, we strolled briefly in the park. Lana glanced up as we passed under the arch, but Maddox stared straight ahead in the same inward and intense way I'd noticed at the restaurant.

"You okay?" I asked as we left the park and headed for the subway.

Again, she offered me her sweet smile. "I'm fine," she said.

We descended the stairs, then one by one we each went through the turnstiles and headed down the long ramp that led to the uptown trains. We were about half-way down when I heard the distant rumble of our train heading into the station. "Come on, girls," I said and instinctively bolted ahead, moving more quickly than I thought, as I realized when I turned to look behind me.

The train had not yet reached the station, but I could see its light as it emerged from the dark tunnel. On the platform, perhaps ten yards behind me, both Lana and Maddox were running. Lana was skirting the edge of the platform, with Maddox to her left, though only by a few inches. I looked at the train, then back at the girls, and suddenly I saw Maddox glance over her shoulder. She must have seen the train barreling out of the tunnel, for then she faced forward again and, at that instant, leaned to her left, bumping her shoulder against Lana's so that Lana briefly stumbled toward the pit before regaining her footing, as if by miracle.

I heard Maddox's voice in my mind: *to be an only child.*

The little girl who'd been the object of Maddox's murderous intent was now a grown woman with children of her own, and I had only to look across the table to reassure myself that I'd done the right thing in sending Maddox away. To have done otherwise would have put Lana at risk. Other children had done dreadful things, after all, and that searing episode in the subway station convinced me that Maddox was capable of such evil, too. She had declared what she'd wanted most in life and then ruthlessly attempted to achieve it. I had no way of knowing if she would make another attempt, but it was a chance I wasn't willing to take, especially since the intended victim was my own daughter.

"Maddox had to go," I repeated now.

Lana didn't argue the point. "I remember the day you took her to the airport," she said. "It was raining, and she was wearing that sad little raincoat she'd brought with her from the South." She looked at me. "Remember? The one with the hood."

I nodded. "That coat made her look even more sinister," I said dryly.

Lana looked at me quizzically. "Sinister? That's not a word I would use to describe Maddox."

"What word would you use?" I asked.

"Damaged," Lana answered. "I would say that Maddox was damaged by life."

"Perhaps so," I said, "but Maddox had done some damage of her own."

"Meaning what?"

"Meaning that she stole an answer sheet at Falcon Academy," I said. "One of her classmates saw her."

"You mean Jesse Traylor?" Lana laughed. "He just got caught himself. Cheating on his taxes." She took a sip from her cup. "Jesse was the school apple-polisher, a tattletale who would have done anything to ingratiate himself with the headmaster."

Cautiously, I said, "Even lie about Maddox?"

"He'd have lied about anyone," Lana said. She saw the disturbance her answer caused me. "What's the matter, Dad?"

I leaned forward. "Did he lie about Maddox?"

Lana shrugged. "I don't know." She glanced toward the street where two little girls stood outside a theater. "She apologized, by the way," she said. "Maddox, I mean. For slapping me. Not a spoken apology." She looked as if she were enjoying a sweet memory. "But I knew what she meant when she did it."

"Did what?" I asked.

"Nudged me," Lana answered. "It was a way we had of telling each other that we were sorry and wanted to be sisters again." She smoothed a wrinkle from her otherwise perfectly pressed sleeve. "After we had pizza at Jake's," she said. "In the subway. We were running for the train, and Maddox gave me that hostile look she used when she was joking with me, and then she just nudged me, and that was her way of saying that she was sorry for hitting me, and that she knew I was sorry for what I'd said to her." She looked at me softly. "And since we were both sorry, things were going to be okay."

With those words, Lana finished her coffee. "Anyway, it's quite sad what happened to Maddox." She folded her napkin and placed it primly beside her plate. "The way she never got her balance after she left us." She smiled. "And so she just . . . finally . . . stumbled into the pit."

"Into the pit," I repeated softly

Shortly after that, we parted, Lana returning to her husband and children, I back to my apartment, where, with Janice out of town, I would spend the next few days alone.

I passed most of that time on the balcony, looking down at the tamed streets of Hell's Kitchen, my attention forever drawn to families moving cheerfully toward the glittering lights of Times Square, fathers and mothers with their children in tow, guiding them, as best they could, through the shifting maze. I saw Maddox in every tiny face, remembered the tender touch of her small hand in mine, her quiet "Thank you," for the little refrigerator magnet she had returned to me; the last bit of kindness I'd shown before sending her out of our lives forever.

Had she been a liar, a cheat, a thief? I don't know. Had I completely misunderstood the little nudge she'd given Lana that day as the two girls raced for the train? Again, I don't know. What children perceive and remember years later can be so different from what adults know . . . or think they know. Perhaps she'd already been doomed to live as she did after she left us, and to die as she did in that bleak, unlighted space. Or perhaps not. I couldn't say. I knew only that for me, as for all parents, the art of controlling damage is one we practice in the dark.

Thomas H. Cook is the international-award-winning author of more than thirty books. Born in Fort Payne, Alabama, he published his first novel, *Blood Innocents*, in. Two years later, after the release of his second novel, *The Orchids*, he turned to writing full-time, and published steadily through the 1980s, penning such works as the Frank Clemons mystery trilogy, starring a jaded cop. He's been nominated for the Mystery Writers of America Edgar Allan Poe Award eight times in five different categories, and his novel *The Chatham School Affair* won the Best Novel Award in 1996. He has twice won the Swedish Academy of Detection's Martin Beck Award, the only novelist ever to have done so. His short story "Fatherhood" won the Herodotus Prize for best historical short story. His works have been translated into more than twenty languages.

Joyride: René Appel

First published in *Alfred Hitchcock's Mystery Magazine, September 2015*

Hans glances quickly to his right. Angela sits slumped beside him. She hasn't buckled her seat belt. It's pointless to insist. *What difference does it make?* She'd say something like that. *You planning to have an accident?* She does things her own way, he's known that for some time. "An independent woman," they said. Some contracted that to "bitch." Whatever they called her, they all agreed that, since her election as mayor, things had gone lots better than under Verhoek, that stuffy old Christian Democratic Party hack who'd occupied the mayoral throne for the previous several decades. He was lily-white and pure, Verhoek, but also bland and boring. Angela's party was the Liberal Democrats, and her gender caused many to mistrust her. They said she was all show and no substance—and she certainly did put on a good show. But within six months of her election she'd made her- self so popular that even the

CDP's chairman seemed eager to get in her good graces, instead of playing his usual opposition-party games.

And now, just like that, she's sitting in his car. She kicks off her stylish heels and raises her feet to the dash, showing off her long, shapely legs to their best advantage. It's hard for Hans to resist running his palm along the sprinkling of freckles that make her tanned flesh even more attractive.

The reception at City Hall lasted longer than he'd expected, and they'd bumped into each other in the parking lot as if by prearrangement. They'd chatted briefly. Ordinary, innocuous chitchat. The new sports fields, the office complex his company is building, the expansion plan for Stallerveld. Maybe there'd be gossip about the two of them, but his business recently landed a couple of major contracts with the city, and naturally they'd have to talk them over from time to time.

He knows he's had too much to drink and shouldn't be driving. Four glasses of wine—or was it five? As they stood there in the parking lot, stalling off the moment they'd have to go their separate ways, she took her cell from her purse. "I have to call a cab," she said. "I'd better not drive. If the mayor gets stopped for a DWI—"

She looked at him, with an expression . . . well, an expression that stirred thoughts he really shouldn't be thinking about the mayor.

"—she loses her influence," Angela went on. "Her political influence."

"Can I give you a lift?" he suggested.

She laid a hand on his arm. "Okay."

As if he knew exactly what was going to happen, he called Marion, but she didn't pick up. He left a message:

"I'll be late. I'm stopping off at Peter's." He'd better remember to warn Peter. He was home alone tonight, guaranteed. He was always home alone since Elly died. Sad. Don't think about it now. Angela had already mentioned that her husband Hugo was spending a long weekend in the Ardennes, biking with a few friends, and that her son wouldn't be home until late. Interesting that she'd brought all that up.

He looks at her again, just as she turns toward him. Their eyes lock.

"The next right?" he says.

"Yes, and then the second left. So you know where I live?"

"Sure, the mayor's residence. We built it for Verhoek, fifteen years ago."

"You know, I don't really feel like going home," she says, before they reach the turn. "It's so warm."

It is indeed unseasonably warm for the time of year, humid, has been for more than a week. The heat gets into your head, into your body. In town, the men are all in shorts, the women in loose-fitting sundresses. "The silent killer." He'd read a newspaper article about the danger the heat wave posed for seniors, and that's what they'd called it.

"Really *so* warm," says Angela again.

He nods. This is a direct invitation. A dare. She's had enough to drink that she won't drive, but this she'll do.

"Let's go to the beach. It'll be wonderful!"

"You want to swim?" he asks.

"Maybe."

The moon dimly illuminates the entrance to a small, dark parking area. All the beachgoers are long gone. A child's bicycle has been left behind, but there are no other cars. It's quiet, peaceful. He glances at his watch. Eleven fifteen.

"You need to get home?" Angela's voice is ironic. "Past your bedtime?"

He clears his throat. "No . . . I'm fine . . . absolutely."

She rests her hand on his thigh. He can feel the electricity course through his body. She looks down and must see that he's aroused. He tries to gather his scattered wits. Alone with Angela . . . an incredible specimen of womanhood. This can't be happening. He can't *let* it happen. But his body disagrees with his mind, and he can't resist. He unbuckles his seat belt and leans toward her. He seems to be on cruise control. He tastes the sweetness of her mouth. She pulls away for just a moment and eyes him greedily. A long soul kiss follows.

And then she pulls away.

Dammit. Too much, too soon. He's ruined it. He can see those city contracts dissolve into nothingness.

Then she gets out of the car. Stands there for a moment, walks around to his side and jerks open the door. A hot kiss, even hotter than before.

"Are you coming?"

Without waiting for an answer, she pulls him out of the car and runs ahead of him toward the sea. He follows her, almost stumbles but manages to keep himself on his feet. She vanishes down the narrow beach path. He gains on her, although he thinks she could run faster if she wanted to. She might break away and outpace him later, just to tease him. He tries to grab her arm. She falls—accidentally on purpose—and pulls him with her.

Fedor and Bente walk hand in hand along the path. They could walk like this for hours. The party at the school was crap, with all those people, all their fellow students. Why should they hang out with that bunch, when all they want is to be alone? It's a little after midnight. Except for the song of a couple of noisy crickets, it's utterly quiet. No people, no sound. Well, sure, a rustling in the distance, as if some bunny or other little animal is hurrying away from their footsteps through the underbrush.

The full moon lights their way, sometimes peeking out from behind a passing cloud, bathing the scene in a strange, almost unreal glow and casting sharp shadows, as if they're moving through the landscape of a video game.

Fedor comes to a stop, draws Bente toward him and kisses her. She runs her hands through his hair.

"I really like you," she whispers.

"How much is 'really'?"

"I'm not telling." Sometimes she can be a real tease—he loves that about her.

They kiss again. Farther on, they come out into an open area, a small parking lot. A solitary car stands there. Its lights are on, and the driver's door is open.

Fedor points to the BMW. "Check it out. It's just sitting there. Doesn't look like anyone's in it."

"I wonder why?" Bente comes to a stop and looks around. "Where's the driver?"

"Maybe in the dunes," Fedor blurts, "with some hot babe."

Bente giggles.

On impulse, Fedor slides behind the wheel. Earlier in the summer, his father let him drive his Renault Mégane around a big empty lot. At first, he'd had trouble shifting gears, and sometimes he gave it too much gas before going into neutral and made the engine roar. But he quickly got the hang of it. Next year, if he passes all his classes, his parents have promised to pay for lessons and the driving exam.

"Hey, the keys are in it!" He turns the ignition key impulsively, and the car comes to life.

Bente slides in beside him. "Let's take a ride!" she says.

The idea shocks him back to reality. "No way!"

"Come on, Feddie, just for a minute. Just here in the parking lot."

"I don't even have a license," he argues.

"Like that matters? Come *on*, don't be chicken!" She covers his face with little kisses, each kiss promising something more if he gives her what she wants.

Reluctantly, he shifts into reverse and backs out of the parking space.

"You really know how to drive?" asks Bente.

"Well, sure. Just watch." He feels powerful behind the wheel of this fancy BMW. The car responds perfectly to his touch. He shifts into first and moves forward. As he approaches the tree line, he turns the wheel and lets up a bit on the gas, easing smoothly into a half circle. The suspension is amazing—they don't even notice the bumps and dips in the road surface.

"This is fun," says Bente. "Keep going!"

He drives on. A beautiful girl, an expensive car—this is a once-in-a- lifetime chance, and he's not about to let it pass him by. He glances over at Bente. Her eyes gleam with excitement in the moonlight.

After a couple of minutes, they come to the main road.

"We better go back," says Fedor. "I just need to find someplace to turn around." He taps the turn signal and makes a right out into the road. Just ahead on the left is the turnoff for the village, but he's not going to take that chance. Traffic, people, maybe cops. Best bet is to stay as far away from all that as possible. There has to be a driveway up here where he can turn. He slows down, and jumps nervously when a horn honks behind him. A convertible roars by, two guys in it. The driver flips him the bird.

"Jerk," mutters Fedor, and Bente pushes the button that lowers the passenger window and screams "Asshole!" into the night.

Fedor's knees begin to tremble, and his hands, suddenly sweaty, almost slip from the steering wheel.

"Let's go back," Bente says. There is anger in her voice.

Maybe he's spoiled everything, Fedor thinks, when all he wanted was to impress her.

"Okay, fine," he says quickly. "Hang on." He turns carefully into a drive- way, then backs out, spinning the wheel the other way. He can't get the shift lever back into first. There's a grinding noise, and the engine stalls.

"What's wrong?" asks Bente.

"Nothing. No problem." He turns the key. The car starts. Clutch in, shift into first, let up on the clutch and give it a little gas.

And then, out of nowhere, there's a bright light and a sudden jolt and a loud crash. Fedor and Bente are frozen in time and space.

Fedor isn't sure how to get back to the parking lot. Bente is no help— she just sits there crying. They can't have been gone more than fifteen minutes, tops.

"He was driving way too fast," says Fedor for the umpteenth time, but it's as if Bente doesn't even hear him. "Crazy fast. I didn't see him. All of a sudden, he just *hit* us."

And then he sees the entrance to the lot, after all. He pulls the car right back into the space where they found it.

He takes a handkerchief from his pocket and wipes the steering wheel. He's surprised that he thinks of this. Then he gets out of the car. Bente sits there, paralyzed. She's shivering, though the evening is still warm. A dark cloud hides the moon, maybe indicating a change in the weather on the way.

"Come on, we gotta get out of here. They might come back any second." Fedor walks around the car, opens the passenger door and pulls Bente's arm.

"We should have done something," she sniffles.

"Are you nuts?" Fedor shakes his head. "Can you imagine the trouble we'd be in?"

"But maybe—" she begins.

"No, really. He was just shaken up a little. Good thing he had his helmet on. He'll be fine, trust me. But there's no way we could stick around and get involved."

As if they're glued together, not ready to break their embrace, Hans and Angela walk back up the path. It's more stumbling than walking, really. Their passion has intoxicated them.

They come in sight of the car. Stupid of him not to lock it. The lights are on, the driver's door wide open. He stops.

"What?" asks Angela.

He searches his trouser pockets. Nope, no keys. He hurries to the BMW and slides in. Whew, they're still in the ignition.

"Is something wrong?" Angela comes up beside him.

He gets out of the car and wraps his arms around her. He resists the urge to talk about the future. No promises, no obligations. He leans against the car, his right hand on the hood. Strange, it feels warm. Must take the engine longer to cool off in this heat.

"We'd better go," he says.

She nods.

When they've been driving for a while, they hear an ambulance's siren.

A hundred meters from her house, Angela says, "I'll get out here."

He tries to pull her to him, but her soft hands hold him off. "You gotta know when to hold 'em and know when to fold 'em," she murmurs.

"You mean—?"

She presses her fingertips to her mouth and then touches his lips gently. Is she kissing him goodbye, or telling him not to speak? Before he can ask, she's gone.

Five minutes later, he's home. Marion has apparently already gone to bed. He pours himself a whiskey, drops in a couple of ice cubes, and goes out to the back terrace. When he closes his eyes, he can call it all back. Her voice, her perfume, her skin, her body. And they did it outside, in the open air. Maybe she gets a kick out of that, taking risks she really ought to avoid.

When his glass is empty, he goes back inside, locks up, and takes a shower. As quietly as possible, he opens the bedroom door and crawls into bed. Marion doesn't stir.

A few minutes later, her voice startles him: "Late."

"Yeah. I had a drink when I got home." The excuse seems superfluous.

"How is he?"

It takes a few seconds for him to realize she means Peter.

"Oh, okay. G'night."

She curls up against him and kisses him. "Sleep tight."

Betrayer, he thinks. *Cheat*.

Fedor hears the first notes of Coldplay's "Atlas," pulls out his cell phone, and sees Bente's name on the screen.

"Have you heard anything?" she says.

"You mean about . . . the guy on the motorbike?"

"Well, *duh*."

He clears his throat. "No, nothing. It'll be in the paper on Monday, I guess."

"I think we should go to the cops," Bente whispers, so low he can barely hear her.

"The cops?"

"We were involved in a hit-and-run, Feddie. That's a crime!"

"*He* hit *us*, we didn't hit him. And if we keep our mouths shut, no one'll ever know we were in the car." The guy on the bike can't possibly have seen *us*. He doesn't say the words aloud.

Neither of them speaks for a while, and then she breaks the silence and asks if they're going to see each other today.

"I've got homework," he says, "and my mom wants me to visit my grand- ma with her this afternoon." He sighs.

There's a sudden rumble of thunder, and within moments the sky is full of dark gray clouds.

"It's gonna rain." As soon as the words leave his mouth, Fedor knows it's a dumb thing to say. Gazing out his bedroom window, he sees the first drops begin to fall. And then it's pouring so hard he can barely make out the houses on the other side of the street.

"I'll see you in school on Monday, I guess."

"Sure, Monday." He presses his lips to the phone and listens for her answering kiss, but it doesn't come.

Half an hour later, she texts him: "We should go to the police."

He texts her back, tells her just to forget about it. "Please, Bente, trust me." And then five x's. Five more than she'd used to close *her* message.

More than once, Hans picks up the phone to call Angela, but each time he forces himself to cradle the receiver without dialing. It was a classic one-night stand, he knows, the sort of thing you always remember but never repeat. She'll remember it, too, he hopes. But it can't go on, that's impossible. Although it seems cruel, almost inhuman, to simply set aside an hour of such utter passion, to replace it with an eternal longing that can never be satisfied. Does he regret what they've done? No, not at all.

While Marion is busy in the kitchen, he calls Peter and quickly fills him in on what's happened. "I told Marion I was with you," he says.

"So I'm your alibi," says Peter.

"Yeah, I suppose you could say that."

"Mr. Bergman? Mr. Bergman!"

He shakes his head to dislodge the memories.

Kim holds up her phone. "I've got the police on the line. Can you speak to them now, or should they call back?"

"I'll take it now."

He lifts his own receiver and hears a few clicks, then a surprisingly high-pitched male voice. "This is John Kemper. Is this Hans Bergman?"

Hans acknowledges his identity. Kemper tells him that he's with the regional police. He'd like to come by and have a look at Mr. Bergman's car.

"My car? Why?" The only thing he can think of is possible traces of Angela's presence. A strand of her hair, a whiff of perfume?

"I can be there in half an hour. Is that okay?"

"Certainly."

After he cradles the phone, he tells Kim that he has to duck out for a second. He goes downstairs and out to the parking lot and has a look at his car. Smells it, runs his hand across the passenger seat. No sign of Angela. As if it never happened.

Then he walks around the car—and, damn, there's a big dent and some deep scratches on the rear panel on the passenger side, and the right taillight is shattered. It looks like someone's rammed into the back of the car. Here in the parking lot? No, not possible. At home, he parks in the driveway, and the car was there all day yesterday. Earlier, then? But when? Is this why the police are coming? The questions echo inside his head.

Back in his office, he sits at his desk, flips open the folder for the shopping-center remodel, and tries to make sense of the blueprints. The minutes tick by slowly. At last the phone rings. A Mr. Kemper is asking for him at reception.

Kemper offers Hans a hand and introduces himself. His voice is pitched deeper than it sounded over the phone.

"Hans Bergman. Pleased to meet you."

"Shall we go have a look at your car?"

Kemper walks around the BMW and examines the damage thoughtfully. "What happened here?"

Hans shrugs. "Looks like somebody hit me when I was parked somewhere. I didn't see it until now."

Kemper runs his fingers along the paint, following the line of the scratches. "Seems pretty recent."

It begins to drizzle.

"Should we go inside?" asks Hans.

It's as if Kemper doesn't hear him. "You weren't on the Tulpstraat around midnight on Saturday?"

"Saturday?" He has to force himself not to turn and run. He doesn't know what exactly is going on, but it must be something serious. The police don't show up at your doorstep just because of a couple of scratches.

"Correct, sir, Saturday night. A car was spotted driving slowly along the Tulpstraat, as if the driver was looking for something. One witness said he thought it was a BMW. Right around that time, a man on a motorcycle ran into a car. He was pretty seriously injured. So we're checking out all the BMWs in the area."

Hans feels as if *he* has been run into.

They sit together at lunch.

"I saw it on the news," says Bente. "A guy on a motor-bike, twenty-four years old. He's in the hospital, hurt bad. Our fault."

He sees that she's holding back tears, and he puts his arm around her. He tries to make it look like they're just having a little argument. Maybe nobody's paying attention to them, but the girls especially always seem to know when something's going on.

"Totally *not* our fault," he says. "We weren't even moving. We had our lights on, and he just smashed right into us. Honestly, it was one hundred percent *his* fault."

"If we hadn't been there, it wouldn't have happened."

"But that doesn't make it our fault." In his mind's eye, he's back on the road. He gets out of the car and checks out the poor dude lying draped over the curb. Ten meters off, the front wheel of the stalled-out motorbike is still spinning. If the guy's dead, there's nothing they can do about it. If he's alive, somebody must have heard the crash and will call an ambulance and the cops. Jesus, the cops! If his parents find out about this, they'll kill him. "The stupid bastard was driving like a maniac, way too fast."

"But—"

Bente loses her fight, and tears stream down her cheeks. "We have to go to the police," she gasps between sobs.

He looks up and sees Viviana, Bente's best friend, watching them.

Hans follows Kemper to the police station "for further investigation of the vehicle," as Kemper puts it. A young officer brings him back to his office in a patrol car. He tells Kim that he has a meeting and can't be disturbed, so he's turning off his cell. He takes a company car and spends several hours just driving. It rains all afternoon. He pulls off the road at a café near the dunes, orders a cappuccino and a cheese sandwich, and tries to get his thoughts straightened out.

He's back at the office at four thirty.

"Mr. Kemper wants you to call him," says Kim.

Kemper is all business. He wants Hans to come to the station.

"Why?"

"We'll discuss that when you get here."

Interesting that Kemper doesn't offer to provide him with transportation. No way to know what that means. Hans calls a cab and has to wait half an hour before it pulls into the parking lot. The driver seems eager to chat about the weather, but Hans returns only the briefest of responses.

This time, Kemper is accompanied by a second man, who introduces himself as Mulder. They get straight down to business. Multiple flakes of paint found on the damaged motorcycle have been matched to the BMW. "But," says Hans, "there are lots of dark gray BMWs." He suddenly remembers the siren he heard while driving Angela home.

"The paint came from *your* BMW, Mr. Bergman, not *a* BMW. And don't forget the dent and the scratches on your car."

Hans shrugs. "I told you, someone must have run into it when it was parked somewhere. And then the jackass drove off without leaving a note."

"Must have happened pretty recently, seeing how you hadn't even noticed the damage until today."

"Maybe Thursday or Friday."

Mulder repeats Hans's words, but with an intonation that makes it obvious he doesn't believe them.

Then the question comes. Hans expects it. Where was he around midnight on Saturday?

"I was with an old friend. Peter Langer."

They write down Peter's name and ask for his address and phone number. As soon as he leaves the station, he'll have to call Peter. Then he realizes that, if he's a suspect, they may not let him go. He'll have to call home and have Marion bring him a change of clothes, a toothbrush, toothpaste.

"So you visited him Saturday evening, after the reception at City Hall?"

They've done their homework. "Yes, he's an old friend. His wife died recently, and he's lonely."

"And Mr. Langer lives in the Peppelstraat." Kemper eyes Hans meaningfully.

It takes a few seconds for the penny to drop: The Peppelstraat intersects with the Tulpstraat.

"Is something wrong?" asks Marion, when Hans has poured himself a stiff shot of whiskey, grabbed the paper, and settled in his favorite armchair.

He takes a sip. "No, nothing."

"You seem so . . . I don't know, preoccupied. Like something's on your mind."

He decides to tell her, since it'll be in the paper tomorrow or the next day. He gives her the same story he gave the police. His visit to Peter, the drive home. Nothing out of the ordinary happened, as far as he knew at the time, but it seems almost certain that some poor guy on a motorbike ran into the BMW at some point, damaging the car, totaling the motorcycle and winding up in intensive care.

"How can that have happened?"

"I don't know. But it did."

And then all at once he sees *how* it did. It's as if some invisible observer whispers an eyewitness account in his ear. While he was in the dunes with Angela, somebody took his car for a joyride. That's when the bike must have collided with the

BMW. He remembers now that the engine was still warm when they got back. Whoever "borrowed" his car must have put it back where Hans had parked it, hoping the car's owner would wind up taking the blame for the collision.

"Goddammit," he whispers.

Marion says again that it doesn't seem possible, must be some kind of a mistake.

"I'm tired of talking about it," he tells her.

After dinner, which they eat in silence, Hans goes into the home office he's turned into a man cave.

Marion brings coffee. "Oh, you're in here?"

"I seem to be, don't I?"

She mumbles an apology and leaves him alone. He really should treat her more nicely, but he just can't manage it.

When he's finished his coffee, he calls Peter, who reports that he was just about to dial Hans's number, since the police have just left.

"And?" asks Hans.

"Well, I backed you up, except I didn't realize your story was meant for the cops."

"It wasn't. It was meant for Marion. In case you ran into her, you know?"

"But now the police. Are you in some kind of trouble?"

Hans tells him the whole truth and nothing but the truth: the BMW, the accident, the injured biker. "And it happened in the Tulpstraat, not far from your place, while I was in fact *not* visiting you."

"You're not going to tell them that, I hope."

"Well, I may have to. If I don't want to take the blame."

"And if they find out you weren't here last Saturday evening, then what happens to *me*? I've lied to the cops, given you a fake alibi." Hans hears the indignation in Peter's voice. "That makes me an accessory after the fact or something."

"Don't be ridiculous. You didn't know it had anything to do with the accident. You thought you were just helping me put one over on Marion."

"But I still turn out to be a liar."

Hans sighs. He doesn't know what to say or think. The whole business is so mixed up in his head, he can't even keep it straight himself. For a long moment he sits there, the room quiet except for the ambient noise of the phone connection.

"Well, fine," he tells his old friend. "You do what you have to do."

And at that Peter hangs up on him.

Hans closes his eyes. Then he opens them and looks up Angela's home phone number. They're going to have to come clean about what really happened Saturday night. There's no other option. If he can't duck responsibility for the accident, then who knows how long a prison term he might be facing? There's only one person who can help him now—not counting whoever it was who stole his damn car, but *that* bastard's not going to own up to the theft, Hans is sure of that much.

Marion's bound to find out the truth sooner or later. She'll be hysterically angry at first. He'll let her scream it all out, he won't say a word while she flings a few place settings at the walls, he'll do whatever penance she imposes on him—and eventually she'll get over it. He fetches the whiskey bottle, a glass, and some ice cubes from downstairs. Marion doesn't seem to be around. A stiff drink gives him the courage to call Angela.

"Hello," a teenaged male voice says.

"This is Hans Bergman. I'd like to speak with your mother. It's urgent."

"I'll get her."

Hans can visualize the boy walking through the house with the cordless phone. He hears a quick rat-a-tat on a door. "Mom, phone. It's urgent."

Hans can't quite make out the response.

"I don't know," says the boy. "I'll ask. Can I tell her who's calling again, please?

"Hans Bergman. I've got to ask her something important."

Now that he's taken the step of calling, he absolutely needs to get Angela on the line.

"Hans Bergman," he hears the boy repeat. "He has to ask you something important."

A full minute passes before he hears Angela's voice. "I was taking a bath.

What is it?"

She was taking a bath. Why would she tell him that? He tries to concentrate on the matter at hand. He tells her about the accident, but he has the impression she's already heard the news. "We have to go to the police—I think we should go in together—and tell them the truth."

"I don't know what you're talking about."

He forces a laugh. "You know exactly what I'm talking about. The empty parking lot by the dunes. You ran toward the sea, I followed you, and then—"

"You've certainly got a vivid imagination. And then *what*? We did it, is that what you're saying?"

"Well, yeah. We did a *lot* of it."

"And you thought this delightful little scenario up all by yourself?" she asks.

"Come on, Angela. Stop playing games. We have to—
"

She hangs up on him. Hans stares at the receiver as if it's to blame for everything. He wants to fling it to the ground and kick it to bits. Instead, he yells out "Bitch!" at the top of his voice.

Fedor and Bente meet up after the last class period of the day.

"Did you see it in the paper?" she asks.

He nods.

"They've arrested that poor man, and he didn't do anything."

"We didn't do anything either," says Fedor.

She lays a hand on his arm. "No, but we took his car. If we hadn't of done that, then—"

"If, if, if," Fedor interrupts her.

"I can't stand it," says Bente. "We *have* to tell them. I can't sleep, I keep thinking about it. That poor man in prison, and he's totally innocent." She looks at him, her eyes wide. "Fedor, you can't want him to suffer?"

"You think *I* want to go to jail?"

"You won't, if we tell the truth how it happened."

"How do you know that?"

"I don't *know* it," she admits, and then a thought strikes her. "We can ask your mom. She knows all about legal stuff. Let's ask her."

Fedor hesitates, but Bente gazes at him with such concern, such love, that he almost loses himself in her eyes. "Okay," he says at last. "She should be home by six."

She puts her hands over his ears, pulls him to her and kisses him full on the mouth.

"No," Fedor's mother says, "I wouldn't say a word to anyone."

"You wouldn't tell the truth?" asks Bente, her head cocked in surprise.

"I don't think it would be a good idea, especially not for Fedor. He doesn't have his license yet, and you were on a public road. That's a pretty serious offense right there. And then he caused the accident—"

"He didn't cause it," Bente protests.

But his mother seems not to have heard her. "And he drove away from the scene without reporting it to the police or calling an ambulance. I don't know what a judge would say about that, but I'm guessing Fedor and you— would wind up in some pretty serious trouble."

"But it's not fair to let that man take the blame!"

"Fair? Sweetheart, life *isn't* always fair. Is it fair for Fedor to lose his future because some idiot on a motorbike was too stupid to watch where he was going?"

Bente stares at the carpet, as if she hopes to find the answer to Fedor's mother's question written there.

"Well? Would *that* be fair?"

Slowly, Bente shakes her head.

The room is quiet for a while. And then the conversation turns to school, to the academic year just begun, the projects and assignments and examinations that lie ahead. At six thirty, Bente says she has to get home.

She stands up to go, relieved, almost happy. "Thanks for talking with us, ma'am," she says.

"'Ma'am'?" says Fedor's mother. "You don't have to be so formal with me, Bente. Please, just call me Angela."

René Appel is not only an award-winning crime novelist, but also an accomplished linguist, receiving a doctorate cum laude in the study of second language acquisition by foreigners and the development of Dutch language education for this group. From 1994 to 2003, he was a professor of Dutch as a second language at the University of Amsterdam. His writing career developed far earlier, however, beginning in the early seventies with short stories he wrote for literary magazines. In 1987, his first psychological thriller, Handicap, was published. Since then, he has written a new novel almost every year. Two of them, *The Third Person* (1990) and *Random Violence* (2001) won The Golden Noose, the prize for the best Dutch crime novel of the year. His most recent titles are The Lawyer and The Shortest Night. He has also written two children's books, three collections of short stories, a series of radio plays, three scripts (for tv and film) and a theater play. His bestselling thriller *Clean Hands* was the basis for a successful feature film which was released in 2015. He lives with his family in Amsterdam.

Rusch & Helfers

The Little Men: Megan Abbott

First published as part of the *Bibliomysteries* series

At night, the sounds from the canyon shifted and changed. The bungalow seemed to lift itself with every echo and the walls were breathing. Panting.

Just after two, she'd wake, her eyes stinging, as if someone had waved a flashlight across them.

And then, she'd hear the noise.

Every night.

The tapping noise, like a small animal trapped behind the wall.

That was what it reminded her of. Like when she was a girl, and that possum got caught in the crawlspace. For weeks, they just heard scratching. They only found it when the walls started to smell. *There's no little men,* she told herself. *It's not.* And then she'd hear a whimper and startle herself. Because it was her whimper and she was so frightened.

I'm not afraid I'm not

It had begun four months ago, the day Penny first set foot in the Canyon Arms. The chocolate and pink bunga-lows, the high arched windows and French doors, the tiled courtyard, cosseted on all sides by eucalyptus, pepper, and olive trees, miniature date palms – it was like a dream of a place, not a place itself.

This is what it was supposed to be, she thought.

The Hollywood she'd always imagined, the Hollywood of her childhood imagination, assembled from newsreels: Kay Francis in silver lame and Clark Gable driving down Sunset in his Duesenberg, everyone beautiful and everything possible.

That world, if it ever really existed, was long gone by the time she'd arrived on that Greyhound a half-dozen years ago. It had been swallowed up by the clatter and color of 1953 Hollywood, when its swooping motel roofs and shiny glare of its hamburger stands and drive-ins, and its descending smog, which made her throat burn at night. Sometimes she could barely breathe.

But here in this tucked away courtyard, deep in Beachwood Canyon, it was as if that Old Hollywood lingered, even bloomed. The smell of apricot hovered, the hush and echoes of the canyons soothed. You couldn't hear a horn honk, a break squeal. Only the distant *ting-ting* of window chimes, somewhere. One might imagine a peignoired Norma Shearer drifting through the rounded doorway of one of the bungalows, cocktail shaker in hand.

"It's perfect," Penny whispered, her heels tapping on the Mexican tiles. "I'll take it."

"That's fine," said the landlady, Mrs. Stahl, placing Penny's cashier's check in the drooping pocket of her satin housecoat and handing her the keyring, heavy in her palm.

The scent, thick with pollen and dew, was enough to make you dizzy with longing.

And so close to the Hollywood sign, visible from every vantage, which had to mean something.

She had found it almost by accident, tripping out of the Carnival Tavern after three stingers.

"We've been stood up," Penny said. After all, Mr. D. had called, the hostess summoning Penny to cone of the hot telephone booths. Penny was still tugging her skirt free from its door hinges when he broke it to her.

He wasn't coming tonight and wouldn't be coming again. He had many reasons why, beginning with his busy work schedule, the demands of the studio, plus negotiations with the union were going badly. By the time he got around to the matter of his wife and six children, she wasn't listening, letting the phone drift from her ear.

Gazing through the booth's glass accordion doors, she looked out at the long row of spinning lanterns strung along the bar's windows. They reminded her of the magic lamp she had when she was small, scattering galloping horses across her bedroom walls.

You could see the Carnival Tavern from miles away because of the lanterns. It was funny seeing them up close, the faded circus clowns silhouetted on each. They looked so much less glamorous, sort of shabby. She wondered how long they'd been here, and if anyone even noticed them anymore.

She was thinking all these things while Mr. D. was still talking, his voice hoards with logic and finality. A faint aggression.

He concluded by saying surely she agreed that all the craziness had to end.

You were a luscious piece of candy, he said, *but now I gotta spit you out.*

After, she walked down the steep exit ramp from the bar, the lanterns shivering in the canyon breeze.

And she walked and walked and that was how she found the Canyon Arms, tucked off behind hedges do deep you could disappear into them. The smell of the jasmine so strong she wanted to cry.

"You're an actress, of course," Mrs. Stahl said, walking her to Bungalow Number Four.

"Yes," she said. "I mean, no." Shaking her head. She felt like she was drunk. It was the apricot. No, Mrs. Stahl's cigarette. No, it was her lipstick. Tangee, with its sweet orange smell, just like Penny's own mother.

"Well," Mrs. Stahl said. "We're all actresses, I suppose."

"I used to be," Penny finally managed. "But I got practical. I do makeup now. Over at Republic."

Mrs. Stahl's eyebrows, thin as seaweed, lifted. "Maybe you could do me sometime."

It was the beginning of something, she was sure.

No more living with sundry starlets stacked bunk-to-bunk in one of those stucco boxes in West Hollywood. The Sham-Rock. The Sun-Kist Villa. The m=smell of cold cream and last night's sweat, a brush of talcum powder between the legs.

She hadn't been sure she could afford to live alone, but Mrs. Stahl's rent was low. Surprisingly low. And, if the job at Republic didn't last, she till had her kitty, which was fat these days on account of those six months with Mr. D., a studio man with a sofa in his office that wheezed and puffed. Even if he really meant what he said, that it really was kaput, she still had that last check he'd given her. He must have been planning the brush off, because it was the biggest yet, and made out to cash.

And the Canyon Arms had other advantages. Number Four, like all the bungalows, was already furnished: sun-bleached zebra print sofa and key lime walls, that bright white kitchen with its cherry sprigged wallpaper. The first place she'd ever lived that didn't have rust stains in the tub or the smell of moth balls everywhere.

And there were the built-in bookshelves filled with novels in crinkling dustjackets.

She liked books, especially the big ones by Lloys C. Douglas or Frances Parkinson Keyes, though the books in Number Four were all at least twenty years old with a sleek, high-tone look about them. The kind without any people on the covers.

In fact, she started with those. Reading them late at night, with a pink gin conjured from grapefruit pees and an old bottle of Gilbey's she found in the cupboard. Those books gave her funny dreams.

"She got one."

Penny turned on her heels, one nearly catching on one of the courtyard tiles. But, looking around, she didn't see anyone. Only an open window, smoke rings emanating like a dragon's mouth.

"She's finally got one," the voice came again.

"Who's there?" Penny said, squinting toward the window.

An old man leaned forward from his perch just inside Number Three, the bungalow next door. He wore a velvet smoking jacket faded to a deep rose.

"And a pretty one at that," he said, smiling with graying teeth. "How do you like Number Four?"

"I like it very much," she said. She could hear something rustling behind him in his bungalow. "It's perfect for me."

"I believe it is," he said, nodding slowly. "Of that I am sure."

The rustle came again. Was it a roommate? A pet? It was too dark to tell. When it came once more, it was almost like a voice shushing.

"I'm late," she said, taking a step back, her heel caving slightly.

"Oh," he said, taking a puff. "Next time."

That night, she woke, her mouth fry from gin, at two o'clock. She had been dreaming she was on an exam table and a doctor with an enormous head mirror was leaning so close to her she could smell his gum: violet. The ringlight at its center seemed to spin, as if to hypnotize her.

She saw spots even when she closed her eyes again.

The next morning, the man from Number Three was there again, shadowed just inside the window frame, watching the comings and goings on the courtyard.

Head thick from last night's gin and two morning cigarettes, Penny was feeling what her mother used to call "the hickedty ticks."

So, when she saw the man, she stopped and said briskly, "What did you mean yesterday? 'She finally got one'?"

He smiled, laughing without any noise, his shoulders shaking.

"Mrs. Stahl got one, got you," he said. "As in: Will you walk into my parlor? said the spider to the fly."

When he leaned forward, she could see the stripes of his pajama top through the shiny threads of his velvet sleeve. His skin was rosy and wet looking.

"I'm no chump, if that's your idea. It's good rent. I know good rent."

"I bet you do, my girl. I bet you do. Why don't you come inside for a cup? I'll tell you a thing or two about this place. And about your Number Four."

The bungalow behind him was dark, with something shining beside him. A bottle, or something else.

"We all need something," he added cryptically, winking.

She looked at him. "Look, mister–"

"Flant. Mr. Flant. Come inside, miss. Open the front door. I'm harmless." He waved his pale pink hand, gesturing toward his lap mysteriously.

Behind him, she thought she saw something moving in the darkness over his slouching shoulders. And music playing softly. An old song about setting the world on fire, or not.

Mr. Flant was humming with it, his body soft with age and stillness, but his milky eyes insistent and penetrating.

A breeze lifted and the front door creaked open several inched, and the scent of tobacco and bay rum nearly overwhelmed her.

"I don't know," she said, even as she moved forward.

Later, she would wonder why, but in that moment, she felt it was definitely the right thing to do.

The other man in Number Three was not as old as Mr. Flant but still much older than Penny. Wearing only an undershirt and trousers, he had a moustache and big round shoulders that looked fray with old sweat. When he smiled, which was often, she could tell he was once matinee-idol handsome, with the outsized head of all movie stars.

"Call me Benny," he said, handing her a coffee cup that smelled strongly of rum.

Mr. Flant was explaining that Number Four had been empty for years because of something that happened here a long time ago.

"Sometimes she gets a tenant," Benny reminded Mr. Flant. "The young musician with the sweaters."

"That did not last long," Mr. Flant said.

"What happened?"

"The police came. He tore out a piece of the wall with his bare hands."

Penny's eyebrows lifted.

Benny nodded. "His fingers were hanging like clothespins."

"But I don't understand. What happened in Number Four?"

"Some people let the story get to them," Benny said, shaking his head.

"What story?"

The two men looked at each other.

Mr. Flant rotated his cup in his hand.

"There was a death," he said softly. "A man who lived there, a dear man. Lawrence was his name. Larry. A talented bookseller. He died."

"Oh."

"Boy did he," Benny said. "Gassed himself."

"At the Canyon Arms?" she asked, feeling sweat on her neck despite all the fans blowing everywhere, lifting motes and old skin. That's what dust really is, one of her roommates once told her, blowing it from her fingertips. "Inside my bungalow?"

They both nodded gravely.

"They carried him out through the courtyard," Mr. Flant said, staring vaguely out the window. "That great sheaf of blond hair of his. Oh, my."

"So it's a challenge for some people," Benny said. "Once they know."

Penny remembered the neighbor boy who fell from their tree and died from blood poisoning two days later. No one would eat its pears after that.

"Well," she said, eyes drifting to the smudgy window, "come people are superstitious."

Soon, Penny began stopping by Number Three a few mornings a week, before work. Then, the occasional evening too. They served rye or applejack.

It helped with her sleep. She didn't remember her dreams, but her eyes still stung lightspots most nights.

Sometimes the spots took odd shapes and she would press her fingers against her lids trying to make them stop.

"You could come to my bungalow," she offered once. But they both shook their heads slowly, and in unison.

Mostly, they spoke of Lawrence. Larry. Who seemed like such a sensitive soul, delicately formed and too fine for this town.

"When did it happen?" Penny asked, feeling dizzy, wishing Benny had put more water in the applejack. "When did he die?"

"Just before the war. A dozen years ago."

"He was only thirty-five."

"That's so sad," Penny said, finding her eyes misting, the liquor starting to tell on her.

"His bookstore is still on Cahuenga Boulevard," Benny told her. "He was so proud when it opened."

"Before that, he sold books for Stanley Rose," Mr. Flant added sliding a handkerchief from under the cuff of his fraying sleeve. "Larry was very popular. Very attractive. An accent soft as a Carolina pine."

"He'd pronounce 'bed' like 'bay-ed'." Benny grinned, leaning against the window sill and smiling that Gable smile. "And he said 'bay-ed' a lot."

"I met him even before he got the job with Stanley," Mr. Flant said, voice speeding up. "Long before Benny."

Benny shrugged, topping off everyone's drinks.

"He was selling books out of the trunk of his old Ford," Mr. Flant continued. "That's where I first bought *Ulysses*."

Benny grinned again. "He sold me my first Tijuana Bible. *Dagwoods Has a Family Party*."

Mr. Flant nodded, laughed. "*Popeye in The Art of Love*. It staggered me. He had an uncanny sense. He knew just what you wanted."

They explained that Mr. Rose, whose bookstore once graced Hollywood Boulevard and had attracted great talents, used to send young Larry to the studios with a suitcase full of books. His job was to trap and mount the big shots. Show them the goods, sell them books by the yard, art books they could show off in their offices, dirty books they could hide in their big gold safes.

Penny nodded. She was thinking about the special books Mr. D. kept in his office, behind the false encyclopedia fronts. The books had pictures of girls doing things with long, fuzzy fans and peacock feathers, a leather crop.

She wondered if Larry had sold them to him.

"To get to those guys, he had to climb the satin rope," Benny said. "The studio secretaries, the script girls, the publicity office, even makeup girls like you. Hell, the grips. He loved the sexy grip."

"This town can make a whore out of anyone," Penny found herself blurting.

She covered her mouth, ashamed, but both men just laughed.

Mr. Flant looked out the window into the courtyard, the *flip-flapping* of banana leaves against the shutter. "I think he loved the actresses the most, famous or not."

"He said he like the feel of a woman's skin in 'bay-ed'," Benny said, rubbing his left arm, his eyes turning dark, soft. "'course, he'd slept with his mammy until he was thirteen."

As she walked back to her own bungalow, she always had the strange feeling she might see Larry. That he might emerge behind the rose bushes or around the statue of Venus.

Once she looked down into the fountain basin and thought she could see his face instead of her own.

But she didn't even know what he looked like.

Back in the bungalow head fuzzy and the canyon so quiet, she thought about him more. The furniture, its fashion at least two decades past, seemed surely the same furniture he'd known. Her hands on the smooth bands of the rattan sofa. Her feet, her toes on the banana silk tassels of the rug. And the old mirror in the bathroom, its tiny black pocks.

In the late hours, lying on the bed, the mattress too soft, with a vague smell of mildew, she found herself waking again and again, each time with a start.

It always began with her eyes stinging, dreaming again of a doctor with the head mirror, or a car careering toward her on the highway, always lights in her face.

One night, she caught the lights moving, her eyes landing on the far wall, the baseboards.

For several moments, she'd see the light spots, fuzzed and floating, as if strung together by the thinnest of threads.

The spots began to look like the darting mice that sometimes snuck inside her childhood home. She never knew mice could be that fast. So fast that if she blinked, she'd miss them, until more came. Was that what it was?

If she squinted hard, they even looked like little men. Could it be mice on their hindfeet?

The next morning, she set traps.

"I'm sorry, he's unavailable," the receptionist said. Even over the phone, Penny knew which one. The beauty marks and giraffe neck.

"But listen," Penny said, "it's not like he thinks. I'm just calling about the check he gave me. The bank stopped payment on it."

So much for Mr. D.'s parting gift for their time together. She was going to use it to make rent, to buy a new girdle, maybe even a television set.

"I've passed along your messages, Miss Smith. That's really all I can do."

"Well, that's not all I can do," Penny said, her voice trembling. "You tell him that."

Keeping bust was the only balm. At work, it was easy, the crush of people, the noise and personality of the crew.

Nights were when the bad thoughts came, and she knew she shouldn't let them.

In the past, she'd had those greasy-skinned room-mates to drown out thinking. They all had rashes from cheap studio makeup and the clap from cheap studio men and beautiful figures like Penny's own. And they never stopped talking, twirling their hair in curlers and licking their fingers to turn the magazine pages. But their chatter-chatter-chatter muffled all Penny's thoughts. And the whole atmosphere – the thick muzz of Woolworth's face powder and nylon nighties when they even shared a bed – made everything seem cheap and lively and dumb and easy and light.

Here, in the bungalow, after leaving Mr. Flant and Benny to drift off into their applejack dreams, Penny had only herself. And the books.

Late into the night, waiting for the lightspots to come, she found her eyes wouldn't shut. They started twitching all the time, and maybe it was the night jasmine, or the beachburr.

But she had the books. All those books, these beauti-ful, brittling books, books that made her feel things, made her long to go places and see things – the River Liffey and Paris, France.

And then there are those in the wrappers, the brown paper soft at the creases, the white baker string slightly fraying.

Her favorite was about a detective recovering stolen jewels from an unlikely hiding spot.

But there was one that frightened her. About a farmer's daughter who fell asleep each night on a bed of hay. And in the night, the hay came alive, poking and stabbing at her.

It was supposed to be funny, but it gave Penny bad dreams.

"Well, she was in love with Larry," Mr. Flant said. "But she was not Larry's kind."

Penny had been telling them how Mrs. Stahl had shown up at her door the night before, in worn satin pajamas and cold cream, to scold her for moving furniture around.

"I don't even know how she saw," Penny said. "I just pushed the bed away from the wall."

She had lied, telling Mrs. Stahl she could hear the oven damper popping at night. She was afraid to tell her about the shadows and lights and other things that made no sense in daytime. Like the mice moving behind the wall on hindfeet, so agile she'd come to think of them as pixies, dwarves. Little men.

"It's not your place to move things," Mrs. Stahl had said, quite loudly, and for a moment Penny thought the woman might cry.

"That's all his furniture, you know," Benny said. "Larry's. Down to the forks and spoons."

Penny felt her teeth rattle slightly in her mouth.

"He gave her books she liked," Benny added. "Stiff British stuff he teased her about. Charmed himself out of rent for months."

"When he died she wailed around the courtyards for weeks," Mr. Flant recalled. "She wanted to scatter the ashes into the canyon."

"But his people came instead," Benny said. "Came on a train all the way from California. A man and woman with cardboard suitcases packed with pimento sandwiches. They took the body home."

"They said Hollywood had killed him."

Benny shook his head, smiled and tobacco toothed smile of his. "They always say that."

"You're awfully pretty for a face-fixer," one of the actors told her, fingers wagging beneath his long makeup bib.

Penny only smiled, and scooted before the pinch came.

It was a Western, so it was mostly men, whickers, lip bristle, thee-day beards filled with dust.

Painting the girls' faces was harder. They all had ideas of how they wanted it. They were hard girls, striving to get to Paramount, to MGM. Or started out there and hit the Republic rung on the long slide down. To Allied, AIP. Then studios no one ever heard of, operating out of some slick guy's house in the Valley.

They had bad teeth and head lice and some had smells on them when they came to the studio, like they hadn't washed properly. The costume assistants always pinched their noses behind their backs.

It was a rough town for pretty girls. The only place it was.

Penny knew she had lost her shine long ago. Many men had rubbed it off, shimmy by shimmy.

But it was just as well, and she'd just as soon be in the warpaint business. When it rubbed off the girls, she could just get out her brushes, her power puffs, and shine them up like new.

As she tapped the powder pots, though, her mind would wander. She began thinking about Larry bounding through the backlots. Would he have come to Republic with his wares? Maybe. Would he have soft-soaped her, hoping her bosses might have a taste for T.S. Eliot or a French deck?

By day, she imagined him as a charmer, a cheery, silver-tongued roué.

But at night, back at the Canyon Arms, it was different.

You see, sometimes she thought she could see him moving, room to room, his face pale, his trousers soiled. Drinking and crying over someone, something, whatever he'd lost that he was sure wasn't ever coming back.

There were sounds now. Sounds to go with the two a.m. lights, or the mice, or whatever they were.

Tap-tap-tap.

At first, she thought she was only hearing the banana trees, brushing against the side of the bungalow. Peering out the window, the moon-filled courtyard, she couldn't tell. The air looked very still.

Maybe, she thought, it's the fan palms outside the kitchen window, so much lush foliage everywhere, just the thing she'd loved, but now it seemed to be touching her constantly, closing in.

And she didn't like to go into the kitchen at night. The white tile glowed eerily, reminded her of something. The wide expanse of Mr. D,'s belly, his shirt pushed up, his watch chain hanging. The coaster of milk she left for the cat the morning she ran away from home. For Hollywood.

The mouse traps never caught anything. Every morning, after the rumpled sleep and all the flits and flickers along the wall, she moved them to different places. She looked for signs.

She never saw any.

One night, three a.m., she knelt down on the floor, running her fingers along the baseboards. With her ear to the wall, she thought the tapping might be coming from inside. A *tap-tap-tap*. Or was it a *tick-tick-tick*?

"I've never heard anything here," Mr. Flant told her the following day, "but I take sedatives."

Benny wrinkled his brow. "Once, I saw pink elephants," he offered. "You think that might be it?"

Penny shook her head. "It's making it hard to sleep."

"Dear," Mr. Flint said, "would you like a little helper?"

He held out his palm, pale and moist. In the center, a white pill shone.

That night, she slept impossibly deeply. So deeply she could barely move, her neck twisted and locked, her body hunched inside itself.

Upon waking, she threw up in the waste basket.

That evening, after work, she waited in the courtyard for Mrs. Stahl.

Smoking cigarette after cigarette, Penny noticed things she hadn't before. Some of the tiles in the courtyard were cracked, some missing. She hadn't noticed that before. Or the chips and gouges on the sculpted lions on the center fountain, clogged with crushed cigarette packs, a used contraceptive.

Finally, he saw Mrs. Stahl saunter into view, a large picture hat wilting across her tiny head.

"Mrs. Stahl," she said, "have you ever had an exterminator come?"

The woman stopped, her whole body still for a moment, her left hand finally rising to her face, brushing her hair back under her mustard-colored scarf.

"I run a clean residence," she said, voice low in the empty, sunlit courtyard. That courtyard, oleander and wisteria everywhere, bright and poisonous, like everything in his town.

"I can hear something behind the wainscoting," Penny replied. "Maybe mice, or maybe it's baby possums caught in the wall between the bedroom and kitchen."

Mrs. Stahl looked at her. "Is it after you bake? It might be the dampers popping again."

"I'm not much of a cook. I haven't even turned on the oven yet."

"That's not true," Mrs. Stahl said, lifting her chin triumphantly. "You had it on the other night."

"What?" Then Penny remembered. It had rained sheets and she had used it to dry her dress. But it had been very late and she didn't see how Mrs. Stahl could know. "Are you peeking in my windows?" she asked, voice tightening.

"I saw the light. The oven door was open. You shouldn't do that," Mrs. Stahl said, shaking her head. "It's very dangerous."

"You're not the first landlord I caught peeping. I guess I need to close my curtains," Penny said coolly. "But it's not the over damper I'm hearing each and every night. I'm telling you: there's something inside my walls. Something in the kitchen."

Mrs. Stahl's mouth seemed to quiver slightly, which emboldened Penny.

"Do I need to get out the ball peen I found under the sink and tear a hole in the kitchen wall, Mrs. Stahl?"

"Don't you dear!" she said, clutching Penny's wrist, her costume digging in. "Don't you dare!"

Penny felt the panic on her, the woman's breath's coming in sputters. She insisted they both sit on the fountain edge."

For a moment, they both just breathed, the apricot-perfumed air thick in Penny's lungs.

"Mrs. Stahl, I'm sorry. It's just – I need to sleep."

Mrs. Stahl took a long breath, then her eyes narrowed again. "It's those chinwags next door, isn't it? They've been filling your ear with bile."

"What? Not about this, I-"

"I had the kitchen cleaned thoroughly after it happened. I had it cleaned, the linoleum stripped out. I put up fresh wallpaper over every square inch after it happened. I covered everything in wallpaper."

"Is that where it happened?" Penny asked. "That poor man who died in Number Four? Larry?"

But Mrs. Stahl couldn't speak, or wouldn't, breathing into her handkerchief, lilac silk, the small square over her mouth suctioning open and closed, open and closed.

"He was very beautiful," she finally whispered. "When they pulled him out of the oven, his face was the most exquisite red, like a ripe, ripe cherry."

Knowing how it happened changed things. Penny had always imagines handsome, melancholy Larry walking around the apartment, turning gas jets on. Settling into that club chair in the living room. Or maybe settling in bed and slowly drifting from earth's fine tethers.

She wondered how she could ever use the oven now, or even look at it.

It had to be the same one. That Magic Chef, which looked like the one from childhood, white porcelain and cast iron. Not like those new slabs, buttercup or mint green.

The last tenant, Mr. Flant told her later, smelled gas all the time.

"She said it gave her headaches," he said. "Then one night she came here, her face white as snow. She said she'd just seen St. Agatha in the kitchen, with her bloody breasts."

"I...I don't see anything like that," Penny said.

Back in the bungalow, trying to sleep, she began picturing herself the week before. How she'd left that over door open, her fine, rainslicked dress draped over the rack. The truth was, she'd forgotten about it, only returning for it hours later. Walking to the closet now, she slid the dress from its hanger pressing it to her face. But she couldn't smell anything.

Mr. D. still had not returned her calls. The bank charged her for the bounced check so she'd have to return the hat she'd bought, and rent was due again in two days.

When all the other crew members were making their way to the commissary for lunch, Penny slipped away and splurged on cab fair to the studio.

As she opened the door to his outer office, the receptionist was already on her feet and walking purposefully toward Penny.

"Miss," she said, nearly blocking Penny, "you're going to have to leave. Mac shouldn't have let you in downstairs."

"Why not? I've been here dozens of-"

"You're not on the appointment list, and that's our system now, Miss."

"Does he have an appointment list now for that squeaking starlet sofa in there?" Penny asked, jerking her arm and pointing at the leather-padded door. A man with a thin moustache and a woman in a feathered hat looked up from their magazines.

The receptionist was already on the phone. "Mac, I need you... Yes, that one."

"If he thinks he can just toss me out like some street trade," she said, marching over and thumping on Mr. D.'s door, "he'll be very, very sorry."

Her knuckles made no noise in the soft leather. Nor did her fist.

"Miss," someone said. It was the security guard striding toward her.

"I'm allowed to be here," she insisted, her voice tight and high. "I did my time. I earned the right."

But the guard had his hand on her arm.

Desperate, she looked down at the man and woman waiting. Maybe she thought they would help. But why would they?

The woman pretended to be absorbed in her *Cinestar* magazine.

But the man smiled at her, hair oil gleaming. And winked.

The next morning she woke bleary eyed but determined. She would forget about Mr. D. She didn't need his money. After all, she had a job, a good one.

It was hot on the lot that afternoon, and none of the makeup crew could keep the dust off the faces. There were so many lines and creases on every face – you never think about it until you're trying to make everything smooth.

"Penny," Gordon, the makeup supervisor said. She had the feeling he'd been watching her for several moments as she pressed the powder into the actor's face, holding it still.

"It's so dusty," she said, "so it's taking a while."

He waited until she had finished then, as the actor walked away, he leaned forward.

"Everything all right, Pen?"

He was looking at something – her neck, her chest.

"What do you mean?" she said, setting the powder down.

But he just kept looking at her.

"Working on your carburetor, beautiful?" one of the grips said, as he walked by.

"What? I ..."

Penny turned to the makeup mirror. That was when she saw the long grease smear on her collarbone. And the line of black soot on across her hairline too.

"I don't know," Penny said, her voice sounding slow and sleepy. "I don't have a car."

Then, it all came to her: the dream she'd had in the early morning hours. That she was in the kitchen, checking on the over damper. The squeak of the door on its hinges, and Mrs. Stahl outside the window, her eyes glowing like a wolf's.

"It was a dream," she said, now. Or was it? Has she been sleepwalking the night before?

Had she been in the kitchen ... at the oven ... in her sleep?

"Penny," Gordon said, looking at her squintily. "Penny, maybe you should go home."

It was so early, and Penny didn't want to go back to Canyon Arms. She didn't want to go inside Number Four, or walk past the kitchen, its cherry wallpaper lately giving her the feeling of blood splatters.

Also, lately, she kept thinking she saw Mrs. Stahl peering at her between the wooden blinds as she watered the banana trees.

Instead, she took the bus downtown to the big library on South Fifths. She had an idea.

The librarian, a boy with a bowtie, helped her find the obituaries.

She found three about Larry, but none had photos, which was disappointing.

The one in the *Mirror* was the only one with any detail, any texture.

It mentioned that the body had been found by the "handsome proprietress, one Mrs. Herman Stahl," who "fell to wailing" so loud it was heard all through the canyons up the promontories and likely high into the mossed caves of the Hollywood sign.

"So what happened to Mrs. Stahl's husband?" Penny asked when she saw Mr. Flant and Benny that night.

"He died just a few months before Larry," Benny said. "Bad heart, they say."

Mr. Flant raised one pale eyebrow. "She never spoke of him. Only of Larry."

"He told me once she watched him, Larry did," Benny said. "She watched him through his bedroom blinds. While he made love."

Instantly, Penny knew this was true. She thought of herself in that same bed each night, the mattress so soft, it's posts sometimes seeming to curl inward.

Mrs. Stahl had insisted Penny move it back against the wall. Penny refused, but the next day she came home to find the woman moving it herself, her short arms spanning the mattress, her face pressed into its applique.

Watching, Penny had felt like the Peeping Tom. It was so intimate.

"Sometimes I wonder," Mr. Flant said now. "There were rumors. Black Widow, or Old Maid."

You can't make someone put his head in the oven," Benny said. "At least not for long. The gas'd get you, too."

"True," Mr. Flant said.

"Maybe it didn't happen at the oven," Penny blurted. "She found the body. What if she just turned on the gas while he was sleeping?"

"And dragged him there, for the cops?"

Mr. Flant and Benny looked at each other.

"She's very strong," Penny said.

Back in her bungalow, Penny sat just inside her bedroom window, waiting.

Peering through the blinds, long after midnight, she finally saw her. Mrs. Stahl, walking along the edges of the courtyard.

She was singing softly and her steps were uneven and Penny thought she might be tight, but it was hard to know.

Penny was developing a theory.

Picking up a book, she make herself stay awake until two.

Then, slipping from bed, she tried to follow the flashes of light, the shadows.

Bending down, she put her hands on the baseboards, as if she could touch those funny shapes, like mice on their haunches. Or tiny men, marching.

"Something's there!" she said out loud, her voice surprising her. "It's in the walls."

In the morning it would all be blurry, but in that moment, clues were coming together in her head, something to do with gas jets and Mrs. Stahl and love gone awry and poison in the walls, and she had figured it out before anything bad had happened.

It made so much sense in the moment, and when the sounds came too, the little *tap-taps* behind the plaster, she nearly cheered.

Mr. Flant poured her glass after glass of amaro. Benny waxed his moustache and showed Penny his soft show.

They were trying to make her feel better about losing her job.

"I never came in late except two or three times. I always did my job," Penny said, biting her lip so hard it bled.

"I think I know who's responsible. He kited me for seven hundred and forty dollars and now he's out to ruin me."

Mr. D. –

I don't write to cause you any trouble. What's mine is mine and I never knew you for an indian giver.

I bought fine dresses to go to Hollywood Park with you, to be on your arm at Willa Capri. I had to buy three stockings a week, your clumsy hands pawing at them. I had to turn down jobs and do two cycles of penicillin because of you. Also because of you, I got the heave-ho from my roommate Pauline who said you fondled her by the dumbwaiter. So that money is the least a gentleman can offer a lady. The least, Mr. D.

Let me ask you: those books you kept behind the false bottom in your desk drawer on the lot – did you buy those from Mr. Stanley Rose, or his handsome assistant Larry?

I wonder if your wife knows the kind of books you keep in your office, the girls you keep there and make do shameful things?

I know Larry would agree with me about you. He was a sensitive man and I live where he did and sleep in his bed and all of you ruined him, drove him to drink and to a perilous act.

How dare you try to take my money away. And you with a wife with ermine, mink, lynx dripping from her plump, sunk shoulders.

Your wife at 312 North Faring Road, Holmby Hills.

Let's be adults, sophisticates. After all, we might not know what we might do if backed against a wall.

- yr lucky penny

It had made more sense when she wrote it than it did now, reading it to them. Benny patted her shoulder. "So he called the cops on ya, huh?"

"The studio cops. Which is bad enough," Penny said.

They had escorted her from the makeup department. Everyone had watched, a few of the girls smiling.

"Sorry, Pen," Gordon had said, taking the powder brush from her hand. "What gives in this business is what takes away."

When he'd hired her two months ago, she'd watched as he wrote on her personnel file: Mr. D.

"Your man, he took this as a threat, you see," Mr. Flant said, shaking his head as he looked at the letter. "He is a hard man. Those men are. They are hard men and you are soft. Like Larry was soft."

Penny knew it was true. She'd never been hard enough, at least not in the right way. The smart way.

It was very late when she left the two men.

She paused before Number Four and found herself unable to move, cold fingertips pressed between her breasts, pushing her back.

That was when she spotted Mrs. Stahl inside the bungalow, fluttering past the picture window in her evening coat.

"Stop!" Penny called out. "I see you!"

And Mrs. Stahl froze. Then, slowly, she turned to face Penny, her face warped through the glass, as if she were under water.

"Dear," a voice came from behind Penny. A voice just like Mrs. Stahl's. *Could she throw her voice?*

Swiveling around, she saw the landlady standing in the courtyard, a few feet away.

It was as if she were a witch, a shapeshifter from one of the fairytales she'd read as a child.

"Dear," she said again.

"I thought you were inside," Penny said, trying to catch her breath. "But it was just your reflection."

Mrs. Stahl did not say anything for a moment, her hands cupped in front of herself.

Penny saw she was holding a scarlet-covered book in her palms.

"I often sit our here at night," she said, voice loose and tipsy, "reading under the stars. Larry used to do that, you know."

She invited Penny into her bungalow, the smallest one, in back.

"I'd like us to talk," she said.

Penny did not pause. She wanted to see it. Wanted to understand.

Walking inside, she realized at last what the strongest smell in the courtyard was. All around were pots of night-blooming jasmine, climbing and vining up the built-in bookshelves, around the window frame, even trained over the arched doorway into the dining room.

They drank jasmine tea, iced. The room was close and Penny had never seen so many books. None of them looked like they'd ever been opened, their spines cool and immaculate.

"I have more," Mrs. Stahl said, waving toward the mint-walled hallway, some space beyond, the air itself so thick with the breath of the jasmine, Penny couldn't see it. "I love books. Larry taught me how. He knew what ones I'd like."

At that, Penny had a grim thought. What if everything smelled like gas and she didn't know it? The strong scent of apricot, eucalyptus, a perpetual perfume suffusing everything. How would one know?

"Dear, do you enjoy living in Larry's bungalow?"

Penny didn't know what to say, so she only nodded, taking a long sip of tea. Was it rum? Some kind of liqueur? It was very sweet and tingled on her tongue.

"He was my favorite tenant. Even after ..." she paused, her head shaking, "what he did."

"And you found him," Penny said. "That must have been awful."

She held up the red-covered book she had been reading in the courtyard.

"This was found on ... on his person. He must've been planning on giving it to me. He gave me so many things. See how it's red, like a heart?"

"What kind of book is it?" Penny asked, leaning closer.

Mrs. Stahl looked at her, but didn't seem to be listening, clasping the book with one hand while with the other stroked her neck, long and unlined.

"Every book he gave me showed how much he understood me. He gave me many things and never asked for anything. That was when his mother was dying from Bright's, her face puffed up like a carnival balloon. Nasty woman."

"Mrs. Stahl," Penny started, her fingers tingling unbearably, the smell so strong. Mrs. Stahl's plants, her strong perfume – sandalwood?

"He just liked everyone. You'd think it was just you. The care he took. Once, he brought me a brass rouge pot from Paramount studios. He told me it belonged to Paulette Goddard. I still have it."

"Mrs. Stahl," Penny tried again, bolder now, "were you in love with him?"

The woman looked at her, and Penny felt her focus loosen, like in those old detective movies, right before the screen went black.

"He really only wanted the stars," Mrs. Stahl said, running her fingers across her décolletage, the satin of her dressing robe, a dragon painted up the front. "He said their skin felt different. They smelled different. He was strange about smells. Sounds. Light. He was very sensitive."

"But you loved him, didn't you?" Penny's voice was more insistent now.

Her eyes narrowed. "Everyone loved him. Everyone. He said yes to everybody. He gave himself to everybody."

"But why did he do it, Mrs. Stahl?"

"He put his head in the oven and died," she said, straightening her back ever so slightly. "He was mad in a way only Southerners and artistic souls are mad. And he was both. You're too young, too simple, to understand."

"Mrs. Stahl, did you do something to Larry?" This is what Penny was trying to say, but the words weren't coming. And Mrs. Stahl kept growing larger and larger, the dragon on her robe, it seemed, somehow, to be speaking to Penny, whispering things to her.

"What's in this tea?"

"What do you mean, dear?"

But the woman's face had gone strange, stretched out. There was a scurrying sound from somewhere, like little paws, animal claws, the sharp feet of sharp-footed men. A gold watch chain swinging and that neighbor hanging from the pear tree.

She woke to the purple creep of dawn. Slumped in the same rattan chair in Mrs. Stahl's living room. Her finger still crooked in the tea cup handle, her arm hanging to one side.

"Mrs. Stahl," she whispered.

But the woman was no longer on the sofa across from her.

Somehow, Penny was on her feet, inching across the room.

The bedroom door was ajar, Mrs. Stahl sprawled on the mattress, the painted dragon on her robe sprawled on top of her.

On the bed beside her was the book she'd been reading in the courtyard. Scarlet red, with a lurid title.

Gaudy Night, it was called.

Opening it with great care, Penny saw the inscription"

To Mrs. Stahl, my dirst murderess.
Love, Lawrence.

She took the book, and the tea cup.

She slept for a few hours in her living room, curled on the zebra print sofa.

She had stopped going into the kitchen two days ago, tacking an old bath towel over the doorway so she couldn't even see inside. The gleaming porcelain of the oven.

She was sure she smelled gas radiating from it. Spotted blue light flickering behind the towel.

But still she didn't go inside.

And now she was afraid the smell was coming through the walls.

It was all connected, you see, and Mrs. Stahl was behind all of it. The lightspots, the shadows on the baseboard, the noises in the walls and now the hiss of the gas.

Mr. Flant looked at the inscription, shaking his head.

"My God, is it possible? He wasn't making much sense those final days. Holed up in Number Four. Maybe he was hiding from her. Because he knew."

"It was found on his body," Penny said, voice trembling. "That's what she told me."

"Then this inscription," he said, reaching out for Penny's wrist, "was meant to be our clue. Like pointing a finger from beyond the grave."

Penny nodded. She knew what she had to do.

"I know how it sounds. But someone needs to do something."

The police detective nodded, drinking his Coca-Cola, his white shirt bright. He had gray hair at the temples and he said his name was Noble, which seemed impossible.

"Well, Miss, let's see what we can do. That was a long time ago. After you called, I had to get the case file from the crypt. I can't say I even remember it." Licking his index finger, he flicked open the file folder, then beginning turning pages. "A gas job, right? We got a lot of them back then. Those months before the war."

"Yes. In the kitchen. My kitchen now." Looking through the slim folder, he pursed his lips a moment, then came a grim smile. "Ah, I remember. I remember. The little men."

"The little men?" Penny felt her spine tighten.

"One of our patrolmen had been out there the week before on a noise complaint. Your bookseller was screaming in the courtyard. Claimed there were little men coming out of the walls so kill him."

Penny didn't say anything at all. Something deep inside herself seemed to be screaming and it took all her effort just to sit there and listen.

"DTs. Said he'd been trying to kick the sauce," he said, reading the report. "He was a drunk, miss. Sounds like it was a whole courtyard full of 'em."

"No," Penny said, head shaking back and forth. "That's not it. Larry wasn't like that."

"Well," he said, "I'll tell what Larry was like. In his bedside table we found a half-dozen catcher's mitts." He stopped himself, looked at her. "Pardon. Female contraceptive devices. Each one, with the name of a different woman. A few big stars. At least they were big then. I can't remember now."

Penny was still thinking a bout the wall. The little men. And her mice on their hindfeet. Pixies, dancing fairies.

"There you go," the detective said, closing the folder. "Guy's a dipso, one of his high-class affairs turned sour. Suicide. Pretty clear cut."

"No," Penny said.

"No?" Eyebrows raised. "He was in that oven waist deep, miss. He even had a hunting knife in his hand for good measure."

"A knife?" Penny said, her fingers pressing her forehead. "Of course. Don't you see? He was trying to protect himself. I told you on the phone, detective. It's imperative that you look into Mrs. Stahl."

"The landlady. Your landlady?"

"She was in love with him. And he rejected her, you see?"

"A woman scorned, eh?" he said, leaning back. "Once saw a jilted lady over on Cheremoya take a clothes iron to her fellow's face while he slept."

"Look at this," Penny said, pulling Mrs. Stahl's little red book from her purse.

"*Gaudy Night*," he said, pronouncing the first word in a funny way.

"I think it's a dirty book."

He looked at her, squinting. "My wife owns this book."

Penny didn't say anything.

"Have you even read it?" he asked, wearily.

Opening the front of the inscription, she held it in front of him.

"'Dirty murderess.'" He shrugged. "So you're saying this fella knew she was going to kill him and, instead of going to say, the police, he writes this little inscription, then lets himself get killed?"

Everything sounded so different when he said it aloud, different than the way everything joined in perfect and horrible symmetry in her head.

"I don't know how it happened. Maybe he was going to go to the police and she beat him to it. And I don't know how she did it," Penny said. "But she's dangerous, don't you get it?"

It was clear he did not.

"I'm telling you, I see her out there at night, doing things," Penny said, her breath coming faster and faster. "She's doing something with the natural gas. If you check the gas jets maybe you can figure it out."

She was aware that she was talking very loudly, and her chest felt damp. Lowering her voice, she leaned toward him.

"I think there might be a clue in my oven," she said.

"Do you?" he said, rubbing his chin. "Any little men in there?"

"It's not like that. It's not. I see them, yes."

She couldn't look him in the eye or she would lose her nerve. "But I know they're not really little men. It's something she's doing. It always starts at two. Two a.m. She's doing something. She did it to Larry and she's doing it to me."

He was rubbing his face with his hand, and she knew she had lost him.

"I told you on the phone," she said, more desperately now. "I think she drugged me. I brought the cup."

Penny reached into her purse again, this time removing the tea cup, its bottom still brown-ringed.

Detective Noble lifted it, took a sniff, set it down.

"Drugged you with Old Grandad, eh?"

"I know there's booze in it. But, detective there's more than booze going on here." Again, her voice rose high and sharp, and other detectives seemed to be watching now from their desks.

But Noble seemed unfazed. There even seemed to be a flicker of a smile on his clean-shaven face.

"So why does she want to harm you?" he asked. "Is she in love with you, too?"

Penny looked at him, and counted quietly in her head, the dampness on her chest gather.

She had been dealing with men like this her whole life. Smug men. Men with fine clothes or shabby ones, all with the same slick ideas, the same impatience, big voice, slap-and-tickle, fast with a back-handed slug. Nice turned to nasty on a dime.

"Detective," she said, taking it slowly, "Mrs. Stahl must suspect that I know. About what she did to Larry. I don't know if she drugged him and staged it. The hunting knife shows there was a struggle. What I do know is there's more than what's in your little file."

He nodded, leaning back in his chair once more. With his right arm, he reached for another folder in the metal tray on his desk.

"Miss, can we talk for a minute about *your* file?"

"My file?"

"When you called, I checked your name. S.O.P. Do you want to tell me about the letters you've been sending to a certain address in Holmby Hills?"

"What? I...There was only one."

"And two years ago, the fellow over at the MCA? Said you slashed his tires?"

"I was never charged."

Penny would never speak about that, or what the man had tried to do to her in the back booth at Chasen's.

He set the file down. "Miss, what exactly are you here for? You got a gripe with Mrs. Stahl? Hey, I don't like my landlord either. What, don't wanna pay the rent?"

A wave of exhaustion shuddered through Penny. For a moment, she did not know if she could stand.

But there was Larry to think about. And how much she belonged in Number Four. Because she did, and it had marked the beginning of things. A new day for Penny.

"No," Penny said, rising. "That's not it. You'll see. You'll see. I'll show you."

"Miss," he said, calling after her. "Please don't show me anything. Just behave yourself, okay? Like a good girl."

Back at Number Four, Penny laid down on the rattan sofa, trying to breathe, to think.

Pulling Mrs. Stahl's book from her dress pocket, she began reading.

But it wasn't like she thought.

It wasn't dirty, not like the brown-papered ones. IT was a detective novel, and it took place in England. A woman recently exonerated for poisoning her lover attends her school reunion. While there, she finds an anonymous poisoned pen note tucked in the sleeve of her gown: "You Dirty Murderess...!"

Penny gasped. But then wondered: Had that inscription just been a wink, Larry to Mrs. Stahl?

He gave her books she liked, Benny had said. *Stiff British stuff that he could tease her about.*

Was that all this was, all the inscriptions had meant?

No, she assured herself, sliding the book back into her pocket. It's a red herring. To confuse me, to keep me from finding the truth. Larry needs me to find out the truth.

It was shortly after that she heard the click of her mail slot. Looking over, she saw a piece of paper slip through the slit and land on the entry-way floor.

Walking over, she picked it up.

Bungalow Four:

You are past due.
—Mrs. H Stahl

"I have to move anyway," she told Benny, showing him the note.

"No, kid, why?" he whispered. Mr. Flant was sleeping in the bedroom, the gentle whistle of his snore.

"I can't prove she's doing it," Penny said. "But it smells like a gas chamber in there."

"Listen, don't let her spook you," Benny said. "I bet the pilot light is out. Want me to take a look? I can come by later."

"Can you come now?"

Looking into the darkened bedroom, Benny smiled, patted her forearm. "I don't mind."

Stripped to his undershirt, Benny ducked under the bath towel Penny had hung over the kitchen door.

"I thought you were inviting me over to keep your bed warm," he said as he kneeled down on the linoleum.

The familiar noise started, the *tick-tick-tick*.

"Do you hear it?" Penny said, voice tight. Except the sound was different in the kitchen than the bedroom. It was closer. Not inside the walls but everywhere.

"It's the igniter," Benny said. "Trying to light the gas."

Peering behind the towel, Penny watched him.

"But you smell it, right?" she said.

"Of course I smell it," he said, his voice strangely high. "God, it's awful."

He put his head to the baseboards, the sink, the shuddering refrigerator.

"What's this?" he said, tugging the oven forward, his arms straining.

He was touching the wall behind the oven, but Penny couldn't see.

"What's what?" she asked. "Did you find something?"

"I don't know," he said, his head turned from her. "I…Christ, you can't think with it. I feel like I'm back in Argonne."

He had to lean backward, palms resting on the floor.

"What is it you saw, back there?" Penny asked, pointing behind the oven.

But he kept shaking his head, breathing into the front of his undershirt, pulled up.

After a minute, both of them breathing hard, he reached up and turned the knob on the front of the oven door.

"I smell it," Penny said, stepping back. "Don't you?"

"That pilot light," he said, covering his face, breathing raspily. "It's gotta be out."

His knees sliding on the linoleum, he inched back toward the oven, white and glowing.

"Are you…are you going to open it?"

He looked at her, his face pale and his mouth stretched like a piece of rubber.

"I'm going to," he said. "We need to light it."

But he didn't stir. There was a feeling of something that door open like a black maw, and neither of them could move.

Penny turned, hearing a knock at the door.

When she turned back around, she gasped.

Benny's head and shoulders were inside the oven, his voice making the most terrible sound, like a cat, its neck caught in a trap.

"Get out," Penny said, not matter how silly it sounded. "Get out!"

Pitching forward, she leaned down and grabbed for him, tugging at his trousers, yanking him back.

Stumbling, they both rose to their feet, Penny nearly huddling against the kitchen wall, its cherry-sprigged paper.

Turning, he took her arms hard, pressing himself against her, pressing Penny against the wall.

She could smell him, and his skin was clammy and goosequilled.

His mouth pressed against her neck roughly and she could feel his teeth, his hands on her hips. Something had changed and she'd missed it.

"But this is what you want, isn't it, honey?" the whisper came, his mouth over her ear. "It's all you've ever wanted."

"No, no, no," she said, and found herself crying. "And you don't like girls. You don't like girls."

"I like everybody," he said, his palm on her chest, hand heel hard.

And she lifted her head and looked at him, and he was Larry.

She knew he was Larry.

Larry.

Until he became Benny again, moustache and grin, but fear in that grin still.

"I'm sorry, Penny," he said, stepping back. "I'm flatter, but I don't go that way."

"What?" She said, looking down, seeing her fingers clamped on his trouser waist. "Oh. Oh."

Back at Number Three, they both drank from tall tumblers, breathing hungrily.

"You shouldn't go back in there," Benny said. "We need to call the gas company in the morning."

Mr. Flant said she could stay on their sofa that night, if they could make room under all the old newspapers.

"You shouldn't have looked in there," he said to Benny, shaking his head. "The oven. It's like whistling in a cemetery."

A towel wrapped around his shoulders. Benny was shivering. He was so white.

"I didn't see anything," he kept saying. "I didn't see a goddamned thing."

She was dreaming.

"You took my book!"

In the dream, she'd risen from Mr. Flant's sofa, slicked with sweat, and opened the door. Although nearly midnight, the courtyard was mysteriously bright, all the plants gaudy and pungent.

Wait. Had someone said something?

"Larry gave it to me!"

Penny's body was moving so slowly, like she was caught in molasses.

The door to Number Four was open, and Mrs. Stahl was emerging from it, something red in her hand.

"You took it while I slept, didn't you? Sneak thief! Thieving whore!"

When Mrs. Stahl began charging at her, her robe billowing like great scarlet wings, Penny thought she was still dreaming.

"Stop," Penny said, but the woman was so close.

It had to be a dream, and in dreams you can't do anything, so Penny raised her arms high, clamping down on those scarlet wings as they came toward her.

The book slid from her pocket, and both of them grappled for it, but Penny was faster, grabbing it and pushing back, pressing the volume against the old woman's neck until she stumbled, hells tangling.

It had to be a dream because Mrs. Stahl was so weak, weaker than any murderess could possibly be, her body like that of a yarn doll, limp and flailing.

There was a flurry of elbows, clawing hands, the fat golden beetle ring on Mrs. Stahl's gnarled hand against Penny's face.

Then, with one hard jerk, the old woman fell to the ground with such ease, her head clacking against the courtyard tiles.

The ratatattat of blood from her mouth, her ear.

"Penny!" A voice came from behind her.

It was Mr. Flant standing in his doorway, hand to his mouth.

"Penny, what did you *do*?"

Her expression when she'd faced Mr. Flant must have been meaningful because he immediately retreated inside his bungalow, the door locking with a click.

But it was time, anyway. Of that she felt sure.

Walking into Number Four, she almost felt herself smiling.

One by one, she removed all the tacks from her makeshift kitchen door, letting the towel drop onto her forearm.

The kitchen was dark, and smelled as it never had. No apricots, no jasmine, and no gas. Instead, the tinny smell of must, wallpaper paste, rusty water.

Moving slowly, purposefully, she walked directly to the oven, the moonlight striking it. White and monstrous, a glowing smear.

Its door shut.

Cold to the touch.

Kneeling down, she crawled behind it, to the spot Benny had been struck by.

What's this? he'd said.

As in a dream, which this had to be, she knew what to do, her palm sliding along the cherry-sprig wallpaper down by the baseboard.

She saw the spot, the wallpaper gaping at its seam, seeming to breathe. Inhale, exhale.

Penny's hand went there, pulling back the paper glue dried to fine dust under her hand.

She was remembering Mrs. Stahl. *I put up fresh wall-paper over every square inch after it happened. I covered everything with wallpaper.*

What did she think she would see, breathing hard, her knees creaking and her forehead pushed against the wall?

The paper did not come off cleanly, came off in pieces, strands, like her hair after the dose Mr. D. passed to her, making her sick for weeks.

A patch of wall exposed, she saw the series of gashes, one after the next, as if someone had jabbed a knife into the plaster. A hunting knife. Though there seemed a pattern, a hieroglyphics.

Squinting, the kitchen so dark, she couldn't see.

Reaching up to the oven, she grabbed for a kitchen match.

Leaning close, the match lit, she could see a faint scrawl etched deep.

The little men come out of my walls. I cut off their heads every night. My mind is gone.
Tonight, I end my life.
I hope you find this.
Goodbye.

Penny leaned forward, pressed her palm on the words. This is what mattered most, nothing else.

"Oh, Larry," she said, her voice catching with grateful tears. "I see them too."

The sound that followed was the loudest she'd ever heard, the fire sweeping up her face.

The detective stood in the center of the courtyard, next to a banana tree with its top shorn off, a smoldering slab of wood, the front door to the blackened bungalow, on the ground in front of him.

The firemen were dragging their equipment past him. The gurney with the dead girl long gone.

"Pilot light. Damn near took the roof off," one of the patrolman said. "The kitchen looks like the Blitz. But only scorched, inside. The girl. Or what's left of her. Could've been much worse."

"That's always true," the detective said, a billow of smoke making them both cover their faces.

Another officer approached him.

"Detective Noble, we talked to the pair next door," he said. "They said they warned the girl not to go back inside. But she'd been drinking all day, saying crazy things."

"How's the landlady?"

"Hospital."

Noble nodded. "We're done."

It was close to two. But he didn't want to go home yet. IT was a long drive to Eagle Rock anyway.

And the smell, and what he'd seen in that kitchen—he didn't want to go home yet.

At the top of the road, he saw the bar, its bright light beckoning.

The Carnival Tavern, the one with the roof shaped like a big top.

Life is a carnival, he said to himself, which is what the detective might say, wryly, in the books his wife loved to read.

He couldn't believe it was still there. He remembered it from before the war. When he used to date that usherette at the Hollywood Bowl.

A quick jerk to the wheel and he was pulling into its small lot, those crazy clown lanterns he remembered from all those years ago.

Inside, everything was warm and inviting, even if the waitress had a sour look.

"Last call," she said, leaving him his rye. "We close in ten minutes."

"I just need to make a quick call," he said.

He stepped into one of the telephone booths in the back, pulling the accordion door shut behind him.

"Yes, I have that one," his wife replied, stifling a yawn. "But it's not a dirty book."

Then she laughed a little in a way that made him bristle.

"So what kind of book is it?" he asked.

"Books mean different things to different people," she said. She was always saying stuff like that, just to show him how smart she was.

"You know what I mean," he said.

She was silent for several seconds. He thought he could hear someone crying, maybe one of the kids.

"It's a mystery," she said, finally. "Not your kind. No one even dies."

"Okay," he said. He wasn't sure what he'd wanted to hear. "I'll be home soon."

"It's a love story, too," she said, almost a whisper, strangely sad. "Not your kind."

After he hung up, he ordered a beer, the night's last tug from the bartenders' tap.

Sitting by the picture window, he looked down into the canyon, and up to the Hollywood sign. Everything about the moment felt familiar. He'd worked this precinct for twenty years, minus three to Uncle Sam, so even the surprises were the same.

He thought about the girl, about her at the station. Her nervous legs, that worn dress of hers, the plea in her voice.

Someone should think of her for a minute, shouldn't they?

He looked at his watch. Two a.m. But she won't see her little men tonight.

A busboy with a pencil moustache came over with a long stick. One by one, he turned all the dingy lanterns that hung in the window. The painted clowns faced the canyon now. Closing time.

"Don't miss me too much," he told the sour waitress as he left.

In the parking lot, looking down into the canyon, he noticed he could see the Canyon Arms, the smoke still settling on the bungalow's shell, black as a mussel. Her bedroom window, glass blown out, curtains shuddering in the night breeze.

He was just about to get in his car when he saw them. The little men.

They were dancing across the hood of his car, the canyon beneath him.

Turning, he looked up at the bar, the lanterns in the window, spinning, sending their dancing clowns across the canyon, across the Canyon Arms, everywhere.

He took a breath.

"That happens every night?" he asked the busboy as the young man hustled down the stairs into the parking lot.

Pausing, the busboy followed his gaze, then nodded.

"Every night," he said. "Like a dream."

Megan Abbott is the Edgar®-winning author of seven crime and mystery novels, including *Queenpin*, *Die a Little*, *Bury Me Deep*, and *The Fever*, which was chosen as one of the Best Books of the Summer by the *The New York Times*, *People Magazine* and *Entertainment Weekly* and one of the Best Books of the Year by Amazon, National Public Radio, the *Boston Globe* and the *Los Angeles Times*. Her writing has appeared in *The New York Times*, *Salon*, *The Guardian*, *The Wall Street Journal*, *The Los Angeles Times Magazine*, *The Believer* and *The Los Angeles Review of Books*. She's also the author of the nonfiction book *The Street Was Mine: White Masculinity in Hardboiled Fiction and Film Noir*, and the editor of *A Hell of a Woman*, an anthology of female crime fiction. Her writing has been nominated for many awards, including three Edgar® Awards, the Hammett Prize, the Shirley Jackson Prize, the Los Angeles Times Book Prize and the Folio Prize. Born in the Detroit area, she graduated from the University of Michigan and received her Ph.D. in English and American literature from New York University. She has taught at NYU, the State University of New York, and the New School University. In 2013-14, she served as the John Grisham Writer in Residence at Ole Miss.

Honorable Mentions

Lee Child, "Small Wars," Amazon.com
Mat Coward, "On Borrowed Time," *EQMM*, June
Paula Daley, "No Remorse," *EQMM*, March-April
O'Neil de Noux, "Just An Old Lady," *AHMM*, September
Dayle A. Dermatis, "The Scent of Amber and Vanilla," *Fiction River: Pulse Pounders*
Brendan DuBois, "The Crossing," *Alfred Hitchcock's Mystery Magazine*, January-February
Brendan DuBois, "The Lake Tenant," *EQMM*, November
C. B. Forrest, "The Runaway Girl from Portland, Oregon," *AHMM*, October
Stephen Gore, "Black Rock," *Ellery Queen's Mystery Magazine*, August
Jane Haddam, "Crazy Cat Ladies," *EQMM*, February
Parnell Hall, "The Dead Client," *Dark City Lights*
Carolyn Hart, "What Goes Around," *EQMM*, November
Chuck Heintzelman, "Three Strikes," *Fiction River: Pulse Pounders*
Julie Hyzy, "White Rabbit," *Manhattan Mayhem*
Shirley Jackson, "Murder on Miss Lederer's Birthday," *Let Me Tell You*
Robert T. Jeschonek, "The Messiah Business," *Fiction River: Risk Takers*
Eve Kagen, "Spit the Truth," *Dark City Lights*
Stephen King, "Drunken Fireworks," *The Bazaar of Bad Dreams*
Michele Lang, "Sucker's Game," *Jewish Noir*
Violet LaVoit, "The Electric Palace," *Hanzai Japan*
Janice Law, "The Dressmaker," *AHMM*, November

Elmore Leonard, "Time of Terror," *Charlie Martz and Other Stories*
David Levien, "Knock-Out Whist," *Dark City Lights*
Kate McLachlan "Seasons of Deception," *Lesbians on the Loose*
Denise Mina, "Seven Years," *Bibliomysteries*
T. Jefferson Parker, "Me and Mikey," *Manhattan Mayhem*
Nancy Pickard, "Three Little Words," *Manhattan Mayhem*
Louis Rakovich, "The Cocoon" *The M.O.*, July
Ian Rankin, "Meet and Greet," *The Strand*, July
Annie Reed, "The Flower of the Tabernacle," *Fiction River: Recycled Pulp*
Jonathan Santlofer, "The Golem of Jericho," *Jewish Noir*
Michael Caleb Tasker, "A Loneliness to the Thought," *EQMM*, May
Brian Tobin, "Entwined," *AHMM*, June
P. J. Ward, "Sylvia Reyes" *Protectors 2*
Shauna Washington, "La Rouge Jolie," *AHMM*, September
Elle Wild, "Playing Dead," *EQMM*, September
Graham Wynd, "Mesquite," *Protectors 2*

CPSIA information can be obtained
at www.ICGtesting.com
Printed in the USA
LVOW07s2237251016
510266LV00016B/80/P